THE
INHERITANCE

A NOVEL

JOANNA GOODMAN

HARPER

NEW YORK • LONDON • TORONTO • SYDNEY

HARPER

THE INHERITANCE. Copyright © 2024 by Joanna Goodman. All rights reserved. Printed in the United States of America. No part of this book may be used or reproduced in any manner whatsoever without written permission except in the case of brief quotations embodied in critical articles and reviews. For information, address HarperCollins Publishers, 195 Broadway, New York, NY 10007.

HarperCollins books may be purchased for educational, business, or sales promotional use. For information, please email the Special Markets Department at SPsales@harpercollins.com.

FIRST EDITION

Designed by Jamie Lynn Kerner

Library of Congress Cataloging-in-Publication Data has been applied for.

ISBN 978-0-06-331939-4 (pbk.)
ISBN 978-0-06-332901-0 (library ed.)
ISBN 978-0-06-337313-6 (international ed.)

24 25 26 27 28 LBC 5 4 3 2 1

For my spirit sisters who carried me through the last few years.

*Say not you know another entirely, till you have
divided an inheritance with him.*

—JOHANN KASPAR LAVATER

PREFACE

VIRGINIA BUNT IS FLAT ON HER BACK, HER LOWER BODY UNNATURALLY twisted on the hardwood, no feeling below her shins. The sheet is wet and sticky underneath her thighs, the duvet tangled around her feet, all of it having come off the bed with her. She can't move. She has no idea how long she's been here. A day? Two days?

Spectacular pain is exploding up and down her left side from her knee to her groin. Her left leg is turned awkwardly, the inner thigh pushed out. The entire leg is deeply bruised, mottled dark purple. The room is quiet; she's alone. She usually doesn't like to be left alone—not by men—but this is different, her perspective having been stunningly altered by the circumstances. She thinks about her girls, though not with the usual crushing remorse or operatic shrieks of guilt in her head. She's failed them utterly and completely, she knows that; but now it just seems so irrelevant. None of it matters anymore—not the kind of mother she's been, or the women they've become—especially Arden, who is so much like her. Tate always manages to land on her feet, but Arden can be so helpless. She worries about Arden—her passivity and codependence, traits Virginia has certainly passed down to her youngest daughter.

Even if Virginia lives, she's already lost the battle. There's a certain overriding clarity to it all, though. This was always going to be her destiny, she sees that now. Not just the violent battering of her body and ego, but the epic humiliation at the hands of a man; the complete aloneness of this moment. *You know you want it, you decrepit old whore.*

She can just imagine how the girls will react to this, her grandest fuckup yet.

Let it go, Virginia. Let go of what they think. Maybe she won't tell them. Maybe she'll die here like this. Wouldn't that be poetic? Dying while still waiting for her life to start.

She can hear the subway rumble outside her window and it's comforting to know that life is going on out there, people are going places, getting on with things. Life is expanding, and though she may not be part of it, the sound of the train makes her feel like she's not alone on the planet.

As she floats in and out of consciousness, she remembers as a little girl waking up one night from a bad dream and calling out for her mother. She must have been about five or six. She couldn't remember what the dream was about, but her heart was beating very fast. Her eyelet curtains were pulled open and the tree branches outside her window looked scarier than usual. She slid her feet out of bed, grabbed her doll, Constance, and hurried out of her room. She was wearing baby-doll pajamas with a scalloped hem, and she felt cold. There were goose bumps up and down her arms and legs, but she wasn't sure if they were from the cold or from being scared.

She padded down the hall to her parents' room, knowing her mother would let her sleep in their bed. Not between them—her father didn't like Virginia in the bed, said it disrupted his sleep—but on her mother's side, curled in a fetal position with her mother's heart beating against her back.

She had one hand on the doorknob—she was holding Constance's hair with the other—and was about to open the door when she heard them arguing.

"You could at least acknowledge her sometimes," her mother was saying.

"I do acknowledge her."

"Oh, Howarth. You barely do. You ignore her most of the time. Can't you at least engage her every now and then? Ask her something about school or watch her do her goddamn Hula-Hoop for five minutes?"

Her father was a professor of English at York University. He didn't have time for Virginia's silly games or her constant "jibber-jabbering." He would always tell her to go and read a book instead. She hated reading, which bothered him. "How did I wind up with a child who doesn't read?" He was often disgusted with her.

Virginia pressed her ear closer to the door.

"She looks up to you, Howarth," her mother said. "So maybe she's not going to be an intellectual, so what? She's only a child."

There was a long silence.

"What am I supposed to do with a pretty moron?" he said at last, sounding genuinely perplexed. "She's useless."

Or maybe he'd said, "It's useless."

Virginia could never be sure. She went back to her room, absorbing what she'd heard. She turned on the bedside lamp and crawled under the covers with Constance. Even then, she knew her father's opinion was the one that mattered most, the only one that counted, really. His words would always shape how she felt about herself and who she became in the world.

Pretty, useless moron.

Lying here now, splayed out on the floor, she wonders about the careless things her girls might have overheard *her* say about them over the years. Might those words have caused a kind of internal damage to which she was completely oblivious?

More than likely, she acknowledges, picturing their beautiful, sad faces as she finally loses consciousness.

THE
INHERITANCE

1

MARCH 2018

A STRONG GUST OF WIND BLOWS OPEN THE SHUTTERS WITH A BANG, waking Arden from an already disturbed sleep. She blinks, blinded by a beam of light from the ill-positioned streetlight shining directly into her window. She looks over at her phone, which is upright in its dock. It's almost three o'clock. She gets up, closes the window, slips back under the duvet. Without even attempting to fall asleep on her own, she reaches into her bedside drawer and grabs a Sublinox. She swallows it with a glass of warm water and lies back down, waiting for the iron clamp of grief to loosen its grip.

Eventually, she falls into a thick, dreamless sleep. Next thing she knows there's an elbow pressing into her lower back. As she slowly begins to come to, groggy and disoriented, she searches for Scott's warm body in the bed. There's a soft moan beside her. She opens one eye and gazes over at her sleeping daughter, remembering. *Scott's dead.*

That's when the tape starts rolling. *Are we going to be okay? Are the kids going to be permanently damaged? Will I figure out life on my own?* And then the more practical matters: *Should I list the house? Should I take a second mortgage? Should I send Ivey to a shrink?*

Arden forces herself awake to make it stop. She turns and looks over at Ali's round, pink face. Her damp hair is fanned out around her, her left arm flung across Wyatt's back, holding him close, the way they must have slept together in the womb. Her precious magpies. She touches his pull-up. It's soaking wet. Almost seven years old and he's back in pull-ups.

On the other side of Wyatt, Ivey is snoring, face skyward. Her chest rises and falls, her nose whistling softly with each exhalation. She's at the edge of the mattress, long legs tangled up in the sheets. Arden reaches across the other two to touch Ivey's cheek. The older she gets, the more she's morphing into her father. She's got the same dark brown eyes and heavy brow, the angular jawline and slightly cleft chin that Wyatt once called "an upside-down fortune cookie." She rarely sleeps in here anymore, but every once in a while, she has a bad dream or gets lonely or misses her father, and she crawls in with them in the middle of the night.

Ali sits up abruptly, squinting and rubbing her eyes. Arden wordlessly hands her the wire-rimmed glasses that make her look so much older than six, kisses her forehead, and gets out of bed to shower. She's going to New York to visit her stepdad, Hal. It's her first time away from the kids since their father died a year and a half ago. Her sister, Tate, booked her a massage in Park Slope and got her two tickets to see a show on Broadway. Tate is spoiling her because she knows Arden is flat broke, and also because she likes to think of herself as Arden's savior.

Arden gets in the shower and lets the hot water wash away the cloudiness of the sleeping pill, the residue of dread. She tips her head back, her mouth opened wide so she can taste the water on her tongue. She stands there for a long time. Just as she's starting to feel human again, the plastic curtain flies open, rattling the metal hooks on the rod, and there's Ali, staring up at her. Arden throws an arm over her bare breasts and is immediately reminded of that morning when Ali barged in on her and Scott showering together. She was five and stood there gaping at Scott's penis for an uncomfortable length of time, until he eventually grabbed a facecloth and shielded himself with it like it was a codpiece.

"What is that thing?" Ali asked him.

"That's my wiener," Scott responded, unprepared. How could you be?

Ali squealed and ran away.

"Your *wiener*?" Arden said to him. "Really? That's what you're going with?"

Scott shrugged and let the washcloth fall to his feet. That turned out to be the last conversation he ever had with his youngest daughter other than the perfunctory goodbye he called out to them before he left to go back to the cottage. Arden wonders if Ali will wind up in therapy one day, sobbing on a shrink's couch over the fact that her father's last words to her were *That's my wiener.*

"Mommy?" Ali says, her glasses fogging. "Please don't leave."

"It's just for two nights, darling."

"That's what Daddy said."

Arden lifts Ali into her arms and goes back under the shower. *How can she sell the fucking house? It will destroy them.*

"My jammies are getting wet!" Ali shrieks, but a moment later, she's splashing around and laughing. Six-year-olds are resilient, their emotions fierce but transient. She sits down on the shower floor and starts making potions with Arden's coconut shampoo and mango conditioner and bright blue shaving cream. Who can blame her for being scared? Her father went away for a weekend and never came home. They all have to live with that for the rest of their lives, every time someone they love walks out the door.

When Arden turns off the shower, she can hear Wyatt and Ivey bickering. She sticks her head out to make sure they don't come to blows. She threatens to take his tablet away if he doesn't leave his sister alone. Ivey is on her phone, making a TikTok video, Snapchatting, and texting all at the same time. She's thirteen and already deep inside the sullen abyss of adolescence. Arden figures she would have been a tough teenager no matter what, but Scott's death has added a depth of anger that complicates everything. Ivey, she's sure, is meaner and sadder than she ever would have been had Scott lived. The worst part for Arden is dealing with all of it alone—the wild hormones, the verbal assaults, the door-slamming and battles over phone time, the school drama, the silent treatments and alarming periods of isolation in her bed. Arden shoulders everything.

After Scott died, someone gave her a book called *Proof of Heaven*. She read it and it provided some fleeting comfort in the moment. In the spirit of it, she tried to "feel" Scott's presence, tried talking to him and waiting for intuitive answers. She went and bought all the books about life after death. She clung to the idea that Scott was still here, *somewhere*, possibly watching over them, helping out where he could. But as the days passed and her loneliness deepened, she began to feel cheated.

Scott wasn't *here*. He wasn't here to binge-watch their favorite shows, or to try the braised short rib and wasabi crema tacos at their favorite taqueria in Liberty Village. He wasn't here to cry with her over the descent into darkness of their beautiful little girl. He wasn't spooning her at night and paying the bills and fixing Wyatt's bike and taking her car in for an oil change and shoveling the front walk and listening to her complain about her sister and her mother. He wasn't touching her and scratching her back and fucking her. Death, it turns out, is just a crater in the hearts and lives of the ones left behind. After she realized that, she decided to get rid of Scott's things. She donated most of his clothes, threw out the sweat-stained workout gear and smelly running shoes, threw out his half-used bar of soap, his hair wax, his last bottle of Kiehl's after-shave balm. All she saved were a few T-shirts that smelled of him, and his favorite pair of jeans, which are folded at the bottom of her sock drawer. She wanted to be rid of the pain, to cleanse the house of him, to banish her grief. She erased his last voice mail and threw away his agenda, which was full of his illegible handwriting. She needed all traces of him out of the house. It hurt too much.

Having never lost anyone before, she failed to anticipate what it would be like not to have him after six weeks, six months, a year. She was dazed and out of her mind with grief in the beginning, so she gave him away in large chunks to try to get rid of her anguish. Gave away his dress shirts and bespoke suits and shaving kit because she didn't appreciate how meaningful all those meaningless things would be down the road. She was numb and impulsive, and so she erased him as a way to move forward. A year and a half later, she regrets all of it. She wishes she had kept all the leftover pieces of him, the things he'd touched and worn, the proof of his aliveness. She read somewhere that Liam Neeson still keeps all his wife's things in their bedroom, even a decade after her death, as though she might come back to him one day. Arden wishes she had done the same.

She realizes now—too late, of course—that she took their marriage for granted. They both did. They were basically waiting out the kids while counting down to the empty-nest years. They trudged through the daily grind, trying to stay afloat, perpetually weary and irritable. Life with three kids was messy, chaotic. There was far too much sarcasm and snark and under-the-breath muttering; too much teeth clenching and eye-rolling. (Scott once mentioned to Arden that he wanted them to "kiss more often," and she almost punched him in the face.) There just wasn't enough time to gaze into each other's eyes and profess their love for each other. Nevertheless, it could all be managed together.

The women in the widows' group she attended exactly once assured her that time would tenderize the pain, but it's been over a year and a half and time still hasn't fulfilled that promise. In her case, the grief is compounded by the financial sinkhole Scott left behind. She still needs a sleeping pill to drown out the fear and worry every night.

Scott was an exuberant spender. He did very well for himself as a stockbroker and they lived a high and frivolous life for several years, even though Arden was always wary of what he called "stretching." She had reservations about the enormous house in Lawrence Park, and then the sweeping home renovation he had planned, the Range Rover for her and Porsche for him, the Muskoka Lake cottage rental at fifteen thousand bucks a week, the speedboat, the endless overpriced restaurants, Italian suits, and maxed-out Platinum cards that she knew were not "stretching" so much as living well beyond their means. Toronto is a competitive city. He wanted to keep up, not just to be in the mix but to be at the top of it. He was always reassuring her, with the blithe arrogance of a successful Bay Street broker, that there was more than enough to go around. And there was, right up until the markets crashed in 2008 and their savings were practically wiped out. Still, Scott was relentless in his optimism, ever confident that he could and would get back to where he'd been. Consequently, he did very little over the ensuing years to curb his spending or alter their lifestyle. He hadn't planned on having twins and then dying suddenly at thirty-six.

In the end, he left Arden with significant debt, an unfinished home, and no college nest egg for their children. Their retirement fund was already significantly depleted after taking a massive hit in '08, so she used Scott's life insurance policy to pay off as much of their line of credit as she could. The Porsche, which he'd been leasing, went back to the dealership, and she traded in her car for something more modest.

Her mother and Tate have been campaigning for her to sell the house for months, but getting rid of it now would be like losing another family member. Besides, in its current state of semidisrepair, she would lose a fortune, *if* it sold at all.

Scott loved this house, a Depression-era Tudor Revival built in 1931 and virtually untouched, inside and out, in its entire eighty-seven-year history. He's the one who jokingly named it "Hackberry Manor," as an ode to the great, rotting hackberry tree on their front lawn. Part sentinel, part attractor of swarming starlings that rain purple shit on their cars, the pretty tree, with its rotted cavity and the nuisance of its fruit, became a metaphor for the house itself.

Arden's never liked the house—it's too medieval for her taste—but Scott was infatuated with it, from its steeply pitched, twin triangular gables and multipaned windows to the arched front door with the heavy wrought-iron knocker. The dark timber trim and white stucco facade on the upper half, he said, set it apart from the other homes on the street, which was true, in the way that a trailer would stick out on a similar street lined with modern limestone mansions. It would be their English country manor in the city, he said persuasively, and she understood then that he'd already made his decision. He was always going to live in Lawrence Park, on tree-lined Cheltenham Street.

Inside, the term "Depression-era" is more apt than Arden would like it to be. When they bought the house, the last renovation had been done by the previous owners in 1979, an attempt to restore it to its 1931 authenticity by staining every wood surface in the house—floors, stairwell, exposed ceiling beams, wall paneling, doors, and cabinetry—in Puritan mahogany. The effect of all that dark wood is heavy and somber, like living in an abandoned castle. Even the sun through the leaded-glass windows fails at its one objective to brighten up the place. Before they could make any aesthetic improvements, all the wiring had to be upgraded from the old knob and tube, the leaking gabled roof needed to be fixed, the decaying timber boards on the front of the house had to be replaced. After all that, there wasn't much money left to tackle the interior.

They eventually managed to update the upstairs bathroom, replacing all the pink tiles with Carrara marble, the rusty tub with a sleek, modern, egg-shaped thing. They did the kitchen as well, with help from a sought-after interior designer who installed a center island and fancy Italian appliances that cost about the same as a car.

Arden had never been exposed to the competitive underbelly of the North Toronto elite, with its crushing pressure to fit in and tick off all the right boxes. Scott, on the other hand, had lived for a time in nearby Lytton Park, with his own box-ticking parents, until they lost everything in the '89 recession. That early loss fueled Scott's determination to reclaim that status for his own family, which meant the big house in one of the Park neighborhoods, membership at one of the exclusive ski clubs in Collingwood, another membership at the Granite Club for tennis and socializing, and private school for all the kids. And then he died.

Now the kids attend the local public school, the club memberships are delinquent, and most of the house is still stuck in the 1930s—outdated, run-down, neglected. Still, the kids are secure here, they're content at their schools, and all their memories of Scott inhabit every room on every floor. To uproot them at this point would be reckless.

Arden stares at herself in the medicine cabinet mirror, shaking her damp brown hair out of its bun and letting it fall in soft waves to her shoulders. She needs to refresh her auburn lowlights, wax her eyebrows. She notices some new freckles on her face that didn't used to be there, the dark blue 3D circles under her eyes. She's only thirty-seven, but her body and spirit have been through a lot. When people find out she's a widow, they typically say, "My God, you're so young."

She does not feel young. She holds up her hand and twirls her wedding band around her finger. Scott put it on her for the first time on a rooftop terrace in Gramercy Park, a lifetime ago. They were married there by a Unitarian minister, with only their families and a handful of close friends in attendance. The apartment belonged to the parents of one of her stepfather's colleagues. The ceremony overlooked Manhattan, and she remembers thinking how strange it was to see people walking their dogs in the park below as she was saying "I do." It was the most momentous day of her life, and just an average day for those dogs and their owners, cleaning up shit and perhaps glancing up at the young couple on the terrace with their whole lives in front of them.

In the kitchen, it's breakfast as usual. "Don't forget to trim my crusts," Ali says, not looking up from whatever YouTube video she's watching. "Yesterday you left the crusts on."

"Why do seagulls live by the sea and not the bay?" Wyatt asks her. "Why?"

"Because then they'd be called *bagels*! Get it? *Bay-gulls?*"

Arden fakes a laugh, checks her watch. There's still time to make more lists for Tate. Rules and instructions, phone numbers, diagrams, and maps. A typical day starts when she kicks the three of them out of the house, entrusting Ivey to get the twins to Blythwood Public School and then herself to the middle school on time. After they're gone, Arden makes beds, throws in three or four loads of laundry, prepares some food, and pays bills—her new full-time job. At three thirty, she picks up the twins and then deposits them at various activities—swimming, karate, acro, soccer—and then home again for snacks and Lego and arts and crafts, always trying to make up for the fact that they don't have a father. The best part of the day is when she hands over their devices and gets some time to herself to make dinner and listen to the news and brace for the night shift. Only after they've gone to bed does she get to collapse on the couch with a show and a cup of tea.

The front door opens, slams shut. Tate appears in the kitchen looking flushed from the cold and irritatingly stunning, two rosy circles above her exquisite cheekbones and big sunglasses to hide her fortysomething eyes. Her long blond hair is pulled back in a low ponytail and her ass in those athleisure yoga pants doesn't look a day over twenty-five.

"You might want to Scotchgard that white jacket while you're here," Arden mutters.

Tate is seven years older than Arden, but they could pass for twins. Tate is the glamorous, successful sister. She's an editor at a home décor magazine and lives with her boyfriend, Tanvir, in a sleek Yorkville condo overlooking Bloor Street. No debt, no mortgage, no kids, although recently she's been contemplating having a baby. Basically, no burdens.

"This old thing?" Tate teases, taking off her shearling jacket and tossing it on the back of Ali's chair.

"Did you bring a sweatsuit?" Arden asks her.

"I'm wearing one."

"Here's the map to their school," Arden says. "And to their swimming lessons."

"The *map*? Isn't the school around the corner? Don't the kids know where they're going?"

"It's just in case." Arden hands her a thick document. "These are some instructions, some phone numbers. And here are the meds."

She opens the pantry door above the coffee machine and starts pulling out all the colored pill bottles. "This is Wyatt's Biphentin. He takes one with breakfast." WYATT is written in black Sharpie on the lid. "If you forget to give it to him, you'll probably get a call from his teacher."

"Got it."

"These are for Ivey," she says. "She gets one Vyvanse and one Zoloft. She has to take them with food. She hasn't been eating lately so you have to force her to have some toast at least, or the Vyvanse won't work."

"The Vyvanse is for the anxiety?"

"No, for the ADHD. The Zoloft is for the anxiety. She can forget to take a Vyvanse, but she *has* to take her Zoloft."

"What about this one?"

"This is my Prozac. I'll be taking it with me. Ivey sometimes takes a Dexedrine after school if she has a lot of homework and she needs some extra focus, but maybe don't give it to her while I'm gone. Sometimes it gives her heart palpitations and the last thing you want is for her to have one of her panic attacks and wind up at the hospital."

"Holy shit, you need a pharmacist, not a babysitter."

"This is the new world," Arden says.

"What about friends?"

"Only Tyler's mother keeps a completely peanut-free house for Wyatt."

"So he can go to Tyler's?"

"Yes, but that's *it*. Otherwise, you'd have to call whoever's mother beforehand and tell her exactly what to do and it's a big pain in the ass—"

Wyatt's brow furrows. Arden quickly puts her arm around him and crouches down to talk to him at eye level. "I shouldn't have said that, Magpie. I just meant it's a lot of trouble for Aunt Tate to explain to your friends' moms—"

"You think I'm a pain in the ass."

"No, I don't," she says. "Now, go put your shoes on or you'll be late for school."

"What else do I need to know?" Tate asks, skimming the documents.

"Wyatt's been having nightmares. I stupidly had a Holocaust documentary on while he was in the room. I didn't realize he was paying attention. If it's a bad one, just give him his iPad till he falls asleep."

"Can I give him a Zoloft?"

Arden looks at her, not sure if she's kidding. You can never tell with nonparents. "No, you can't give him a Zoloft."

"What about screen time?"

"The twins get an hour after dinner. Ivey only after all her homework is done."

"Ah yes, I see that here in your four-hundred-page tome."

"I'd be happy to stay home and let you go to New York in my place."

"It's been over a year," Tate says. "You need this. And so do *they*."

The phone rings before Arden has a chance to argue. She hunts around for it, silently cursing whichever kid—because it's *always* a kid—carelessly misplaced it. She finally finds it on the built-in desk in the butler's pantry, buried under the *Globe and Mail*. "Hello?"

"Arden Moore?"

"Yes."

"This is Larry Lasker. I'm the estate lawyer—"

"My husband's estate has already been settled," Arden interrupts. "It was settled right after he died."

"Actually, I'm calling from Westchester County, New York."

Arden drops into the Gobi barstool, suddenly placing his name. *Uncle Larry.*

"I represented your mother many years ago in the Ashforth hearings."

"Of course," she manages, and it all comes back at once, a deluge of confusion and pain.

"I knew you when you were a little girl," he says, and of course she remembers driving around in his navy blue Corvette, eating Dunkin' Donuts and singing along to the Everly Brothers. There was no back seat in that car, so her mother and Uncle Larry used to squeeze her into the crawl space whenever they had to drive between Rye and Manhattan.

She loved it at first, until those donuts and fun rides led to the ruin of her snug little life in Brooklyn.

"The petitions were over your right to inherit from your father's estate," he reminds her.

"That was a long time ago. We've all moved on."

"I've been following another, related estate case in the Surrogate's Court," he explains. "I was waiting on that verdict before reaching out to you. The decision just came in and I thought you might be interested. It affects you a great deal, Arden."

The way he calls her by her first name makes it seem like they're old friends. She's not eight anymore; he can't win her over with donuts. "I can't do this," she says.

"Arden—"

"It's been over for a long time, Mr. Lasker. My mother gave it all she had, and she lost. It cost us a great deal, and I won't make that same mistake."

"This time it has to do with Bruce Ashforth," he says. "Your half brother. You may or may not know he died?"

A caterpillar of excitement crawls up the back of her neck.

"Can I at least give you my number?" Lasker says. "I think you'll want to hear what I have to say. You know how much money is at stake."

"How much exactly?"

"They're estimating Bruce's estate to be worth about sixty million, which would put your share at thirty, give or take."

She sputters something, an attempt to speak that fails and comes out sounding like a burp.

"Your Uber's here!" Tate calls from the other room.

"Give me your number," Arden says. "I'm actually on my way to New York right now. I could meet with you Sunday before I fly home?"

She reaches for a pen and scribbles his number on the corner of the newspaper.

"I look forward to seeing you again," he says.

She hangs up and calls her mother. No answer.

"Are you coming?" Tate says, barging into the butler's pantry. "The Uber driver is about to leave."

"Have you heard from Mom?"

"Not today. Why?"

"Her old lawyer just called me. Remember Larry Lasker? The short guy with the perm and the Village People moustache?"

"Yeah, of course. The one with the donuts."

"He just called," Arden says. "He wants to talk to me about the Ashforth inheritance again."

"Why now?"

"It has to do with my half brother, Bruce's, death. Apparently, I may be able to inherit from him."

Tate sighs unhappily. Arden can't blame her; they all have terrible memories from their mother's legal crusade against the Ashforths.

"It's thirty million dollars," Arden adds, and Tate's expression changes.

"So here we go again," Arden says, and they stare at each other in silence, understanding perfectly, without having to say a word, the full implication of what that means.

2

The first picture Arden ever saw of her father fell out of one of her mother's books, *The Sensuous Woman*, when she was six. They were packing to move from their basement apartment in Astoria to the house in Brooklyn that belonged to her mother's boyfriend, Hal. It was very hot that day. *Today in New York* was announcing ninety-four degrees for the second day in a row. There was a noisy fan oscillating slowly, like an old man having trouble breathing. The fan was sitting on a plastic folding chair their mother had dragged into the middle of the room. Arden was scooping books from the bookcase and dumping them into file boxes. Her mother wasn't a big reader—in fact, Arden had never seen her mother read anything before, although it's possible she read after Arden went to sleep—but she was very attached to the books she did have. She had given Arden very specific instructions about which books went into which boxes. The boxes were labeled "Sexuality," "Diet," and "Self-Help." Arden had to figure out which ones went where. Some were more obvious than others—*The Complete Scarsdale Medical Diet, The Save Your Life Diet, The Beverly Hills Diet, The Hite Report: A Nationwide Study of Female Sexuality, The Joy of Sex, The Sensuous Woman.*

Arden stopped to flip through *The Sensuous Woman*, which is when the photograph fell into her lap. She gazed it for a moment, sitting there on her bare thigh, and she knew it was her father. The date at the bottom said July 1979.

"Is this our dad?" she asked her mother, holding up the picture.

Virginia was in the kitchenette, wrapping dishes in newspaper. She stopped what she was doing and lowered *Phil Donahue* on her little ten-inch TV. "Where did you find that?"

"In this book," Arden said, holding it up.

Virginia threw her head back and laughed. "Isn't moving fun?" she said. "All the things you find!"

"So, he *is* our dad?" Arden asked again, studying the man in the picture. He had a dark suntan and deep creases fanning out around eyes, which were squinting into the sun. He was on a boat, wearing a blue windbreaker and white pants. A pair of sunglasses was perched on his head, tamping down his windblown white hair.

"That's him," Virginia said, climbing over some boxes to get to her. "I forgot about that picture."

"He's so old."

"He was handsome, though. You had to see him in person."

"How did he die?" She never thought to ask until now.

"He died in a plane crash," her mother said. "When I was pregnant with you."

"It was his own plane," Tate added, coming out of her bedroom. She was wearing her boxer shorts, the ones that said RAD on the bottom and a cropped Madonna T-shirt from the Who's That Girl concert in July. Tate and Virginia had had a huge fight about it because the T-shirt had cost a fortune and Tate went and cut it up, so that now it showed off a strip of her stomach. She had grown tall and skinny over the summer. She was almost fourteen, and their mother kept saying, "Things are about to get interesting around here."

"He was one of the richest men in America," Tate said.

"He was?"

"She's exaggerating," Virginia said. "He was nowhere near one of the richest men in America."

"He was a billionaire," Tate said.

"He was not a billionaire," Virginia corrected, starting to sound exasperated. "He probably had a hundred million or so, yes, that's true. But a billion dollars is a thousand million, and Wallace did not have that much."

"*Sorryyyy*," Tate said. "I stand corrected. He was a hundred millionaire then." She was leaning against the bookcase with her usual surly expression. *Looking to cause trouble*, Virginia used to say. "Our dad was really a hundred millionaire?" Arden said, turning to her mother.

"He wasn't *our* dad," Tate corrected her matter-of-factly. "Uncle Wally was *your* dad. We don't have the same father."

Virginia's head twisted around like a Barbie doll's.

"We're not sisters?" Arden cried, and the world as she knew it collapsed around her, leaving her sitting there among her mother's sex books and the rubble of her formerly safe universe.

"We're *half* sisters," Tate said. "We have the same mother, but different fathers. Your father was, like, the richest man in the America, and mine was the poorest."

"For God's sake, Tate."

Arden began to cry.

Tate looked stricken and rushed over to her. "We're still sisters," she said, pulling Arden into her arms. "Having the same mother basically makes us real sisters."

"Why do you have to be so mean?" Virginia said to Tate. "She didn't need to know that today."

Tate rolled her eyes. She was angry because she didn't want to go live with Uncle Hal, who was going to marry their mother in the fall. She wanted to stay in their little apartment, just the three of them. Arden understood that Tate had meant to hurt their mother, not her, but it still felt like Tate had kicked her in the stomach.

"Why don't Tate and I have the same father?" she asked her mother.

"Because I loved two men," Virginia explained. Tate rolled her eyes again.

Arden couldn't explain what exactly she felt she'd lost—her sister? Her father? Her mother? Probably all of them. Or maybe it was the *idea* of her mother, who was no longer perfect and solid and trustworthy in her eyes, but somehow smudged, like an ink blob on a beautiful drawing. What if her mother had another baby with Uncle Hal? There would be three of them, connected by one mother and yet fundamentally disconnected, with fathers scattered everywhere.

"You also have two brothers," Tate said.

Arden looked over at her mother. Virginia was glaring at Tate. "Is that true?"

"Yes, hon. Two half brothers."

"Can I play with them?"

"They're grown-ups," Tate chimed in. "They're Mom's age."

"A few years younger than me," Virginia said. "They'd be in their twenties now."

"Why don't we ever see them?"

"They hate Mom," Tate said. "They think she's a gold digger, so they act like you don't exist."

"Oh, Tate!" Virginia cried. "Stop it now. Just stop it."

Virginia took both of Arden's hands in her own and said, "One day, you will get your share of the Ashforth fortune."

"Arden's going to be a billionaire?" Tate cried.

"Wallace Ashforth was your father," Virginia said, ignoring Tate. "And no matter what your half brothers say or do, I will *never* stop fighting for what belongs to you, Arden. Do you hear me?"

Arden nodded, confused.

"Now, I can put this picture in a frame for you if you like," Virginia said, making her voice sound light and bubbly. "And you can keep it in your new room."

Arden nodded again, not sure why it mattered. She felt nothing at all for the old man in the photograph, but she did latch onto the good parts of the story and embellish them. A couple of years later, when she was in third grade at her new school in Midwood, she told her classmates her father had been the richest man in the world. No one believed her, though. They knew she lived in a small house on Avenue K, no different from the rest of them. When she asked her mother about this, Virginia said, "Your father didn't have a will, which is why you got nothing. But one day you'll get everything you deserve."

Arden's teacher, Mrs. Rosenstern, kept Arden after school one day and told her to stop talking about how rich her dead father was. She said that no one liked a braggart. Arden thought the word "braggart" was hilarious. She had no intention of stopping; the bragging was all she had. But then one day she made some comment about her father being Wallace Ashforth, the millionaire. Normally the other kids just ignored her, but this time, someone from her class—a popular girl named Carrie Stein—took a few steps closer to her. They were in the schoolyard for recess, playing dodgeball. Carrie was holding the red dimpled ball against her chest. She was wearing a black Monsters of Rock T-shirt and had a scary look on her face. The other kids from the game gathered in closer when she approached Arden. "My mom knows who your mom is," Carrie said. "Your mom was in the newspaper because she's a *con artist*."

The other kids snickered. Arden remembers their laughing faces floating around her. "She is not," Arden said, her face getting hot.

"My mom says your mother is a scammer and that you're a bastard," Carrie went on. "She says your mom doesn't have a clue who your real father is and that she's just using you to get the money. So, stop saying Wallace Ashforth is your father because the truth is you're *nobody*."

That was the last time Arden ever bragged about being an Ashforth.

3

Arden is on the bathroom floor at her stepfather Hal's with her laptop and a mug of lukewarm Earl Grey tea perched on the ledge of the tub. She's used to working in the bathroom, which, it turns out, is a viable office when you have three kids clamoring after you or your stepfather won't leave you alone in his small house. Whatever positive mental health benefits she gained during her spa day yesterday are now just vapors, the replenished energy already depleted. She opens the laptop and ignores all the bills collecting in her inbox, with no plan to deal with them anytime soon. She hates everything to do with managing their finances: writing checks, transferring money, paying bills. It's even worse when there's no money to shuffle, so she procrastinates, letting the "nonperilous" stuff languish, accruing late fees and unnecessary interest charges, and paying what has to be paid at the last possible moment. She can't remember if it was always like this for them, or if Scott just kept her safely buffered from it all. Until he died, she didn't even know her online banking password. She just blithely handed it over to him, as though she were the fourth child in their family. How could she have known? There was no contingency plan for losing him. Her part-time job and survivor's pension won't sustain them forever, let alone cover three college tuitions.

Some days she blames herself for their debt, other days she thinks it's her mother's fault for modeling codependence, but it was Scott who was so consumed by status and power and spending that he was never able to rebuild their savings after the recession. He died trying. She asked him once why status was so damn important to him.

"Because that's how I was raised," he said.

That conversation happened early in their marriage, before kids, when they were house-hunting in neighborhoods they couldn't afford. Arden was trying to warn him. He knew about how *she*'d been raised— specifically that her mother's obsession with the Ashforth inheritance had ultimately robbed Arden of her mother, her beloved stepfather, and the first home where she had finally felt secure and normal. "I would have traded all the money in the world to stay with Hal in Brooklyn," she told Scott.

"That's completely different," he argued. "Your mother was chasing a castle in the sky! It was always a long shot. Inheritances like that only happen in the movies. *I'm* the one making my own money here. I'm already earning a ton and there's only going to be more and more of it."

"My point is that her obsession with money ruined my life."

"That will never happen to us, Arden. You know what I earned this year. We're good, babe. We're *really* good."

She realized then she would either have to embrace his values or fight him every step of the way, so she capitulated and joined him on the ladder. It was fun for a while. It was a trick ladder, though, she soon discovered. Every time they reached the top rung and paused to catch their breath, a new rung appeared out of nowhere, and the climb had to continue. You either continue climbing, panting and weary, or you free-fall.

Arden reaches for her phone and calls home for the routine family FaceTime. Wyatt answers on the first ring. "Knock-knock!"

"Who's there?"

"Urine."

"Urine who?"

"*Urine* trouble if you don't open the door!"

Peels of laughter from Wyatt. They're all there except Ivey, squashed together around Tate's laptop. Arden can hear the faint thumping of Ivey's angry music from her bedroom.

"Speaking of urine," Tate says, "tell your mom what you did."

"I urined in my underwear."

"Oh, Wyatt. I'm sorry, Tate."

"Aunty Tate made me wash them myself."

"Good for her," Arden says. "How long have they been on their screens?" she asks Tate. The twins both look a little dazed.

"I don't know. An hour, maybe?"

"Like, five hours?" Ali says.

Arden frowns. "You have to set boundaries for them, Tate. They could be watching porn for all you know."

"What's porn?"

"I'm trying," Tate says wearily.

"Where's Ivey?" Arden asks. "She's not answering my texts."

Tate calls up to Ivey through the ceiling. "Your mom's on the phone!" Nothing.

"She probably doesn't want you to see her," Wyatt says.

"Why not?"

"Her hair is green," Ali says. "And all the white towels are green, too."

"She dyed her hair?"

"She didn't tell me she was going to do it," Tate says. "She's always locked in her room or the bathroom. I'm not equipped to handle a teenager. The little ones, sure. But Ivey is above my pay grade."

"Mine too," Arden says, defeated.

"Did you speak to the lawyer?"

"Tomorrow. He's meeting us for lunch before I fly home. I'm taking Hal."

"Be careful, Arden. Remember what happened to Mom."

"I can't go there yet."

"What does Mom say?"

"I haven't been able to reach her all weekend," Arden says. "You?"

"No."

"Can we go now, Mom?"

"I miss you, my magpies."

"Bye, Mom."

One by one, the twins sign off.

"No more devices tonight!" Arden shouts, and she can see Tate wink at them, thinking she's off camera.

After the call, Arden Googles Wallace Ashforth on her laptop. A handful of search results pop up, many of them linked to inheritance proceedings. She clicks Wikipedia and takes a long gulp of tea, hoping to discover more about her father and brothers. The truth is, she knows almost nothing about them from Virginia, and she herself made a decision long ago never to delve.

Wallace Archibald Ashforth, son of "Tin Plate Magnate" Dugald Ashforth, was killed in a plane crash September 1, 1980, with his wife, Geraldine.

The patriarch of the family, Dugald Ashforth, was born in Glasgow, County Lanarkshire, in the Central Lowlands of Scotland in 1880. At eighteen, he immigrated to America and began an apprenticeship at a small tin-plating firm in New York City. Within five years, he had not only purchased it but also grown it into the leading tin-plate company in the industry. Just shy of thirty, Dugald—now known as the "Tin Plate Magnate"—sold his company to U.S. Steel for more than fifty million dollars. He married at the age of fifty and had a son, Wallace Ashforth, his only heir.

After graduating from Princeton, Wallace, who shared his father's instinct for business, took a risk and invested in a forty-story tower on West Fifty-Fifth Street, which he named the Ashforth Building. Soon he was at the forefront of the postwar Midtown Manhattan building boom. By the early sixties, he had founded Ashforth Development Group and was working alongside David Rockefeller on the urban renewal of Lower Manhattan, steadfastly amassing his own fortune. In 1950, he married Geraldine Lammers, the daughter of a Dutch diplomat, and they had their first son, Bruce, in 1957. The following year, Geraldine gave birth to James.

In the midseventies, when New York City was on the brink of bankruptcy and crime rates were soaring, Wallace made two bold moves: he purchased 2 million square feet of real estate on the Upper West Side, and he relocated his family to Denby, in Westchester County, New York, a wealthy town on the Long Island Sound, cozily nestled between New Rochelle and Rye. They lived there until Wallace and Geri's Cessna crashed into the White Mountains of New Hampshire on Labor Day 1980. They were both just one year shy of fifty.

The most noteworthy circumstance surrounding their deaths was that neither Wallace nor Geraldine had a will, which was unconventional given Wallace's sizable estate, but widely explained by the combination of his youth and hubris. Whatever the reason for the intestacy, the entire fortune quietly passed to his only two heirs, Jamie and Bruce.

Arden reads a few stories about Jamie's petition for control of his brother Bruce's estate, and the ensuing legal battle with the Parkinson's Foundation, and then, feeling sleepy, she closes her laptop. She dumps the rest of her tea down the toilet, stretches her legs on the tiled floor, and leans back against the tub. She tries her mother one more time—she hasn't been able to reach her since before she left for New York—but it goes straight to voice mail again.

"*Where are you?*" she says. "I need to speak to you about my father."

This is the third voice mail she's left in two days, along with multiple texts, all of them unanswered. Arden knows Virginia is with a man—Virginia is *always* with a man when she goes MIA—but the timing couldn't be more inconvenient.

She texts Tate. I think Mom is in a Manhole again.

4

The next day, Arden and Hal enter the dark foyer of Beijing Palace in Midtown. Arden approaches the maître d' while Hal hangs back to grab a handful of loose pastel mints from a glass jar. "We have a reservation for three under Lasker," Arden says, looking around.

Before Virginia divorced Hal and moved the girls back to Toronto, Hal used to take them here on very special occasions—Virginia's thirty-fifth, his first vernissage. He brought Arden for lunch on her tenth birthday, just the two of them, while Virginia was in court. He told the waiter it was his daughter's first double-digit birthday, and then he ordered half a dozen dishes, including her favorite, Three-Nut Chicken. Afterward, they rode home on the subway, each with a doggie bag on their lap. The place hasn't changed at all since she was last here, its décor immune to trend. Every detail is implicitly choreographed to capture the quintessential Chinese fine-dining experience—the dark leather booths, blood-red carpet, fire-breathing dragon murals, and napkins blooming like flowers in the water glasses on every table, the lazy Susans and the assemblage of waiters in their pristine white jackets ready to spring into action at their captain's signal. It could be the sixties or the eighties; no one would know the difference.

The maître d' leads them wordlessly to the back of the restaurant, padding softly on the carpet as though his shoes were slippers, and then points to an older man in one of the booths.

"Is he paying?" Hal whispers in Arden's ear.

"Mr. Lasker?" Arden says tentatively.

The lawyer looks up from his menu and breaks into a smile. "Arden Bunt," he says, looking her over, incredulous. "The last time I saw you, you were what? Six? Seven?"

"Eight or nine, I think."

"Christ."

He jumps to his feet and leans in to peck her cheek. She flinches slightly, not expecting the kiss, and they stand there awkwardly for a moment, contemplating each other with disbelief, corralling their memories.

"I felt old before I saw you," he says, still staring at her. "You look so much like your mother."

She smiles, knowing he means it as a compliment—Virginia is a beautiful woman—but nevertheless begrudging any comparison to her mother. "You've met my stepdad, Hal Koffler."

They shake hands vigorously, looking each other directly in the eyes. "It was a long time ago," Hal says.

"You were in court a few times back in the late eighties," Lasker says.

"I was," Hal answers, with uncharacteristic coldness. He doesn't elaborate.

"He had hair back then so you may not remember him," Arden joked.

"So did I," Lasker laments.

In contrast to Hal's baggy Old Navy jeans and Brooklyn College sweatshirt, Larry Lasker is wearing a starched white shirt with a purple striped tie, chunky gold cuff links, and an elegant Patek Philippe watch. His silver-gray suit jacket, slung over the back of the booth, is obviously bespoke, as are his bluish-white teeth. He's shorter than she remembered, with thinning silver hair, no longer permed, and a deeply suntanned face. His unnaturally smooth forehead suggests injections. He's certainly using his abundant resources to wage war against aging.

"You shaved your moustache," she says, sliding into the booth and wrecking the perfect napkin flower as she lays it on her lap.

"I got rid of it back in the midnineties," he says. "My wife told me I looked like a porn star, so off it went."

She remembers his shirts were always open one button too many, and if he moved a certain way, she would glimpse a nipple. He always wore around his neck a gold Star of David, which used to get tangled in his chest hair.

"Thank you for meeting me," he says, flagging the waiter. He orders a Tsingtao beer. "Would you like one?"

Hal nods and Arden orders a glass of white wine.

"I'm sorry about your husband," Lasker says. "Virginia told me. Such a loss." He shakes his head, brown eyes clouding over. "Thirty-six years old. You never know, do you?"

"You spoke to Virginia?" Hal says edgily.

"Yes. Briefly. Before I called Arden."

"She didn't mention it."

"It was just a courtesy call," he explains lightly. "She said she'd help you any way she could."

The headwaiter returns with their drinks, and Lasker takes it upon himself to order for the table—egg foo young, Hunan filet mignon, and crispy shrimp. "Anything you want to add?" he asks them.

"Moo goo gai pan," Hal says, pointing to the "Old Favorites—Food from the Fifties" section of the menu.

"And the Three-Nut Chicken, please," Arden adds.

When the waiter leaves, Lasker turns to Arden with that familiar, pitying look in his eyes and says, "So, how are your kids doing? You've got two?"

"Three."

"Three kids," he murmurs, shaking his head. "They must miss their dad. You must be having a hell of a time."

"We're managing," she says, annoyed at having her current pain probed by someone who caused so much of it in the past.

"Good for you. You're a brave lady."

The word "lady" jars, a relic of a word. Arden attempts a polite smile, thinking Lasker may look current, but his soul belongs to a bygone era. Hal looks like he's holding back an eye roll. Arden can sense he can't stand Larry Lasker.

"You probably want to know why we're here," Lasker continues, reaching for his gray-on-gray checkered Louis Vuitton briefcase. "As I mentioned on the phone, there's been a new development. Your half brother, Bruce, died of complications from Parkinson's disease almost two years ago. Just before he died, he revoked his will—actually, he had his lawyer burn it—and then he named his nurse as sole executor and left his entire estate to the Parkinson's Foundation."

"And I fit in how?" Arden wants to know.

"Jamie Ashforth contested his brother's new will, claiming that Bruce was not of sound mind when he changed it. I've been following that hearing since it began, and the good news is Jamie Ashforth just won his petition on final appeal."

Lasker smiles, his eyes shining triumphantly. Arden and Hal are silent, lost.

"To make a long story short," Lasker explains, "Bruce Ashforth died *intestate*. Do you see? He essentially died without a will, which means, for all intents and purposes, that his sixty-million-dollar estate is up for grabs."

Arden looks over at Hal, who suddenly has bulging cartoon eyes.

"Egg foo young, sir."

The three of them look up, startled to discover a team of eager waiters standing over them with silver-domed platters. The captain proceeds to remove each cloche and painstakingly distribute the food onto all three of their plates in equal measure.

"Moo goo gai pan," he announces, formally doling out each spoonful as though he were a footman serving the royal family. "And Three-Nut Chicken."

Arden's mind is racing.

"Hunan-style filet mignon . . ."

When the parade of food finally comes to an end, Lasker resumes talking. "Bottom line," he says, leaning in closer, "the door is open for you."

"Doesn't Jamie inherit his brother's estate?" Hal asks. "Since Bruce had no other family?"

"Yes and no," Lasker responds. "There's one caveat." He pauses to take a bite of his food and then, with a mouthful of prawn, says, *"Arden."*

"How?"

"You're Bruce's half sister, Arden. You're entitled to an equal share of the estate."

"But you've been down this road before with Virginia," Hal reminds him sharply. "And you lost every time. *I was there.* We all lost."

Arden looks over at Hal, who's glaring across the table at Lasker with open hostility. She forgets sometimes that Hal lost as much as she did and that Virginia's history with the Ashforths is also *Hal's* history. Arden was a little girl. She doesn't remember very much, other than its final consequence. Most of what she knows was told to her, or she read it online.

In 1981, Virginia, who was the former secretary and lover of Wallace Ashforth, applied for Letters of Administration at the Surrogate's Court in White Plains, New York, on behalf of her baby daughter, Arden, claiming the infant was the biological child of Wallace Ashforth. Given that Wallace had died intestate, Virginia argued that her daughter should be a beneficiary. That argument unfolded in the Surrogate's Court over the next four years, at great cost to Virginia.

In the end, she was not able to establish Wallace's paternity of Arden by clear and convincing evidence, and her application was denied, as was Arden's right to inherit. In the words of the surrogate, the child, Arden, was considered a filius nullius, child of no one. It was 1985. The following year, Virginia and the girls moved in with Hal in Brooklyn. It might have been a fresh start for them all but for Larry Lasker's chutzpah and refusal to quit. Any loophole he could find—the repealing of an obscure clause that related to illegitimate children, the possibility of a change of venue—he seized and filed a new petition.

Arden's few memories of her mother from that period are mostly of being picked up after school to ride the train to Rye, and then playing on the floor of Lasker's office. He used to bring her things, probably to get her out of the way and keep her quiet—donuts, jacks, a Feeling Fun Barbie doll that was dressed in a fringed denim jacket and lace miniskirt. Arden doesn't remember being inside the courtroom, or seeing her two half brothers, the "greedy tightwads," Virginia used to call them, but there's a vague recollection of serious conversations in hushed voices happening around her. She does remember thinking how boring grownups were and wishing Tate were there to play with her, but Tate was getting older and didn't have time for her anymore.

Arden remembers a terrible argument between Hal and Virginia during that time. Arden was about eight or nine, it was near the end, so it would have been the late eighties. Virginia had been filing petitions and appeals in every court right on up to the Court of Appeals in Albany for nearly a decade. Her latest petition sought to move the proceedings out of Westchester County, where, Lasker had convinced her, the Ashforths' influence was insurmountable.

"When do we get to start living?" Hal asked her. They were making dinner in the kitchen. Hal rarely ever got mad or yelled, but that night Arden remembers she could hear him yelling from her bedroom. She crept to the top of the stairs.

"Larry thinks if my claim could just be heard outside of Westchester County—"

"Larry thinks, Larry says, Larry, Larry, Larry. He's the reason we're still in this nightmare! Maybe if he would just accept defeat and let you move on, we'd be free of this albatross."

"He has a lot to lose, Hal. He's already invested so much of his time and money."

"That's *his* problem," Hal shouted. "No one forced him to work on contingency. What about how much *we've* lost?"

"We haven't lost anything."

"Virginia, really? Take a look around you. You've lost almost a decade of your life already! A decade of your daughters' lives! I'm the one raising Arden!"

"I'm doing this for *them*!"

"They would rather have a mother, trust me."

"They have a mother."

"No they don't. You're not really here with us. You're too busy living in the future. *When we get the money, when we win the claim, when we make the Ashforth brothers pay . . .*"

Hal must have thrown something then—Arden heard a smash, like glass shattering—or maybe it was an accident or Virginia was the one who threw it, but Arden was frightened. She loved Hal and didn't want him to leave them.

"When is it time to move on?" he asked Virginia, lowering his voice. "Tell me. When do we get to live in the present again? I can't take much more of this, living on pause. Everything is always on hold. We can't even go on vacation '*until we get the money*'!"

"We're broke, Hal. Everything is on hold because we're broke."

"We're broke because every cent we make goes to your 'extra' out-of-pocket legal fees. Contingency, my ass."

"We're close this time, Hal. Larry is convinced if I can file in—"

"Stop, Virginia. You're always close. You've been close for eight years. Can't you just move on?" he pleaded. "Isn't it time?"

Virginia eventually lost her motion to move the proceedings to a different county. She went on to lose two more appeals before finally raising the white flag, but by then it was too late. She'd blown up her marriage. Hal filed for divorce in 1989 and Virginia and the girls moved out, to a small apartment on a nearby street.

Two years later, in the summer of 1991, Virginia—single again—decided to move back to Toronto with Tate and Arden. She had to physically leave New York in order to thoroughly and effectively put Larry Lasker and the Ashforths behind her. Arden was almost eleven at the time, Tate eighteen. Arden was devastated. She didn't want to leave Hal, who had raised her as his own since she was six. She couldn't have loved him more if he'd been her real father. She also had some good friends at PS 193 and had been looking forward to going into sixth grade with them, their final year before starting junior high; she was happy in Midwood, with Hal just a few blocks away. Unlike Tate, her life in Brooklyn was the only life she'd ever known or remembered.

The timing was perfect for Tate, though, who was about to start college. It was decided she would study journalism at Carleton University in Ottawa, where the tuition was cheap compared to the States. Virginia was a dual citizen—she'd been filing taxes and using her parents' address as her own for years—so she was entitled to Canadian health care and a school loan for Tate. Tate, who was born in Toronto, started telling people she was moving "back home," which infuriated Arden.

They moved in with Virginia's parents, the dour Bunts, who lived in a narrow, three-bedroom house on Cortland Avenue. It was a cul-de-sac with a sprawling Catholic church on the corner and lots of parks nearby—a "good" neighborhood with "good" schools, Virginia kept saying. In the end, their transition across the border was quiet, seamless. Arden started sixth grade, Tate went off to college, and Virginia threw herself into finding a job. Brooklyn began to recede. New friends were made. Eventually, Virginia got a job at Stewart's, an upscale department store in the Yorkdale Mall, and they moved to an apartment near the school. Puberty assailed Arden's body and became its own demarcation in the history of her life, overshadowing the move from New York and everything else that had happened before it.

"Why couldn't you ever prove paternity between my father and me?" Arden asks Lasker.

"New York probably has the most complicated law of descent of distribution," Lasker explains, sighing profoundly. "Unfortunately, up until very recently, illegitimate children have been harshly discriminated against in the courts. Obviously, the belief was that extramarital relationships could be discouraged by penalizing the illegitimate child."

Illegitimate. Arden hates that word almost as much as she hates the word "bastard." She can still hear Carrie Stein belting her with it in the schoolyard. She hasn't thought of herself that way in a long time. After Scott and the kids, she thought it had stopped defining her. *Child of no one.*

"Wallace never knew about you; he died before you were born. There was no proof of paternity without exhumation and no surrogate in the state would have allowed the body to be exhumed for a postmortem paternity test."

"Why did you agree to take on the case, then?" Arden asks him. "It sounds like it was a total waste of time from the start."

"Not at all," he says. "I was quite optimistic. I believed we could win a motion to order blood tests for your half brothers, which I felt could be very persuasive in establishing kinship."

"But you never did prove kinship."

"No. Even after the law became a little friendlier to nonmarital children in the late eighties, I couldn't convince the Westchester Surrogate's Court to compel blood or DNA testing on either of the Ashforth brothers."

"And now?"

"Great question. There are three factors that improve your odds significantly if we were to file a petition today. One, the law has changed. As I mentioned, it's a hell of a lot friendlier to nonmarital children. Two, there have been tremendous advances in genetic marker testing. You either are or you aren't a distributee, and with a simple DNA test, we don't have to waste the court's time with an expensive, drawn-out kinship hearing. And finally, although the Surrogate's Court denied your right to inherit from Wallace Ashforth in the eighties, we're dealing with a different decedent now."

"But how do we get Bruce's DNA?"

"Glad you asked," Lasker says excitedly. "Bruce's brain, which is full of viable tissue, just happens to be sitting in a jar in Florida."

"My God. Why?"

"Bruce donated his brain to the Parkinson's Foundation for research," Lasker says. "Which means no exhumation is necessary to get a DNA sample."

"Would the DNA be reliable from embalmed brain tissue?"

"According to my expert, an extraction and washing procedure was developed that significantly increases the quantity and quality of the embalmed DNA. Given that Bruce passed away quite recently, I think the chances are excellent that his DNA will be well preserved. A lot of posthumous cases are proving kinship these days; yours wouldn't be the first. Of course, this will all be thoroughly investigated by a team of scientists, should you decide to proceed."

After a protracted silence, Hal says, "Do you really think you can win this time? That there's a real possibility Arden could inherit?"

"I won't go down the same road my mother went down," Arden adds. "I can't do that to my kids."

She remembers all the promises Virginia made over the years—the three-story brownstone in Park Slope she was going to buy, the convertible Corvette for summer drives, the Hamptons beach house, which, she promised the girls, would have a swimming pool with a slide and a trampoline out back and built-in bunk beds and a rec room in the basement for pinball and Ping-Pong. She was going to take them to Disneyland *and* Disney World, and they were going to fly to Florida and California first-class, which sounded rich and impressive even though Arden had no idea what it meant. Virginia used to cut pictures out of magazines of Corvettes and mansions and pools that belonged to famous actresses and stick them on the fridge with magnets. She'd gotten that idea from a book called *Creative Visualization*. She was going to buy them banana-seat bicycles and Barbie Dream Campers and Sega consoles and take them on a shopping spree to FAO Schwarz at Christmas. It turned into a game she called When We're Millionaires, and over the first ten years of Arden's life, that list grew in scope, lavishness, and imagination. That none of those things ever materialized was extremely disappointing, but not tragic. On some level, Arden understood that it was just a game.

It was the other unfilled promises that left Arden resentful, the promise of Virginia herself. All the time she was going to spend with them when it was over; the museums and zoos they would visit, the movies they would see, the cookies they would bake, the endless snuggles at bedtime. Instead, Virginia was perpetually at the courthouse in White Plains, or in Rye, working on her case with Lasker. It was Hal who picked Arden up from school most days and took her to MoMA and the zoo and let her paint with him in the basement for hours on end.

"Chasing this bloody inheritance cost us our marriage," Hal says, glowering at Larry. "I will not watch the same thing happen to my daughter."

"I'll be honest with you," Lasker says. "We both got a bit . . . *mired*. There was a lot of money at stake and your mother knew Wallace was your father, Arden. Can you imagine her frustration, knowing how much money was within your reach? The deeper we got, the harder it was to walk away. I was a thirtysomething *schmuck*. I was arrogant, cocky. I really believed we could win. I believed you were—*are*—entitled to a share of that estate. That's why I approached her and offered to file her petition."

Lasker puts on his bifocals and begins to read aloud from one of his documents. *"The statute also provides that half-blood relatives are to be treated*, and I quote, *as if they were relatives of the whole blood."*

He puts the paper down and removes his glasses.

"I know you worked pro bono for my mother," Arden says. "Will you have the same arrangement with me?"

"I worked on contingency. Pro bono makes it sound a lot more noble than it is," Lasker says. "I was more like a personal injury lawyer. I stood to earn fifteen percent on your inheritance, which would have been a handsome payday."

Arden picks at her food, not really tasting anything. "So, you'll work on contingency again?"

Lasker's expression changes and Arden immediately deflates.

"I can't," he says. "I would be willing to come down in my fees if you were to compensate me with a percentage of the inheritance at the end."

"Come down how much?"

"I could shave off twenty percent of my hourly rate."

"Which is?"

"Eight hundred."

Hal's jaw falls open and he makes a noise that sounds like air seeping out of a tire. "That's criminal," he mutters.

Arden adds, "I may as well just sign over my house."

"I'm sorry, but I don't do contingency anymore."

"Don't you owe it to her?" Hal says, his voice layered with rancor and accusation.

Lasker doesn't respond.

"But you're basically saying it's a sure thing," Arden points out.

"I've learned enough over the years to know there's never a sure thing," he says, suddenly changing his tune from opportunism to one of sage pragmatism. "At the end of the day, decisions are subjective. It's the law. They're not always based on fact or fairness. I wish they were. I just can't guarantee a judge will order the posthumous DNA test on Bruce's brain. Jamie's lawyer will argue collateral estoppel, which means that because the surrogate decided you weren't entitled to inherit from Wallace's estate thirty years ago, you have no standing now to lay claim to Bruce's estate. In other words, if you're not Wallace's daughter, you can't be Bruce's sister."

"You said it was a straightforward decision."

"It is, but Jamie Ashforth won't go down without a fight. His lawyer will force a kinship hearing. These probates are time-consuming. It will go on for a long time, that much I can guarantee. I am willing to promise that I will fight all the way to the Appellate Court until they do, just not for free."

"I told you, I'm completely broke."

"Look, Jamie Ashforth's appeal was just denied," Lasker informs her. "Bruce's intestacy stands. His only other living fiduciary is Jamie, which means, by New York law, you are entitled to half of his estate. Don't you think it's worth it to *try* to compel a genetic marker test?"

"Not if it isn't a guarantee."

"Nothing's a guarantee," Lasker says. "But here's another thing in your favor: Bruce was a resident of New York City when he died, which means any petition will have to be filed at the New York County Surrogate's Court, as opposed to in Westchester County. That's a coup for you, Arden. Your mother and I fought for that in the eighties. This is a gift! The Ashforth name holds no influence on Chambers Street. Jamie may be a big fish in White Plains but filing in Manhattan is a game changer."

"I don't think you understand," Arden says. "I've got no money, Mr. Lasker. I can't afford to pay for a lawyer on a hope and a prayer that I *might* win."

"There's another piece here that I haven't told you, which may change your mind."

Arden feels the stirring of a migraine. She presses her fingers to her temple to contain the throbbing.

"When Jamie filed for Letters of Administration, he listed you as a potential, alleged distributee."

"Why would he do that?" Hal asks. "And how do you even know this?"

"I know because, as I told you, I've been following the case very closely. I had an intern down at the Hall of Records every day waiting on this petition."

"Why would Jamie list me as a distributee if he doesn't want me to inherit?"

"*Alleged distributee.* He has no choice. Your mother's claims are all on record. They're assuming you're going to show up with your hand out again, this time for a piece of Bruce's estate. This way, they list you as someone who is probably going to file a claim, and at the end of their petition, they've asked the court to find that you're *not* a distributee, based on the surrogate's decision thirty years ago."

"So they're being proactive."

"Exactly."

"Now what? I *have* to file a claim? Even if I don't want to?"

"Absolutely not. The court is going to issue you a citation, with a return date to show up in court. You either sign it or you don't. That's why I called you when I did. You can expect to receive the citation any day."

"They have Hal's address in Brooklyn as my last residence."

"Then, Hal, you can expect a process server to show up on your doorstep in the next few weeks with that citation. *I've* also been proactive."

"You mean presumptuous," Hal mutters.

"One needs to be a little presumptuous when dealing with this kind of money."

"So then what? After I get the citation."

"It will move quite quickly. There will be a court date, probably about thirty days out from the date of the citation. If you choose not to show up, that's it. You give up your right to file a claim, and you don't inherit. Ever. It's over."

"And if I do show up?"

"We object to the citation and ask for a DNA test. And then Jamie's lawyer will refuse consent, and we go from there."

"It sounds expensive."

"Can you really afford to just walk away, Arden?"

"If it's as simple as you claim it is," Hal says, "why not at least handle that first court proceeding on contingency for her? Wouldn't it be worth it to you if she wins?"

"I never said it would be simple," Lasker points out. "I think you have an excellent chance of inheriting *in the end*. But simple? No. It's never simple. Like I said, even if we win the right to do a DNA test and you're a match, Jamie will demand a kinship hearing and then an appeal, and another appeal."

"It's a risk for you, too, but—"

"It's not *my* risk to take," Lasker reminds her. "I've brought this to you for your consideration. I'm giving you a heads-up, if you will. If you decide it's worth pursuing and you show up to court, I think you'll be well rewarded in the long run. But again, it's *your* risk to take."

"You did it for my mother."

"We all know why," Hal mutters.

"It was a long time ago and I was a hell of a lot more reckless back then," he says. "I was hungry for the PR, way more ambitious. There's also the legal side of contingency, Arden. If we win and then you decide to challenge our contingency agreement—even if it is in writing—there's a chance it wouldn't hold up in court."

"I would never do that."

"I'm not a daredevil anymore," he says, sounding slightly weary. "An intestate estate case is time-consuming—even if there is a good outcome."

"Arden, you can walk away," Hal says.

"Can I? I'm in serious debt."

"It's like déjà vu," Hal says, visibly sweating.

"The only thing I've got is our line of credit," Arden says, thinking out loud. "Or a second mortgage?" Her chest tightens even as the words leave her mouth, but the gauntlet's been thrown down, and the path before her feels pretty much irrevocable.

"I don't want you to do anything you're not comfortable with," Lasker says, his demeanor sanguine. "For what it's worth, I think you'll regret not fighting for what's rightfully yours. Wouldn't you always wonder 'What if . . . ?'"

Arden looks over at Hal, who simply shakes his head.

Larry is looking at her meaningfully. "Your mother was horribly mistreated by the Ashforths," he says. "This money is her legacy to you, Arden."

"I need to think about it," Arden says. "I vowed I would never go down the road my mother went down over this inheritance."

"Things have changed."

"I need some time," Arden says, the red-and-orange-striped seating upholstery dancing dizzyingly in front of her like ribbons. She's not a decision-maker. That was Scott's role. "This is as big a risk as I'm ever going to take."

Arden's phone vibrates on the table. "It's Virginia," she says, reaching for it. "Hey, Mom—"

"It's Tate."

"Tate? Why do you have mom's phone?" Arden says, panic engulfing her. Something in Tate's voice reminds her of the day she got the call that Scott was dead.

"Mom's in the hospital. I'm at St. Mike's with her—"

"What happened?"

"She's in the emergency—"

"Did she fall?"

"She was—I think she was assaulted."

"*Assaulted*?" Arden's heart is racing. She tries to steady her breath, to let the word land. "Assaulted *at home*? In her apartment?"

"I think so. She called 911. We don't know much else—"

"Is she okay?"

"You should come home," Tate says. "Right away."

5

APRIL 2018

VIRGINIA TURNS HER HEAD TO LOOK OUT THE WINDOW. THE RED OAKS ON Arden's street are finally starting to bloom, the canopy returning to its leafy glory. Just a couple of years ago, Scott spearheaded a campaign to save hundreds of the majestic old trees in the neighborhood. Virginia marveled at his passion for the trees, but he eventually confessed it was a matter of protecting his investment: he hadn't paid two million dollars to live on a street with wider sidewalks and fewer trees. He'd paid to live under the impressive Lawrence Park canopy, and he wasn't about to let the city cut down three hundred and fifty of its most cherished oaks. It is a lovely street, full of contemporary new builds, traditional center-hall mansions, and generous lots. Aside from Arden's house—the only sad, unkempt Tudor on the block—it would have been a lovely upbringing for the children. But Arden is going to have to sell it unless she wants to lose it entirely.

It's been almost three weeks since it happened. She has a femoral neck fracture and broken rotator cuff, which, the doctor explained, could have been life-threatening at her age. She had to have a full hip replacement. A partial replacement was discussed, but the doctor felt that a complete replacement would give her better mobility and less pain walking in the long run. Her body suffered a tremendous shock. She was transferred to the Holland Orthopedic Center for a full week and will likely be bedridden for months. She'll need physiotherapy three or four times a week for at least the next six months.

It was decided by the girls that she's to live with Arden while she convalesces. Arden converted her downstairs guest room into a bedroom and Tate and Arden have been sharing nursing duties. The good news is her physiotherapy is covered by OHIP. That's what the girls keep telling her, as though she gives a shit. She'd rather not have to do physiotherapy.

The girls are still trying to piece together what happened, probing and grilling her every day. One morning, when she was still in the hospital, she could hear them talking about her. She was groggy and dopey, but she was awake.

"What do you think really happened?" Arden said.

"She was assaulted, like the doctor said. Maybe raped."

Virginia had refused the rape kit when she was admitted. She swore to them the sex had been consensual.

"Who rapes a woman?" Arden whispered.

"It happens all the time," Tate said. "Besides, she's still so beautiful. She doesn't look her age at all."

Virginia appreciated that. It's true, if you caught a glimpse of her walking down the street, you'd never know her actual age. She takes impeccable care of herself—practices yoga, works hard, has lots of sex. All of it keeps her fit and healthy. She only ever injects her forehead so that it has that smooth, wax paper feel she likes, but her face isn't absurdly filled and lifted like a lot of women her age. She uses restraint and subtlety. Good genes help too—flawless pores, enviable bone structure, soft blond hair that defies age.

"Why lie about it?"

"She's afraid to tell us the truth," Arden said. "She probably thinks we'll think it was her fault."

They're clever, her daughters. They know her. But Virginia will continue to stick to her story. It was consensual sex that got out of hand; she and her lover fell off the bed, him landing on top of her and crushing her left side. She's very petite, and he was a very large man, tall, heavy-boned, muscular. (All true.) She was in pain after they fell, but she didn't realize how bad it was. She fell asleep right there on the floor and he was gone when she woke up. The pain was crippling, and she realized something was very wrong. She managed to reach for the phone and call 911.

Implausible, the doctor told Arden and Tate. Virginia could hear that conversation as well while she pretended to sleep. Gauging by the shattered hip, broken rotator cuff, and severe bruising, the doctor said it was more likely she'd been thrown across the room like a football.

Virginia stirred and blinked open one eye. "Girls?" she croaked, taking their attention from the doctor.

"We're here, Mom."

"I'm sorry," Virginia said. "I'm so sorry for everything I've put you through."

"It's not your fault, Mom," Arden said, her eyes tearing up. "Just sleep."

Virginia can hear the grandkids in the kitchen, making their usual commotion. They flit in and out of her room every so often to say hello or kiss her cheek. She's embarrassed for them to see her like this, fractured and helpless, hobbling with her walker to the bathroom in her nightgown. The list of recent humiliations is endless. *You know you want it.*

She's been thinking that when this is all over, she might move to one of those isolated Buddhist monasteries. There's one in Nova Scotia that sounds wonderful. She could meditate all day and have a quiet, peaceful life. A monastery feels like a safe place to live out her days, as long as she doesn't have to shave her head. Her long blond hair is her crown, the last vestige of her youthful beauty. Men or no men, she's not willing to be bald as part of her penitence.

Anyway, there will be *no more men.* Her sexual recklessness has cost her all her self-pride, her confidence, her openness. It very nearly cost her her life. What Lou Geffen did to her will forever mark the pivotal juncture between her old self and this thing she's become in its aftermath—profoundly disillusioned, scared, ashamed.

There it is. She's a victim now.

The old Virginia was a free spirit, as open-minded as she was openhearted. She was trusting, relentless, fearless. She bungee jumped off a cliff in Costa Rica on her sixtieth birthday. She jumped out of a stripper cake wearing nothing but pasties for Hal's fortieth. She was a lover of men. She was a lover. Comfortable in her skin—a rarity, she knew—and sexually empowered right into her midsixties. She was never afraid to ask a man for what she needed. She could tell him how she felt, how she wanted to feel, teach him what to do to get her there. Hal once called her a walking sexual revolution. She was as self-assured in her physical being as a Zen master is enlightened.

Oh sure, she's always had her share of foibles—the codependency issues, the boundary setting, the restless spirit—but, despite all that, she was an irredeemable optimist, especially about love.

Until now.

It feels like a lifetime ago that she was sitting across from Tate and Arden over a potluck dinner, discussing with great enthusiasm her brilliant idea to sign up for a seniors' dating app. The conversation began the usual way, with Arden asking if she was seeing anyone.

"She's always seeing someone," Tate muttered.

"Actually, I ended it with Miguel," Virginia said. "Turns out I'm not comfortable in a polygamous relationship. I've been thinking about joining Tinder."

"Oh God, Mom."

"Why not? Because I'm in my sixties?"

"Yes!" both girls cried at the same time.

"So, I'm a cougar. Big deal."

"You're not a cougar," Tate said, shredding her arctic char with her fingers. "*I'm* a cougar. You're a panther."

"A panther?"

"You're over sixty. That's a panther."

"I read somewhere it's a saber-toothed tiger," Arden said.

"I don't need your approval," Virginia huffed. She was used to their teasing. From the time they were little, they've always ganged up on her. Together, they're bolder, more critical.

"Why don't you try being single for a bit," Tate suggested.

"You say the same thing every time I get out of a relationship."

"It's not healthy to go from one guy to the next."

"Oh please. Can we not start with the codependent love addict shit? I like men! I enjoy sex. Besides, I'm almost sixty-five. It's too late for me to change."

"It doesn't have to be."

"Why do you even care who I'm dating?" she asked them. "I like being with a man. There are worse things."

"Not for us."

Virginia joined SilvrFoxes the next day. Her soulmate was out there; she believed that in the throbbing recesses of her heart. In the meantime, she was determined to have a hell of a fun time finding him. And once she did, then the life she had always envisioned for herself would begin—listening to smooth jazz and sipping gin and tonics on the veranda of their cottage at sunset; long, languid dinners that they'd cook together with fresh herbs from their garden; lazy Sunday mornings in bed, reading the paper with CBC radio on in the background, handholding strolls, matinees, weekend trips to Prince Edward County and Cambridge. This person, whoever and wherever he might be, held the key to her happy twilight years.

She should have listened to the girls. Had she heeded their advice, she'd still have her independence, her mobility. Her idealism. But maybe that's missing the point. Maybe joining SilvrFoxes wasn't the problem, any more than desiring to be in a loving relationship was a problem. Maybe something else is fundamentally wrong with her. The truth is she *had* a stable marriage to a stable man in a stable home. And what did she do? She didn't sip gin and tonics with him on the veranda or laze around in bed reading the paper. She went after Arden's inheritance money. What choice did she have? Before she even found out she was pregnant, Wallace had promised her he would always take care of her. She believed him, just as she believed he loved her. In her mind, Arden's birth only deepened his obligation to them, regardless of whether he was alive to carry out his promise. She would file the same claim again today if she had to—perhaps not the same way, at the expense of Hal and her daughters, but Wallace had made her a promise and her intention was only ever to hold the Ashforths to it on his behalf.

When Hal finally ended it, he said to her, "You had it all, Virginia. Two beautiful children, a man who adores you, a happy home. *What's wrong with you?*"

Her father also used to ask to her that; he was so frequently perplexed by her. *What's wrong with you, Virginia?* She would often catch him staring at her, his expression a blend of disappointment and confusion, the way Tate and Arden sometimes look at her now. She baffled him. She was too pretty and not smart enough, both of which made him equally uncomfortable. It was like he could never comprehend how someone of his intellect—a professor of literature—had managed to produce a creature of such little value, a feckless scrap of a girl with no discernible talent other than being pretty.

On his deathbed, he held her hand and said, "I never knew what to do with you, Virginia."

"Why is that?" she asked him, genuinely curious.

She waited in silence for several minutes while he thought about his answer. Finally, he said, "You weren't what I'd hoped for."

"Grandma?"

Virginia turns. Little Wyatt is in the doorway, peering at her with a curious look on his face. "Are you going to do your exercises now?" he asks her. "It's ten."

He likes doing the physio with her. He thinks it's fun. His favorite is the buttock contractions. He gets a real kick out of it. Virginia, not so much. The worst is the step climbing and descending, which she does on his plastic bathroom stool, the one he uses for brushing his teeth.

"I'm a little stiff this morning," she says. "How about you come back a bit later?"

He approaches. "Mommy says you have to do them or you're going to be an inbalid."

"I'll do them," she promises. "I just need my medicine first."

"Okay. I'll come back after *Wild Kratts*," he says, and off he goes.

He's like a hologram: she can see him and hear him, but he's not real, she can't *feel* him. She wants to feel something—tenderness, affection—but there's nothing. She's hollow. The doctor says that's normal with depression, which, he says, is also normal after what she's been through.

"Wyatt says you don't want to do your exercises," Arden says, marching into the room like an army general.

"I need my meds. I'm in a lot of pain."

Arden pulls a bottle of morphine out of the front pocket of her hoodie and drops two pills into her mother's open palm. "You can't stay on these much longer," she says, handing her a glass of water. "You have to switch to the codeine."

"Can't you let me have some pleasure?"

"That's not even funny," Arden says, sitting down on the side of the bed.

"I'm not trying to be funny."

Arden takes the glass from Virginia and sets it down on the adjustable tray. "Can I talk to you about something?" she asks. "While you're still coherent?"

"Depends."

"It's about the inheritance."

Virginia relaxes.

"I haven't really talked to you about my meeting with Larry Lasker. I need some advice."

"Arden, you're Wallace Ashforth's daughter. You're entitled to your share of his estate. Don't you think there's a reason this has just landed in your lap?"

"But after everything you went through, everything you lost—"

"From what you've said—and, admittedly, I only retained bits and pieces—it sounds like Larry thinks you can win this time. Enough has changed with DNA and all that. One simple test and the money is yours."

"Lasker says it's never open-and-shut with estate cases, especially when there's no will."

"You have to try, Arden. You need the money, don't you?"

"Desperately. I mean, we really, *really* need it."

"It's that bad?"

"It's really bad," Arden admits. "I'm scared."

Virginia's chest tightens. You never want to hear your adult child tell you she's scared, especially when you're trapped in a hospital bed with a broken hip. "What was Scott thinking, getting himself into such a mess?" she says.

"He thought he could get himself out. He was doing his best . . ." Her voice trails off and she looks away. "He just ran out of time."

"It sounds like you don't have a choice, then, unless you sell the house."

"I'm not selling the house."

Virginia sighs. She gets it, there are memories here, but the house itself is not worth hanging on to, not in this state, half-finished, rotting in places.

"Here's what I haven't told you," Arden says. "Lasker won't do contingency. Hiring him would be a huge financial risk. What if it goes on as long as it did for you? I've got the kids, I'm broke—"

"That prick," Virginia says. "Why won't he work on contingency?"

Arden shrugs.

"He's the one who came to you."

"It doesn't matter," Arden says, nervously folding and refolding the napkin on her mother's breakfast tray. "It's off the table, so I'd have to re-mortgage the house or go back into debt. Or both, depending on how far it goes. And what if I don't win? I'm worried it's too much of a gamble."

"It sounds to me like you can't afford *not* to," Virginia says, touching Arden's hand.

Arden is quiet for a moment. She looks so young in her sweatshirt and jeans, with her freckled nose and her hair in two loose pigtails. She's always complaining that she feels old, but, to Virginia, she looks like she could still be in college.

"Wallace Ashforth really was my father, right, Mom?"

"Arden! Of course he was. What kind of a question is that?"

"It's just . . . I can't file this claim and then have it turn out he's not really my father."

"What are you saying? That I made it all up? You think I spent all those years in court, filing petition after petition *on your behalf* as part of some big scam I concocted? I'm not smart enough for that."

"Relax, Mom. I know you were seeing him."

"We loved each other."

"I just need to be sure there's no other possibility—"

"He was the only man I'd been with when I got pregnant with you."

"Can you blame me for wanting to be sure?"

"File the petition," Virginia says. "They owe you. One simple DNA test and this will finally be over."

Arden nods, not looking entirely convinced. She rips off a corner of Virginia's untouched raisin bread and pops it in her mouth. "Can I ask you something else before you get loopy?"

"The window is closing."

"What happened that night?" Pouncing on her just as the morphine is kicking in.

"I'm tired, Arden."

"I promise I won't tell Tate. Please, just tell me what he did to you."

"I've told you a hundred times."

"Did he rape you?"

"Don't be ridiculous."

"If he did, you know he'll do it again to other women."

"Not now, Arden. Please."

"Just tell me his name."

"Why? You can't press charges. It was just sex."

"Look at you! It wasn't 'just sex.' You were assaulted; we all know it. We just don't know if it was rape or elder abuse or all of the above!"

"I told you, I don't remember anything from that night. And I'm sure he didn't give me his real name anyway," Virginia says, grateful she'd had the wherewithal to delete her SilvrFox account and almost all traces of that monster from her phone while she was still in the hospital. "No one gives their real name."

"You did."

Virginia closes her eyes and waits for the sweet narcotic oblivion to wash over her. She's done talking. She would rather die than tell her daughters the truth about what happened or reveal any of the fragments of memories he left inside her skull, like the shards of that smashed wineglass.

6

Arden reaches across the table for the bottle of Chianti and pours Tate a refill. "How's the article coming along for the *Trussed-Up Home*?" she asks, grasping for some normalcy in the aftermath of Virginia's assault. It's the first time in weeks they've had a chance to sit and catch up.

"I wish I could truss up my home," Arden says, replenishing her own glass. They're at the kitchen table, working on a schedule for Virginia.

"My house needs trussing, don't you think?"

"I haven't written a single word since you went to New York," Tate says. "Between Mom and your kids, I barely had time to pee when you were away. I don't know how you do it."

"Three kids is a lot," Arden admits. "Especially twins and a teenager."

"*One* kid is a lot. Three is absurd."

Tate has been on the fence about having children for years. She froze eggs in her late thirties, but when she and Tanvir decided to try for a baby at forty, none of them took. She was philosophical about it, figured the universe was confirming that her ambivalence about motherhood really meant she didn't want kids.

"I was going to tackle the article tonight," Tate says. "If you'd stop plying me with wine."

"You're much better company when you're drunk."

"Tell me more about your meeting with Lasker."

"He's still a sleazeball. A very polished, well-dressed sleazeball."

"What about the inheritance?" Tate says. "Do you think it's for real? Are you going to lose a decade of your life like Mom did? Or are we going to be rich?"

"It's far from a sure thing," Arden says. "Behind curtain one, I could win thirty million dollars. Behind curtain two, I lose everything—my house, my kids' education, the clothes off my back, *plus* God knows how many years of my life."

"Maybe this isn't the time for you to take a stand."

"What's that supposed to mean?"

"Your style is more laissez-faire. You like to go with the flow. I'm just saying maybe this isn't the right situation for you to finally make a big life decision."

"That feels like an insult."

"Not at all. I'm worried about you, that's all. I don't want you to get sucked into a long, drawn-out lawsuit that will only benefit the lawyers."

"Would you just walk away from thirty million bucks?"

Tate frowns, swishes the wine around in her glass. "Isn't it crazy how things have turned out for us?"

"Meaning?"

"Your dead billionaire father and my deadbeat father."

"When's the last time you heard from West?"

"A birthday card when I turned thirty-three. He thought I was thirty. He was only off by three years." She takes a sip of her wine and looks out the window. "I haven't seen him since we moved to Toronto," she says, sounding a little forlorn.

"You mean since Mom lost the inheritance and he lost his meal ticket."

"He's still living in Vermont."

"Do you ever want to see him again?"

"I'm indifferent. I've made it this far without him."

"Remember when he took us to see *Top Gun*?" Arden says, laughing at the memory. It was right before they moved to Brooklyn to live with Hal. Arden was only five, but West somehow managed to smuggle her in. She'd wanted to see *Crocodile Dundee*, but she was outvoted.

"I wanted to cut my hair like Kelly McGillis," Tate reminisces.

It was Arden's first movie in a theater. Virginia had given West money for the tickets and some treats. He bought them Coke and Raisinets and buttered popcorn, even though their mother forbade popcorn. A boy from the Bronx had choked on some the summer before and died, but

West said that was just an urban legend and not to worry about it. Arden doesn't remember the movie at all—other than that it was loud and boring—but she remembers how the Raisinets melted on her tongue and tasted delicious mixed with the salty popcorn.

When Tate told her mother that she wanted to cut her hair in a curly bob, like the actress in the movie, Virginia refused, saying, "Your long hair is your crown."

Tate had straight blond hair that fell like a blanket to the middle of her back, just like her father's. Tate's father was a hippie. He wore jeans with holes in the knees and a blue undershirt with sweat stains under his armpits. His feet were bare, his long hair was a tangled mess, his beard smelled faintly of sour milk. Arden thought he was creepy, but Virginia would often say to Tate, "You're so beautiful, just like your father."

The way she said it made Arden wonder if it was a compliment or a warning. Beauty mattered a great deal to Virginia. Tate was named after another very beautiful person, Sharon Tate. At the time, they didn't know that Sharon Tate been stabbed to death, only that she was gorgeous. The weird thing was Virginia was the most beautiful of all of them, and yet she spoke of beauty as though it were an unattainable prize, a gift bestowed upon a chosen few, of which she was not one.

"Why is your name West?" Arden asked him that day.

"Why is your name Arden?"

"Because it rhymes with garden." (She'd made that up.)

West's eyes narrowed and smoke came out of his nostrils. "I was reborn when I went West," he said. "I moved to California and there was no me before that." That's how he spoke, in poetic fragments.

"But what's your *real* name?"

"Bryce."

Tate and Arden giggled. "You don't look like a Bryce."

"What does a Bryce look like?"

"Like a preppy."

"What's that?"

"You don't know what a preppy is?" Tate roared. "Like, from the *Preppy Handbook*?"

He was a strange man, Tate's father. In and out of their lives, a beguiling drifter, a moocher, a thief. Virginia got pregnant with Tate when she was just eighteen. Her father immediately kicked her out of the house, so she went to squat with West in the basement of a dilapidated Victorian row house on the corner of Hazelton and Yorkville, smack in the city's counterculture epicenter. In the late sixties, Yorkville had come to be known as the Haight-Ashbury of Canada—crawling with long-haired teenagers and festering with drugs, smoky music venues, art galleries, and psychedelic clothing stores. Virginia and West busked on the streets—he played guitar, she sang—and gigged at whatever coffeehouses would pay them. They were young and gorgeous, and the coffeehouses were still flourishing, and they managed to scrounge enough money to eat and buy weed and, occasionally, to catch Joni Mitchell or Gordon Lightfoot at the Riverboat. Tate was born in that run-down basement apartment, with only Virginia's mother and a midwife present. West wasn't even there. He came and went, and Virginia was used to that. All that mattered to Virginia was that Tate was fat and healthy and remarkably beautiful. At least, that's the story Virginia always tells.

When Tate was about three, West announced he was moving to New York. He had a friend who lived there who kept writing to him about a burgeoning underground rock scene. Apparently, the folk scene was over. Now it was the Ramones, Lou Reed, Iggy Pop, Debbie Harry, and Patti Smith. It was CBGB in the Bowery. West was excited to go and try his luck there. Virginia doesn't recall if West even asked her to go with him, but she wound up hitching to New York City with Tate in her arms and not much else, and then staying on the friend's couch for several months. Eventually, they got their own apartment in Queens. West had earned some money selling weed and mushrooms—Virginia has always been very frank about this—and Virginia's mother also sent her enough money for six months' rent.

West continued to come and go. Eventually, he was gone most of the time. Luckily, their landlady, an elderly Greek woman named Mrs. K.—neither Tate nor Virginia can remember her last name anymore—was able to help. Mrs. K. was a seamstress. She worked from home, making wedding dresses and drapes, and she agreed to care for Tate during the day so that Virginia could work full-time. Tate loved those afternoons, listening to the soothing whir of the sewing machine while they watched *The Price Is Right* and *Hollywood Squares* and *The $20,000 Pyramid*.

Tate's job was to get up and change the channel, hopping from show to show all day long, so that Mrs. K. wouldn't have to get up from her sewing machine. Tate got used to seeing her mother only at night and on weekends, and to basically not having a father at all, save for sporadic, unannounced visits that usually ended with something of theirs being stolen.

On one of those surprise visits, West stole Virginia's jewelry and the cash from her wallet. Another time, he even cleaned out the girls' piggy banks so that they had to hide them the next time he showed up. He was always pressuring Virginia about the inheritance, as though he were entitled to Arden's father's money as much as they were. When the lawsuits ended, he vanished for good.

"Mom sure sealed our fate when she chose our fathers," Arden says.

"Every guy she ever met was always going to be the knight in shining armor."

"She *had* her knight and she fucked it up."

"At least Hal is still in your life," Tate points out.

"He's in your life too."

"I should head back," Tate says, standing. She dumps the remains of her wine in the sink and blows Arden an air kiss. "Get some sleep," she says, letting herself out the back door.

Arden stays at the kitchen table for a little while, savoring the quiet, the aloneness; reflecting on her own dual experiences of "father"—the one who died and abandoned her, the other who stepped in and took his place. Blood, she thinks, would be utterly extraneous to her if not for the strange circumstance of her real father's fortune.

She once gave Hal a birthday card that said, *It is a wise father that knows his own child*. It was a Shakespeare quote that made Hal bawl, and yet it was and still is the truth. No matter how things unfold with the petition and the DNA test, the only father who will ever truly matter is the one that knows her.

7

Arden wakes up from yet another agitated sleep and squints at her phone. *Five thirty in the morning.* She glances over at the twins, both of them snoring next to her in a tangle of limbs and sheets, and is comforted by their presence. She touches one of their arms, not sure whose it is.

Knowing she won't be able to fall back to sleep, Arden slips out of bed and goes downstairs, straight to Scott's office. She opens the top drawer of his desk—her desk now—and reaches into the very back, searching for the small key. She finds it buried under months of clutter and neglected papers, and then unlocks the bottom file drawer. She retrieves the manila envelope and holds it on her lap for a few moments before sliding out the report.

Case Report. Thomas Ngo, M.D., Chief Medical Examiner Coroner.
Case #____ Reported as: Myocardial Infarction.
Location: Lake Joseph—Seguin Township.
Moore, Scott Alexander. Found: 09-05-16.

MR. MOORE'S BODY WAS FOUND ON THE BOAT, APPROXIMATELY 200 YARDS OFF REEF ISLAND, LAKE JOSEPH. ZOLPIDEM LEVEL IN BLOOD WAS .22. NO OTHER TRAUMA NOTED AND FOUL PLAY NOT SUSPECTED.

Arden glances up as the sun splashes into the office, bathing it with its soft morning glow. No one knows she does this. It's become her secret fetish, reading and rereading the coroner's report. She can't explain why she does it, why she *needs* to, other than it being some kind of morbid connection to Scott.

The zolpidem was a surprise. She thought he'd stopped taking the sleeping pills. He told her he had. *What other secrets were you keeping, Scott?*

She didn't know about the pills or how bad their debt had become. There's also the matter of the woman Scott had lunch with right before he died. Arden hasn't mentioned that to anyone, not even to Tate or her mother. She's done a damn fine job of not allowing herself to think too much about it either, but it's *there*. A faint whisper at the bottom of her psyche, a soft and persistent nagging that won't relent, especially when she's alone. Witnesses described her as "an attractive woman in her early thirties." Shoulder-length blond hair, white Bermuda shorts, heather-gray tank top, flip-flops. They were seen at a table for two on the lakefront patio at Turtle Jack's, not too far from where his boat was docked.

Arden has no idea who the mystery woman could be, other than possibly a client who happened to be up at her cottage that weekend. It was not uncommon for Scott to meet with clients in Muskoka. Most of them have summer homes up there, so when Arden is more mentally fit, she trusts that the simplest answer is usually the right answer.

It's when she loosens the grip on her thoughts, usually in the middle of the night or when she's very tired, that she can spin out on more salacious versions of what transpired the day Scott died. Her worst-case scenario is that the mystery woman told Scott something dramatic and alarming over lunch—perhaps she threatened to tell Arden they were having an affair, or that she was pregnant with his child—which later caused him to have a heart attack on his boat.

Arden knows better than to indulge in that sort of morbid fantasy, but she does occasionally get hijacked. In the end, she has no choice but to go on her faith in Scott's moral compass and in their marriage, a union that lasted fifteen years.

They met on New Year's Eve 1999. It was Y2K and there was an anxious buzz in the air, people fretting about everything from a global power failure to the end of the world. At nineteen, even Arden was feeling more anxious than excited. They were at a house party in the Annex, the residential neighborhood adjacent to the university, which felt safer than being at a bar.

She spotted Scott sitting alone on the couch and was immediately drawn to him. He had dark hair parted in the middle and falling messily over either side of his face. He was wearing a frayed Soundgarden T-shirt and ripped jeans, seemed more on the fringe of the gathering than part of it. He wasn't making moves on any of the women or chugging beer or talking loudly to get noticed. He didn't dance. He didn't have douchey bleached-blond hair, which was a trend among a lot of the guys back then who were into Sugar Ray and thought Mark McGrath was cool.

She noticed him noticing her and when she was sufficiently intoxicated she plunked herself down beside him on the brown corduroy couch and said, "You don't have a drink."

He smiled. His eyes were a little glassy and she realized he was probably high. For some reason, this intrigued her even more.

"I'm Arden."

"*Garden?*"

The music was loud.

"Arden!" she repeated.

"Arden?"

"Yes. Arden."

"Cool name," he said. "Scott."

He held out his hand and they shook hands formally, like they were at a business meeting, and then they both laughed.

Someone put on *1999* and everyone started screaming and rushing over to the dance floor. Arden and Scott didn't move. She pretended like she didn't want to join in, even though she kind of did, because Scott seemed like the kind of guy who was too cool to dance to a Prince song. He was just watching all the idiots with his hot little smirk and his lidded eyes.

"Do you go to U of T?" he asked her.

"Ryerson. I'm in Art History but, honestly, I hate it. I'm thinking of switching to another program or another school. Or even taking some time off. You?"

"I'm in Business at U of T."

He didn't mention that he was going to be a stockbroker, that he'd already mapped out his path and its timeline, that he had five- and ten-year plans. It was probably a good thing, or he might have scared her away. She was as aimless and adrift as he was driven, but she didn't know that yet.

The clock was ticking down to a new millennium and there was a simmering undercurrent of tension in the air, a collective, palpable nervousness that people were trying to drown out with booze and coke and stupid antics. There were so many theories circulating, so much paranoia. Even Arden was becoming a little more agitated as midnight approached.

"What do you think?" she asked him. "Is the world about to end?"

Scott smiled again, his lips holding a secret. His eyes shone. He was so beautiful. Chill, self-contained. He wasn't even trying hard. This is important—and she told him this later, after they'd slept together: she knew he was *genuinely* not trying hard; he wasn't trying to look as though he wasn't trying, which was what most guys their age did. She understood this about him immediately: *he didn't care what they thought.* He had other, more important things on his mind, even then.

"It's going to be fine," he told her. "I promise."

She believed him. She'd felt safe with him the moment she sat down beside him. She felt, inexplicably, that everything was finally going to be all right.

He was hired at an investment bank straight out of college. He proposed to her that summer, on a weekend trip to Niagara-on-the-Lake. One year later, he became a certified stockbroker, and they were married. His ambition suited her as much as her malleability suited him. Scott was galvanized by life. The future excited him. *His* future excited him. Arden found herself completely swept up in it, riding the crest of his enthusiasm. And then the money started rolling in.

She told herself she'd go back to college when she really knew what she wanted to do with her life. She didn't want to waste more time floundering in some random program and then graduate with yet another useless certificate. She figured she'd wait, mature, zero in on what really turned her on, and then go back to school.

Whenever she mentioned the possibility of a career, when it nagged at her the way she thought it was supposed to, Scott would say supportively, "You'll figure it out."

The truth was she didn't have to figure anything out because *he* had it all figured out for them. His desire to start a family dovetailed beautifully with hers, and Ivey came along when Arden was only twenty-four, followed by a couple of miscarriages, and then finally, six years later, the twins. During that time, she'd been content as a full-time mother. Her job was to make more babies, and it really did become a job, which consumed her for the entire second half of the oughts.

During those years, Arden got very used to not having to take the lead—not with the big things, like where they would live or how many kids they would have—nor with the little things—where to travel over March break, what car to buy. Scott was simply on top of everything. He was so damn capable and enterprising, he facilitated her life. He did it lovingly, too, always making her feel cared for and safe.

She places the coroner's report back inside the desk and locks the drawer. Larry Lasker's number is still sitting there, scribbled on the corner of the newspaper. She knows she has to get back to him about the petition, but she's quite proficient at procrastinating major life decisions.

She's always lived mostly by default, making haphazard choices, allowing her life to unfold without a map or a plan, and instead following the most clearly demarcated or brightly illumined path, or, more often, the person with the best idea. She let Scott make all the big decisions. She got quite comfortable in her role as the follower. It was a role she knew well, one she had always played with Tate and Virginia.

When it suited him, Scott liked to say she was easygoing. Other times, when he got annoyed or frustrated with her indecisiveness, he'd say she was too noncommittal.

"I committed to *you*," she'd remind him.

She'd never thought of herself as noncommittal so much as unambitious. She never really considered the future in a cohesive way the way Scott and Tate always had. After graduating high school, she went to Ryerson to study art history. It was the only university she applied to because she couldn't afford to go to college in the States—New York would have been her obvious first choice—and there was nowhere else in Canada that appealed to her. She hadn't fully thought out what would have happened had she not been accepted at Ryerson, so it was a good thing she was. But she was bored there, and after two years of aimless floundering, she switched to Centennial College to study art education. Her classes were in the same building where *Degrassi* was filmed, which was cool for a minute, but she never felt like she was aligned with what she was studying. She had no interest in teaching, but she stuck it out and earned her certificate—not as prestigious as a degree, but at least she finished. She dabbled as an assistant art teacher at the Visual Arts Center downtown and then decided to switch again and study museum and gallery practices at a different college, which led to another certificate in a field that left her as ambivalent as the others. By this time, she was a newlywed. Scott was about to be certified as a broker and already had a well-paying job. It was only a matter of time before she got pregnant, so putting in the work to build a career felt like a waste of energy.

If she had to lay her lack of ambition at anyone's feet, it would be Virginia's. Virginia never talked about her own interests or passions or hobbies, never discussed career, fulfillment, possibility. She only ever filed petitions to acquire her share of the Ashforth money. Maybe Arden inadvertently absorbed that the money would one day be hers, so she didn't have to try too hard at anything else. Maybe she'd always just been waiting. Not consciously—certainly not consciously—but on some deeper level just waiting for her windfall. Tate, not having a dead billionaire father of her own to rely on, went in the opposite direction. Her career—the pursuit of it, the nurturing of it—had always been her fuel.

The best things in Arden's life seem to have just landed in her lap: marriage to a solid man whom she adored, a comfortable home, a positive pregnancy stick, followed by another and—surprise—twins! She never did pursue any of her fleeting interests—photography, painting, curating—though she would occasionally spitball ideas with Scott to test his reaction.

"What do you think about me taking some photography courses at the College of Art and Design?" she ventured, one night in bed while she was breastfeeding the twins.

"To do what with?"

"I enjoy photography," she said. "I actually think I have a really good eye."

He put his book down on his chest and turned to face her. "If that's what you want," he said, in a tone she immediately recognized as patronizing. "I want you to do whatever makes you happy."

She was annoyed at being placated but couldn't really blame him. She hadn't ever shown herself to be big on follow-through. Ideas buzzed in her head like mosquitoes and then vanished just as quickly. "I've always loved taking pictures," she said, without much conviction. "I know it'll be hard to start a career in my thirties, especially with the kids, but—"

"Being an at-home mother of three is a worthy calling, Arden."

"I never said it wasn't." That term "at-home mother" irritated her. As though removing the word "stay" somehow elevated it, made it sound more modern.

"You shouldn't feel bad about what you do."

"I don't feel bad," she said. "Maybe just a bit . . . unfulfilled."

She looked down at Ali's and Wyatt's tiny bobbing heads as they sucked hungrily on both of her chafed nipples, and she felt guilty for saying such a thing out loud, for even thinking it. It was maternal blasphemy. "Maybe I could start with one course to test it out." Already she was backtracking. "I'll have to find someone to watch our little magpies . . ."

"Absolutely," Scott said, and resumed reading.

The next day, he came home from work with a gorgeous coffee-table book called *Photography Across Time*. It had wonderful glossy pages that inspired and demoralized her at the same time. On the inside flap, he'd written: *To my beautiful Arden, the best wife and mother I know. May you never doubt your true vocation.*

She never took the photography course. She decided it would be best to wait until the kids were a bit older. That made more sense. Scott bought her a professional Nikon camera that Christmas, but she rarely touched it. She used her phone for taking pictures, like the rest of the world. She did get a part-time job at a gallery on Davenport, and for a time, in tandem with her other job—motherhood—it felt like a significant achievement. Still, it was Scott who had the monopoly on initiative. He was enterprising enough for the both of them, and from that point on she settled complacently into her role.

And then, tragedy.

Had Arden known that life could be so short and arbitrary, she might have seized more of it at a younger age, been greedier about her ambitions. Instead, she poured everything she had into her husband and children.

She'd observed her mother's love life with a certain amount of contempt. She'd witnessed Virginia hunt for a soulmate with unabashed zealousness, and then, when each romantic enthusiasm fizzled, move on to the next one. Even after the failure of her marriage to Hal, Virginia quickly recalibrated and returned doggedly to her original crusade for love. New city, new home, same desperate Virginia.

Arden never wanted to be that woman. From a young age she saw there was no grace in all the hustle, the expending of energy on transient, shifting targets. There was no dignity in the chase. She would rather patiently *allow* than grasp, which has always felt less greedy.

But that was then. Now that Scott is gone, she has no choice but to hustle. He was the one who always steered the ship. His choices, his decisions—these navigated the course of their lives. In the absence of his motivation and energy, their family is at a standstill; it's up to Arden now to become the decision-maker, the leader, the one who propels them forward.

She still occasionally wonders if being a wife and mother truly is her "vocation." Is there only one anyway, or can you have several? If being Scott's wife was part of her vocation, where does that leave her today? One question leads to another, leads to another, tumbling forward like dominoes. She has to stop herself because that sort of musing is a luxury of the self-centered.

To file the petition or not, that is the question. It's the *only* question.

She gazes upward, as though Scott might be there, hovering above her, ready for her to bounce some more ideas off him.

"What do I do, babe?" She says this out loud, to the ceiling. "Do I file the claim?"

How silly we are, she thinks, *pretending the dead are somehow watching over us from above, or that they're here with us "in spirit," whatever the hell that means.*

And then a memory comes to her, whooshing out of nowhere to the forefront of her mind, of a fight they once had over her inheritance. It was a couple of years after the '08 recession; Ivey was about five years old. They didn't have the twins yet. Scott was up late, crunching numbers. Financially, they were hurting. They'd lost a lot of money and they weren't rebounding as quickly as Scott had hoped. He came into their bedroom and woke her up in the middle of the night. She'd dozed off by herself, waiting for him to come to bed.

"You up?" he said, gently shaking her. "I had an idea."

"Tell me tomorrow," she murmured, but he turned on her bedside table lamp and repeated, "I have an idea."

"What?"

"I was reading about a probate case in the States."

"What are you talking about?"

"I was reading about a guy who was denied inheriting from his paternal father back in the eighties, just like you. But with all the new DNA testing, he filed again, and he won. I mean, it's more complicated than that, obviously, but I was thinking maybe you should revisit filing a petition in New York."

"Are you kidding me?" she said, abruptly sitting up.

"So much has changed on the DNA frontier—"

"Have you lost your mind?" She was seriously concerned about his mental state. His eyes were bloodshot and slightly wild, his hair disheveled. There was something manic in the way he was talking to her. She felt utterly betrayed. He knew her history and she thought he would have understood what filing a new claim would mean for her.

"Arden, your father was a goddamn billionaire and here we are struggling to get out of debt—"

"He wasn't a billionaire."

"He was close to it! Why wouldn't we try again? With DNA—"

"Stop this," she said. "You weren't there. It's a dead end."

"Why? DNA is a game changer—"

"You know what happened to my family," she said, resenting that she should have to explain to him again how the Ashforth inheritance had robbed her of both her mother and the only real father she'd ever had.

"And you know what happened to *mine*," he countered.

Scott's father had had a very successful drapery business but went bankrupt in the early nineties, right after the recession. Scott was about eleven or twelve when they sold their beloved home on Alexandra Boulevard and moved to a small apartment in Scarborough. His parents never recovered emotionally or financially, leaving Scott with a sizable resentment and a burning desire to recoup what his parents had lost.

"My mother's lawsuit went on for more than a decade and it ruined my life," Arden said. "We are not filing a new petition. It's not happening."

"Your life wasn't exactly ruined, Arden. No one died. You're still close with Hal."

Her jaw fell open and she just stared at him in disbelief. She'd never felt so angry with him.

"Arden, think about it," he begged. "Think about what we could do with that money."

"That money isn't ours!" she snapped. "My mother lost her last appeal. Like I said, it's a dead end. Scott, how bad is our debt? Why are you even thinking about this? You're scaring me."

"Don't worry about our finances," he said dismissively. "I just had a great month. We're going to be fine, but why not have a cushion? A nest egg we'd never touch? Why shouldn't you get your share of his estate?"

"I can't even believe you're bringing this up," she said. "After everything I've shared with you about my past, about how it impacted me. The divorce from Hal, being dragged to live in Toronto, essentially losing my mother for the first ten years of my life—"

"I'm only thinking about *our* family," he said, trying to take her hand.

"Bullshit," she said, pulling her hand away. "You're thinking about how to get your hands on more money. That's all that matters to you."

"That's not fair."

"Asking me to file a lawsuit in New York is not fair," she said. "I don't like this side of you, Scott."

"It didn't bother you when we were in Maui and Paris."

"Fuck you," she said. She kicked him out of the room then and cried herself to sleep. She didn't speak to him for a full week after that—it was the longest they'd ever gone without speaking—until he finally came and apologized to her and promised he would never bring it up again. He never did.

Arden stares at Lasker's phone number until the numbers begin to blur and she knows *exactly* what Scott would want her to do right now.

He would have her file the petition and risk everything for her share of the inheritance. It's what he wanted for her when he was alive; it's what he'd want now. Strangely, realizing that does not make her more inclined to do it.

In the end, all she really has to go on is her *mother's* experience. Virginia got sucked into a vortex of court hearings, lawyers, false hope, and greed. Hal also got sucked in, paying for whatever he could to help. He lost most of his savings trying to keep Virginia's petition alive. Theirs was a life postponed, one in which all their problems were going to be solved with the inheritance. For years, they all existed in a strange purgatory—impermanent, untethered—until Virginia finally walked away empty-handed, her crusade having cost them whatever money they did have, her marriage, her best years, and her spirit. It feels at best unsound and at worst sadistic for Arden to even contemplate embarking on a similar journey. Besides, it's totally antithetical to the stance she's taken her entire life.

Maybe this isn't the time for her to plant a stake in the ground or make a seismic life decision. Maybe Tate's right, and her next step shouldn't be bold or risky or dramatically out of character.

She turns on her phone and dials Lasker's number. His receptionist puts her right through, as though he's been expecting her call, which he probably has.

"Mr. Lasker? It's Arden Moore."

"Larry, please. We're old friends."

"Larry, I've thought about it, and I don't think I can go through with the petition. There's too much at stake, especially for such an uncertain outcome. I'm just not a gambler. My kids are very fragile right now; they're still grieving. We're all grieving. I don't have the bandwidth or the money right now, and taking care of my children is my number one priority. It's my only priority."

"But you need money to take care of them, and the opportunity is *right now*."

"I just can't take a chance on sinking us deeper into a hole."

Lasker is quiet. He may even have sighed. "I think you're making a big mistake. Especially given how dire your finances are."

"I guess it's a catch-22," she says. "I'm sorry I wasted your time."

"I've got a proposition for you," he says, one he's obviously had in his back pocket all along. "I've discussed your situation with my stepson—"

"Your stepson?"

"Joshua. He's a smart kid."

"Kid?"

"He's ambitious, energetic, hungry. He's young, yes, but he would work on contingency. The only caveat is he practices family and divorce law, which is why I didn't bring it up when we met."

"Could he win? Does he have any experience with estate law?"

"He's got me. I'm always here as a resource, and I know the case back to front. You'd have my help. I'm just not prepared to take it on full-time on a contingency basis. Joshua is."

"I appreciate this."

"Can you meet with him?"

She looks over at Virginia. "I'm not sure I can get back to New York right now. My mother had an accident and she's living with me. My sister and I are caring for her—"

"Virginia had an accident? Is she okay?"

"She broke her hip."

"That's never a good thing at our age. Give her my best, will you?"

"Of course, yes."

"Joshua will come to you, then."

"Really?"

"For Virginia Bunt's daughter? Absolutely. He'll be there."

More like for thirty million bucks he'll be there.

She suspects she's just been played. Larry Lasker was going to get her to file this claim one way or another—with him in the lead, or as puppet master for his stepson. Either way, she's sure he'll be getting a generous kickback if they win. Still, if the stepson is willing to work on contingency, who cares if they've set her up? She's got almost nothing to lose and everything to gain.

8

Arden steps back to admire the photograph she's just installed, marveling at its breadth and quiet ambition. It's called *Woman in Limbo 2*, part of a series of women photographed in such soft focus and minimal light as to obscure the line between photography and painting. In this one, a woman in a green dress is standing at her window, gazing off in the distance at a colorless sky. Only the green dress stands out against the muted colors and the soft blur of window and sky and woman. Arden can practically *feel* the woman's indecision as she moodily contemplates what lies beyond.

This is Arden's happy place, the gallery. Her haven of inspiration and creative magic.

"You're going to kill me," Hana says, coming up behind her, a whir of dark lipstick, citrus perfume, jangling bracelets. "I have a client who wants this one for her bathroom."

"Her *bathroom*?"

"We're in the business of selling art," Hana says. "Not telling them where to put it."

Arden reluctantly removes *Woman in Limbo 2* from its hooks and leans it up against the wall. If she could afford it, she'd buy it.

"I find it a bit insipid anyway," Hana says, heading for the door. "Do you mind wrapping it for me? I've got a meeting with Della Feasby. She's in from Calgary."

"Does she have new work to show you?"

"I wish," Hana says. "She sent me a terse email last week. She found out I sold one of her paintings at a discount, so she's a little disgruntled. Hopefully, I can smooth things over with a bottle of expensive wine and some ego stroking."

Arden's been working part-time at the Emerging Artist Gallery on and off for the past few years. Hana opened with the philosophy that everyone should be able to own at least one piece of art. Now she travels the world looking for undiscovered artists, always endeavoring to launch their careers and ignite a passion for art in people who don't think they can afford it. EAG's collection is humble and brilliantly curated, and Hana's vision has found a niche among Toronto's status-seeking millennials.

Arden Bubble-Wraps the photograph, sets it aside in the back room, and goes off in search of a replacement. The gallery floor is lined with rows of paintings twenty-deep leaning up against every inch of wall space, which was Hana's idea to take the formality out of shopping for art and make the pieces more accessible. The freedom to browse the ample inventory yard-sale style is part of the whole EAG experience. Hana likes to say she "disrupted" the art world before disrupting was a thing. To her credit, Hana truly loves art and reveres her artists. Her gallery is a shrine to them.

Arden's always had a fraught relationship with art. She loves it, but at the same time she experiences this passion through an observer's filter of longing and envy, the built-in pain point that she's never been good enough to make her own art. She paints occasionally, nothing very good. The *Who the hell do you think you are?* voice has consistently been the loudest in her head. She loves everything about the art world, but she's only ever dabbled. She's settled for a spot on the periphery, watching from the bench, just so long as she gets to somehow be a part of it.

Hal had hoped at one point that her interest in painting would bloom into an actual talent, but it never happened. She's had to come to terms with the fact that appreciation is not ability. Hal never gives up, though, which is why he bought her the expensive Winsor & Newton oil paints and an easel for her thirty-fifth birthday. He's always wanted them to have a special bond that could transcend their lack of a biological connection. He settled on painting because Arden was always so spellbound by his work. She loved being in his basement studio while he painted; loved the piney smell of turpentine, the bright blobs of color on his white porcelain palette, his paint-caked easel and empty Del Monte tomato cans of used paintbrushes. His discarded sketches lay all over the concrete floor like fallen leaves, which she would sometimes sign and take to school and pretend were her own. She used to lie on her stomach for hours and finger-paint or color with pastels that stained her skin. She wore a plastic smock and was allowed to be as messy as she wanted.

When she was sixteen, she moved back to Brooklyn to spend the summer with Hal, organizing and cataloguing his body of work. He paid her ten dollars an hour to sort everything by medium and then store it in archival boxes by subject matter for a gallery on Long Island that was going to be featuring his work that fall.

She returned to Toronto at the end of that summer more aware than ever that she was missing some inherent seed of motivation or confidence that propelled others forward. Maybe it was because the first decade of her life had been built on a sandcastle of fantasy, a fairyland in which all their dreams would come true *when they magically became millionaires.* Even at sixteen, she was already strangely detached from any sense of intrinsic pressure to achieve or plan for her future.

"Arden?"

She turns, startled. "Is it one already?" she says, checking her watch and looking at the man standing in front of her.

"It is." He holds out his hand. "Joshua James. Larry's stepson."

"Arden," she says, shaking his hand.

Joshua has dark, wide-set eyes and straight black hair pulled back in a low man bun. He's fit but slight, wearing a snug gray hoodie with jeans and Vans. "Thanks for coming to Toronto," she says, nervously buzzing. "Just give me a minute to grab my bag."

She disappears into the back to freshen up. She's wearing an un-flattering boyfriend cardigan borrowed from Ivey, serviceable leggings, and ballet flats. The only makeup she has with her is a clear lip gloss, not even tinted or shimmery. Her hair is flat and not especially clean, so she has to settle for looking like a middle-aged mother, which makes her feel self-conscious about her appearance—something she has not experienced in a very long time—and which, in turn, launches a second arrow of guilt. She didn't expect him to be so good-looking. If anything, she'd been expecting a younger, crasser Larry Lasker.

They head over to the Brasserie next door for lunch, grabbing two spots on the leather banquette near the front door. Joshua orders a St-

Ambroise pale, and she orders a glass of Sancerre. Tate is looking after Virginia and the kids today, so she thinks, *Why not?*

"You don't look old enough to be a lawyer," she says, realizing she's been staring at his face. She quickly looks away.

"I'm thirty-four. I've been practicing for five years. The first three with Fine, Bleekman and Sharma. They're one of the most prominent law firms in New York."

"What made you want to leave the security of a big firm?"

"I wanted to have more autonomy than I had as a fifth-year associate there."

"And do you?"

"Absolutely. I can choose the cases I want, the people I want to represent. It's way less money, but I'm working on that."

She likes him. No flashy gold cuff links or starched bespoke shirts. He's got some of Larry's confidence, without the affectation. His ambition and exuberance remind her of a young Scott, back when he was studying to be a broker.

"Larry's filled me in on everything," Joshua says.

"Did he mention that my father was served two days ago?"

"He did, which is great. We've got a court date for, I believe, middle of May?"

She nods, feeling a little dread over that looming date.

"Let's get right to the reason I'm here," he says. "To discuss contingency."

Their drinks come and Joshua orders steak frites. Arden has no appetite.

"I'll be honest with you," he says as their waiter disappears behind the bar. "I don't have unlimited resources. I can't foot the entire bill and fully commit my time with absolutely zero income."

"Like I told Larry, I'm completely broke and already in debt."

"Your share of the Ashforth estate would solve all those problems and more, Arden. Forever."

He rolls up his sleeves, revealing two intricate tattoos covering the insides of both forearms from his wrists to his elbows. One of them looks like a bearded god sitting on top of an erupting volcano; the other is of a long-haired warrior with a tattooed torso and a sword in his hand. Arden tries not to gape, but his attractiveness quotient has just risen exponentially. If Joshua notices her noticing, he doesn't acknowledge it.

"I'm willing to work with you," he continues. "I'd need a retainer of fifteen thousand to get me through the next couple of months, but I'll forgo my hourly rate. All I'm asking is to outline a schedule of payments to cover court fees, my research assistant, my time."

"How much do you take if we win?"

"Twenty percent."

She does some quick math. "That's about six million, if Bruce's estate is actually worth sixty million."

"Keep in mind," he says, "if the court agrees to test Bruce's DNA right away and you're a match, we may win right then and there. Jamie may just want to get rid of us."

"I'll still have to come up with your money before I have the inheritance."

"Short term, yes."

"And the first step if I go forward?"

"We go to court and I argue for a DNA test on Bruce's brain tissue."

She lets out a long breath.

"Larry's wheelhouse is kinship and intestacy," Joshua says. "And we've got him in our corner. I genuinely don't think we can lose, Arden."

After lunch, Joshua takes an Uber back to his hotel and Arden strolls along Davenport, enjoying the mild weather. Maybe it's the sun in her face or the two glasses of wine or the stirring of sexual attraction, but she feels exhilarated. The crazy part is she believes him. Over the course of their hour-long lunch, he somehow made her realize that complacency is no longer an option. It's time to take a risk. What the hell could be more motivating than being able to send the kids to college? Or being able to support her mother and get Hal a proper art studio? If not now, *when?*

She stops in the middle of the street and shoots off an emphatic text to Joshua. I'll see you in court. Let's do this!

Her heart is pounding as she hits Send, but she's still laughing. Her next call is to the branch manager at her bank. She'll start with a loan of twenty thousand dollars against her line of credit. If the judge agrees to test Bruce Ashforth's pickled brain, maybe that's all she'll need.

9

"It looks like a crime scene," Arden says, turning on the lights.

"It probably *is* a crime scene," Tate reminds her.

Virginia's bedroom is still exactly as it was left the night of the assault. The duvet and sheets are still in a heap on the floor, with pillows and clothes strewn everywhere. Also on the floor are the lamp from her bedside table, some books, the portable phone and base, and shards of broken glass stained with red wine. There's still blood on the sheets and mattress.

Arden's been here once to collect a bunch of her mother's things, but she didn't have time to clean up. It was the day after the assault and she was still in a daze. She grabbed as much as she could for her mother and fled. It's the first time Tate is seeing it.

"I'm going to wash all the bedding," Arden says, bending down to collect the pieces of glass on the floor.

"Do you think you should?" Tate says. "What if his DNA is on it?"

"Really? This isn't an episode of *CSI*."

"Seriously, Arden. Who knows? Just put the fitted sheet in a plastic bag. You can wash everything else."

Tate puts the lamp back on the table, gathers the books in a pile. "What the hell do you think happened here?" she mutters, more to herself.

"She may never tell us," Arden says, going to the kitchen to look for a plastic bag. The whole place stinks of garbage, but the kitchen is unbearable. She has to hold her nose looking for a bag, broom, and dustpan. When she returns to the bedroom, Tate has already stripped the duvet and pillows.

"How much longer can she afford to keep this place, you think?"

"She won't be able to go back to work for a while."

Virginia sells women's shoes at Stewart's. She's been there for almost twenty-five years, has an established and loyal clientele of wealthy customers, and has been able to earn an impressive living off her commissions. Her monthly disability checks will barely cover her rent.

"I don't see her ever wanting to come back here anyway," Tate says, examining the torn, bloodstained shirt her mother must have worn that night—a pretty pink J.Crew sweater—and then stuffing it into the plastic bag with the DNA-stained sheet.

"We should speak to her about subletting the apartment. We could use the money."

They snap pictures of the room and then sweep up the glass, scrub the wine off the floor and the blood off the kilim rug near the dresser, and throw all the remaining linens into the washing machine. They find a mop and bucket in the walk-in pantry and Arden cleans the bedroom floor, trying not to think about what happened here that night.

"I'll empty the fridge and pack up some more of her things," Tate says. "Why don't you grab what you're looking for?"

Virginia still has a half dozen file boxes filled with court transcripts and legal notes going back about thirty years. Arden finds the boxes neatly stacked and labeled ASHFORTH–LEGAL in the storage unit. She hauls them out one by one and then drags them over to the elevator, fighting the urge to rip them open right here. It's pizza night and she's got to get home to the kids, but she plans to dig into them as soon she's alone tonight.

Friday pizza night is a tradition Scott and Arden established after the twins were born, one Arden is determined to uphold for the sake of normalcy. She loves when the house smells of pepperoni and sausage, when the kids gather in the family room with plates on their laps, talking over one another. It reminds her of when their family was whole.

She pokes her head into her mother's room, discouraged to find Virginia still lying there, staring up at the ceiling. "Pizza's here!"

"No, thanks."

"It'll be good for you to get out of bed."

"It's too much of a hassle."

"You're going to get bedsores."

No answer.

"I'll bring you a slice?"

"I'm not hungry, darling."

They've been through a lot, Virginia and the girls, but Arden's never seen her mother this depressed, not even when a boyfriend left her and broke her heart. She'd smoke a pack of cigarettes, sulk for a few days, and then pick herself up. Wallowing was never her way.

"Maybe later, then," Arden says. "I'll make sure we save you a slice."

She closes the door and joins the kids in what Scott and Arden generously christened the "family room." It was originally the maid's quarters, just a sunken room off the kitchen with shag carpet, wood-paneled walls, and a low, water-damaged ceiling that looks as though it could cave in on them at any moment. Scott had dreamt of building in wall-to-wall bookcases—the kind you see on Pinterest, white with a sliding ladder—a movie screen, and an oversized sectional that would fill the entire space. For now, they make do with a red IKEA couch and Hal's hand-me-down La-Z-Boy.

Arden takes an oily disc of pepperoni and pops it in her mouth while the kids jostle each other for the "best" pieces. Tate is nibbling on her own gluten-free crust with no cheese or toppings.

"Where's Ivey?"

"Where do you think?" Ali says, falling back on the couch with a sagging, grease-stained paper plate on her lap.

Arden yells up to Ivey's room a couple of times. When there's no answer, she goes upstairs to get her. No one is allowed to opt out of pizza night.

She finds Ivey in bed in the dark, the only light coming from her phone.

"Ive? Supper's here."

No answer.

Arden sits down on the edge of the bed, having recently read in one of her many parenting books that you're supposed to speak to your kid eye to eye to show them respect. She gently pulls back the duvet.

"What are you doing?" Ivey shrieks.

"Supper's here," she says, looking her right in the eye. *Respect.*

"Why is your face so close to me?" Ivey says, turning away. "Your breath smells like pepperoni."

"We're eating."

"I don't like pizza."

"Since when? You had it last week."

"I think I'm lactose intolerant," she says. "About seventy-five percent of the world can't digest dairy, you know."

"You're not lactose intolerant."

"Dairy increases the body's level of insulin, which can cause cancer."

"I wish you'd stop Googling everything."

"Why? I like to be informed."

"The internet can be dangerous."

"Oh please!" Ivey moans, pulling the duvet back over her head. "Not this again."

Arden's heart lurches. She wants to shake her. *Why can't you go back to how you used to be?*

Maybe two well-adjusted kids out of three isn't a bad ratio. "Do you want something else?" Arden asks her. "I can make you a tomato sandwich?"

"Can you please just go?" Ivey says.

Don't take her personally. Another nugget from the book *Don't Take Your Teenager Personally!*

Arden swallows her hurt feelings and goes back downstairs. She plunks down on the couch between Ali and Wyatt, her sweet and loveable six-year-olds.

"Tyler's dad invited me to go camping at Algonquin Park," Wyatt says. "Can I go?"

"We'll see," Arden says wearily. "When?"

"Canada Day weekend."

"That's three months out. Let's revisit it when school's over."

"That means no."

"I said we'll see. It means *we'll see*."

Everyone is looking at her. Tate has that judgy "nonparent" face.

"Tyler's dad knows how to use an Epi-Pen," Wyatt perseveres.

"I haven't said no. It's months away."

They both know she will say no. It's almost always no. How can she let him go out into the middle of the woods with someone who knows nothing about deadly allergies?

Two red splotches pop up on both his cheeks and a dark vein is pulsating on his forehead, a telltale precursor to the storm that's coming. He is so much like his father—same expressions and temperament—it makes all their arguments bittersweet.

"Daddy would let me go!" he cries, his voice cracking. "He used to stand up to you so I could have a normal life!"

"Calm down, Wy. I haven't said no." She can feel the familiar tide of guilt rising up inside her. What if she's causing him more damage than the peanut allergy?

"You're ruining my life!" he screams. "You're trying to make me afraid to live because *you're* afraid! It's not fair!" He turns to Tate and throws up his arms in frustration. "Tell her it's not fair, Aunty Tate!"

Tate looks horrified at being drawn in. She looks over at Arden for help. When no one says anything, Wyatt runs out of the room. A door slams.

"You're not the only one who can use the Epi-Pen, you know, Mom," says Ali.

"I never said no."

"You would have, though," Ali says, her face covered in tomato sauce. "You always do. Whenever you say 'We'll revisit' you mean no."

The peanut allergy is yet another complication in their already complicated lives. She worries enough about him growing up father-less, knowing as she does that no matter how good a job she does, the absence of Scott to balance out all her neuroses will probably under-mine all her best efforts to ensure he has a happy, carefree life. She's already lost her husband; she's not going lose her son to a fucking trace of peanut butter.

The memory of Wyatt's first anaphylactic reaction is always with her, as constant as her own shadow. He was fifteen months old. She was eating peanut butter on toast for breakfast and he reached over from his high chair and snatched it from her. She watched him eat it, laughing, unconcerned. Moments later, he started coughing and wheezing. She thought he must have choked on a small piece of toast, but then he started screaming—a terrifying cry she'd never heard before—and she froze. He was in pain, she could see that, but she didn't know why or what to do. He was starting to break out in white hives and having trouble breathing. She lifted him out of his high chair and he hung limply in her arms. She screamed for Scott. By the time he got to the kitchen, Wyatt's face was so swollen they couldn't see his eyes. His bottom lip was slack, his body lifeless. He was drifting in and out of consciousness.

Scott called 911. When the paramedics arrived, Arden wailed, "He's dying!"

And he was. She knew it.

One of the paramedics grabbed Wyatt from her arms and yelled out to his partner, *"Grab me an Epi-Pen or we're going to lose this little guy."*

Those words haunt her to this day. Yet, in trying to keep him safe, she knows she's depriving him of a normal life. Camping, sleepovers, Halloween—all are potentially deadly for him. It was Scott who always advocated for Wyatt's freedom. Some of their worst fights were about how to deal with his allergy. Scott believed in a boy having freedom, normalcy. He wanted Wyatt to grow up fearless and confident, not paranoid that death lurked around every corner.

Arden is in charge now and in some ways it's a relief. She has much more control over things. She can say no and have the final word. She can keep Wyatt out of danger at her discretion. Sometimes he hates her for it, but she'd rather him be angry and alive.

Later, when it's just the two of them, Tate and Arden pull out a container of ice cream and some Chips Ahoy cookies. When they were kids, waiting up for Virginia to get home from a date, they would always make ice cream sandwiches with whatever cookies they could find in the pantry. They do this now wordlessly, side by side in the kitchen, as though no time has passed at all, and then return to the family room.

When Tate first arrived with her suitcase and announced she would be staying here for a few days to help care for Virginia, Arden worried they'd get on each other's nerves and bicker, like they used to when they were younger. But so far she's enjoyed having Tate around. They've found a rhythm, have fallen back into the comfortable routines of the old days. Arden likes the company too. It's easy, familiar. Tate fills the void left by Scott, especially at night, when the silence used to drive Arden out of her mind.

"I'm wiped out," Tate says, stretching out on the La-Z-Boy.

"What do you want to watch?" Arden asks, licking around the ice cream center of her sandwich. "Old movie? Cheesy reality show?"

"We're like an old married couple."

"How about *The Outsiders*. I haven't seen it in years."

When Virginia bought their first DVD player, they must have rented that movie at least thirty times. Their room was papered in posters of Matt Dillon and C. Thomas Howell. Tate was a Dallas fan; Arden loved Ponyboy. She used to go around saying, "*Stay gold, Ponyboy.*"

"Tanvir and I have decided to have a baby before it's too late," Tate says.

Arden looks up from her ice cream sandwich. "You're pregnant?"

"No. But I want to be."

Arden is quiet for a moment, careful of how to phrase her next question. "Aren't you too old?"

"We're going to use a donor egg."

"You've already started the process and you're only telling me now?"

"We're going to Colorado for a preliminary appointment. We've found a fertility clinic there with incredible success rates."

"Have you picked a donor?"

"The clinic picks for us. We don't get to see pictures of her."

"And you trust them?"

"We do. They vet all their donors, and they'll try to match us with someone who ticks off all our criteria."

"What if she's . . ."

"Ugly?"

"I mean . . . or anything, really. You're trusting a clinic to pick your kid's DNA?"

"Yes. I trust them more than I trust myself. I'd pick the prettiest donor. They'll pick the most suitable donor."

"You're starting this now, though? With mom incapacitated?"

"I don't exactly have all the time in the world," Tate says. "It may not be my egg, but I don't want to be seventy and raising a teenager."

Arden has so much more to say, but she can sense that Tate has made up her mind and the only appropriate response here is unbridled support. "Wow," she says, feeling slightly off-kilter. "This is exciting!"

"Me as a mom, right?"

"And you're sure you want kids now?" Arden says, worrying that this decision is going to somehow upend *her* life. "Even after you've babysat mine?"

"I figure I can manage just one," Tate says. "Besides, it's probably a good thing it won't have my DNA. It'll be spared the Bunt baggage."

"You think our baggage is really in the DNA?"

"I guess not."

After a moment, Arden says, "Since we're dropping bombshells . . ."

"You fucked your lawyer."

"Tate! Seriously?"

Tate shrugs. "I Googled him. He's hot."

Arden shrugs, acting like she hadn't noticed.

"I'm right, aren't I?"

"No, you're not right. Please. Get real."

"What, then?"

Arden's cheeks feel as hot as pancakes. She looks down, trying to conceal her goofy smile, her redness. "I mean, you're in the realm," she admits.

"You *want* to fuck him?"

"I'm attracted to him, yes."

"Translation: you want to fuck him."

Arden starts to laugh, a deep belly laugh, and can't stop. *When's the last time I laughed like this?* She can't remember.

"Is it mutual?"

"I doubt it," Arden says, settling down. "He's younger than me. I'm a middle-aged widow. I'm his client."

"You're gorgeous, what are you talking about?"

"I don't *actually* want to sleep with him," Arden clarifies. "I'm just enjoying *wanting* to sleep with him. Does that make sense?"

"Not one bit."

"I feel like maybe I'm coming back to life." She lowers her voice in case any of the kids are lurking. "Something inside me stirred when I met Joshua."

"Good for you. I don't see why you wouldn't just go for it."

"Because he's my lawyer," Arden says, still whispering. "Besides, it would be like cheating on Scott. I already feel guilty enough just *having* these thoughts."

"Scott's not here," Tate says. "And he wouldn't want you to stay celibate for the rest of your life."

"It hasn't even been two years."

"It's been almost two years."

Arden sits with that a moment. Hearing it reframed like that makes her wonder if she's waited long enough. *What is long enough, anyway?* There should be a handbook. How long before you're allowed to laugh again without feeling guilty? How long before you can start fantasizing about other men without feeling guilty? How long before you can have sex with someone who isn't the man to whom you committed your entire life?

Tate leans forward, takes Arden's hands, and says emphatically, "Live, damnit. *Live!*" The George Costanza line from their favorite *Seinfeld* episode, the one where Elaine's boyfriend is going bald.

Arden smiles. She needed this tonight. "Thank you, sis."

After Tate goes to sleep, Arden decides to tackle the boxes that have been calling to her all day. She slices through the packing tape of the first one with a paring knife and empties everything onto the kitchen table. It's mostly file folders of statements and invoices, court transcripts, precedents. *New York County Surrogate's Court '87. White Plains '88.* She finds a book, *Estate Law for Dummies*, and flips through. Virginia has highlighted paragraphs here and there, which Arden skims. The one that captures her interest is a section called *Identity & the Non-Marital Heir.*

An individual's sense of identity is deeply connected to the awareness and acceptance of their parentage and family history . . .

Arden's never given it much thought before, but that word—"identity"—triggers something uncomfortable inside her. She's always been ambivalent about looking inward, but it occurs to her, maybe for the first time, that the Ashforths' unflinching rejection of her existence may have caused more damage to her morale than she's been willing to acknowledge.

She closes the book and reaches for a thick manila envelope, the contents of which she spreads out on the table. Here it is, then, she thinks, looking down at the photographs and mementos, proof of her mother's relationship with Wallace Ashforth. The sum total of their history together amounts to this: a collection of ticket stubs from the Kenmore Theatre, preserved in a Ziploc bag; a yellowed newspaper clipping from 1980 about Wallace and Geraldine Ashforth's plane crash; a dead flower pressed between a book of poetry by Lydia Virginia, the woman for whom her mother was named; two photographs and a single letter written on onionskin airmail paper.

Arden remembers the Kenmore in Brooklyn; Hal used to take her there when she was a kid. It's where they saw *Indiana Jones* together. It seems strange to her now that Wallace Ashforth would have taken her mother there, rather than to a theater in Manhattan.

She stares at the photographs of Wallace Ashforth for a long time, looking for some resemblance to herself. She often wonders if things would have been different had he lived. Would he have acknowledged her? Supported her? Or would he have flat-out rejected her, the way his sons did? Virginia always believed he would leave his wife for her, but that was never going to happen. He had two young sons—heirs to his business, his estate, his legacy. He was never going to walk away from their mother, the Ashforth matriarch, to be with his secretary and their illegitimate daughter.

Arden sets the photos aside and takes out the letter, which she reads to herself. She's always had her doubts about Virginia's version of their affair. Virginia has a tendency to romanticize all her relationships, remembering them as being greater and more impassioned than they actually were. Most of the time, she got completely lost in them, like a method actress going deep into character. When she was dating Davinder Bakshi she started wearing a sari, cooking curry, and watching Bollywood movies. When it was over between them, the saris disappeared and so did the Indian food. Even when she was married to Hal, she immersed herself in the role of Brooklyn housewife, at least until she was hijacked by the Ashforth inheritance. Arden was never really sure who her mother was without the men. Virginia may not have known herself, but this is something Arden only recently became aware of. Between boyfriends, Virginia would return to her girls, prioritizing motherhood, as though everything were normal. The girls would sleep in her bed every night, one on either side of her. Arden used to intertwine her legs around Virginia's, locking her there so she couldn't escape.

When a new man came around—and a new man always came around—Virginia would slip away from them again. Arden always had the feeling that she and Tate were stand-ins for something far more exciting.

She puts everything back in the box except for *Estate Law for Dummies*, which she takes to bed with her. God knows why, but she finds it fascinating. As for the rest of the stuff, she's not quite sure she knows any more than she did before. Photos and a few promises written in a letter—can those be trusted? On their own, they're certainly not going to win her an inheritance.

10

MAY 2018

"YOU GOOD?" JOSHUA ASKS HER, SQUINTING UP AT THE SKY.

They're standing on the corner of Chambers Street, facing Surrogate's Court directly across the street. It's humid and sunny, more like summer. Today is the first hearing. She flew in last night and she'll be heading back when she's finished in court this afternoon. As she anxiously contemplates what's about to unfold, she finds herself wishing Virginia were here with her. Having been through the same thing thirty years ago, her mother's presence in the courtroom would have been good moral support. "I'm nervous," she admits.

"My strategy is to keep it simple today," Joshua explains, straightening his tie. He looks older and more sophisticated in his dark suit and pocket square, with his chin-length black hair tucked neatly behind his ears. She has to remind herself not to let herself get distracted by him, no matter how good he looks dressed up for court. She's not sure she's managed to conceal her attraction very well to this point, but her feelings for him seem to be escalating from the harmless crush she confessed to Tate into actual lust. This is either a serious complication or a welcome distraction; she hasn't decided yet.

"We're going to argue that you have a right to file a new claim with a new decedent," he says. "There's no reason you shouldn't be able to take advantage of the advances in DNA testing since your mother's claim thirty years ago. And if you're not a match, we'll withdraw and go away."

"And you've run this by Larry?"

"Absolutely."

"I thought he might be here."

"He's not your lawyer," Joshua says. "I am, remember? You can't afford Larry."

They cross Chambers Street in silence. Surrogate's Court, which is devoted primarily to wills and adoptions, as well as housing the Hall of Records, draws far less traffic than the other court buildings. As they climb the front steps, Arden is aware that she and Joshua are the only two people in the vicinity of the entrance. Inside, the three-story atrium is bathed in golden light and as grand as a castle, with ornate arches and columns, a spectacular marble staircase, and garlands carved onto two tiers of cornices. Arden gazes up at the coffered roof, with its hundreds of panes of leaded glass, marveling at the majesty of the work that must have gone into it.

They head up to the fifth floor, where the hearing will be. Upstairs, there's no soft amber glow, no gold-and-caramel-swirled marble, not a trace of Beaux-Arts architecture, just ugly tiled floors, beige walls, and fluorescent white lighting. Arden studies the motion calendar outside their room. *Two fifteen, before Surrogate Dale Lull: The Matter of Ashforth.* They're early.

She draws a breath as they step inside the courtroom. Everything is dark mahogany—the walls panels, the floor, the furniture. The only color is the deep, blood red of the carpet, the puddling velvet drapes, and the leather chair seats.

"No one's here," she says.

"I like to be first."

They sit down at a long mahogany table facing the judge's bench. The jury box is caged in wire mesh, like a chicken coop. Everything is perfectly symmetrical: two marble fireplaces on either side of the room, three chandeliers hanging above the table, portraits of former surrogates alternating with wood panels, each one carved with a single word: FORCE, DEGRADATION, TRUTH, CIVILIZATION, WISDOM.

"My hands are shaking."

"Don't be intimidated. You're not in criminal court."

She looks behind her at the empty gallery. Hopefully it stays that way; she doesn't want an audience. Joshua empties his briefcase, starts scribbling notes on a pad. Another man enters the courtroom. Serious, self-important, expensive suit. He sits down at the other end of the table without acknowledging Arden and Joshua.

"Ashforth's lawyer," Joshua whispers. "Myron Fistler."

"Where's Jamie?"

"The clients rarely show up for the first hearings," he says. "Nothing much is going to happen."

"And I'm here why?"

"To get comfortable."

The Honorable Judge Lull enters the room with his clerk in tow. Everyone rises. The judge nods to acknowledge them and then takes his seat. Everyone else sits back down while the judge arranges a pack of Kleenex, Halls lozenges, and bifocals in a straight line next to his gavel. He looks to be in his late sixties, possibly older, with thinning hair in a washed-out hue that may have been red in his youth, a neatly trimmed white beard, and a prominently bulbous nose that looks like an avocado pit.

"The dispute before this court," he begins, "involves Arden Bunt Moore, an alleged decedent of Bruce Alastair Ashforth. The executor of the estate, James Ashforth, is requesting the court to find that Mrs. Bunt Moore is not a distributee and has no interest in Bruce Ashforth's estate as per a previous ruling by the Westchester surrogate in 1985."

The judge looks up and locks eyes with Arden. She shrinks in her chair. The way he says her maiden and married names together sounds like Buntmore.

"Counsel, I have some concerns about this matter," the judge continues. "We're still blazing a relatively new trail here, and I want to be thoughtful about how we proceed. One of the shortcomings of New York's approach to kinship is the complex and expensive procedure itself. Kinship hearings are intended to prevent false claims of heirship. However, in the past, they've proved quite restrictive, often denying inheritance rights to the nonmarital children—"

"Your Honor, we're nowhere near a kinship hearing, and I believe we can avoid one altogether," Fistler says. "Ms. Buntmore has no standing in this court. As you can see in the claim attached to our petition, the Surrogate's Court of Westchester County ruled more than thirty years ago that Arden Bunt was not the daughter of Wallace Ashforth and had no right to inherit, which means she can't be the half sister of Bruce Ashforth. On the grounds of collateral estoppel, we do not consent to a genetic marker test and move to dismiss."

"Your Honor," Joshua says, standing, "the change in law allows my client to try again with a new decedent and to take advantage of recent advances in science. We ask the court not to hold a decision from 1985 against her. Do not preclude her access to a genetic marker test, where scientific evidence can and will prevail."

"We'll get there, Mr. James," the judge says. "We haven't even begun."

"In the old days," Joshua continues, "illegitimate children were discriminated against as a way to discourage extramarital affairs. Nowadays, that no longer justifies limiting the rights of nonmarital children to get advanced DNA testing."

"That's irrelevant," Fistler argues. "The collateral estoppel argument makes the sanctioning of posthumous DNA testing unreasonable."

"Is the tissue sample for DNA testing easily available?" the judge wants to know. "And are there privacy concerns?"

"I can tell you right now that privacy is one of the main concerns for the Ashforth family," Fistler says.

"There is no need for exhumation," Joshua says. "The brain tissue is accessible."

"Exhumation or not, there is no good and substantial reason to compel DNA testing here. This is a cash grab, plain and simple."

"Your Honor?" Joshua says. "A review of several recent decisions in the New York County Surrogate's Court shows a legal trend that makes it easier for nonmarital children to inherit—"

"Which invites untold opportunistic individuals to file fraudulent claims," Fistler counters. "It would be a free-for-all!"

"With the accuracy of current genetic testing," Joshua resumes, "why would anyone bother to file a fraudulent claim knowing that DNA will quickly and conclusively rule them out as an heir? In fact, compelling DNA testing would make these proceedings that much more efficient by eliminating the frauds before they ever crawl out of the woodwork."

Arden glances up at Joshua. He's impressive, charismatic.

"This is a binary decision," Joshua states, sitting back down. "If you consent to the genetic marker testing, we don't have to waste another moment of the court's time."

"The court appreciates your generosity," Judge Lull quips.

"If she's not a match," Joshua continues, "we will withdraw and not file any objections. Arden Moore has a right to DNA testing. The Ashforths should not be permitted to suppress her search for the truth."

"Paternity has already been denied," Fistler says, sounding bored. "Therefore, there is no reason to compel a genetic marker test."

"All right, Counsel," the judge interrupts. "We're going in circles here."

"Your Honor, if I may?" Joshua says. "The advances in DNA technology give us a very useful tool in postdeath kinship proceedings. There's absolutely no sound basis in the legislature that warrants depriving a nonmarital child of the right to legitimization through posthumous genetic testing. A simple chromosome test would effectively establish Arden Moore's kinship to Bruce Ashforth once and for all."

"Let me be clear," Fistler says. "As per the Surrogate's Court of Westchester County, Ms. Buntmore is *not* a distributee of Bruce Ashforth's estate, and Mr. Ashforth certainly never intended for his estate to be left to a complete stranger."

Joshua turns to face Fistler, impressively staring him down. "He also didn't intend for his estate to be left to his *brother*."

"None of this is relevant here," Judge Lull interrupts.

Joshua turns away from Fistler and back to the judge. "Your Honor, you are correct in saying we're still blazing a relatively new trail here, but this should still be a relatively simple decision. We are merely asking for a DNA test to rule our client in or out."

"Let's stop wading through all this rhetoric, Mr. James. What I would like to know is how the petitioner has standing. Out of curiosity, has there been any contact at all between the petitioner and the Ashforth family prior to or since Bruce's death?"

"None whatsoever," Fistler says. "This is a woman whose mother had a lifelong obsession with a fortune that never belonged to her. Go back in history and you'll find countless failed petitions and appeals, and now the spurned lover has passed her gold-digging crusade on to her daughter. We've been here before, Your Honor. This is a shakedown, nothing more."

"Mr. Fistler, enough with the ad hominem remarks," the judge says. "Keep your arguments to the facts, please."

Arden blinks back tears. *Gold-digging crusade? A shakedown?*

The judge's gaze lingers on Arden, their eyes lock for a split second, and then he turns his attention to Joshua. "Give me something to justify consenting to posthumous testing, Counselor, given that the Westchester court already decided the petitioner was not a distributee and therefore not entitled to inherit."

"That was before the amendment in 2010," Joshua says. "Quite simply, the law has changed. She deserves a chance—"

"That amendment was not intended to open the door to every money-grubbing scam artist," Fistler mutters.

"Your Honor!" Joshua cries, jumping to his feet again. At the same time, Judge Lull says, "Mr. Fistler! You've been warned once. Your opinion here is irrelevant; now stick to the facts."

"Apologies, Your Honor." But Fistler doesn't seem remotely apologetic to Arden. Quite the opposite.

"Permit me to get away from the polite legalese here," Joshua says, settling down. "I know an open courtroom hearing isn't the place to express my personal beliefs, but I believe, Your Honor, that Mr. Fistler is wrong in his assessment of my client. There has never been any evidence to prove she *isn't* Wallace Ashforth's daughter. She is now seeking legitimization in the courts, which is her right."

"Okay, Mr. James. Without the consent of a known family member, I need evidence here. If you want to make a motion to compel access to DNA testing, I'll allow it. But this is a court of record, so if you want a court order, you need to make your motion in writing. I'm not going to entertain an oral application for DNA material."

"Your Honor—" Fistler says.

"Mr. Fistler, you're welcome to file a cross-motion to dismiss, based on collateral estoppel that Arden Moore is not a member of the Ashforth family. This is as far as we're going to go today."

Arden looks over at Joshua, utterly confused. "What's happening?" she whispers.

"We're still charting a new course here with regard to DNA technology as it applies to nonmarital children claiming the right to inherit,"

Judge Lull acknowledges. "This case may in fact present a novel issue—"

"I object to that!" Fistler shouts, looking somewhat unraveled. "The law must rely on precedent—"

"And as I've just stated, this may be a case of First Impression." The judge removes his bifocals and stares out into the gallery. "File your motions, and I'll do a deep dive into whatever precedent I can find. In the interest of efficacy, we'll meet back in court to hear both motions at the same time."

Arden tunes out the rest. She can feel the beginning of a migraine. *What the hell has she gotten herself into?*

The judge stands abruptly and exits the room. Arden looks over at Joshua. "That went extremely well," he says, smiling. "You can relax, Ms. Buntmore."

11

Virginia's physiotherapist is a super-fit millennial with impressive abs and carved ice-cream-scoop biceps. Her name is Hayley Foil and she's never not aggressively chewing a wad of peppermint gum. "Eight, nine, ten," she says, looking a little bored, moving Virginia's leg around like a stick shift. "Other ankle."

Virginia rotates her left foot inward and then out, drawing circles with her big toe while Hayley counts out loud. "One, two, three, four, five—"

Virginia wants to tell her to shut up. *I can fucking count to ten!*

"Are you doing the ankle pumps and rotations three times a day?" Hayley asks her, a feather of accusation in her tone.

"Most days."

"I know it's monotonous, but it's really important," she says. "We want you walking normally again without that walker. Right?"

"I guess."

"Okay," Hayley chirps. "Butt contractions." She places her hand lightly on Virginia's left glute to make sure she's doing the work.

"I used to do two hours of yoga a day." Virginia says this more to herself, remembering. She used to care about her body, to have discipline and strive for health. Hayley wouldn't know that about her.

"Tighten. Hold for five, four, three, two, and one. Good. Again."

Virginia's progress has been slow. She's not the least bit motivated. She wants to walk on her own again, but not quite enough to work for it. For once, she'd rather lie around and be cared for by the girls. She's lost her freedom and her enthusiasm, but the most crushing blow has been the loss of her raison d'être—the dream of finding someone with whom to spend the rest of her life. She misses the pursuit of that dream, the excitement of the first date, the first kiss, the first fuck. She misses *men*. Their strong hands, their games, her power over them, their power over her, the hunt, the promise. The very idea of love could always invigorate her. Without any of that, she's nothing.

She once confided in the girls that she often thought of herself as the heroine in a romantic comedy—Meg Ryan awaiting her Tom Hanks.

Tate rolled her eyes and said, "That is so fucked up, Mom."

Arden said, "You're such a romantic. Life isn't a Nora Ephron movie." This was *before* Scott's death, so Virginia was surprised by Arden's pragmatism. She had mistakenly presumed, given Arden's love story with Scott, that Arden—unlike Tate—had inherited her romantic idealism.

"I don't think it's such a bad outlook on life," Virginia said, unwilling to relinquish her sense of hopefulness or her expectation of love.

"That's because you're delusional," Tate responded.

That's the word that keeps coming back to her now—"delusional." Each and every one of them—West, Wallace, Hal, and everyone in between, culminating with Lou Geffen—was just a pearl of delusion in the endless strand that has made up her life. The great delusion, she sees now, being love itself.

The drugs help and don't help. They mute the pain and shame, but leave her listless, a shell.

"All right," Hayley says, "we're going to do knee bends and leg raises, and then we're hitting the stairs."

Virginia groans, longing to smack the pep out of her.

"The more exercise you do, the less pain you'll be in."

"So you keep saying."

"Attitude is so much a part of the recovery process," Hayley says. Virginia braces herself for more nuggets from *The Secret*. Hayley likes to oversimplify even the most complex universal concepts to accommodate her worldview. "I know a lot of people are skeptical about the law of attraction, but the principle of positive thinking and how much it impacts our physical health—both good and bad—is totally valid."

Hayley places both hands on Virginia's knee and slowly bends it. "Hold for one, two, three, four, five." She eases Virginia's leg back down on the bed. "And the other one. Good. I really believe there's a strong correlation between your current vibration and your progress, or lack thereof."

"I didn't realize I was vibrating."

"We're all vibrating, Virginia. Humans vibrate energy, and yours is very low. I can feel it. All your negative thinking and self-pity has lowered your vibration, which is hindering your physical recovery."

"I think it's my age that's hindering my physical recovery," Virginia says. "Old people just don't bounce back as quickly."

"See what I mean?" Hayley says, lowering Virginia's leg and going back to the other one. "That's exactly the kind of negative self-talk I mean. If you keep telling yourself you're old—"

"I *am* old." Even as she says it, she's aware she sounds defeatist and self-pitying, completely out of character. She doesn't know herself anymore.

"Age is a mindset."

"Said the twenty-six-year-old to the sixty-five-year-old."

"Your generation is too practical," Hayley says. "You're too focused on what you can see. Sorry, do you mind if I check my phone? Someone's texting me."

"Of course not," Virginia says, relieved to get a break from Hayley's unsolicited TED Talk.

She continues on her own with the knee bends. One, two, three, four, five. Look at that. She can count by herself.

"Sorry about that," Hayley says, tucking the phone into her JanSport backpack. "My boyfriend has a scabbing mole and he's freaking out."

"Did his vibration cause it?"

"Very funny. The sun caused it. Your generation ruined the sun for us, remember?" Hayley resumes the knee bends. "What was I saying?"

"My bad vibration . . ."

"Not bad—*low*. Have you read *The Varieties of Religious Experience*?"

"No."

"William James wrote about what he called healthy mindedness versus the sick soul. He claimed that healthy-minded people saw sickness as an illusion."

"This doesn't feel like an illusion," Virginia says, pointing to her bluish-purple leg.

"But it can be healed by your thinking. James believed in the 'mind-cure' over medicine, but both together are even better."

Virginia doesn't have the energy to argue with this helium balloon. She just lies there, quiet.

Hayley digs around in her purse and pulls out a pamphlet. "Here," she says. "I think this might help."

She hands Virginia the pamphlet, at the top of which it says, *Healing from Elder Abuse*.

"It's a support group," Hayley says. "You're not alone, Virginia."

Virginia shoves the pamphlet inside the bedside table drawer without a word. Hayley robustly claps her hands together and says, "Now let's hit those stairs!" Her breath is a fresh cloud of mint in the air.

Later, when Virginia is alone, reading the elder abuse pamphlet and enjoying a Nespresso, Tate and Arden barge into her room without knocking. She quickly shoves the pamphlet under the covers as they sit down on the rented hospital bed, one on either side of her, looking solemn. "We need to talk to you," Tate says.

"Why so grim, Nurse Ratched?"

"It's about money."

"What about it?" she says, glad to talk about anything other than what happened That Night.

"We're worried about your finances," Tate says.

"I don't have any finances."

"That's the problem."

Virginia closes her eyes, not wanting to look at them looking at her. Their disappointment in her is unbearable.

"Your employment insurance checks don't even cover your rent," Tate explains. "And next year, if you want to retire, your pension checks won't be enough either."

"You want me to give up my apartment."

"It's not that we want you to," Arden says. "There's no other option, unless you have some savings we don't know about it."

"There are no savings," Virginia snaps. "You know there are no savings. I sell shoes. I make just enough to live."

"Without your sales commission, you can't afford to keep your apartment. We're going to have to sublet it."

"Arden, is this what you want? You want me living here for the rest of my life?"

"It's not for the rest of your life, Mom. You'll get back on your feet. You may be able to go back to work in a few months. You can find a cheaper apartment—"

"Cheaper? It's a six-hundred-square-foot one-bedroom apartment. How much cheaper could I go?"

"Arden may have her inheritance money by then and she'll be able to buy you a house."

Virginia looks at Arden. "Is it going well? What does your lawyer say?"

"He's optimistic. It's fifty-fifty, I guess."

"Let's not worry about the future right now," Tate says. "Let's just stay in today. Today, we can't afford your apartment, so we have to sublet it. Are you okay with that?"

"Do I have a choice?"

"Not really," Arden says. "But it's short-term. Tate's right, Mom. By next year, you could be living in your dream house."

"The house Wallace Ashforth promised you," Tate adds.

Virginia forces a smile, recalling with an ache of guilt how often she'd said those exact words to the girls when they were little. "One day we'll be living in our dream house," she'd muse while cutting pictures out of *Architectural Digest*. "The house Wallace Ashforth promised me."

12

Wallace made Virginia a multitude of promises. Some he kept, most he didn't. She wasn't the type to demand or threaten. Her way was the way of patience, acquiescence. She held herself steady in the belief that he genuinely loved her, that he would eventually choose love over obligation and leave his wife. That was his biggest promise of all. Had he not been killed in the plane crash, Virginia believes he would have done it too. She tells herself that, anyway. Tells herself he would have changed his mind about everything.

She's finally going through the box Arden left in her room. She hasn't looked inside it in decades, not since she moved into her apartment building and shoved it in the storage locker. She had Ivey spread everything out on her bed so she wouldn't have to get up, and now she's engrossed in the past, sorting through dozens of old movie ticket stubs. *The Deer Hunter, Jaws 2, Alien, Midnight Express*. Wallace used to choose the movies. She preferred romantic comedies, would have loved to see the Woody Allen movies, but she was content to get dressed up for Wallace, curl her blond hair, spritz her neck and wrists with Opium perfume, and put on the gold necklace he bought her with the ivory elephant pendant that fell snugly in the valley of her cleavage. Even though it was only to hide in a dark theater in Flatbush where no one would see her, she knew Wallace appreciated the effort. She was always okay when at least someone was appreciating her.

She pulls two photographs from the manila envelope. In the first, Wallace is sitting on a park bench in the promenade of Carl Schurz Park, gazing solemnly out at the East River. They were having one of their clandestine lunches away from the office. He's wearing a trench coat and fedora, and he has that sexy Burt Reynolds moustache, but he looks so serious. Maybe they were fighting, or he didn't want her to take his picture. She can't quite remember. He used to get very upset with her over things like that.

In the other photo, he looks more relaxed, more himself. He's on a whitewashed deck somewhere, with a view of the ocean behind him. It looks like his summerhouse in Maine, if Virginia had to guess. His wife, Geraldine, must have taken this one. He probably gave it to Virginia, thinking he looked handsome in it. He's smiling for the camera, wearing a button-down shirt, a crested blazer, and a paisley ascot. He used to wear ascots.

Virginia always thought Wallace would have impressed her father. She couldn't wait for their relationship to be official so she could introduce them. What an upgrade he would have been after West. Her father had despised West, from his long, tangled hair to his dirty, sandaled feet. The first time he met him, her father said, "He's even worse than I would have expected from you, Virginia."

Still, West was the reason she wound up in New York, working in the secretarial pool at Ashforth Development Group. She'd taken typing courses in high school and was still surprisingly fast, even after all that time. The office manager was impressed with her. "Pretty and quick," she said. "They'll love you here."

ADG was a great place to work. The men all wanted to date her; she was popular with the other secretaries; she was a star typist. Within a few months, she was promoted to Wallace's private pool. Previously, she had admired him from afar. He was very attractive—not in the conventional way, but in the way powerful men are attractive. When he walked into a room, everyone fell silent, sat up a little straighter, tried a bit harder. He had good, thick hair and a steely gaze that made Virginia's pulse speed up when he fixed it on her, which was often. He wasn't extroverted or magnetic like some leaders—she had sensed he was a bit of a loner—but he was always very polite. People feared him, which made him especially desirable to her.

When Wallace started flirting with her, she felt like she'd won a beauty pageant. Wallace Ashforth had picked *her*. Although their flirty banter was discreet, the other secretaries noticed the attention he paid her, and she felt like a movie star. Their first kiss happened when she was in his office one afternoon, taking dictation.

"I can't concentrate," he said. "I can't even work around you anymore. What's that perfume you're wearing?"

"Love's Baby Soft," she said, feeling her cheeks flush.

He came around the desk and sat on the edge of it, pulling her toward him so that her chair rolled right between his legs. He touched her hair gently at first and then tugged her head back with a forceful little jerk that excited her. She was looking up at him like a pup waiting to be fed a scrap of meat. And then he bent down and kissed her on the mouth. When he pulled her to her feet and pressed her body tightly to his, she could feel him under his expensive dress pants, hard and eager. He was kissing her neck, her shoulder, moving his hands from her breasts to her rear end like he couldn't decide where to go first, like he wanted to devour her.

Their affair began that night at the Hotel Bossert. It was an out-of-the-way hotel on the corner of Montague Street in Brooklyn Heights, so Wallace didn't have to worry about being recognized. They would slip into his limo in the Financial District and cross the Brooklyn Bridge into anonymity. In its glory days—somewhere between the flapper years and the fifties—the Bossert had been known as the Waldorf-Astoria of Brooklyn. Wallace told her this the first time he brought her there. On first appraisal, she was dazzled by its grandeur and opulence. *Italian Renaissance*, he described it, trying to impress her. The lobby's carpet had a traditional floral pattern in emerald green and peach, and there was a row of white marble and gilt columns that rose to the dramatically high ceiling, where clusters of brass chandeliers hung twinkling overhead. There was a bar at the other end of the lobby and they could hear disco music playing, which felt anachronistic to her. It was like the Bee Gees playing at a Great Gatsby party.

When they got up to the room, Virginia was disappointed. It was shabby, neglected, with an outdated décor and stains on the carpet. The tub had a ring of rust around the drain and there was a strong musty smell, possibly mold in the walls. She looked at Wallace, wondering if he would suggest they go elsewhere, somewhere more in keeping with his status, but he said nothing. He seemed perfectly happy, and not surprised at all by the caliber of the room.

He looked her up and down and said, "I wish you'd worn a skirt."

She suddenly felt foolish. She was dressed like Annie Hall—wide-leg pants and a white blouse with a black vest over her top. Thankfully, she'd decided against the tie and bowler hat.

He threw her down onto the bed and they made love on the bedspread. He didn't even remove it beforehand. That was 1977, late autumn. She'll never forget the bite in the air when he tucked her into the cab at the end of the night, pecking her forehead like he was her uncle. "Good night, sweetheart," he said, his cigar breath hanging in the air between them. She understood he was acting like an uncle on purpose, pretending they weren't lovers for the cabdriver's benefit. He could never be sure who might recognize him. He used to worry about that a lot. He was often in the newspapers, and they were rarely kind to him.

Wallace tapped the roof of the cab with a leather-gloved hand, signaling he was ready for Virginia to be driven off, and then she watched him walk toward Hicks Street, where his driver was patiently waiting to take him home to Denby.

She didn't think it would happen a second time. She figured he was done with her and would be moving on to the next secretary, especially because of the Annie Hall outfit, but he surprised her a few days later when he called her into his office, bent her over his desk, hoisted up her denim skirt, and plunged himself inside her. He caught her off guard, but the sex was good. There was something about him—his certainty about everything, his entitlement, his power. She couldn't stop thinking about him at work, at home. All the time. They returned again and again to the Bossert, sometimes several nights in a week. It became their special place. That and the Kenmore Theatre. Virginia grew very fond of the hotel, even with its dingy rooms, moldy odor, and air of decline. When they tore the building down about a year after Wallace died, it felt like her entire history with him had been demolished, erased. She remembers making a special trip to Brooklyn just to see the space where it had once stood, which was now just rubble, and she grieved deeply not just for her lover but for that entire era of her life, which had been so special.

While they were sleeping together, Wallace gave her money to compensate Mrs. K., who was babysitting Tate several nights a week as well as during the day. Mrs. K. thought Virginia's job must be very important and encouraged her to work late as often as necessary. She was always praising Virginia for doing what she had to do to make a good life for Tate. And Virginia did believe she was building a future for her and Tate—with Wallace. She thought she was being clever dating a man like him, especially after West. Wallace Ashforth was the antithesis of West. The fact that Wallace was married, well, Virginia was confident she could overcome that obstacle. She believed she had some intangible hold over men that even Geraldine Ashforth could not match. Wallace also made her think it was possible. Not just possible but inevitable.

She never could have imagined him dying and leaving her alone with two fatherless daughters.

Out of the quiet, the front door slams and Virginia jumps. From her room, she can hear someone's shoes being kicked off, landing with two thuds on the wood floor. "Arden?" she calls out.

Moments later, Arden appears in the doorway, looking mascara-smudged and stressed.

"I thought you had a shift at the gallery?" Virginia says. "What's wrong?"

"I was laid off."

"Oh no. Arden. Why? You've been there for years."

"Hana's being sued by one of her artists," Arden explains, sounding distraught. It turns out Della Feasby was more than just a little disgruntled. "She can't afford to keep me because I'm only part-time."

"Can't you work full-time to keep your job?"

Arden shakes her head. "Not with the kids and the lawsuit and . . . you like this." She starts to cry.

"I'm sorry, darling. I know how much you love it there."

"It's not just that," Arden says. "It's the money. It wasn't much, but it was something. The timing couldn't be worse."

"I wish I could help," Virginia says. "I feel terrible adding to your burden."

"I'm going to have a bath," Arden says, looking and sounding far too weary for someone her age. "Hopefully the inheritance comes through sooner rather than later."

"Oh, Arden. You sound just like I used to sound—"

Arden's eyes flash with anger and Virginia immediately shuts her mouth. She hasn't seen a look like that on Arden's face in years. It's an adolescent's rage, feral and unresolved. Arden looks about to say something and Virginia braces herself, but instead she just turns and leaves without a word.

When she's alone, Virginia slides the photographs she was looking at back inside the manila envelope and reaches for the letter from Wallace. She takes it out of its Air Mail envelope, unfolding the thin paper with tingling fingers. Ever since the assault, her fingertips frequently go numb, which seems to coincide with more intense waves of lower back pain.

Greetings from Vaasa.

My dear Bunt, the days and nights without you are unbearable. Six weeks at sea with a bunch of septuagenarian Finns and Estonians . . . Where's an iceberg when you need one?

I've already told Geri this is my last cruise. I'm going through the motions. The only thing I'm enjoying is the breakfast smorgasbord. Pickled whitefish, Dutch hard rolls, and cloudberry preserves. (The vodka's good too. I'll bring back a bottle of Koskenkorva.)

I think about you—the way your skin feels when I touch you, the way you throw your arms around my neck when I show up at our place, that thing you do to me in the theater. I never planned on falling in love with you, but it's happened anyway. I want you to know that my feelings are genuine, Bunt. The longer I'm trapped on this ship, the more certain I am. Here I sit gazing out at the Baltic Sea and all I can think about is jumping off and swimming back to you!

We fly home from Stockholm on the 4th. I will be knocking at your door shortly thereafter, vodka and herring in hand.

With love,
Baldie

She presses the letter to her chest, remembering. *Bunt and Baldie.* She was starting to doubt that he'd ever really loved her. It buoys her to read this now and know that she was once the kind of woman for whom even the most powerful of men would swim across the Baltic Sea.

13

"Tell me about your finances," Joshua says, diving into her least favorite subject. Arden appreciates his directness, the way he skips over the small talk, which was more Larry's style, but she'd rather talk about anything other than her humiliating financial debt.

"Fistler will go there," he warns, reaching for the edamame. "I want you to be ready, Arden." The next court date is set for the last day of June, which gives them about five weeks to prepare. "You know he's going to make you out to be a gold digger. That's his M.O."

She gets a bit distracted watching Joshua's lips close around the edamame shell and then suck out each bean, one, two, three. Those beautiful lips. They're at Hazakura on Harbord, close to Joshua's hotel. He arrived this morning to interview Virginia. Arden is so damn happy to be out of the house, away from her mother and the kids. Just having a drink alone while she waited for Joshua was like a spiritual retreat. Being with him now, she's practically giddy.

"He's going to dredge up your husband's debts," Joshua says. "The three kids with no college fund—"

"I get it," she says.

"I want you to be prepared because my plan is to go there first. I don't want you to take it personally."

"I'm getting used to it."

"When the time comes, I'm going to acknowledge that your husband left you with a lot of debt," he says. "Which should have no bearing whatsoever on your petition to test Ashforth's DNA. I just need you to tell me everything."

Arden sighs, looks away from him.

"I don't want Fistler to make an ass out of me in court," he says. "So please don't hold back."

"It's embarrassing."

"I'm your lawyer," he says. "Think of me as a priest or an AA sponsor. You can tell me absolutely anything without guilt or shame. No judgment."

"Well, the latest is I was just laid off from the gallery."

"I'm sorry to hear that."

"Me too," she says, still reeling from the news. "My boss is being sued by one of her artists so she can't afford to keep her part-timers."

"Does she have a good art lawyer?"

"Is that a thing?"

"Absolutely. Art lawyers represent artists, art organizations, private collectors, galleries, museums. Some firms will have a specialized art law department, or you can work for an in-house legal team at an auction house. Kind of right up your alley, come to think of it."

"Maybe if I was twenty years younger."

"You'd be great at something like that. Art lawyers have to understand artists. Art, as I'm sure you know, is extremely personal, and art deals can be really complex and emotional."

"More complex and emotional than estate law?"

"Nothing is more complex and emotional than estate law."

She traces the hand-painted cherry blossom on her cup with the tip of her finger. "As for Scott," she says, choosing her words carefully, "he was a very savvy, successful stockbroker but he spent all his money on the things he wanted for himself and our family. Not the most important things, like, say, the kids' education, but the things that mattered most to him. Club memberships, impressive cars, a *boat*."

Her follow-up question, if she were Joshua, would be, *And where the hell were you?*

She thinks about that a lot. *Where the hell was she?* When Scott was spending their money faster than he could make it, why was she so silent, so compliant? Of course, she was simply playing the role she'd been assigned. Even when it was a matter of life and death, neither of them really wanted her to disrupt the status quo. They were both entrenched in Arden's obliging passivity.

She remembers him coming home late from work every night in a bad mood, pale and drawn, dark circles under his eyes, and then he'd be gone again when she woke up in the morning. He ate poorly or not at all, snuck cigarettes in his car, put himself to sleep at night with pills. She watched it go on for a long time and did nothing more than plead with him to slow down, quit smoking, try yoga, eat better. Once, she even said, "You're going to have a heart attack!" But she never actually *did* anything about it. She should have intervened, given him an ultimatum. *Cut back at work or we'll leave. Start a college fund for the kids or we'll leave. Clean up your lifestyle or we'll leave . . .*

She should have booked the damn doctor's appointment herself, thrown away his pills, stood up to him. Instead, she dismissed her own worries. She let him talk her out of her fears over and over again. She let herself be placated because she wanted to believe that everything would be *okay*. She not only watched him die; she allowed it to happen, just like she allows everything to happen. It's not exactly a leap to conclude that her pattern of inaction contributed to his death. While she may not have caused it, she certainly didn't do anything to prevent it.

She itemizes her long list of debts for Joshua while he taps notes into his phone. When she's done, he looks up and says, "That wasn't so bad, was it? I'm starving. Let's eat."

He orders pork bao, shishito peppers, and roast duck ramen, all her favorites. She actually feels a little lighter, as though she's just confessed her sins and been absolved. She splashes back a cup of sake and relaxes.

"I've spoken to Bruce's lawyer," Joshua says. "I want to make sure no other copies of the original will turn up. Our whole case hangs on the intestacy."

Arden hadn't even considered that. "And?"

"No other copies as far as the lawyer knows," he says. "I also spoke with Bruce's nurse, a guy name Casmir Slominski. He said Bruce was a decent guy, an eccentric-uncle type. He told me Bruce despised his brother. They didn't speak."

"Did something happen between them?"

"He just said Jamie was exactly like their father. He only cared about money and fucking people over. And fucking."

Joshua pulls a legal pad out of his messenger bag and flips back a few pages, looking for something in his notes. "He said Bruce knew his brother would challenge the new will and probably win. He said if that happened, the 'vultures would swarm.'"

"What vultures? *Me?*"

"All of Wallace Ashforth's illegitimate children."

"*All of them?* Was he implying Wallace had others? Not just me?"

"That's the assumption," Joshua says. "But there's no proof."

Arden leans back against her chair, winded. "I don't know what's worse," she says. "Being thought of as a vulture, or the fact that I might have a bunch of half siblings scattered around New York."

"No one has come forward, Arden. Right now, you're the only vulture."

"Very funny."

"None of this affects your petition. It's just a reconnaissance mission. The more we know about the Ashforths, the stronger our case will be."

He tucks the notepad back in his bag and says, "Larry mentioned there was a housekeeper who was supposedly very close to Bruce and Jamie. She lived with them for about twenty years and was fired in the late seventies."

"Did he give you a name?"

"He did. My investigator is looking for her, which brings me to my next point. I'm going to need a little more money."

"How much?"

"A few thousand at least."

"My retainer didn't go very far."

"This is what's called the discovery phase, which is necessary in the very likely event that we end up in a kinship hearing. Looking for key people, interviewing them, gathering information. It always costs more than you expect, but it will be worth it."

"I wish I was guaranteed to inherit at the end of all this."

"If Wallace really is your father, I'm willing to guarantee you'll inherit. I just can't say when."

She smiles weakly but isn't sure if she should feel reassured by his certainty or terrified by his cockiness. She vacillates between the two. His attitude is on the razor edge of reckless overconfidence, which makes her nervous. He's smart and competent and sure-footed, but he's also young and inexperienced. Even Larry wouldn't go as far as to guarantee a win. It's like a doctor guaranteeing a full recovery after cancer. It's just not done.

A family of five walks past them on their way to a table at the very back of the restaurant—a young couple with three boys under the age of about six, each with a tablet tucked under his arm. Arden watches them as they're seated between the kitchen and men's bathroom, the table typically reserved for families with young kids.

"How's your mother?" Joshua asks her, pulling her attention from the family. "Is she ready for tomorrow?"

"I think so. She's looking forward to telling her story."

"Larry says to say hello."

"How did your mother meet Larry?" she asks. Joshua reveals very little of himself, which makes her even more curious about him.

"She was his legal assistant."

"Were your parents already divorced? I mean . . . sorry. That's none of my business—"

"My dad took off when I was twelve. Larry and my mom started seeing each other about a year after he left. Married two years after that."

"Is your father still in your life?"

"Not really. He lives in Seattle, has a new family. He just got in a cab one morning and never came back."

"A cab? That's awful."

Joshua shrugs.

"How do you and Larry get along?"

"It was rough at first," Joshua admits. "I despised him. I actually ran away when my mother told me we were moving in with him. Turns out I'm not cut out for living on the street. I came home the next day and had a long bubble bath and cried in my mother's arms while she fed me soup." He laughs at the memory, an adorable, self-deprecating laugh. "We moved in with Larry a month later."

"So you're a mama's boy."

"Absolutely. Shameless. I worship her."

"How do you and Larry get on now?"

"Larry's all right. He can be obnoxious and arrogant, but he's stable. He's been good to my mother and that's all that matters to me. If it wasn't for him, I wouldn't be a lawyer."

"You didn't want to be a lawyer before he came into your life?"

"Hell no. I had no idea what I wanted to do. I wasn't on a good path, let's just put it that way."

"I guess you've got a lot to prove," she says, and he looks surprised, as though he didn't think he could be so easily read. People tend to think they're a lot more complex than they really are. She witnessed Scott's youthful ambition mushroom into something more self-conscious and socially motivated as he got older; she often worried that his prosperity and acquisitions simply could not keep up with his desire to impress, which was profound. He, too, had a lot to prove.

"I suppose I do," Joshua concedes, reaching for the ceramic flask. "My mother emigrated from the Philippines with absolutely nothing. She married my father and then he left us with nothing."

"And now you're motivated by wanting to make her proud and him regret abandoning you."

"You read me," Joshua says, gazing into his cup. His cheeks are softly flushed. "One time, when I was in law school, I was huddled in a doorway outside NYU waiting for a friend. It was winter and I had a coffee in my hand. This woman was walking by and she stopped and tossed a coin in my cup. I was so humiliated. She assumed I couldn't be a student. To her, I looked like a guy begging for money. That lit a fire under my ass."

"Why, though?"

"Because I already felt like I didn't belong in law school. I didn't think I was as smart or as pedigreed as the other students. I was half Filipino, the kid who was so underwhelming, his own father got in a cab one day and took off for good. When that woman tossed her coin in my cup, I made one of those self-important vows to myself, you know? *As God is my witness, no one will ever mistake Joshua James for a beggar again!*"

Arden chuckles at the image of him on his knees, fist melodramatically upraised to the sky.

"Did I mention she was wearing a fur coat?" Joshua says, replenishing both their cups. "What an entitled bitch."

The food arrives and keeps coming, dish after dish, filling the air with the smell of ginger and Asian five spice. Outside, the sky turns a soft purple as the afternoon slips away. Arden is feeling calmer than she's felt in a long time, and unless she's completely delusional, it seems like Joshua has been outright flirty with her.

A commotion at the back of the restaurant interrupts the moment. Arden turns around just as the father of the three young boys is jumping up from the table, covered in ramen broth from the crotch of his pants to his ankles. On the floor at his feet, the porcelain ramen bowl is spinning like a dreidel next to a heaping pile of noodles. All three boys are crying while the poor mother crouches down on her hands and knees, simultaneously yelling at the kids and mopping up their mess with her napkin.

"Why do parents drag their kids to adult restaurants?" Joshua says, sounding put out.

"What's an *adult* restaurant?"

"A sake bar," he says. "Those kids don't want to be here. *We* don't really want them here. What are the parents trying to prove? That little kids can still fit into their hip, urban lifestyle?"

"They're just having ramen," Arden says, guilty of occasionally bringing her children to adult restaurants.

"It's a sake *bar*," he repeats. "Why does every corner of the city need to be family-friendly?"

"You know I have three children. Where would you like us all to live? The suburbs? A leper colony?"

"Sorry," he says, smiling. "I'm not exactly a kid person, but I won't hold yours against you. And, yes, for the record, I'd like you all to live in the suburbs. A leper colony isn't necessary. I'm not a monster."

"People say they're not kid people until they have their own," Arden points out. "You're young. One day—"

"It's never going to happen."

"Never say never. You might meet someone who wants children. What if it's a deal-breaker for her?"

"People with kids always think people who don't want kids will change their minds. Why is that? Can you not fathom that some people just might not be good at it and prefer not to inflict themselves on an innocent creature?"

"'Inflict' is a strong word," she remarks.

"I don't want to disappoint anyone."

"Why would you?"

"Fatherhood is not for me," he states, clearly attempting to shut down the conversation.

"I'm just saying you're still young."

"I just don't have the gene. Can we leave it at that?"

"I'm not sure there's a gene."

"*That* is the last thing I want," he says, looking past her at the offending family.

Arden turns to look at them again. All three kids have settled back in their chairs and are hunched over their devices, quiet little zombies.

"Why bring them out if you're just going to stick a tablet under their nose?" Joshua continues, his irritation and outspokenness on the subject suggesting to Arden some kind of personal wound.

She drops it, but her gaze lingers on the family. The husband and wife are laughing now, sharing a bottle of wine. Arden gets it; they're just trying to survive another day, to feel part of the world again. She feels a stirring of envy, a darkness descending.

"I should get home," she says, pulling her eyes away. "I'll walk you back to your hotel and grab a cab there."

They walk in silence for a block or two, past a smattering of hookers on Jarvis, sad girls in short faux-fur jackets, high-heeled boots, and Value Village miniskirts, loitering in front of the Keg steak house. "There are better neighborhoods," she says.

"I like it here. It's fine during the day. It's close to everything."

They reach his hotel and stand facing each other on the sidewalk, as though it's the end of a first date that was full of potential and possibility. "I'll see you tomorrow," she says, navigating the awkwardness.

"Hey, there's a cab," he says, suddenly jumping out in front of her and flagging it down.

For a split second she wonders if he's going to kiss her, but as he politely holds the door open for her, she realizes she's entirely misconstrued the moment.

"Good night," he says.

"You've got my address, right?"

"Yep. I'll be there first thing in the morning."

He slams the car door and steps back onto the sidewalk with a friendly wave. Alone in the cab, Arden lets her head fall back against the seat. She closes her eyes, feeling a little tipsy and disappointed, a lot guilty. As the taxi pulls into the street, she wonders if her feelings for other men will always be tangled up with guilt—if, in fact, guilt is the unavoidable destiny of widowhood.

14

Joshua's laptop is set up at Arden's dining-room table, the video camera facing Virginia. Arden dragged in a floor lamp to brighten up the room as much as she could, but it's made little improvement: the forest-green wallpaper and mahogany wood absorb all the natural light. It's also pouring rain, so the entire house feels gloomier than normal.

"I'm sorry it's so dark," she says, turning the lamp to its brightest setting.

"It's fine," Joshua says. "It's very gothic."

"We were going to renovate," she says apologetically. "It's the first thing I'm going to do with the money—"

She's been catching herself more often lately spending that money in her head; the other night, she lulled herself to sleep playing "When I'm a Millionaire."

She quickly picks up on Joshua's disinterest in her renovation plans and doesn't elaborate. He's busy sorting through his notes, preparing.

"The kids are out," she tells him, wanting him to know they won't be getting in the way. Tate took them to a movie—all except Ivey, who refused and went to a friend's house instead, probably to vape weed all afternoon.

Joshua looks up vaguely and nods. "Ready?" he says, fiddling with the camera.

The rain is coming down heavily now, pelting the leaded-glass windows. Virginia is seated at the head of the table, with Arden and Joshua on either side of her. She smiles, flirty, enchanting. Her hair is freshly brushed and she's wearing pink lipstick and a pink cardigan with pearls. Even her cheeks are pink. It's the best she's looked since the accident.

Maybe she's slowly getting back to her old self. All it took was bringing a man into the house.

"Can you state your name, please?" Joshua asks her.

"Why so formal?"

"It's good practice," Joshua says. "Fistler is most likely going to subpoena you. Virginia, I'm going to ask you some very personal questions, okay? I'm going to act as if I'm the opposing counsel, so you may find my demeanor a bit hostile. Don't take it personally. The goal here is to get you comfortable with this line of questioning, what you can expect from Jamie's lawyer, that sort of thing."

Virginia nods.

"State your name, please."

"Virginia Bunt."

"And you're Arden Moore's mother?"

"Yes."

"What was your relationship with Wallace Ashforth?"

"We were lovers. Well, first he was my employer. I was in the secretarial pool at Ashforth Development Group."

"How long were you lovers?"

"From 1977 to 1980. Right up until he died."

"Did you have any other lovers during that time?"

"I did not. I was in love with Wallace and very loyal."

"And you got pregnant with your daughter, Arden, during that time?"

"Yes, I did. I got pregnant in 1980. I remember the night I took the home pregnancy test because I had just been to see the movie *Urban Cowboy* with Debra Winger and John Travolta. I realized during the film that my period was late, so I bought a test at the pharmacy on my way home. That was in June, I think."

"Did you tell Wallace Ashforth you were pregnant?"

"No, I did not."

"And why is that?"

"He was in Cape Elizabeth at the time. He summered there."

"Cape Elizabeth, Maine?"

"Yes. Maine."

"With his family?"

"Yes."

"Wallace Ashforth was married at the time, correct?"

"Correct."

"When were you planning on telling him you were pregnant?"

"After Labor Day, when he came back from Maine."

"And what happened?"

"He died in a plane crash."

"So he never knew you were pregnant?"

"No."

"And obviously neither you nor your child stood to inherit."

"There was no will."

"You've been down this road before, haven't you, Ms. Bunt?"

"What road?"

"You've been trying to get your hands on Wallace Ashforth's money for three decades, haven't you?"

"Joshua!" Arden says, glaring at him. "Is that really necessary?"

"I'm Fistler right now. Ms. Bunt, please answer my question."

"I've been trying to prove paternity so that my daughter can get what she deserves," Virginia says, "which is her share of *her father's* estate. He promised me he would always take care of me. You read his letter. He loved me."

"You've lost every petition and appeal you've filed since 1980, correct?"

"The laws changed."

"Just answer the question, please."

"Yes."

"The bottom line is there's really nothing to prove you and Wallace were ever lovers, is there, aside from a letter submitted in previous court documents? Letters signed Baldie, not Wallace?"

"Baldie was short for Archibald, his middle name."

"It's a stretch."

"It's the truth," Virginia says.

"Ms. Bunt, I'll ask you again: Do you have any *real* proof of your alleged affair with one of the wealthiest men in the country?"

"My *daughter* is my proof!"

"Something a little more substantial? So far, this is all very thin."

"I was his secret," Virginia says, shifting around on her chair. "We went to movies and hid in the dark. We stayed at the Hotel Bossert in

Brooklyn, where no one knew him. But he loved me. He was going to leave Geraldine."

"Let's talk about those photos. They're not even photographs of you and Wallace together, are they? In fact, there are no photographs of the two of you together."

"I was a secret," she repeats softly. "He would never allow it."

"How do we know you didn't steal those pictures from his desk at work?"

"I took one of those pictures!"

"Even if you did, what does that really prove? He was your boss. Let's say you took a picture of him. How does that prove you were sleeping together? Isn't that quite a leap?"

"Analyze the handwriting. My former lawyer did, and it's a match."

"Excellent, Virginia. Great answer."

Virginia smiles, straightens up.

"You knew Wallace was married, yes?"

"Yes."

"Fidelity isn't really an issue for you, though, is it?"

"Really, Joshua?" Arden interrupts.

"It speaks to an overall lack of integrity," Joshua says. "Fistler will go there."

"You're right," Virginia says, her voice strong and unwavering. "My moral standards were questionable. I had an affair with a married man, but a DNA test would still prove that Wallace Ashforth is Arden's father. That has nothing to do with my lack of integrity."

Arden smiles. Every so often, her mother impresses the hell out of her.

"Do you have any proof that you had no other lovers at the time you got pregnant?" Joshua asks, undeterred.

"Of course not."

"Do you recognize this man?" Joshua asks, pulling a newspaper clipping out of a file folder. Virginia squints to get a better look, and then her expression changes.

"Ms. Bunt?"

Suddenly, she looks much less pink than she did at the start of the interview.

"Please answer the question, Ms. Bunt."

"Yes," she says, her voice a tremor. "I recognize him."

Arden looks over at Joshua and grabs the newspaper clipping. It's from the *Toronto Daily Star*, dated July 7, 1970. The headline reads YORKVILLE'S HIPPIE HOTBED.

Below the headline is a photograph of some hippies sitting on a stoop at the corner of what looks to be Yorkville and Avenue Road. At the center of the group, a teenage boy with long blond hair and an angelic face is playing guitar. He's looking down at the chords, a cigarette between his lips. The paper identifies him as "high school dropout Bryce Beekhoff, better known as West to the hippies and beatniks of his Yorkville haunt."

Arden recognizes him immediately. Her heart drops.

"Can you tell me who this person is?" Joshua asks Virginia.

"His name is West."

"He changed his name to West, correct? His real name is Bryce Beekhoff?"

"Yes."

"And who is he to you?"

"An ex-boyfriend."

"He's more than that, isn't he?"

"How did you find that?" Virginia wants to know.

"Virginia, Jamie's lawyer will surely get his hands on this, just like I did. Can you answer my question?"

"You know who he is, or you wouldn't be showing me this."

"Answer the question," Joshua says softly.

"He's my other daughter's father."

"Your elder daughter, Tate?"

"Yes."

"And how long were you and Mr. Beekhoff together?"

"A few years, but he was in and out of our lives."

"Let me rephrase. When was the last time you saw Mr. Beekhoff?"

Virginia blinks nervously, looks over at Arden. "I don't know exactly. Maybe the mid-eighties?"

"After Arden was born?'

"I guess so."

"This is very important, Ms. Bunt. You stated under penalty of perjury that the only man in your life—the only man with whom you were sexually active from at least 1977 to 1980—was Wallace Ashforth. Yet now you're saying Mr. Beekhoff was also in your life at least until the mid-eighties?"

"We were not sexually active," Virginia says.

"You're saying that this man, your longtime boyfriend and the father of your first child, was in your life *but the two of you were not sexually active?*"

"That's correct. He would show up once in a while to see Tate, that's all. I was always loyal to Wallace."

"Loyal to Wallace," Joshua repeats, letting the absurdity of the statement marinate.

Virginia is close to tears. Her thin hands are shaking.

"Can she have a break?" Arden asks impatiently. "She's still recovering from her accident."

Joshua agrees to a break. He stops the camera and Arden jumps up to get her mother a glass of water. Joshua follows her into the kitchen.

"This is awful," Arden says, turning on the tap. "You're bullying her."

"I thought your mother was very poised. Fistler will be much harder on her. He'll be a hell of a lot more graphic as well."

"Meaning?"

"There will be questions about penetration, ejaculation—"

"That's humiliating!"

"That's the whole point."

"What about the photo of Tate's father? Why didn't you tell me about it? Why did you accuse her of sleeping with him at the same time she was sleeping with Wallace?"

"For all we know, that hippie could be *your* father too," he says. "I just got my hands on that bit of information and frankly I would have preferred to have heard it from your mother. You and Tate need to get DNA tests right away."

"Why?"

"If your mother was sleeping with both men at the same time, don't you think we should rule out the possibility that West is your father? A

DNA marker test will tell us if you and Tate are half or full siblings. We need a fifty percent match to go forward without any concerns."

"My mother swears she wasn't sleeping with West when she was with Wallace."

"You trust her? I don't want there to be any surprises."

"This is . . . *Shit.*"

Arden leans back against the sink for support. *Could West be my father?* With Virginia, anything is possible. It would mean the end of the inheritance; it would mean Tate is her full sister.

"If your mother is telling the truth," Joshua says, "we have nothing to worry about."

Arden nods absently and decides to give her mother the benefit of the doubt. Virginia may be a lot of things—promiscuous, flaky, unreliable—but Arden has never known her to be a liar.

"This is why we do these depositions," Joshua says, coming closer to her. "Due diligence."

"Assuming Tate and I are half sisters, will that be enough to compel the judge to let us test Bruce's DNA?"

"I don't think so. Fistler will just suggest there were multiple men. He'll paint her as a slut."

"How can I put my mother through that?"

"You have no choice," he says, infuriatingly pragmatic. "We're not stopping now, unless you and Tate turn out to be full-blood sisters."

"I'm starting to think this whole thing was a bad idea." She turns to face him. "After hearing you today—"

"*Already?*"

"What?"

"We're just getting started."

"You terrorized my poor mother. If Fistler gets hold of her, it will be a shit show."

"Estate proceedings are always a shit show. Fistler will do some grandstanding, but ultimately there's no valid reason not to compel a DNA test in this day and age, especially with so much at stake. You're going to need a thicker skin, Arden. We're in this for the long haul."

He lays a hand on her forearm and says, "Go and get a DNA test."

Then he takes the glass of water from her and leaves the kitchen. She looks down at her arm where his hand was touching her a moment ago. She can hear her mother thanking him for the water from the dining room, using that high-pitched voice she reserves for men. Arden hasn't heard that voice since Virginia was assaulted; she's reassured to hear it making a comeback.

Arden fills the kettle for tea, not wanting to go back to the dining room. She's in a mood now. Everything is getting to her—the rain, the possibility of West being her father, her dilapidated house, the pending court date, her loneliness. What she'd really like to do is kick everyone out and sink into a hot bath with one of those edible gummies Tate gave her.

"You coming, Arden?" her mother calls from the other room. "We're waiting!"

Arden piles the teacups on a tray and grabs the sugar and milk. "In a minute!" she says, making her voice sound as upbeat and solicitous as she can.

15

Ever since the mock deposition, Virginia's been having this recurring nightmare where she's falling in slow motion, falling and falling out of the sky, until she crashes onto her bedroom floor in a deafening cacophony of smashing bones. When she opens her eyes, there's a shadowy, featureless figure standing above her. *You know you want it, you decrepit old whore.* That's when she wakes up for real, usually with a stunning pain in her hip.

She hasn't told anyone about her dreams. The girls have been relentless trying to get her to talk, to report him, to press charges. Virginia understands why, of course. She knows he's still out there, probably preying on other desperate old women, but the shame of coming forward is unimaginable. Her silence is self-preservation, simple as that.

She remembers all of it, though, in vivid detail, from the easy, convivial conversation over dinner to the agonizing minutiae of the assault. The name he gave her was Lou Geffen, which, it turns out, was not his real name. She looked him up online before their date and all she found was his Facebook account—gone now—most likely created for the purpose of joining SilvrFoxes. She wasn't concerned at the time. Plenty of people in her generation—*old people*—don't have a presence online.

They met at a coffee shop called the Beanerie, west of Liberty Village. It was very out-of-the-way, but Virginia didn't mind. He insisted it be an independent place because he did not support coffee chains, he said, and she admired his righteousness.

She was pleased with his appearance. He was very tall, well over six feet, possibly as tall as six five. She wasn't lying about how big he was.

He was heavyset, husky, completely bald, with features that were slightly too long for his face—a long, straight nose, long teeth, prominent chin. Still, she found him attractive. His user profile said he was fifty-five, but he looked much younger in person. He looked like he was in his early forties. He had no business being on SilvrFoxes. Another red flag? She didn't think so. She thought it spoke to an open mind and a noble indifference to the superficialities of youth culture.

She ordered her usual, a small black coffee in a large cup. Lou Geffen was extremely vexed. "Why a large cup?" he wanted to know, sounding troubled.

"I like the extra space."

"For milk?"

"No, I take it black."

"Hm. Small coffee, large cup. You're an enigma."

Virginia couldn't tell if he was teasing her. Maybe he was. She's not very good with deadpan humor. He ordered himself a regular coffee in a regular-sized cup, which he made a point of saying to the barista.

Lou chose a table in the far back and immediately started talking about himself. He had a restless energy; ideas and thoughts seemed to pop into his head and fly out his mouth simultaneously. He jumped all over the place, enjoying the sound of his own voice, which was deep and confident. It took all the pressure off Virginia. There weren't any awkward silences or stilted exchanges. He had a bottomless magician's hat of stories about himself, which he pulled out, one after another, like colorful handkerchiefs. She remembers thinking how quirky and bewitching he was, how weirdly magnetic.

Now she keeps going over everything he said to her, excavating their entire conversation, searching for clues she might have ignored that would have revealed him to be a monster. The truth is, just about everything he said was odd or self-aggrandizing or controversial.

When she asked him if he'd ever been married, he said, "Marriage is a death knell. It's a cage. Why would anyone willingly get into a cage? My ex spent her days uploading dog memes to Facebook. Relationships are confining. I don't want to be in a cage. I'm too old. My remaining years are too precious."

"You look much younger than fifty-five."

"I've got a good plastic surgeon." He winked. "I used to be a plastic surgeon, actually."

"You did? Your profile said pharmaceuticals."

"*Now*. But I did a three-month residency in plastic surgery."

"You're a doctor?"

"Not practicing," he said. "There's more money in pharmaceuticals. Any idiot can be a doctor. Any idiot can be a surgeon, for that matter. The plastic surgery was the worst. I hated the women, hated the breasts. You're dealing with problems that can't be fixed with a knife. It was a factory of emptiness. I considered being a psychiatrist for a time."

"Psychiatrists make me nervous."

"They're all very pseudoscientific, right? For psychotherapy to be of any value, you need an analyst who's the opposite sex, so you can get insight into *you*. Someone who is the same sex can't give you real insight. You see what I mean?"

She did not.

"You can gauge someone's intellect and acumen in one session," he said. "Just like a first date." He smiled. Was he joking again? Was she supposed to laugh? He made her feel a bit dumb, which was also a little titillating.

"I was very blunt in my youth," he said, not bothering with context. "I was a blunt instrument. Now I understand the nuances of conversation, at least. I can still be blunt, but I've learned to communicate. I don't have to react to everything anymore. I have plenty of friends who are emotional animals."

Emotional animals. She hadn't known what to respond, but it didn't really matter. He went right on talking. "My father was the opposite," he said. "He never spoke. Once a year he said a few words, to make sure I was seeing the world correctly."

He laughed at his own joke and she followed suit, so he wouldn't think she was stupid.

"My father was above religion, if you know what I mean. I don't take religion seriously myself. It's a nice distraction. I'm responsible to everyone in my life at all times, not because God gives a shit. If religious people carried that message to their flocks, I'd be okay with religion. You know what I mean?"

"My father wasn't much of a talker either," Virginia said. Lou ignored her.

"Are you of German origin?" he wanted to know. It was the first question he'd put to her since they'd sat down, other than the question about the small coffee in the large cup.

"I'm not sure," she said. "I always thought Bunt was Anglo-Saxon."

"It's actually Austrian and/or German. I looked it up. It's a great name. Sporty, succinct. Straight to the point. Blunt Bunt. Pow."

She was totally riveted, waiting to see where he'd go next. His brain was like a pinball machine.

"Let's talk about your first name," he said. "You were named for Virginia Woolf, I assume?"

"Yes, my father was a lit professor. He loved her. How did you know?"

"Who else would you be named after?" He used his napkin to pat down his scalp, on which a dew of sweat had formed. "One of the perils of baldness," he said, smiling apologetically. "I just came from playing tennis. My head will continue to sweat for at least another hour."

"You play tennis," she said. It wasn't even a question.

"I don't think you would have been impressed with me today," he said. "Normally, I have a massive serve. Hundred-and-five-mile-an-hour serve. I'm a great baseline player, great at the net. But today I had nothing. Maybe I was nervous about meeting you." He chuckled, continuing to pat his damp pate. "I also bike. I biked Hawaii last year with a few friends. Hawaii, Kauai, Oahu, Mauna Loa. Nineteen days with a bunch of fortysomething guys from my tennis club."

"Fortysomething?" she said. "You're in your forties, I knew it!"

He smiled broadly, revealing all those long teeth. "You caught me," he said, not the least bit embarrassed.

"Why lie about being older?" she asked him.

"It intimidates women of a certain age. I've noticed that women in their sixties tend to feel more comfortable with men their own age or older. I put fifty-five because it's as old as I can get away with."

"I still don't understand why you do it."

"What you don't understand is why I want to be with older women."

"Well, there's older, and then there's *old*."

"I don't make that distinction," he said. "I like women in their mid- to late sixties. That's my sweet spot, right before they turn decrepit. The fact that you struggle to make sense of that reveals more about how *you* feel about your age."

"I'm not sure I agree with that," she said, but she admired his conviction, the way she admired his refusal to set foot in a coffee shop chain.

"Back to my Hawaiian bike trip," he said. "We weren't doing Jewish biking either, by the way!"

She hoped he was Jewish and not anti-Semitic. She was too scared to ask. Geffen sounded Jewish. He might have been Jewish.

"We were doing 'goy' biking. You know what I mean?"

"Not really, no."

"Goy biking is where you put your bag on your back and you bike up the hills, five-thousand-foot climbs with forty pounds on your back. We camped like goys too—freezing our arses off at night and baking all day in the heat. Ever since I came back, I appreciate the little things. Like small coffees in large cups." He winked.

Did that he mean he liked her? It was hard to tell with him.

"Part of their culture is to let men be men," he said.

"Whose culture?"

"Non-Jews. Jewish men are coddled. Like Italian men."

Did he mean himself? And if he did, which was he? The coddled Jew, or the manly goy?

"You have nice, full lips," he said. "I don't trust women with thin lips."

In retrospect, she doesn't know how to rationalize what happened to her judgment around Lou Geffen, or why she ignored all common sense and logic, other than that his interest in her, as with all men, had some kind of euphoric, dopamine-spiking effect on her brain. The challenge of enthralling a guy like Lou Geffen, who was younger by twenty years, opinionated, and, she thought, brilliant, did what it always did for her—it soothed any malcontent she may have been feeling and refueled her worthiness tank.

"Can I take a photo of us?" she asked, sliding her chair over beside him.

"You mean a 'selfie'?" he said, mocking her.

"Do you mind?"

"I do mind."

"Oh." She was surprised. She slid her chair away from him.

"Don't get me wrong," he said. "I've got nothing to hide. I only object on principle. Selfie culture is so moronic."

"I just like to have a souvenir," Virginia said, embarrassed.

"Can't your memory be the souvenir? What did you do before you had a smartphone?" He waited a beat and then answered his own question. "You used your *imagination*."

"I guess so."

"We're not twelve-year old girls, are we?" he said.

The next morning, after he'd raped her and beaten her and left her for dead, Lou Geffen sent her a text. She was in the hospital when she got it, semiawake. It said: Thanks for the wild night. You're an animal, old gal! I'm still black and blue from our tumble off the bed. LMK if u ever want to do it again.

Covering his ass. She deleted the message. Deleted his contact information. His username was OldDogNewTricks. Hers was Bangin'Boomer. Gone. The only thing she did save was a screenshot of his SilvrFoxes profile page with his photo and his fake name. She doesn't know why she saved it, but it's still there, in the album on her phone.

A jury would say she asked for it with a username like Bangin'Boomer. She's seen *The Accused*.

There's a knock on her door and then Ivey's sweet voice from outside her room.

"Come in."

Ivey lopes in, wearing a tiny, cropped T-shirt with baggy sweatpants, her long hair parted down the middle, the way Virginia used to wear hers in the late sixties. Ivey's phone is dinging and buzzing and she's typing as she sits down in the chair next to Virginia's bed.

"Hi, Ives," Virginia says. Her mouth is dry.

"Hey, Gram."

"Can you pass me that water, hon?"

Ivey hands her the glass from the bedside table and then resumes her frenetic, double-thumbed typing. Virginia notices a coin-sized burn on Ivey's slender forearm. "What happened there, Ives?"

"I burned myself taking cookies out of the oven."

"Oh, Ivey. You have to be more careful. That looks like a second-degree burn. Did you put Polysporin on it?"

Ivey is so absorbed with her phone, madly typing, giggling to herself, she doesn't even hear the question.

"Did you come in here to be on your phone?" Virginia says irritably.

"Sorry, it's just that I'm blowing up."

"I beg your pardon?"

"A picture I posted is blowing up. Look." Ivey thrusts her phone at Virginia, not at all concerned with the blistering wound on her arm. "I already have a hundred and seventy-four likes and I only posted it, like, half an hour ago."

Virginia squints at the photo of Ivey in a see-through white tank top over a butterfly-patterned bra, her pale white tummy exposed, making exaggerated kissy lips and peace fingers next to her face. "Very pretty," Virginia says. "But why do you do that with your lips?"

"That's what we do."

"Does your mother know you post these pictures of yourself in your brassiere?"

"Of course not: I blocked her. Plus, I'm not just in a bra, I'm wearing a tank top."

"I don't have a problem with you being proud of your body and wanting to show it off, but your mom isn't as liberal as I am about these things."

"Everyone does it."

"I probably would have too."

"Oh my God, I just reached twelve hundred followers!"

"For that photo?"

"No, Gram. On Instagram. My account has twelve hundred followers."

"Is that a lot?"

"I mean, like, not influencer a lot but, yeah. It's decent."

"You just be careful," Virginia says. "There are bad people out there."

Ivey sets her phone down and rests her head on Virginia's arm. "Who did this to you, Gram?"

The question, coming from Ivey, her firstborn and favorite grandchild, feels like an ambush. "Did your mother send you in here to ask me that?"

Ivey sits up, confused. "No."

"Are you sure?"

"I'm sure. *I* want to know, Gram. He should be punished."

"I did it to myself," Virginia says. "I went on a date with a much younger man, and things got—well, let's say they got vigorous—and we fell—"

"The doctor told Mom and Aunt Tate that it looked like he threw you across the room."

"They weren't there, hon."

"Gram, did he rape you? That's what Mom thinks."

Virginia shakes her head emphatically no.

"If he did, he shouldn't get away with it, Gram."

"Oh, sweet, sweet girl," Virginia says, reaching for Ivey's hand. "Men misread cues, Ivey. I should never have been with a man so much younger than me; he had expectations and I wasn't clear enough—"

"It's not your fault, Gram. That kind of thinking is, like, really old-fashioned. Whatever he did, it wasn't your fault."

Virginia turns away, not wanting Ivey to see the tears pooling in the corners of her eyes.

"If he did rape you," Ivey says, her voice strong and clear, sounding much older than her thirteen years, "he should be in jail."

"Yes, of course, darling. I know that. Now, will you please go and put some Polysporin on that burn?"

Ivey leaves the room and Virginia immediately reaches for that elder abuse support group pamphlet in her drawer.

16

Arden dumps a bag of lime tortilla chips into a plastic bowl, remembering the way Scott's face lit up the first time he tasted them. "You can really taste the lime!" he'd declared, and then proceeded to polish off the entire bag.

"Burgers are almost ready," Tate says, bursting through the back door.

Arden hands her the bowl of chips, relieved to have the confirmation, as of Thursday, that they are in fact half sisters. A quick visit to Ontario Forensics, a cheek swab, a full-sibling DNA test, and ten days later, the results: they do not share the same father. Virginia was smug about it, and slightly offended that they'd taken the test at all, but they managed to convince her that the surrogate needs the actual DNA proof and that it had nothing to do with not trusting Virginia's word.

"How are you?" Tate asks her, before heading back outside.

"As okay as I can be."

Alone in the kitchen, Arden leans against the counter and stares out the window into her backyard. It's a decent size and beautifully landscaped, shaded and intimate, with pink roses, enormous peonies, and two cherry trees that provide a perfect canopy. About five years ago, fed up with the overgrown lot, Scott hired a landscaper to create a cozy English garden surrounding a limestone patio where they could barbecue and entertain, with a generous expanse of grass for a swing set and trampoline. Arden had wanted to start decorating inside the house, but Scott insisted on doing the yard so the kids would have somewhere to play. In the end, she had to admit it was the right call.

As she watches Tanvir flipping patties with Scott's barbecue tongs, she can't help feeling melancholic. The kids are playing around him—

even Ivey is tossing the Frisbee with Hal and Wyatt—but all she can think is *It should be Scott*. Scott should be the one out there in his Grill Dad apron, flipping burgers. It's Father's Day, and the kids should have their father.

Last year was the worst, their first without Scott. Ivey never came out of her room and Arden spent most of the day hiding in the bathroom, sobbing quietly so no one would hear her. They ignored everything to do with Father's Day and tried to pretend it wasn't happening, but it was impossible. The messages and reminders were everywhere, and she kept having to turn off the television.

This year, Hal decided to come spend the weekend with them. They planned a barbecue with Tate and Tanvir and Virginia and Hal, figuring it might be better to face the occasion headlong rather than try to avoid it. Arden is hoping the festivities will at least distract the kids. She's relieved to see Ivey outside, in her pajama bottoms and a snug tank top. Even Virginia has hobbled out to the patio to be with them.

"Condiments?"

Arden pulls herself away from the window and grabs ketchup and mustard from the fridge.

"Relish?" Tate says.

"Scott hated relish. We never buy it."

Tate hesitates a moment by the back door before going outside. "I know this is a hard day," she says.

Arden wipes her eyes. "I hate today. I hate that my kids don't have a father. I just want to be in my bed."

"I know."

Instead, Arden puts on a smile like it's a fresh coat of lipstick and follows Tate outside, forcing herself to be peppy and animated—always acting!—because that's what the kids need from her. They need lightness today.

"Here come the burgers!" Tanvir cries, a little overwrought, as he carries a stack of them to the table.

"Would you look at that!" Hal says, stopping the game of Frisbee to look upward, where the pink sky, a layered trifle of blush, coral and salmon, is starting to turn purple at the edges, giving it a spectacular ombré effect. "I've never seen a sky like this," he says as a sultry pink glow falls over the yard.

Arden thinks they're all behaving with just a little too much zest and enthusiasm, but she can appreciate their effort. As she lays everything out, the wasps immediately swarm the table, landing on the soft drinks, condiment lids, and paper plates. She places a Father's Day card in front of Hal's seat and calls everyone to the table.

"Who ordered a cheeseburger?" Tate says as Tanvir distributes them accordingly. The kids crawl over one another to snatch overflowing handfuls of lime chips, ketchup, Sprite. *They seem okay*, Arden observes, searching for signs of grief on their little faces. Ivey is a little sullen, but no more than usual. "Aren't you hot in those pajama pants?" she asks her.

"They're comfy."

"Don't you want to put on shorts?"

"Can you please just *not*?" Ivey snaps.

Arden sits down, stung.

"I know this is a tough day," Virginia says, defusing the tension. "But Scott is here with us. He's watching over us and he's happy we're together."

Ali and Wyatt look at each other and then up at the sky as though they might spot their father up there, waving down at them from a cloud.

"To Scott," Hal says, raising his glass.

"And to Grandpa Hal," Arden adds.

The burgers are overcooked, which makes her miss Scott even more. He was masterful on the barbecue, knew how to cook a burger to juicy, medium-rare perfection. Not that it matters. She has no appetite. She nibbles the edge of her bun so as not to draw any attention. And then, from the hedge of shrubbery that divides their yards, she hears the neighbors, Mr. and Mrs. Foote. "Hello, Moore family!"

Arden stands and waves, peeking at them through the gaps in the untrimmed bushes. "How are you?" she asks them.

"Waiting for the grandkids to arrive," Mr. Foote says. "How are you all doing today?"

"Oh, you know." She smiles, looking at the kids, not wanting to say too much. Neither lying nor telling the truth feels appropriate.

"Listen, if you'd like, I can have my gardener do your yard the next time he's here. Thursdays, he comes. I'm sure it's at the very bottom of your list, so I'm happy to lend him to you over the summer."

"Oh, don't be silly," Arden says. "It's not necessary. Really. I'll get to it."

The truth is she decided in the spring not to continue with their landscape company, which was outrageously expensive. She was going to hire one of the kids in the neighborhood to do it, but now she's thinking the Footes are bothered by how unkempt and derelict her property looks. Or maybe they're just being thoughtful. She can't tell.

"Did you get a chance to sign Wyatt up for hockey next season at the LPAA?" Mr. Foote asks her. She can just see the glistening, sunburnt pate of his head. "He's, what, seven now? He's getting up there. You don't want to miss that window."

"Our boys were on skates at four," Mrs. Foote says. "It's a wonderful way to meet people, Arden. I'm still friends with the hockey moms from thirty years ago."

Arden can feel her neck pulsating. It's June, for Christ's sake. Why are they bullying her about hockey? Wyatt can't get through the night without peeing in his bed and she should be worrying about his hockey career?

"Happy Father's Day, Mr. Foote. Have a wonderful day with your family."

"You as well, Arden. Let me know if you change your mind about the yard."

Arden sits back down, feeling gloomy and agitated, berating herself for letting the yard go and the kids' activities slide. She's failing. She's letting Scott down. All the things he wanted for their family, she's neglecting or ignoring or fucking up.

"Why do they even give a shit if your lawn needs mowing?" Virginia says.

"And why are they talking about hockey in June?" Tate adds.

"If you want to have a kid, you're going to have to talk about hockey in June," Arden snaps, a little meaner than she intended to sound.

"I don't want to play hockey," Wyatt says.

"Perfect, because I don't want to be a hockey mom."

"I'm going to go to Canadian Tire tomorrow and buy you a lawn mower and a hedge clipper," Hal says. "And I'm going to get those old pricks off your back."

Arden laughs, feeling a little more heartened.

"What about my camping trip?" Wyatt says, with two globs of ketchup in either corner of his mouth. "Can I go with Tyler or what? It's in less than two weeks."

"Wyatt, don't talk with your mouth full" is all she can think to respond. "We'll discuss it later."

"I knew it," he says, tears springing to his eyes.

"I haven't said no."

"You keep saying we'll talk about it later, but then we never do!"

"Maybe Grandpa Hal can go with you as a chaperone," Arden suggests, looking over at Hal. "He's planning to be here for Canada Day anyway."

"He's not handicapped," Ivey mutters.

"Ivey, please."

"I'm not handicapped!" Wyatt echoes. "I don't need a chaperone!"

"You have a very dangerous allergy, Wyatt."

"Why do you always have to make him feel like a freak?" Ivey accuses.

Wyatt is looking at her now, with plump tears sliding down his flushed cheeks, ketchup and dirt all over his face.

Arden turns to her eldest daughter. "I don't make him feel like a freak," she says tightly.

"Yes you do!" Wyatt shouts. "You ruin everything!"

"Mommy didn't ruin anything," Ali defends. "*Ivey* ruins everything."

"No one ruins anything," Virginia says. "Ivey, this has nothing to do with you, darling."

Ivey shoves her plate away and gets up from the table dramatically, her face bright red. "Fine!" she says, and stomps off into the house, slamming the screen door behind her. Wyatt jumps up after her and follows suit.

"Well, this is lovely," Arden says.

"Mommy," Ali says, "Aunt Tate is on her phone at the table."

"Aunt Tate is a grown-up."

Tate puts down her phone. "Sorry, Ali. I just got a work text. No more phone."

"Eat your burger," Arden says, miserable.

"We brought roasted marshmallow ice cream for dessert," Tanvir says brightly.

"I'm sure you can teach the father how to use an Epi-Pen," Tate says. "Maybe you should let him go, Arden."

"Maybe you should wait to have your own kid before you judge the way I parent," she says.

"Why are you so passive-aggressive about my having a kid?"

Arden is quiet, squeezing back tears. Virginia reaches for the mustard and pats her hand.

"Tate, why don't you finish telling us about that article you're working on," Hal says. "About the Leslieville revival."

"There's a revival in Leslieville?" Virginia says, sounding overly interested.

"There's a revival everywhere," Tate says. "I'm doing a piece for *Ontario Home & Garden* on restored plaster ceilings and wainscoting in the East End."

"Fascinating."

"It is, actually. Wainscoting would look so great in your dining room, Arden. Your house has the right feel for it. When you're ready to do it, I mean. If you get your inheritance money."

The way Tate says *"If you get your money"* instead of *"When . . ."* seems deliberate and slyly malicious. It annoys Arden and she feels something much bigger simmering between them.

"Meanwhile," Arden says, "Wyatt is still sleeping in a pull-up. It's not just about the peanut allergy. How can he go on a camping trip when he still needs a goddamn pull-up?"

"He's still wetting the bed?" Virginia says.

"It's been off and on ever since Scott died."

"You need to get a Chummie," Tate says. "I did a post on them for one of those Mommy blogs. Apparently three nights with a Chummie and they never wet the bed again."

"Who's Chummie?" Hal asks.

"It's this little alarm that goes off whenever the kid starts to pee in the middle of the night," Tate explains. "It wakes them up so they can go to the bathroom in time."

"I didn't need a Chummie," Ali says.

"Girls are different," Tate says, as though she's an authority because she wrote one post for a mommy blog.

Arden rolls her eyes.

"I'm just trying to help."

Tanvir gives Tate a look, which shuts her up.

"How was your flight, Hal?" Virginia asks, her voice sounding strained.

"Fine. Easy," Hal says. "Flying out of Newark is the only way to go."

"I miss New York," Virginia says. "Who knows when I'll ever get back there."

"How's the physio going?"

"Oh, fine."

"It's not really fine," Arden mutters. The physiotherapist says Virginia's not very motivated, often skipping her daily exercises. She recommended psychotherapy in addition to the antidepressants Virginia's already been prescribed, but Virginia refused. She still won't talk to anyone.

"What happened, Virginia?" Hal asks her. "What the hell did this guy do to you?"

Ali looks up from her burger.

"Ali, you can go inside and have some time on your devices," Arden says. "Take your burger with you."

"I want to know what happened to Grammy."

"I fell off the bed," Virginia says impatiently. "Just like I keep telling everyone. Grammy has old bones and that's why my hip broke."

Ali looks to Arden for confirmation. Arden nods and smiles, more acting. "Go on," she says. "Before I change my mind."

Ali reluctantly gets up from the table, the last of the kids to disappear.

"I want you to tell me what happened," Hal says, turning to Virginia.

"Oh, not you, too, Hal," Virginia mutters. "Did the girls put you up to this?"

"I haven't said a word to Hal," Tate says.

"What's his name?" Hal wants to know. "At least tell me that. He shouldn't be allowed to get away with this, Virginia. What if he's already done it to someone else?"

"Hal, this is none of your business," Virginia says.

"It is my business."

"How is it your business? We haven't been married in thirty years."

"I still care about you. You're the mother of my daughters."

"We got carried away. The sex was too rough. That's it. This is not the time or place for this conversation—"

"*When is?*" Arden cries.

"Mom, your hip was shattered," Tate says. "You were black-and-blue. We all know it wasn't a sexual romp gone awry. Please, just tell us his name and let us do the rest."

"There's nothing for you to do! Even if he crossed a line, nothing could ever be proved."

"You don't know that," Tate argues. "And by 'crossed a line,' do you mean *he raped and almost killed you?*"

"Tate, calm down," Tanvir says softly, laying his hand over hers.

"My username was Bangin'Boomer," Virginia blurts. "I invited him up to my place, intending to sleep with him. I have a track record, you know. My history with men is literally public record."

"So this monster is allowed to get away with assaulting you?"

"He didn't assault me."

"Didn't he?"

"I don't know anymore!" she cries. "We had sex. It was consensual. It was rough, but I'm pretty sure it was consensual. You all know I have terrible judgment when it comes to men." She glances over at Hal and adds, as an afterthought, "Except you, Hal."

Arden remembers when she was about eleven or twelve, Virginia was in one of her postbreakup depressions. It was after Hal, when they were living in Toronto. Virginia had fallen in love with a sculptor, had shed all the trappings of her own identity the way a snake sheds its skin, and immersed herself utterly in the boyfriend's world.

When he left her because she was "stifling him," she fell apart. She took to her bed, smoking cigarettes and listening to Edith Piaf, despondent. She took a week off work to "mourn the relationship," so she was home day and night, her bedroom a perpetual cloud of smoke, ashes in her sheets, on her nightstand. The whole thing had baffled Arden.

Normally, Virginia bounced back quickly after a break-up. Her recoveries were dramatic, but brief. The guy had also been sort of a jerk, not very friendly, not especially successful or attractive. He had awful breath and there was always clay under his fingernails. Tate was away at university at the time, and Arden remembers feeling profoundly lonely, having to bear the burden of her mother's anguish by herself. One day she came home after school and went to check on Virginia to make sure she hadn't overdosed on sleeping pills or jumped out the window of their apartment.

Virginia was sobbing softly under the covers, a cigarette burning in the ashtray beside her. Arden stood in the doorway, watching her. Virginia must have heard her breathing or simply sensed her presence. "I'm sorry you have to see me like this," she whimpered.

"He wasn't that great," Arden said. "Why are you so upset?"

Virginia stopped crying and sat up, looking indignant and misunderstood. She was wearing a dirty sweatshirt and her hair was so greasy the dark roots looked wet. "You don't understand," she said. "It's not about him! There's nothing worse than being alone, Arden."

This is what Arden is thinking about now while Tate is going on about the police and the rape. "Maybe we should just go to SilvrFoxes," she's saying. "Tell them what happened to you and force them to give us his name."

"You can't report anything if I say nothing happened," Virginia says. "You can't go to the police, you can't go to him, you can't go to SilvrFoxes."

"Stop bullying her," Arden says to Tate.

"Hopefully he doesn't kill the next woman."

"Tate!"

"I'm sorry, but I'm tired of tiptoeing around this. There's a serial rapist out there and Mom is just letting him get away with it!"

"Do we have to do this tonight?" Arden says wearily, looking around the table at the debris from their failed party.

"No," Tate says, standing up. "We don't."

She bends down and kisses Hal on the cheek, wishes him a happy Father's Day, and then leaves without a word to Arden or Virginia. Tanvir quietly apologizes on her behalf and then scurries after her, clearly embarrassed.

"And then there were three," Hal says. Virginia starts to cry.

Hal offers to take care of the cleanup so that Arden can do damage control with the kids. Virginia goes back to her room. Arden tried to console her, but Tate's tongue-lashing left her traumatized. *Don't frighten the squirrel*, Arden keeps telling her.

She knocks on Ivey's door and goes in without waiting for a response. Ivey doesn't look up from her phone. *What's wrong with this generation?*

Scott didn't think Ivey having her own phone at eleven was a problem. *Meth is a problem*, he'd say. *Opioids are a problem. Let her have a phone.* But he isn't here now to see how the powerful triumvirate of Instagram, Snapchat, and TikTok have brainwashed his sweet daughter; how it's shaped her personality, reprogrammed her developing mind, afflicted her self-esteem, taught her to live and die by the number of likes and comments and the twin gods of comparison and FOMO.

"Can you please just get out of my room?" she says coolly.

"I know this isn't about Wyatt's camping trip," Arden perseveres, guardedly sitting on the edge of the bed. *Don't frighten the squirrel.*

Ivey rolls her eyes. She smells of Bath & Body Works vanilla hand sanitizer.

"I know this is about Daddy."

"Oh my *Gawd!*" Ivey shouts. "Get out!"

"Ives, I know this is a hard day—"

"*Get out!* Leave me alone!"

Arden wants to shake her, rattle her around until she snaps back to her old self, or else pound her on the back until a part of the sweet, loving little girl she used to be comes back up to the surface, releasing itself from wherever it's lodged inside her. Arden looks helplessly around Ivey's room, her eyes darting wildly from the closet to the backpack on the floor to the drawers of her desk, wishing she could tear it all apart and uncover some piece of her child, something stashed away, hidden. Letters, a diary, poems, notes she's passed to friends in class. Arden used to do that, save all her notes in a shoebox, but she won't find any of that in here. Kids don't write anymore. There are no more paper trails. Everything is on their phones now, locked behind impenetrable passcodes or messages that evaporate into thin air. Technology makes them as slippery as eels. Arden has never felt so powerless.

She stands up, defeated.

"Dad would never let you do this to Wyatt," Ivey says, still staring at her phone.

"This doesn't even involve you, Ivey."

"He's my brother and I hate watching you deprive him of a normal life." Scott's exact words. "It's not fair. It's selfish. Plenty of kids have peanut allergies. Why don't you just lock him in a goddamn cage? Or keep him in a bubble so you'll feel better."

Arden fights the urge to defend herself. *Today is not the day*, she reminds herself. She takes a breath and says gently, "I know you miss Daddy, and that's probably what this is about."

Ivey ignores her. Arden gives up and leaves the room, closing the door behind her with a swell of despair. She stands there for a long time staring at that fucking closed door.

"*Go away!*" Ivey screams from inside her room, sensing Arden's hovering presence.

Bereft, Arden goes down the hall to the twins' room, trying to pinpoint exactly when it happened, when she lost Ivey. It feels like she lay down beside her in bed one night, scratched her back for a little while, giggled with her, kissed her warm cheek, and whispered, "I love you, my angel." And in her squeaky little voice, Ivey replied, "I love you too, Mama."

The next morning, when Ivey came downstairs, she was utterly unrecognizable—angry, cold, snarky, sullen. The little girl was gone; even her roundness had vanished overnight. That's what it felt like, anyway, or at least how Arden remembers it transpiring—spontaneously, without any warning. She would have needed time to prepare, emotionally and spiritually. Instead, it happened like a death, exactly the way it happened with Scott. She still hasn't managed to regain her footing, to accept this churlish, bad-tempered creature who sucks the positive life force out of the household.

"Magpie?"

She finds Wyatt lying facedown on his lower bunk, crying beneath his Maple Leafs comforter. She pulls the blanket off his head and lies down beside him. He hiccups loudly once, twice, and then the hiccups settle into a soft, steady rhythm.

"I thought having Grandpa Hal there with you was a reasonable compromise," she says. "I thought you'd be happy."

"Happy that I need a babysitter?"

"I'll feel better, Wyatt."

"What about how *I* feel?"

How *Wyatt* feels has never occurred to her, not when it comes to ensuring his survival; keeping him safe has always trumped whatever psychological damage her overprotectiveness might incur. "I do care how you feel," she lies.

"No you don't."

She smooths his hair, which is damp from playing outside all afternoon. He smells of grass and dirt. She inhales him deeply. At least with the twins she knows what's coming; she knows to appreciate and savor them as they are now.

"I miss Daddy," he sputters between hiccups. "He was the one who let me be normal. He wanted me to be a regular kid. Now that he's gone, you're turning me into a freak."

"Those are Ivey's words."

"It's true, though. And it's always going to be like this without Daddy here."

"I just want you to be safe, Wy."

"I don't want to be *safe!*" he cries, rolling over to face her. "I want to have fun! I want to be normal!"

"I want that for you, too, but we have to work together."

"But you don't ever work with me," he sulks. "You just make me do what you say."

It's called parenting. That's how it works. But even as she's thinking it, she's questioning herself. Maybe Scott was right about giving Wyatt more freedom; maybe her relentless management of his allergy will end up creating an anxious, antisocial weirdo.

"Wy-Wy—"

"Don't call me that," he says, wiping his nose. "I'm not a baby."

"You can go camping with Tyler."

Wyatt sniffles a few times, his expression uncertain. "Without Grandpa Hal?"

"Without Grandpa Hal."

"How come?"

"Because you've made an excellent case."

"I did?"

"Yep."

He throws his arm around her and burrows his wet face in her neck, soaking her with his tears and snot. "I love you," he says, his voice muffled in her skin. She loves him back so hard there is no language even to express it to him.

"Super fun day," Arden says, joining Hal in the family room. He's reclined on his old La-Z-Boy watching baseball.

"How'd it go?" he asks her.

"Ivey's not speaking to me, but Wyatt and I are friends."

"One out of two isn't bad."

"I'm letting him go camping."

"Good for you."

"You think it's the right call?"

"I think everyone knows how to use an Epi-Pen."

"Ivey hates me."

"She's supposed to. Do you remember how you used to treat your mother when you were her age?"

"No."

"Well, I do. Both you and Tate were awful."

"Tate was worse."

Arden flops down on the stained red couch and stares up at the ceiling, which seems to be sagging even more than usual. One of the first things she's going to do with her money is gut this house to the studs. She'll rent an apartment while the house is under construction and then move back into her dream house when it's all done.

"I know this is a really difficult time for you," Hal says. "And for what it's worth, you're a fantastic mother."

"Am I?"

"The best I've ever seen."

"Thank you for that. This feels like a perfect segue into something I have to ask you."

Hal lowers the volume on the Jays game. "You need one of my kidneys?"

"I need money."

"Really?" He sounds surprised.

"Ivey needs a jaw expander before she gets braces," she explains. "And the twins are going to day camp in August. It's ridiculously expensive."

"How much?"

"I need about two grand."

Hal whistles.

"It's just that I'm backed up on my Visas."

"Visas? Plural?"

"I had to get a second one to pay for Ali's gymnastics and Wyatt's karate and Ivey's guitar lessons," she says. "Maybe fifteen hundred would tide me over—"

"It's not about the amount," he says. "I'm happy to lend you two thousand dollars."

"What, then?"

"I'm concerned. You're struggling this much, even with the contingency arrangement?"

"Everything is just hitting at once," she says, feeling defensive. "The court fees, the DNA tests, the flights back and forth to New York. The kids need so much. I'm going to go back to the gallery and see if Hana can give me any shift—"

"Go *back*?"

"I was laid off," Arden admits.

"Arden, I had no idea you weren't working."

"Hana said it was temporary."

Hal furrows his wiry brow. His mouth is a thin, tight line; his angry face. "And you haven't followed up with her? Or looked for something else?"

"I've been busy focusing on the petition."

"You need to work, Arden."

"It's fine," she says. "Besides, I'm going to be a millionaire soon." Joking, but not really.

"When?"

"I don't know yet. I'll know more at the end of the month, after the next hearing."

"Where have I heard this before?"

"It's not the same."

"It's exactly the same. Your life is on hold until—and *if!*—you get that inheritance, just like Virginia's was. It's a total déjà vu."

"That money is mine, Dad."

"It's not, though! Don't you see?" Hal shakes his head, exasperated. "Do you remember when you wanted that Sega video game thing? You were about eight or nine?"

"It was a Sega Genesis, and I don't see how that has anything to do with this—"

"Just the other day, I heard you tell Wyatt you'd buy him a Nintendo Switch 'after you win the lawsuit.' Don't you remember what that was like? You kept asking your mother for that Sega and she kept saying, 'As soon as we win our case.' A few months would pass, and you'd ask about it again, and she'd say, 'When we get our inheritance money.' Eventually, you'd bring it up again, and she'd say, 'Soon! Soon! It's coming.' Instead of just saying it was too expensive, she kept promising she'd buy it for you. Two Christmases went by, two birthdays; you waited and waited. Your disappointment broke my heart so much I almost went out and bought you the goddamn thing myself, but it was about two hundred bucks, and I didn't want to teach you or Virginia to spend money we didn't have."

"And?"

"And that's exactly what you're doing now. Making promises and spending money you don't have."

"It's not like I'm being frivolous," Arden says. "Ivey needs an expander for her teeth, and summer camp—"

"Camp is a luxury you can't afford right now, especially since you're not working."

Arden blinks back tears.

"I'm just worried about you," Hal says, softening. "I don't like where this is going."

"Noted."

"I'll write you a check."

"Never mind. It's fine. I'll manage."

"Don't be a baby. I want to help you. This isn't about that," he says, pulling the lever of the recliner and shooting forward to an upright position. "I just want to know that you'll stop with the petitions if you lose in the first round."

"It's not a boxing match."

"You know what I mean," he says.

"I'll stop if my DNA isn't a match to Wallace Ashforth."

"That's not what I said."

"Are you asking if I'll stop if the judge doesn't allow the DNA test?"

"Yes."

"Joshua won't give up that easily."

"Are you sure this kid is a good lawyer?"

"Yes, he's good."

"Because his stepfather is an arsehole."

"Joshua is very good."

"You'd better be an Ashforth," he mutters. "I can't bear to watch this happen to you too."

In the early morning limbo before sunrise, Arden roams the house, going from room to room, ghostlike, purposeless. She can't sleep, which is hardly out of the ordinary, but this time there was a restless quality to her insomnia that propelled her out of bed. She checks on each of the kids, then on her mother and Hal, envying them the miraculous oblivion of sleep. Eventually, she finds herself in Scott's office, which, although it's now technically her office, will always belong to him. There's a troubling accumulation of mail on the desk, all of it unopened. She's gotten in the habit of dumping it on the desk without even sorting through it, sometimes for weeks. She's slightly more responsible with the e-bills, lest she wake up one day with no electricity or, worse, no cable or cell phone data.

With nothing else to do, she starts separating the mail into two piles: trash and low-priority, which includes bills from their gardener, the gutter cleaner, her yoga studio, the Volvo dealership, and a couple from Leaside Storage that don't ring a bell but also don't seem very important.

Once a good portion of the neglected mail is in the recycling bin, the remaining pile feels a lot more manageable and can be dealt with when she has the emotional bandwidth for it. Satisfied with herself, she unlocks the top drawer of the desk and reaches for the coroner's report. She holds it in her hand for a moment or two, running her fingers along the flap of the manila envelope, but resisting the urge to open it. She's very aware this has become a bad habit. It's morbid and secretive and sadomasochist. She has no idea why she still does it, what twisted comfort she gets from seeing those terrible words on paper, but the early days of clinging to the report as tangible proof of something she could not believe or accept are long gone. The reality of his death has taken hold.

Instead of putting the report away, she gets up and goes to the kitchen, where she's relieved to see the sky through the window is smudged with pink light. The sun rising makes her feel a little less lonely, and as she hunts for the birthday cake lighter and then goes over to the sink, she is full of resolve. *It ends now*, she vows, holding the lighter to the corner of the manila envelope.

She watches it catch fire, transfixed by the slowly unfurling flame and the smell of singed paper, thinking how beautiful and dramatic it is, even as it burns her fingertips.

The kids deserve more, she thinks, turning on the tap to wash away the ashes. Yesterday was a gong show, but what if they don't have to settle for a background of perpetual sadness? What if she can do better than just help them cope with loss and survive grief? What if they could create new happy memories *right now*? Not later, after they've sufficiently "healed," but *now*.

She marches upstairs, starting in Ivey's room. She doesn't even give Ivey an option. "Important family meeting," she says. "Attendance is mandatory."

The twins wake easily and scramble downstairs.

When the three of them are at the kitchen table, some more alert than others, Arden says, "Father's Day may have sucked, and maybe it always will, but the day after Father's Day doesn't have to suck also."

The twins giggle, excited.

"I'm going to make crepes—"

"Crepes!" Ali squeals. "With brown sugar inside?"

"Whatever you want, Magpie. Raid the pantry, choose whatever you want."

"Nutella?!"

"Whatever. While I cook, you're going to DJ, Ivey. I want to hear some good tunes to get this party going."

"Party?"

"Yes, it's our annual Post–Father's Day Crepe Dance Party."

The twins are jumping up and down and even Ivey is trying to conceal a little smile. "I'll get my phone," she says, and it's her way of saying she's in.

The twins help make the crepes while Ivey plays music, blasting it through the kitchen speakers like they're at a nightclub. At one point, being cheeky, Ivey plays Strauss's "Blue Danube," and Arden and Wyatt grab onto each other and start waltzing around the table. Then it's Ali's turn to pick a song and she picks country music, and they all do-si-do with linked arms until the smoke alarm starts to beep and they realize they've burned a batch of crepes.

When they finally sit down to eat, Ivey says with great exuberance, "Let's all say what we want to buy when we get our inheritance money."

Arden's heart drops and she instinctively jumps up from the table to make sure Hal isn't on his way to the kitchen. Normally he's up by now, with his coffee and his sketch pad, so it's lucky he isn't here to witness this conversation. The last thing she needs is an "I told you so" from him.

"I want a Nintendo Switch!" Wyatt announces.

Arden's guilt balloons.

"I want the Hogwarts Great Hall Lego set!" Ali says. "And the Hatchimals Hatchibabies. How much things are we allowed to get?"

"That's plenty," Arden says, sitting back down.

"Obviously I want the new iPhone," Ivey says. "I still have your old one from three years ago. And I want to get, like, some really cool clothes and a proper camera, and a rose-gold necklace with my name on it. What about you, Mom?"

"I just want to put some money aside so that you can all go to college."

Ivey rolls her eyes.

"Why do we need to go to college if we're millionaires?" Wyatt says.

"For an education!" she cries, realizing Hal was right. She *is* a shit parent. She hasn't instilled them with any values! Instead, she's allowed Scott's materialistic values to win the day. "College is a wonderful and important life experience," she scrambles. "You get to choose what you want to study, you make lifelong friendships . . ."

"Mom, come on," Ivey says. "People only go to college so they can get a good job and make money. If we're already millionaires, why would we keep going to school?"

Arden doesn't have the energy to continue this right now. It's a much more involved undertaking than she planned for this morning. Besides, she's determined to keep things light and fun. *I'll instill all the correct values in them after I win the lawsuit.*

Instead, she rustles them from the table with the idea of going to Muir Park in their pajamas. They all grab a mode of transportation—the twins hop on their scooters, Ivey takes her skateboard, Arden grabs her bike. She hasn't ridden it in two years and it has a semiflat tire, which she chooses to ignore, and off they go, down the ravine and into the woods that run alongside the tennis courts to the park.

The kids stay on the dirt path, but Arden is feeling expansive and brazen, and she decides to go off road into the woods, the way she used to with Scott when they would go mountain biking together. She gets so caught up in the ride—the wind whooshing her hair, the smell of the dirt beneath her tires, the rushing stream flowing alongside her—she lifts her arms in the air and lets out a carefree "*Whoop!*"

In her newfound jubilation, she doesn't see the enormous root protruding from the ground, and her front tire hits it, and next thing she knows, she's flat on her face in the dirt.

She looks up to find all three kids standing over her, skateboard and scooters in hand, their expressions halfway between concern and amusement. "Are you okay, Mom?"

Arden wipes some dirt from her chin, spits some out of her mouth, and then bursts out laughing. The kids join in, relieved.

"You went right over your handlebars!" Ivey gasps, clutching her stomach. "It was like a cartoon!"

"Your face!" Wyatt roars. "It's covered in mud!"

"The best part is you were showing off and trying to impress us!" Ivey is crying now from laughing so hard. "When you flung your hands in the air and yelled '*Whoop!*'? Oh my God! *I can't!* That was *epic!*"

Ivey snaps a picture of Arden lying on the ground with the bike half on top of her.

"Don't post that," Arden says.

"As if I *wouldn't!*"

They help Arden to her feet and she hoists up her bike and climbs back on, aware that in trying to lift their spirits and give them a semi-normal day with some laughter and lightness, *she* feels a lot less anxious. Somewhere along the way, between the waltz and landing flat on her face in the dirt, she forgot to take everything so seriously; she forgot herself.

17

ARDEN ARRIVES AT HAL'S PLACE IN BROOKLYN ON A CLEAR MORNING AT the end of June, the sun already bearing down on the tree-lined street without apology. Looking up at the small semidetached house, Arden winces at its chipped, celery-green facade, which Hal hasn't touched in at least two decades. The shabbiness of his house instantly makes her feel like shit. How could she have asked *him* for money when his own home is in such disarray and he's living off a *teacher's* salary in Brooklyn?

When she first moved in, the house had seemed so big to her. Compared to their apartment in Queens, even just having her own room made her feel like a princess. Now everything about the place feels neglected, cramped. She's been telling Hal for years that if he'd just invest in a paint job, a new floor—they're doing amazing things with laminate these days—and some modern appliances, the place would be worth a million bucks.

"What do I care what I could get for it?" he said the last time she brought it up. "I'm not going anywhere. I like it just the way it is."

"You like brown linoleum and brown kitchen cabinets and dirty beige carpets?"

"Yes, I do. Besides, I'm always at school or in my studio."

She knows he's too proud to admit he can't afford any major renovations. The fact that he agreed to lend her money anyway makes him a saint and she vows to buy him a beautiful detached redbrick house in the affluent pocket between Avenue J and Avenue I as soon as she gets her inheritance money.

She drags her wheeled suitcase up the three concrete steps and knocks on the front door. When he doesn't answer, she lets herself in with her key.

"Dad?"

She can feel his music vibrating through the broadloom carpeted floor, CCR lyrics drifting up from the basement. Before heading down to see him, she runs up to the second floor to put her suitcase away and splash some water on her face. Her old room—a tiny cubicle at the end of the beige hallway—hasn't changed in thirty years. It still has the same navy blue plaid Ralph Lauren wallpaper and denim futon folded into a couch. She remembers Virginia trying to sell her on the futon concept— "It's a bed *and* a sofa all in one!" At the time, it had seemed both revolutionary and grown-up to Arden.

She opens the window to let in some fresh air, but it's muggy outside and the effort yields nothing. She checks the closet for a fan, wondering if she wouldn't be better off at an air-conditioned hotel, but then Hal would be hurt, and she wouldn't be able to justify spending money she doesn't have.

The basement is half laundry room, half art studio. Like the rest of the house, Hal's studio is also a lot less marvelous than Arden thought it was as a kid. It's still unfinished, with raw concrete walls and floor, exposed plywood ceiling beams, and pink insulation sticking out like the stuffing of an old sofa. There's a mustard-colored washer and dryer from the seventies shoved in the corner, and Hal's vintage CD player set up on a TV tray with the CDs themselves in a milk crate on the floor. An earlier suggestion that he hook up to Spotify was met with bemused derision.

The average room temperature down here swings from subzero in winter to an inferno in summer, when the smell of turpentine, which she once loved because it reminded her of Hal, mingles with the much more alarming smell of mold.

"Can it hurt you?" Hal asks her, without looking up from his painting. He's working on a horizon landscape in oil, blending a moody sky of blues and grays into the glazed layers of swelling water as it meets land, which is, by contrast, warm and sandy and sunlit. She watches him work from her seat on the dryer, mesmerized by his finesse as he dabs wet on wet to achieve the soft, diaphanous effect of light and dark. She recognizes Cupsogue Beach in Westhampton without even having to ask.

"The fact that Virginia didn't name Wallace as your father," he says. "Can Fistler use that against you?"

"Joshua says no. It's as useless to Fistler as it is to us. Wallace didn't sign it because he *died*, not because he refused to acknowledge me."

"Why bring it up at all?"

"To establish timeline."

"This is all a very unpleasant déjà vu," he says.

"You've mentioned that numerous times."

"I wish I had the money to help you so you wouldn't have to go through with this lawsuit."

"I wish I had the money to help *you*," she says. "And as soon as I get my inheritance, I'm buying you a new house whether you like it or not."

"Stop talking like that. I don't want a new house."

"Of course you do. You just don't know it yet. It'll have a light-filled studio—"

"I like my cave."

"Bullshit. It's Hades down here and it reeks of mold. I'm worried about you inhaling this all day."

He waves his hand in the air dismissively. "I've been breathing in chemicals for almost seventy years. You think a little mold is going to kill me?"

"I'm serious, Dad. It's not safe down here."

"I don't want to sound like a broken record, but let's not live in the future like your mother did," he tells her, pointing the end of his paintbrush at her.

"I get it," Arden says. "You're bitter. I still want to buy you a house."

"I'm not bitter. I'm worried."

"You don't need to be. It's going well."

"If you're being honest, how many times a day do you say some version of that to yourself? '*When I get the money, when I win, when I inherit . . .*'"

Too many to count.

"I thought so," he says in response to her silence.

She slides off the dryer and dusts herself off. There's a film of grime along every surface of his studio. "I have to go meet my lawyer in Queens."

"I'm saying this because I care about you," Hal says. "And I know your mother won't."

"I know."

"Do you want to take my car?"

"It's fine. I'll call an Uber."

"Shrimp tacos for dinner?" he says, trying to smooth things over. "I found a great recipe in the *Times*."

"Sure."

"Good luck," he tells her, turning back to his easel with a soft, almost imperceptible sigh.

Jane Knoppers lives in Astoria, on a street that happens to be very close to Arden's childhood home, which triggers in her a slew of sensory memories—the smell of fresh bread from Fotoula's Greek bakery on the corner, garlic emanating from the souvlaki cart on her way home from school, the briny smell of the East River on a muggy morning, the confident feeling of walking down Ditmars or Broadway with one hand in her mother's and the other in Tate's.

Joshua is waiting for her outside. Jane lives in a white row house with a red gabled roof. The house next to hers on the right is blue and brown, the one on the other side yellow and green, all of them attached to one another like a Technicolor train. Arden hasn't seen Joshua since his last trip to Toronto, and he looks suntanned and relaxed, his black hair curling softly around his face from the humidity. His handsomeness flusters her.

Joshua knocks on the crossbuck screen door, peering through its scalloped window. The door swings open mid-knock and he steps back, startled. Jane Knoppers smiles, revealing a half-inch gap between her front teeth. Her skin is pale and loose, falling at the neck like pancake batter. She's wearing an oversized cable-knit cardigan, beige knee-high stockings, and serviceable Wallabies.

"Thanks for speaking with us," Joshua says, shaking her hand.

"Oh, not at all. I'm happy for the company."

The house is shabby but well-appointed, with a slipcovered sofa of faded cabbage roses and plenty of antiques crammed into every nook—a mahogany coffee table with turned legs, a console table buried beneath white doilies and ornate silver picture frames, two drum tables on either side of the couch, a rocking chair with a lumpy brocade seat cushion, an oval dining table and a buffet buried under mismatched china. The walls are covered with photographs and memorabilia of British royalty—plates with Queen Elizabeth's face; framed newspaper articles about Charles and Diana; birth announcements for Princes William and Harry, little George and baby Charlotte; a Union Jack thumbtacked above her kitchen table.

"Are you from the UK?" Arden asks her.

"Oh no, just a devout Anglophile. I've been obsessed with the royals since I was little. Margaret was always my favorite. Did you watch *The Crown*?"

"I've been meaning to—"

"They've done an excellent job," Jane says. "They're a little hard on Elizabeth in some episodes, but overall, very well researched. And the acting is superb. Impeccable. You must watch it."

Jane Knoppers crouches down on her knees and plugs in a Glade air freshener. "I apologize for the smell," she says, wrinkling her nose. "Curry from the Indian restaurant. You get used to it."

"It's a great neighborhood," Arden says, turning to look out the window. "I used to live in Astoria when I was very young. You've got a great view of Hell Gate Bridge."

"It's gorgeous when the light hits it right." Jane rushes over to the window and grandly pulls the chintz drapes wide open for the full effect.

"Can I offer you some tea?" she says, turning to Arden.

"That would be lovely," Arden says, and Joshua shoots her a look.

"Sit, please."

Joshua and Arden sink into the couch, causing a cloud of feathers and dust mites to float up around them. Joshua sneezes. Jane disappears into the kitchen, and they can hear the tap go on and off, the chiming of teacups and saucers, the whistle of the kettle. When she reappears, she's carrying a frosted glass tray loaded with Social Tea cookies, sugar cubes, and a Delft blue-willow tea set.

"What a pretty teapot," Arden remarks, and she can feel the impatience emanating from Joshua's gaze.

Jane pours them each a cup, plops a sugar cube in hers, and settles into the rocking chair, which is painstakingly wedged between the coffee table and buffet like a puzzle piece.

"As I mentioned over the phone," Joshua says, "this is my client, Arden Moore."

"You're Wallace's daughter," Jane says, appraising her.

"Yes. Do you see a resemblance?"

Jane tips her head to the side, squints behind her bifocals. "It's been almost forty years," she says. "I can hardly remember."

"How long did you work for the Ashforths?"

"Nearly sixteen years. I was hired to be the housekeeper, but I wound up taking care of the boys. Bruce was five and Jamie four when I started. I was very attached to them. I practically raised them. Geraldine was never around. The boys were more like props for her, to be dragged out when she was entertaining. She'd make them perform for her guests— they'd have to play the piano or recite a poem—and then she'd send them off. That was the sum total of their relationship."

"And Wallace?"

"Wallace? He saw them even less, but that was understandable. He was the man of the house. He was a very busy, very important man."

"When were you were fired?"

"In 1979. By Geraldine."

"Geraldine? Why?"

Jane averts her eyes.

"Anything you tell us could really help us down the road, Mrs. Knoppers."

"Wallace and I were in love," she says, lifting her cup to her mouth. She seems quite pleased with her disclosure, Arden thinks.

"You were having an affair?"

"I was in my early twenties when it began. I worshipped him. I thought he'd marry me when the boys went off to college."

"How long did it go on?"

"Years. Right up until Geraldine fired me."

"She knew about your affair?"

"I guess she did. I don't know how long she knew, but one afternoon I heard them arguing. She told him she was fed up. Said it was humiliating, that he wasn't even being discreet anymore. But I was just the collateral damage. It was the other woman she was so furious about, the secretary. She couldn't fire his secretary, though, so she fired me."

"Did you ever hear her say the secretary's name?" Joshua asks her. "Do you remember?"

"Of course I remember. I was devastated. I thought I was the only one he loved."

Arden holds her breath. The room is quiet except for the ticking of an antique mantel clock tucked away in the bookcase on top of a hardcover book called 17 *Carnations: The Royals, the Nazis, and the Biggest Cover-Up in History.*

"I thought he loved me," Jane says, dunking the edge of her cookie in tea. "The secretary's name was Virginia."

Joshua looks over at Arden.

"Virginia is my mother," Arden says.

"I assumed."

"Were you ever asked to testify as a witness in the early eighties?" Joshua asks her. "I know you spoke with Virginia's lawyer at the time."

"I told him Wallace and I had been lovers in the sixties and seventies, and that when Geraldine found out, she fired me. But I didn't say anything about the secretary."

"Why not?"

"I was forty years old, and I'd given my whole life to Wallace," she says, an unmistakable current of bitterness in her tone. "I had no husband, no children, no income. I had nothing to show for all the years I'd devoted to him. I didn't think it was fair that *she* should get his money just because she was lucky enough to get pregnant. If you can call it luck."

It takes Arden a moment to understand the implication of Jane Knoppers's remark, so sweetly and underhandedly was it delivered. She sets down her cup of tea, infuriated by this frumpy Queen Mother fangirl. "Are you implying my mother got pregnant *on purpose*?"

"It always seemed to me like it was calculated."

"To be clear," Joshua says, leaning closer to her. "You told Mr. Lasker back in the eighties that you'd had an affair with Wallace?"

"Yes."

"But you deliberately *left out* the part about overhearing Geraldine accuse him of having an affair with his secretary, Virginia Bunt?"

"Correct."

"And Mr. Lasker never asked you to give a deposition, even though your testimony would have been proof of their affair?"

"He didn't know to know, I suppose."

Joshua runs a hand through his hair and stands up, attempting to pace in the small patch of space between the sofa and the rocking chair. He ends up turning around in a circle but staying in the same spot, like a dog chasing his tail.

"Did you reach out to Bruce and Jamie after Wallace and Geraldine died?"

"I went to the funeral, of course. The boys were in their early twenties by then. Adults. I hadn't really seen much of them since they went off to college."

"And after the funeral?"

"I wrote to them a few times, but they never responded. I sent Christmas and birthday cards. Eventually, you give up. Besides," she says, reflecting, "they'd have thought I was after something. Everybody wanted something from the Ashforths. I'll say that in their defense. It can't have been easy. They were hardened against it, if you know what I mean. They didn't trust many people, didn't let anyone in or allow themselves to get close to anyone. Except for Wallace, and then only in the conjugal way."

"Mrs. Knoppers, are you willing to give a deposition for the court this time, basically restating everything you've just told us? Specifically, the part about Wallace's affair with Virginia could be very persuasive."

Jane Knoppers hesitates a moment, her cookie perched over the teacup. "Would there be any compensation?" she asks, ever so innocently, as though the thought just popped into her head. "There is a lot of money at stake."

"I'm afraid not," Joshua tells her. "We can subpoena you, though."

A splotch of red travels from her cheeks to her neck. "Of course, I'm happy to help either way," she says, grinning sweetly.

"Is there anything you can tell me about my father?" Arden ventures, figuring it's her only shot.

Jane Knoppers considers the request for several seconds. She's self-serving, Arden thinks, so anything she reveals will have its own ulterior motive.

"He was a very controlling man," Jane offers. "He used his money to control them all—Geraldine, the boys. Especially the boys. He withheld the money when it suited him, manipulated them into becoming who he expected them to be. If they didn't go to this school or that school, he would threaten to cut them off. If they didn't do the internships he'd arranged for them, he'd threaten to cut them off. If one of them dated a girl he didn't like, grew his hair too long, took the wrong job, they would be out on their own. And he meant it. He could be very, very cold."

The way Tate used to describe "Uncle Wally" made him sound like a generous man, warm and charming, always with a present and a free after-noon to take young Tate to the movies or Central Park or Coney Island. Tate's stories about Wallace planted a seed in Arden that her father had been a kind man, a man who might have loved her had he lived.

"When he wanted something from you," Jane goes on, "he could cast a spell. He was charismatic and brilliant; his attention was intoxicating. You never knew which Wallace you were going to get."

It's hard to imagine young Jane Knoppers, with her bad teeth and dumpling-shaped body, being compelling enough to have captured the attention of a man like Wallace Ashforth. Virginia was at least beautiful.

"Jamie Ashforth is a lot like his father," Jane adds, setting her teacup down on the saucer with a clang. "I'd be careful if I were you, going up against him in court. They get what they want, those men. At any cost."

18

"Why are there so many people here?" Arden asks Joshua, glancing behind her at the gallery full of spectators. "Who are they?"

"The press, law journals."

"The *press*?"

"The *Daily News*, the *Post*, Fox5, ABC7, PIX11."

"Already? This isn't even the kinship hearing."

"The Ashforths are iconic in New York," he says. "I told you."

"They're all staring at me," she says. "And why is it so hot in here?" Her sundress is damp; her hair is starting to frizz. She can already feel herself wilting.

"Broken air conditioner," he says. "This hearing is a big deal, Arden. That's why everyone is here."

Since the last hearing forty-five days ago, Joshua has filed a motion to compel DNA testing, and Jamie Ashforth's lawyer has filed a cross-motion to dismiss.

Fistler is seated at his usual place on the other side of the long table, gold rings gleaming under the fluorescent light. Still no sign of Jamie Ashforth.

"I don't want my picture in the paper," she whispers, touching her hair.

"They're not allowed to take photographs in here."

"And after? Outside?"

"We'll wait them out," he says, and she realizes he's enjoying this. This is exactly why he wanted to represent her, why he agreed to contingency. It's not just about the money; it's about the notoriety, the prestige, the boon to his brand.

"Why are the law journals here?"

"Your case presents a novel issue, which means there is no precedent. It gives the judge an opportunity to render a more trailblazing decision, something the courts have never considered before."

On cue, Judge Lull sweeps into the courtroom and takes his seat at the bench. "Good morning," he says, breathing on the lenses of his glasses, rubbing them with the sleeve of his robe, and then adjusting them on his face. "I have some concerns right off the bat," he says, looking directly at Joshua. "The documentation provided here, Mr. James, is quite . . . *thin.*"

"Your Honor, I don't need a thick file of evidence," Joshua responds calmly. "The law no longer requires it."

"The change in the law concerning nonmarital children was not created to grant rights to *all* nonmarital relatives. It would be inconsistent with the state's policy to minimize needless expense."

"Your Honor," Joshua says, "genetic testing has progressed to the point where biological relations can now be ascertained with absolute accuracy. Which is why the law has determined, in its amendment, that *biology* should be the only relevant factor and not the nature of the relationship."

"I do recognize that special consideration must be given to the sensitive and sometimes competing interests in these types of proceedings. However, the surrogate's decision in a previous case required the party seeking posthumous genetic marker testing to provide *some* evidence—"

"Your Honor, the point of our motion is to *get* that evidence."

"Mr. James, you have provided very little specific information regarding Bruce Ashforth's kinship to Mrs. Buntmore that would convince me to grant access to a genetic marker test of his brain tissue."

"Moore. Her name is Mrs. *Moore.*"

"There are no certified documents here. No death records, no marriage or birth certificates."

"According to the amendment in—"

"Yes, I know. In 2010. I am well aware of the amendment to which you have pinned your entire motion, Mr. James. But given that it is *your client's* legal burden to prove kinship status—"

"We're not here to prove kinship yet," Joshua reminds him, his voice rising in frustration. "We're here to obtain evidence so that we *can* prove status. That's why we need access to Bruce Ashforth's brain tissue."

"If I may, Your Honor?" Fistler interrupts, suddenly coming to life. "The obvious conclusion here is that the petitioner's request for a genetic marker test is totally without legal merit and that this motion must be dismissed on the grounds of collateral estoppel. I remind the court that the Westchester Surrogate already decided in 1985 that Wallace Ashforth was not Arden Moore's father and denied her right to inherit. Even opposing counsel knows that without the consent of a known family member, we shouldn't even be here."

"Your Honor, Arden Moore was never even granted a paternity test in the eighties," Joshua argues. "We are asking the court to allow her access to all the scientific advances available to her today. This is a different estate with a new decedent, under a new law. It's a perfect storm of circumstances that *must* compel access to DNA testing."

"This is just another shakedown by a desperate widow in serious debt!" Fistler shouts.

"Mrs. Moore either *is* or *is not* a biological match to Bruce Ashforth," Joshua says, countering Fistler's rage with measured calm. "She has the right to know."

Judge Lull raises a hand in the air, like a teacher trying to settle an unruly class. His expression reads mild annoyance, boredom. "I'll be ready to give my decision on August sixth," he says, with a lackadaisical bang of the gavel. "Enjoy your summer."

"*So that's it?*" Hal says, dredging a handful of shrimp in flour. "He just cut you off and set the date?"

"It's fine," Joshua says coolly, gazing out the kitchen window into Hal's backyard. "I have total faith in Judge Lull. He knows exactly how this is going to play out, and there was no point going around in circles all morning."

"And how is it going to play out?" Arden asks him, mashing avocados. The three of them are crowded around the Formica table in Hal's small kitchen, which smells strongly of cilantro and seafood.

"He has to grant us access to the DNA test," Joshua says. "Denying you that right would never hold up in appeals, not with the advances they've made since your mother's petition."

"But what about that unstoppable collateral thing?"

"You mean the collateral estoppel?"

"My colleague says that could end this whole thing," Hal says, dropping the breaded shrimp into a pan of hot oil.

"Is he a lawyer?"

"No, he's an art teacher."

"Lull won't dismiss Arden's request," Joshua says, turning away from the window to look at them. "There are too many compelling and controversial arguments, most notably the unprecedented advances in science over the last thirty years. I'm not concerned about collateral estoppel. You deserve to know the truth about your father, Arden. I really believe that, and I'll fight until you get that DNA test."

"I like him better than his stepfather," Hal says to Arden. "I'm sorry, Joshua, I was never a fan of Larry Lasker."

"He's not everyone's cup of tea," Joshua admits. "Arden needs to prepare for a kinship hearing. That DNA test is only the first hoop we have to jump through."

"I'm prepared," Arden says, grabbing a crispy shrimp fresh out of the pan and popping it in her mouth.

"Leave those alone," Hal scolds. "What about the fact that I adopted Arden? I remember that being a problem back in the day."

"I told you, Dad. That domestic relations clause was repealed in eighty-seven. The fact that you adopted me is no longer an issue."

Joshua and Hal both look impressed.

"I'm kind of getting into all this legal stuff," Arden says. "I find it really interesting. In another life, I might have been a lawyer."

"What 'in another life,'" Hal says. "You're still a baby. Go to law school."

"I'm almost forty. Hardly a baby."

"Joshua, would you grab me a Corona from the fridge? And help yourself to another."

Joshua gets up and takes three bottles of Corona from the fridge, opens them, and squeezes a lime wedge inside each bottle neck. "What else can I do?"

Hal looks up from his fry pan and gestures at a red onion sitting on the counter. "You can chop that son of a bitch," he says. "Knives are over there."

"Wait till you taste Hal's jalapeño crema," Arden says, dumping a rough-chopped hill of tomatoes into her bowl of guacamole.

"When does Wyatt go on his camping trip?" Hal asks her, which immediately causes Arden's chest to constrict.

"Friday," she says, rinsing a bunch of cilantro. "I don't want to talk about it."

"He'll be fine."

"You afraid he'll get eaten by a bear?" Joshua says.

"He has a severe nut allergy. I worry every time he leaves the house."

"Oh shit. Sorry, I didn't realize—"

"Don't worry."

"Millions of kids have peanut allergies and still go camping," Hal says. "That's what Epi-Pens are for. His friend's father is not going to let anything happen to him. The kid needs his freedom, Arden."

"You good with cilantro?" she asks Joshua, not willing to admit to Hal that he's right.

"The more the better," he says, and she scrubs the dirt off the leaves, and the subject of the peanut allergy is dropped.

After dinner, Hal disappears into the basement to paint, and Arden and Joshua decide to go for a sunset walk along Avenue K to burn off some of the tacos and postmortem their day at court. Arden is full, a bit drunk, and unusually content. It's a muggy evening and the scent of the June-blooming lilacs follows them for most of the block. At the high school, they turn onto East Seventeenth at Midwood Field, where Arden used to hang out with her friends whenever she was staying with Hal.

"I'm assuming you get your love of art from Hal?" Joshua says, looking out at the field, with its pristine new track and bombastic HOME OF THE HORNETS sign.

"I used to love to watch him paint."

"Do you paint?"

"I don't have the talent to match my enthusiasm. I'm a better photographer."

"Serious?"

"About photography?" She slaps a mosquito on her arm and then licks her thumb to wipe away a smudge of blood. "No. I don't have the time. I haven't had time since my first pregnancy."

Joshua looks at her but doesn't say anything.

"Between the kids and the lawsuit and now being a single mother . . ." She doesn't finish her sentence.

"What do you see yourself doing once they're all out of the house?" he asks her. "Maybe you should go to law school."

Oh, how simple is the mind of a bachelor.

"I have at least ten years to figure that out," she says. "I'll let you know."

"Do you think you have a calling?"

"Motherhood," she answers, not entirely sure if that's true. Joshua seems determined to make her claim something—*anything*. "Is law *your* calling?" she asks him.

"I don't see myself ever doing anything else, so I guess maybe it is. Listen, I'm not trying to disparage what you do—"

"Oh, I know," she says. "Believe me, I've been asking myself the same questions a lot lately. I always just kind of figured Scott and I would decide our next moves together." Meaning *Scott* would decide for them, but she doesn't tell him that.

They cross the street at Avenue L, heading toward the park. "This was my playground when I used to live here," she says. "Except it didn't look anything like this."

The brand-new playscape is bright blue, freshly painted, a far cry from the rusty metal death traps of her childhood. They sit down on one of the benches next to the basketball court, where a group of boys is playing three-on-three, filling the evening with their jeering and cheers, the steady *thunk* of the ball on the ground.

"You feeling okay about today?" Joshua asks her.

"I'm trusting you right now," she says. "So, yes. What surprises me is that Jamie Ashforth hasn't made an appearance in court yet."

"He wants us to know he doesn't have time to waste on this. Like you're an annoying fly his lawyer can just kill and be rid of."

"But how is he not the least bit curious about me? I'm his *half sister*. *I'm* curious about *him*. I want to know what he looks like in person; I want to meet his kids. They're my nieces and nephews, for God's sake. We're blood."

"He doesn't believe that."

"He's going to have to believe it when we get the DNA results. Then what'll he do?"

"I wouldn't get my hopes up about a family reunion," he says. "There's nothing quite like the rejection of your own family to light a fire under your ass."

"Sounds like something you've also experienced."

"I think I mentioned my father has a new family in Seattle? I showed up there once. My dad answered the door. I hadn't seen him in over a decade and he looked kind of annoyed to see me. Nervously scooted me out the door and took me for a beer so he wouldn't have to introduce me to his new family. I asked him if they knew about me."

"Did they?"

"They knew he'd been married before. And I said, 'But do they know about *me*?' And he said, 'They don't ask about my old life.' *His 'old life'!* So, I said, 'I'm your son, asshole. I'm still alive. You don't get to decide if I'm part of your *old* life or your current life.'"

"What did he say to that?"

"He said—and this is the heartwarming part—'I get to decide whatever the fuck I want.' So, that's when I decided to make a shit ton of money that I can shove in his blue-collar face one day."

"Did he ever tell you why he left?"

"Just that he should never have been with my mother. They were wrong for each other. The pregnancy was an accident, he felt trapped, blah-blah. He hated New York. He said he was either going to kill himself or get out, but not to take it personally."

"Why would you take that personally?" she quips.

"Right? My mom always says sperm does not a father make."

"Nor blood," Arden says, standing up. "Let's swing."

She runs over to the swing set and gets on one, the rubber seat squeezing her hips like a vise. When she and Hal used to come here together, when she was very little, he used to push her back and forth for hours. Her mother would get bored after two or three pushes, but not Hal. He had all the time in the world for her. The memory makes her emotional. To have had the unconditional love of a man to whom she did not belong, and none at all from her *real* family, makes so many of her childhood memories bittersweet.

Joshua is watching her from the bench, and as his eyes meet hers, she clues in to the glaringly obvious fact that *he* has feelings for *her* too.

She can see it clearly now in his complicated expression, a combination of desire and abject terror—the same lens through which she often looks at him. She waves him over.

He gets up and approaches the swings, rolling up his sleeves. Sits down and starts swinging to catch up to her.

"Tell me about the tattoos," she says as they pass each other in the air.

"This is the Philippine god Kan-Laon," he explains, extending his left arm. "He's the Eternal One, the Ruler of Time. I used to be obsessed with Philippine mythology when I was a teenager. See how he's covered in tattoos? Those are pintados. The natives used to tattoo their entire bodies with these incredibly intricate drawings. They were like medals of honor."

"Very cool," she says, breathing heavily as she kicks her legs straight out in front of her and throws her head back, letting her hair almost touch the ground. She feels sexy, playful. She lets herself enjoy the feeling, doesn't resist it or try to squelch it out of guilt or grief.

They swing side by side for a while, softly panting from the effort, legs straightening and bending in unison, torsos plunging forward and then tipping backward until they're gazing upside down at the papaya-colored sky. The only sound is the squeak of the swings' metal hinges.

Finally, the sun disappears, blanketing the park in darkness. Joshua slows down his swing's momentum by dragging his feet on the ground. Arden soon follows suit, stopping completely, and turns to face him. "Are we going to win?" she asks him, her voice crashing the silence.

"I think so."

"I *have* to win."

He doesn't say anything.

"I can't let my kids down," she says. "I just can't."

They walk back the way they came, saying little. There's a different energy between them now, a perceptible, exquisite tension, almost as if their swinging together had been sexual.

When they reach Hal's house, Joshua wishes her a safe flight home and gets into his car with an awkward wave.

Arden watches him drive off and then looks up at the house, where Hal is watching her from his bedroom window. He sees her see him and quickly closes the curtains. When she used to visit him as a teenager, he would stand there waiting for her to come home every night when she went out with friends. He never went to bed until he saw her from his window, and then he would close the curtains and disappear. He'd always be snoring soundly by the time she got upstairs, or at least pretending.

19

Virginia stares glumly out the window at the sprawling, gray-brick Angli-
can church next to the old folks' home, both of which are set back from
the road on a lush green corner lot in Lytton Park. When Tate pulls
open the car door for her, Virginia doesn't budge.

"It would be so much less off-putting if they held these things in a
hotel lobby or a coffee shop," Virginia says.

"It'll be fine," Tate assures her.

"Can I change my mind?"

"Let me grab your cane and I'll help you out."

"I can't."

"Of course you can," Tate says matter-of-factly. "I'll come with you
if you want."

"I don't want."

Tate reaches for her mother's elbow and gently tugs her out of the
car. Virginia leans heavily on Tate's shoulder with one hand and on her
cane with the other, finally managing to free her body from the car.

"Do you need my help walking you into the building?"

Virginia shakes her head, dangerously close to tears.

"I'm going to do some errands and then I'll meet you right here at this
bench," Tate says, using the same maternal voice Virginia used to use on
her decades ago when she would drop her off on the first day of school or
at a new ballet class. *Mommy will be back to pick you up at three.* What a
twisted sense of humor the universe has, bringing old people full circle
like this.

All of this is Hayley's fault. Hayley, with her spiritual sound bites and
her minty-fresh optimism.

"Happiness is a habit, you know." That's what Hayley said to Virginia the day she brought up the group again.

Virginia looked up at her with a sudden intense craving for a cigarette.

"You're giving me that look, Virginia."

"What look?"

"You know exactly what look," Hayley said, unstrapping the weights from Virginia's ankles. She sat down cross-legged on the floor next to Virginia's prostrate upper body. "Have you given any thought to the elder abuse group?"

"Some."

"I know I'm your physiotherapist, but the mental and emotional work is super important for your physical recovery as well. You're not exactly recovering at an impressive clip, if you don't mind my saying so."

A cool draft of peppermint wafted around Virginia's face.

"At some point, you have to *want* to get better," Hayley said. "And I don't just mean walking normally again."

"I'm old. It takes longer."

Hayley rolled her eyes and sighed. "It's not your age," she said. "It's your attitude. I've worked with plenty of clients older than you and they've made more progress in less time."

Virginia lolled her head away petulantly and didn't respond.

"Your body has experienced a serious trauma," Hayley said, softening her tone. "And so has your psyche. *All* of you needs to heal."

"I don't belong in an elder abuse group," Virginia muttered. "I'm not an elder."

"You just said yourself you're old."

Virginia frowned.

"Have you ever heard of *Psycho-Cybernetics*?"

"I hate science."

"God, Virginia, can you please just open your mind a *crack*? It's a *book*."

"Fine. No, I haven't heard of it. Please tell me about it while I'm trapped here on my back."

"*Psycho-Cybernetics* is essentially about how our self-image—good or bad—determines the outcome of our lives. The guy who wrote it was a plastic surgeon, and he noticed in his practice that after getting plastic surgery, some patients went on to feel great about themselves, and others, in spite of having a new nose or better boobs, still felt like shit."

"What's that got to do with my broken hip?"

"Your recovery is connected to your self-image," Hayley explained, her voice teetering on pedantry. "Your mind is like a machine that you get to control, but if you're constantly plugging in crappy thoughts about yourself, your life is going to be crappy. William James said we could alter our lives if we alter our attitudes of mind."

"Help me up," Virginia said, holding out her arms. Hayley popped up, planted her legs on either side of Virginia, and gently puller her up to a sitting position.

"I appreciate what you're saying," Virginia said. "It makes sense. I mean, it's not exactly revolutionary, is it? The power of positive thinking and all that? But maybe I'm just not in a rush to go anywhere. I've got no apartment, I can't work, and I'm alone."

"Do you hear yourself? How about getting well for *you*? Ever think of that?"

Virginia was quiet.

"This isn't just about your broken hip," Hayley said, placing her hands underneath Virginia's armpits to help hoist her up on her feet. "It's about your entire life."

"What do you know about my life?" Virginia said, panting from the effort to stand.

"You just said you've got no home, no partner, and no job. Plus, your body and your spirit are broken. Frankly, your life is a perfect reflection of your thoughts."

"Stop quoting me back to myself," Virginia said. "Besides, I know this is all my fault. I don't need to be reminded."

"There you go again with your victim paradigm. I didn't say it was your fault. I said your situation is a reflection of your mindset."

"Same thing."

"It's not the same thing at all. Reprogram your thoughts and your life will change. You'll recover faster. It's very straightforward."

"I don't understand how sitting around with a bunch of abused old people is going to help me," she said stubbornly. "Won't that just make me more miserable?"

"No, Virginia, it won't. You won't be alone with this anymore. You'll finally be able to open up and talk about what happened to you without any fear of judgment. You'll be able to start working through some of your shame and guilt. You'll see you're not so bad off and that others have it way worse than you do. You'll be out in the world again, with people who have been through what you're going through."

Virginia lowered herself onto the bed and looked out the window. Another goddamn perfect day. Her moods were becoming more and more diametrically at odds with the weather. If it was sunny and clear and she could hear birds singing, she felt intensely depressed, as though summer were reproaching her, antagonizing her useless body. On the other hand, a rainy day legitimatized her lethargy, gave her permission to stay in bed without guilt. Unfortunately, it's been a record-breaking July for sunshine, which, thanks to Hayley's prodding and poking, brought about the crushing realization that she's changed at the core into some-one whose natural default is misery. "My God," she said to Hayley. "I didn't used to be like this."

"Like what?"

Virginia turned away from the window, her eyes filling with tears. "I wish you could have known me before," she says. "I was a totally different person."

"Like how?"

"I was fearless, for one thing. I once did a one-woman show at the Howland Theatre. It was a sold-out show about my life. Mostly men I'd dated, but they gave me an ovation. I used to sing at the Riverboat coffee house in the early seventies. It was *the* place to be back then. And when I was dating Jean-Claude from Montreal, I used to dance to the Tam-Tam drums on Mont-Royal every Sunday, free as a bird, wearing just a bikini. I was in my late forties or early fifties, but I didn't care. I never felt old around all those young people."

"I can't picture you like that," Hayley says.

"How could you? But I tell you, I used to be hopeful. That was my thing. I was always full of hope. I was an annoyingly optimistic person. I loved the summer! Ask my girls. I believed in love. I believed I would *find* love. But now . . . now I feel defeated, pessimistic. And it's not just the accident—"

She stopped herself at the word "accident." Even as it left her mouth, it felt wrong; not just inaccurate or understated, but deceptive. "It's not just the *assault*," she said. "It was a little bit before too. I could feel myself giving up, quietly becoming more cynical. All my efforts over the years, and for what? I had started saying that to myself, more than I ever had before. Even while I was dating and going on the app, I kept thinking it. What's it all been for? Why am I still at this? And then I met Lou and it all came to a catastrophic head, but it was as though I was expecting it. It was like the inevitable climax to . . . I don't know what . . ."

"A lifetime of thinking certain thoughts and believing certain things about yourself?"

"Unwanted things. Like maybe I really don't deserve a good man. Or to be happy."

Hayley folded a fresh stick of Extra in half and stuffed it in her mouth.

"How would I get there, if I were to go?" Virginia said. "To the group?"

"Wheel-Trans. They'll pick you up at your front door and they can accommodate your walker."

"I don't need the walker. I'm fine with my cane."

"Either way, they're totally accessible."

Virginia shuddered at the image of herself on a Wheel-Trans bus. "I'll think about it," she said, lying back against her pillow.

And now here she is.

Inside, there's a sign at the reception desk that says ELDER ABUSE MEETING 3RD FLOOR BEHIND THE MUSIC ROOM.

Virginia shuffles over to the elevator, still contemplating whether she should go. There's always the option to sit outside the room and play solitaire on her phone until it's time to meet Tate, but before she can turn and flee, a young woman reaches past her and presses the up button. "Are you here for the support group?" she asks Virginia. She looks about Arden's age, midthirties at the outside.

Virginia nods, thinking to herself, *Why the hell else would I be in this place?*

"Welcome," the woman says. "I'm Leah."

"You don't look old enough to be a victim of elder abuse," Virginia says.

"I'm the facilitator," Leah clarifies. "I work for the CNPEA."

"The what?

"The Canadian Network for the Prevention of Elder Abuse."

"There's a network for that?"

Leah smiles gently and says, "You don't look old enough to be here either."

Virginia softens, dropping her guard. "I'm Virginia."

"Follow me," Leah says. "I'll give you our newcomer package. This is a lovely group. You're in the right place, Virginia."

How would she know?

The meeting is in a small room with a conference table and no windows. There are a couple of walkers parked by the door and a whiteboard in the corner that says, in erasable blue marker:

> *If you say, "The Lord is my refuge," and you make the*
> *Most High your dwelling, no harm will overtake you,*
> *no disaster will come near your tent.*
> PSALM 91

There are seven people seated around the table in threadbare upholstered armchairs. The people look rather threadbare themselves, Virginia observes. She guesses the average age to be about eighty, which makes her feel positively pubescent. She leans her cane against the table and lowers herself with some difficulty into one of the chairs. Everyone smiles at her. The woman to her left is white-haired, slender, well dressed in a crisp chambray blue button-down and chino capris. She reaches out and pats Virginia's hand. "I'm glad you're here," she whispers, which shocks Virginia, who's not used to this kind of openness and hospitality from strangers.

Her eyes light on a pile of books in the center of the table—*Elder Abuse: Reduced to NOTHING*; *The Worldwide Face of Elder Abuse*; *Elder Abuse: The Insidious Scourge Affecting Our Elderly*—and she wishes she could disappear. Someone hands her a pamphlet.

They go around the room and introduce themselves. Bonnie, Lois, Maria, Elaine, Malcolm, Alfred, and Jean, the woman beside her.

"We have a newcomer today," Leah says. "Would you like to introduce yourself?"

"I'm Virginia."

"Welcome, Virginia." Everyone at once, smiling at her.

It feels more like a book club or a knitting circle, and she has to remind herself that all these people have been abused. That's why they're here; that's why *she's* here. She glances around the room, looking for signs of external damage, but everyone looks pretty healthy and normal. Turns out you can't see the real wounds after the bruises heal.

While the facilitator reads something from a book called *"Today I See the Sunrise": Daily Meditations for Survivors of Torture and Abuse*, Virginia peeks inside the pamphlet. *It is estimated that one in ten seniors in Canada will experience some form of physical, emotional or sexual abuse in their later years. Elder abuse occurs when an older adult is abused, typically by a person they should be able to trust. It can happen once, or it may be repeated over time.*

"We haven't had a newcomer in a while," Leah says, when she's finished reading. "Let's start by going around the room and sharing our stories."

The group likes this idea very much, and Jean lifts her hand and says, "I'll start."

Virginia listens rapt as Jean tells her story. First, the stage 2 breast cancer diagnosis at eighty, followed by six months of physical and psychological abuse at the hands of her son-in-law while she was living with her daughter and going through chemo.

"At first he was just hostile," Jean says, dry-eyed, neutral. "He didn't want me there, but my daughter insisted, so he decided to make my life a living hell. It started with eye rolls and rude comments behind my daughter's back. 'Get your bony ass off the couch, you old leech.' Like that. Then he started to slap me and pinch me. I was terrified of him."

"Did you say anything to your daughter?" Virginia interrupts.

"Virginia, there's no cross talk here," Leah says gently. "We don't comment on or address anyone while they're sharing."

"I'm sorry," Virginia mumbles, flushing with embarrassment.

"It's fine," Jean says. "He said if I told my daughter what he was doing, he'd take my grandchildren away and we'd never see them again. I was so sick from the chemo, too, so I didn't have the energy to fight him or stand up to him. I was just trying to get through the treatments. In retrospect, I should have stayed in my own home and hired a nurse, but my daughter wouldn't hear of it.

"Finally, after my last treatment, when I was at my weakest and most frail, he slapped me so hard I lost consciousness and hit my head on the floor. I woke up in the hospital with a concussion. That's when I told my daughter everything. She wouldn't let me go to the police, and she stayed with him, and I have to live with that, but at least my daughter and grandchildren are still in my life, and he's in counseling. That was five years ago. I've been in therapy ever since, and I'm cancer-free, and I believe this group is a big part of my recovery. I don't think I'd be here without the love and support I've received here."

Virginia's mouth is hanging open. This woman was assaulted by her own son-in-law while going through chemo and *he's still in her life*, and here she is talking about it with the serenity and gratitude of someone describing a six-month retreat at an ashram. *Is she drugged? Does she have Alzheimer's?*

"Thank you for sharing, Jean."

Malcolm goes next, and then Lois, and then Bonnie—tales of neglect in nursing homes, starvation and dehydration, physical and mental beatings. By the time it gets to Alfred, Virginia's used up half a box of Kleenex.

"It was my wife who was abused at her nursing home," he says, with a hint of a Scottish brogue. He has fading orange hair, sunken blue eyes, shoulders that are folding in on themselves. Something about the way he's got his thumbs hooked inside the tops of his suspenders, nervously tugging and stretching them, fills Virginia with pity.

"Annie had Alzheimer's and couldn't speak," he says. "An orderly raped her, and she couldn't even tell me. She just kept hittin' herself between the legs whenever I went to visit, tears comin' down her face. I don't know how long it was goin' on. Finally, a nurse reported him. He got eight years in jail, but Rose had a stroke and died before he was convicted. My last memory of her is she's punchin' herself between the legs and cryin' silently while she's lookin' up at me. This group has helped me to stop blamin' m'self—at least some of the time. Thank you for listenin'."

Alfred snaps his suspenders against his belly and bows his head. Virginia blows her nose. When it's her turn to share, she keeps her eyes glued to the table. "My story is nothing like any of yours," she says apologetically. "Nothing at all. I really don't think I should even be here, so I'll just pass, thank you."

"Virginia, we recommend you commit to at least six meetings," Leah says warmly. "You may yet hear your story."

Virginia nods, unable to imagine ever being brave enough to share her story out loud. Still, she's surprised at how comfortable she feels in this cramped little room on the third floor of an old folks' home. Maybe Hayley was right and she does belong here; she's feeling something she's not sure she's ever felt before, which is the opposite of alone.

After the meeting, Jean stops her at the door and invites her to sit outside in the garden and talk. Virginia agrees until her daughter gets there.

"May I ask what brought you to the group?" Jean probes as they move slowly toward one of the benches on the church lawn.

"My physiotherapist nagged me about it until she finally wore me down."

"I mean, what happened to you."

"Oh, nothing like the horrible things that have happened to you," Virginia says dismissively. "Mine was more like a date gone wrong."

"No need to diminish the impact it's had on you, whatever happened."

"It only happened once. It was mostly my fault. I led him on. When I replay it in my mind, I'm not even sure it wasn't simply rough sex that got a bit out of hand."

"Did you consent?"

"I don't remember."

"So, he raped you."

Jean helps Virginia lower herself onto the bench, which is humbling, given Virginia is about twenty years younger than Jean.

"Let's say he did rape me," Virginia says. "That's a date rape. Elder abuse is much more prolonged."

"Says who? If a child is molested once, is that not sexual abuse?"

"Oh, but that's different."

"Is it the word 'elder' that bothers you, or the word 'abuse'?"

"Both, I guess. They both make me feel a little ashamed."

"You'll come back, won't you?" Jean asks her, and Virginia can hear the soft click of Jean's false teeth. "You know what they say, don't you? If you don't deal with *it*, it will deal with *you*."

"I've never heard that before."

"Well, I hope to see you again, kiddo. You owe it to yourself."

Kiddo. "Yes," Virginia says, feeling deeply seen. "I guess I could try a few more meetings."

"You're very wise for such a young woman."

20

IT'S BEDLAM IN THE STREET BEHIND THE SURROGATE'S COURT WHERE AN episode of *Law & Order: SVU* is being filmed. Foley Square is clogged with trailers, film equipment, spectators, and a few self-important crew members pushing through the crowds with headsets and clipboards, acting like Manhattan is their personal studio and everyone is in their way. Arden hasn't spotted any of the lead actors, but she's got her phone handy in case Mariska Hargitay or Ice-T show up.

"You nervous?" Joshua asks her.

"Very," she says, watching one of the crew members shepherd a handful of extras wearing orange prison jumpsuits onto a Corrections Department bus headed for Rikers Island.

"We've got this," Joshua says.

"Don't say that. You're going to jinx it."

"*Jinx* it?" he laughs. "The law is not jinxable."

"Everything is jinxable," she says. "I think I'm having a panic attack. My fingers are numb. I don't think that's okay. Maybe I should just wait outside for you?"

"We're good, Arden. Can you trust me?"

She looks down at the cute mules she borrowed from Ivey, with her pink, freshly pedicured toes peeking out the ends, and tries to ground herself on the sidewalk.

"Arden, look at me." She looks up at him. "Can you trust me?"

"I'll try."

"Relax."

"It's impossible."

"We're still at the beginning of this ride. There's a long way to go, so you've got to figure out how to get through these situations as calmly and sanely as possible."

"There's too much at stake."

"There always is. But it's money we're talking about, right? It's just money."

Just money. She lets the words land. Joshua is right, of course. They're not waiting for the results of a biopsy or anything. It's just a request for a DNA test. It's just thirty million bucks. It's just her children's futures, her entire bloodline, her identity.

"I see your wheels spinning," he says. "Stop it."

"It's just money," she repeats.

"Don't get me wrong, it's a *shit ton* of money—"

"But it's just money."

Judge Lull enters and takes his seat at the front of the room. "Let me get straight to it so as not to waste any more of the court's time," he says, looking directly into the gallery. Arden closes her eyes. "I've reviewed all the information that was submitted to the court and I'm ready to give my decision."

Her heart drops. Joshua touches her leg, which is shaking.

"In my opening, I said I had a few concerns."

"As do we," Fistler mutters, loud enough for everyone in court to hear.

She feels like she may throw up. She can't have come this far only to be denied now. She imagines Bruce Ashforth's brain, preserved inside that pickling jar, just waiting to be tested and make this all go away once and for all. Could it be that, even with all the great advances in DNA testing and the absurdly convenient access to Bruce's brain tissue, she might still wind up with nothing? Could the universe be that cruel? The fact of Scott's death is her response to that question, and she realizes, foolishly, *Of course the universe would be that cruel.*

"In fact," Fistler adds, in that self-righteous tone that Arden has come to despise, "we have more than a few concerns."

"Mr. Fistler, you've had your opportunity to lay those concerns out for the court," Judge Lull says. "Now, if I may be permitted to give my decision?"

Arden looks over at Fistler, who's giving off his usual smugness, and she's secretly pleased he's been put in his place.

"Had I been permitted to finish that statement," the judge resumes, "I would have said that, despite my concerns, this is a different world from the one in which the petitioner's mother first sought to establish paternity."

"One still needs to present *some* evidence," Fistler interrupts. "Opposing counsel has presented *no* evidence whatsoever to compel testing."

Ignoring Fistler, the judge turns his attention to Arden's side of the table and says, "Mrs. Moore began this pretrial hearing seeking an order for genetic marker testing to establish kinship with Bruce Ashforth, her alleged half brother. Given the advances in genetic testing, it is my opinion that imposing too high an evidentiary standard to even *obtain* access to the technology that provides us with the most reliable evidence of kinship is counterproductive."

Arden looks over at Joshua.

"Your Honor," Fistler says, standing. "That high evidentiary standard is what keeps the frauds and interlopers from crawling out of the woodwork!"

"Mr. Fistler, sit down. I'm not suggesting that every claim has merit. But how does preventing access to accurate DNA testing help to avoid fraudulent claims? Logic dictates that an opportunistic individual will be *dissuaded* from filing a false claim, knowing that family members will use DNA proof to conclusively defeat his or her claim.

"While the statute clearly sets forth the standard of proof in determining kinship, it does not establish the burden to be imposed upon anyone seeking a *pretrial order* for posthumous genetic marker testing."

Arden looks over at Joshua again, trying to read his expression. His face is inscrutable, other than an almost imperceptible moustache of perspiration above his lip.

"Of particular significance here," the judge continues, "is that the tissue specimens of the decedent are readily available for testing and will not require the exhumation of the decedent's body. I see here that the samples were secured by the chief medical examiner prior to the contemplation of litigation."

"The fact that the tissue samples are available does not constitute 'evidence' to compel testing," Fistler complains. "My client is adamantly against postmortem testing, Your Honor, for a number of reasons, most of them emotional."

Joshua looks over at Fistler and laughs out loud.

"Mr. James," the judge reprimands, glaring at Joshua. Joshua settles back in his chair, point made.

"I'm very troubled that what you're doing here is opening a Pandora's box of greedy money-grubbers!" Fistler says, starting to sound unhinged.

"Mr. Fistler, I've just about had it with this line of name-calling. You've been warned multiple times about your excessive ad hominem remarks. I'm telling you now, I'm not going to tolerate this rhetoric in my courtroom."

"My client's claim is meritorious," Joshua adds. "The DNA testing will prove that."

"All right, Counsel. Let's not devolve into more circular arguments. We've been at this long enough. The fact is DNA evidence affords our court system the rare opportunity to move beyond the murkiness of testamentary evidence into the territory of concrete, scientific evidence."

He glances up, makes direct eye contact with Fistler, and then resumes. "To that end," he says, "I find that the evidence presented in this motion *does* establish that the petitioner's request for posthumous DNA testing is reasonable and practicable under the totality of the circumstances, and I am granting the order for posthumous genetic marker testing posthaste—"

"Your Honor," Fistler interrupts. "We request a kinship hearing."

Judge Lull nods placidly, expecting the request. A date is set and the gavel comes down on his mahogany desk. It's over.

Joshua turns to Arden, beaming. Her whole body is vibrating. "What's happening?" she asks him.

"We won our motion, Arden. Fistler must have really pissed him off. Normally, the surrogate just signs his decision and then it's available in the record room. It's highly unusual for the decision to be announced like that."

"Now what?"

"There's going to be a kinship hearing, which we knew was inevitable. What matters is they're going to give us access to Bruce's DNA. There's a lab downtown where you can get a siblingship analysis to determine whether you and Bruce have the same father."

"You want me to do the test here in New York?"

"Yep. I want you to use the lab Larry recommended. It's accredited, which will guarantee admissibility and secure your chance of inheriting. I've already requested Bruce's DNA sample be sent there."

"Is this really happening?" she says, dazed. "We won?"

"Round one."

21

Emerging onto the street in the afternoon sunlight immediately following their triumphant verdict, Joshua and Arden were both giddy, buzzing.
He'd bought a bottle of champagne in anticipation of a win and invited
Arden over for a celebratory drink after her DNA test. The lab, conve-
niently, wasn't too far from his place. An effusive offer, harmless.

Absolutely, she said, totally caught up in the moment. It was all surreal; she was stunned with relief and excitement. A drink was exactly
what she was in the mood for.

"This is the first motion that's ever been won in this inheritance," she
gushes. "I honestly can't believe it. It's finally going our way!"

"I told you it would be different from your mother's experience."

They set off for Battery Park on foot, matching strides, reliving the
moment when Judge Lull announced his decision, laughing over the look
on Fistler's face when he realized he'd lost, imagining the uncomfortable
conversation he would have to have with his client, Jamie Ashforth. They
touched briefly on next steps, but when Arden pressed him for more information about what was to come, Joshua wisely said, "Let's just enjoy
our victory today. No more legal talk."

Wonderful. Everything was wonderful. She called her sister, her
mother, and Hal with the good news. She texted the kids. Ivey responded
right away. Does that mean we're millionaires??? Can I get a Gucci hoodie?

Joshua asked her what the first thing was she was going to buy with
the inheritance money. "I can't even think about that," she responded,
but even as she said the words out loud, she knew they were disingen-
uous. She was already spending the money in her head. There would
be a house for her mother and another one for Hal; the completion of

the lagging reno on her own home; a family trip to Hawaii; a shopping spree with Tate. And of course thoughtful investments and charitable donations. *Values.*

Twenty minutes later, they arrived at the Albany Street Tower, a red-brick high-rise at the corner of South End Avenue. Joshua wanted to pick up some food for dinner, so they stopped at the deli on the main floor of his building, and he bought a couple of Philly cheesesteaks and a bag of salt-and-vinegar chips. "The perfect companion to a bottle of Dom," he said, and she appreciated that confluence of pretension and down-to-earthness, which reminded her of Scott. Her mood was light as they rode the elevator up to his apartment on the ninth floor. She was aware of feeling unencumbered, hopeful—a state of being that, while pleasant, was also jarringly unfamiliar. A thought flickered in her mind: *Am I even allowed to feel this good?*

She shut it down with impressive alacrity. *You can be happy just for today.* She was determined to enjoy her win in court, the first win she'd had in a long time, and if that meant forgetting she was a widow with three kids waiting for her at home, and instead eating chips and drinking Dom Pérignon with Joshua and making plans to spend her millions, so be it.

She runs her fingertip along the inside of his arm, which is splayed across the mattress, his hand in a loose fist. His head tips to the other side but he doesn't wake up. His breathing is steady, quiet. He really is beautiful, she thinks, marveling at his lovely sleeping face.

She knows that lust is for less-complicated women and maybe better left unexplored; that all her decisions must be funneled through the very narrow aperture of what's best for her children. *And yet.* This is the first thing she's wanted for herself in such a long time. Her sexuality has been padlocked for the exact amount of days Scott's been dead, possibly longer. Someone had to break that widow's seal; why not Joshua? Even contemplating it now, the morning after, she can already feel the desire galvanizing inside her. She isn't done with him yet.

She gets up and pads softly to the kitchen, wearing only the white T-shirt she ripped off him last night. The apartment is small but open concept, with high ceilings and a glorious view of the Hudson River, all of which create an illusion of more space. It has the usual trappings of a modern bachelor pad—industrial lighting, polished concrete floors, an exposed brick wall, stainless steel appliances, and a black granite island separating the kitchen from the living room. There's a colossal flat-screen TV wall-mounted above a sleek electric fireplace, the only furniture a suede L-shaped sofa, a barnwood coffee table, and a treadmill.

She pops a pod into the Nespresso machine and sits down on one of the barstools with her espresso shot. *Good morning, Lady Liberty.*

"What a view," she told him last night, gazing out at the twinkling Manhattan skylight and the Statue of Liberty in the distance.

"I know what you're thinking," he said. "I can't be doing too badly if I can afford a place like this."

It was exactly what she'd been thinking.

"Larry bought it in 2003," he explained. "It was a rental apartment before September eleventh. Larry was shrewd. He bought it for pennies right before the reconstruction started. A lot of people had already fled Lower Manhattan. No one wanted to live in all that dust and debris, but Larry saw an opportunity. They ended up converting a lot of the older buildings into modern condos. It's worth millions now. He lets me rent it for half what a place like this goes for. If it wasn't for Larry, I'd be in a hovel somewhere."

"It could use some art," she said, looking around at the bare walls.

"Maybe you could hook me up."

He disappeared into his bedroom and reemerged a few minutes later in sweatpants and a fitted white T-shirt. "You don't mind, do you?"

She did not.

He put on some music—a hip-hop mash-up of Drake, Lil Wayne, Jay-Z—and popped open the champagne. They sat down on the couch—her on one side of the L, him a safe distance apart on the other side—with their flutes of Dom and their Philly cheesesteaks, and she could not recall the last time she'd felt so goddamn free, or at least the last time her head had been that quiet. What a relief it was to be able to compartmentalize reality for a change. It's never been her strong suit, that ability to block out obligation, anxiety, guilt, but last night she found herself enjoying lengthy patches of oblivion, moments of absolute forgetting.

"I'm starving," she said, unwrapping her sandwich. She hadn't eaten since the bite of dry toast she'd had in the morning to quell her precourt nausea.

"They make a pretty good sandwich downstairs," Joshua said, studying the innards of his cheesesteak. "I think it's because they use mozzarella."

"Isn't that a sacrilege? Not using provolone?"

"You know your cheesesteaks."

"We spent a couple of summers in Kennebunk," she explained. "There was this little shack right near the beach where we got the most delicious cheesesteaks. Scott could eat two at a time. He was such a foodie. He once brought a personal chef on a camping trip to Algonquin Park. Everyone else was eating wieners and mac and cheese and we had Mississippi pot roast out of a Dutch oven."

"Hey, speaking of," Joshua said. "I keep meaning to ask you: How was your kid's camping trip last month? You were worried."

He remembered.

"He survived," Arden said, reaching for her phone to find a picture. "Here. This is Wyatt building his own tent." She scrolled through a few more, enjoying them immensely. "This was his first time fishing. He caught a bass. Doesn't he look so proud here? And roasting marshmallows."

She looked over at Joshua and realized his expression was one of polite disinterest. She put away her phone. "I'm glad he got to go," she said. "Scott was always the one to let Wyatt have his freedom. I was so traumatized by that first allergic reaction I always expect the worst. Scott was the calming force in our lives."

"Did you have a good marriage?"

"We're going there?"

"Sorry. Too forward?"

"A little."

"I just want to know more about you. Your marriage feels like an important piece of who you are."

"Who I *was*."

"You sure about that?"

"Meaning?"

"I think you're still defined by your marriage," he said. "Maybe now it's morphed into widowhood, but it still defines you."

"You're probably right," she said. "And, yes, to answer your question, it was a good marriage. It wasn't perfect, but we were best friends; we had a rhythm. He made me laugh. All the check marks."

"That's pretty rare."

"Is it?"

"I have no idea," he admitted, flushing. "I guess I imagine it is, but I may be projecting."

"At least I *think* we were happy," she said, reassessing.

"Say more."

"There was something," she said, not sure why she was even bringing it up, especially to Joshua. "I haven't told anyone this, not even my mother or sister." She took a gulp of champagne. "The day Scott died he was seen having lunch with an attractive blond woman just before he went out on the boat."

"What boat?"

"He had a heart attack on his rental boat."

"But the woman wasn't on the boat with him?"

"No. They just had lunch together."

"Hmm."

"The obvious assumption is he was having an affair."

"Is it? Whose?"

"I'm not sure."

"It's not mine," Joshua said, replenishing their flutes. "And why? Because she was attractive and blond?"

"Yes," Arden confessed. "Maybe he was trying to end it with her that day and she threatened to tell me everything. What if the stress caused him to have a heart attack?"

"That's a stretch," he said. "You got all that from one lunch?"

"He didn't tell me he was meeting a client. He texted me when he woke up that morning, and then again when he got on the boat. He never mentioned having lunch with anyone, let alone a woman, which makes me think he didn't want me to know."

"You're catastrophizing."

"Am I catastrophizing or being pragmatic?"

"It was a lunch. Are there no alternate theories?"

"I'd like to believe he was probably just meeting a client. They all have cottages up there, it was summer. He'd met with clients in Muskoka before."

"There you go."

"It makes me wonder, though. How well did I really know him?" She was thinking about how dire their debt had become, how many pills he was taking at the end.

"I don't see the point in going there," he said.

"I should have been with him in Muskoka. We'd rented a cottage for a month, but I was bored out of my mind. I booked the kids' dentist appointments so I could have an excuse to come back to the city for a couple of days. Ali wanted to stay up there with Scott, but I made him drive us back home. We told her it was just for two days . . ."

Joshua was quiet. He was looking at her, but she couldn't read his expression. It made her uncomfortable and she immediately regretted exposing him to her neuroses when they could have kept talking about Philly cheesesteaks. She bit into her sandwich to shut herself up.

"You've been through a lot."

She nodded, her mouth full of steak and onions. If something happened between them, her breath would be terrible. His, too.

"I'm sorry," he said.

"No, I'm sorry," she countered, reaching for a paper napkin. "That was a lot for a celebratory drink."

"I asked you about him."

That was true.

"Well, thank you for listening. We can change the subject now."

"We don't have to. I just feel a little out of my depth. I'm not sure what to say to you. I feel like I'm coming off trite. You lost your husband. I've never experienced a death."

"It's nice that you're just listening."

"What if he *was* cheating on you?" Joshua asked her.

She stared at him, a little irritated.

"Would it change anything?" he said.

"Absolutely."

"But when I asked you if you had a good marriage, you said yes."

"If he *was* having an affair, then we obviously didn't have a good marriage."

"Is it that black-and-white?"

She stared at him as though he were speaking a different language and didn't answer.

"I guess it is," he said, a little sheepish.

"I'll never know; that's the worst part."

"It was just a lunch, though. It's not like you found their love letters or like the other woman showed up on your doorstep."

"But it was just enough to plant a seed of doubt."

A moment of awkwardness punctured the conversation. Joshua looked like he wanted to crawl under the couch. Maybe he was bored. She was feeling mortified that they'd wound up there. "On a brighter note," she said, forcing lightness, "I'm one step closer to becoming a millionaire."

Joshua relaxed and smiled. "Cheers to that!" he said, and they finished their sandwiches and most of the bottle of champagne. They talked about safe things like music, real estate, the best pizza in New York, his sneaker collection—he has seventeen pair of Jordans—and even a bit about her kids. He went so far as to compare his sneakers—he called them his "babies"—to her children, in terms of how much he loves them. She let it slide because nonparents have no concept of what it's like to love a child, how messy and tortured and consuming it is. *He probably doesn't worry about his sneakers dying from a reaction to peanut butter*, she thought, but she didn't say anything.

After their uncomfortable conversation about Scott, they talked for hours—lightly, easily, enthralled with each other, or at least that's how it felt to Arden. Just before midnight, she remembered she'd never texted Hal. "My dad will be waiting up for me," she said.

He laughed. "You still have a curfew?"

She laughed with him, realizing how absurd it sounded. The way he was looking at her made her insides feel like Jell-O, and so she did the craziest thing she's ever done: she leaned in and kissed him on the mouth. A real kiss. A tongue kiss. Her first tongue other than Scott's in almost twenty years.

"Is this a good idea?" he asked her, making no move to stop it.

"I think so," she said, surprising herself.

"There may be a line here we're stepping dangerously close to, don't you think?"

"You don't want to cross that line?" she asked him, feeling as though she could live with whatever he decided.

"Oh, I do. I definitely do. I mean . . . if you're okay with it, I guess I could cross that line," he said.

"I'm totally okay with it," she said. "I just kissed you."

"What should I do here?" he asked softly, taking her hand. He lightly tickled the inside of her wrist, which caused a tingle between her legs. *It's been so long*, she thought, with a mixture of panic and excitement. There was a sensation in her belly, like the moment right before the roller coaster plunges and all you can do is close your eyes, grip the bar, and let out a primal scream for your life.

"What do *you* want to do?" she asked him. *Gripping the bar and plunging*.

"To hell with it," he said, and this time he kissed her, and she realized, *Shit, this is happening*.

Her first thought was of the bikini wax she'd canceled before her trip; her next was of the birth control pill she went off two years ago. And then she let go and yielded to his lips, to the moment, to what was happening inside her body. Some parts were hardening, others opening.

She sat down on him, her legs straddling him, and removed his shirt without saying a word. She did not want to talk lest the sound of her own voice disrupt her trance. She was pressing into him, and his hardness against her pelvis made her cry out. He lifted her dress over her head and then she pulled down his sweatpants—it was a mad scramble, a lot of heavy breathing and unclasping and arms flailing—and then his hand made his way between her legs and it was as though she'd never been touched down there before. She curled her back like a cat. He teased her a bit with his fingers, but then she grew impatient and grabbed his hand with her own and forced it all the way up inside her, as deep as it would go, and still it didn't feel deep enough. She wanted to feel it in her throat. There was no thought of Scott in her head while they fucked. When it was over and she'd come, not once but twice—the first time before he even entered her—she collapsed on top of him, panting against his chest, utterly drained. She'd held nothing back from him, *nothing*. Not physical or emotional or spiritual, but afterward, lying on him, she literally felt hollow, depleted of energy, depleted of feelings and fluid. Perhaps "numb" was a better word than "hollow."

"I've wanted to do that since the day I walked into your gallery," he said, scratching her back, his lips millimeters from hers. "Even in that big granny sweater you were wearing, with no makeup on, you were so fucking gorgeous."

"I've got to throw that sweater away," she murmured, lifting her head.

"You have no clue how beautiful you are," he said, and his expression was so earnest and so ordinary at the same time, like he was stating a fact and not just paying her a post-sex compliment. She felt the difference.

"I'm happy right now," she told him.

"You are? That makes me happy."

"I'm so used to feeling like . . . a widow."

"How does a widow feel? Aside from sad."

"Invisible."

"You're not invisible," he said. "Trust me."

She kissed him again and it felt like her head was coming loose, disconnecting from the rest of her body and floating up to his industrial ceiling.

"Will you stay the night?" he asked her.

"I have to call Hal."

"Ask him if you can sleep over."

She slid off the couch and went over to the kitchen to call Hal, feeling a little nervous. Her plan was to tell him she was going to spend the night at a hotel, that she was too tired to get a cab all the way back to Brooklyn, but he was having none of it.

"Jesus Christ, Arden."

"What?"

"You're with him, aren't you? You're with Joshua."

"We're celebrating. So what?"

"Don't sleep in the city," he pleaded. "Just come home."

"I'm fine, Dad. It's all good."

"This is a terrible idea, Arden. The two of you. He's your lawyer and you're in the middle of a major lawsuit. Besides, you're still grieving—"

"Stop. Please. I'm not a child." *It's too late for that anyway,* she was thinking.

"But you're acting like a child—"

"I'll see you tomorrow."

She hung up on him, but when she returned to the couch, she was very shaken. Hal had really upset her.

"You okay?" Joshua asked her.

"Hal is pissed."

"You're a grown woman."

"He thinks this is a very bad idea."

"Well," Joshua said. "It is."

And they both laughed.

From where she's sitting, it looks like the Statue of Liberty is waving at her. *Oh hi! That was quite a night you had last night. Wink, wink.* She imagines this little conversation with the statue, and it makes her chuckle to herself.

She feels genuinely alive for the first time in a long time. She still can't quite believe that she's the one who made the first move. She never makes the first move! Rarely makes any move, period. She's not even sure Joshua was planning to sleep with her when he invited her over. *She* was the one who leaned in and kissed him on the mouth. She was horny and she wanted him, figured she had nothing to lose. She was feeling so high and empowered off their win in court, she forgot to weigh all the pros and cons of sleeping with him, forgot to doubt herself and fear his rejection and ultimately talk herself out of it. She was just in the moment; she went for it. And now something has been awakened inside her; not just her sexuality—though definitely that, too—but a new confidence in herself. She wanted Joshua, she went after him, and it feels fucking exhilarating.

"Good morning," Joshua says, joining her in the kitchen. He's barechested, wearing only his sweatpants, which are hanging low on his hips. He kisses the back of her neck. "Do you want breakfast?"

"I really should get home," she says. "Hal is probably freaking out."

He twirls a strand of her hair around his finger. "Come to Rye with me today. It's my mother and Larry's twentieth anniversary."

"Rye?"

"Yes, Rye."

"Rye is near Denby, isn't it?"

"It is," he says. "But why would you go to Denby?"

"You know why."

"That's not a good idea."

"I just want to see his house."

"Arden, stay away from Jamie Ashforth. We don't want him any more pissed off than he already is."

"Obviously I'm not going to bang on his door and introduce myself. I just want to see the town my father is from, the house where my brother lives. I mean, if I'm going to be in Rye . . ."

"So you'll come with me?"

"If we can drive through Denby."

"All right, but I'm not letting you out of the car."

"You're sure your parents won't mind? Or think it's weird that I'm coming?"

"Absolutely not. I already told Mom you were in town for the hearing and that I have stuff to discuss with Larry."

"Do you?"

"I want to talk to him about Jane Knoppers."

"Okay, then."

"Great. I'll let my mom know I'm bringing a plus-one."

A *plus-one*. She lets herself love the sound of that.

22

Virginia settles back against her pillow and waits for the cannabis-infused gummy bear to kick in. Her doctor cut off her morphine supply a while back, but Hayley came to the rescue with an enormous jar of delicious orange, yellow, and green gummy bears, one hundred of them to "take the edge off" and help her sleep. It's not morphine, but it gets the job done. One sweet little bear and she stops giving a shit about everything and eventually drifts off to sleep.

Lately she's been remembering more details about the night of the assault, which is what she's calling it now. As the haze of morphine clears and her shock begins to dissipate, the memories are sharper, more in focus. What previously came as murky, surreal fragments are beginning to crystallize into irrefutable facts.

She remembers inviting Lou Geffen back to her place for a bite to eat and a "nightcap." They'd been at the coffee shop all afternoon, Lou doing most of the talking, and she was intrigued by him. He didn't have a socially appropriate filter and he came off as arrogant and tended toward condescension, but she was strangely captivated. After swimming in a dating pool of reverential septua- and octogenarians for so long, the confidence of Lou Geffen's fortysomething energy was exciting. So she invited him over. It was her idea. She made the move.

"A *nightcap*?" he repeated, laughing at her. "This isn't the seventies, Virginia."

They took an Uber, using her account because he didn't have one. "I refuse to support a company that bullies the local cabs, ignores basic rules and regulations of fair competition, and jacks or cuts their fares at their whim."

Virginia suggested they could take a regular taxi, but he said he was fine using her Uber account, since she didn't seem to have a problem with it. "I don't want to be difficult," he said.

When they got to her apartment, she offered him a glass of wine. She had a bottle of Merlot in the fridge and couldn't wait to pour herself a glass. Lou declined. "My enzymes don't metabolize alcohol."

"I see."

"Which means my body isn't able to efficiently eliminate the alcohol molecules."

"Well, I'm going to have a glass if you don't mind."

"Don't let me stop you."

She went into the kitchen, took out the bottle, poured herself a robust glass, and gulped most of it standing by the sink. She replenished her glass and then returned to the living room. Lou was nowhere to be found. She called out to him.

"In here!" he responded from her bedroom. She didn't know what to think about this. Part of her was excited—he was attractive and much younger than her—but even for Virginia it seemed forward.

She found him in her room, examining the framed photos of Tate, Arden, and the grandchildren, which were set up on her bureau. "Nice-looking family," he said. "Your daughters?"

"Yes."

"They're both hot," he commented, looking Virginia up and down. "You must have been something back in the day, eh?"

Virginia smiled awkwardly, unsure how to respond. He had a way of complimenting her with insults—or insulting her with compliments—that was confusing. Was he attracted to her or repulsed by her? She wasn't sure.

He stepped away from the bureau and moved toward her.

"Should we go into the living room?" she suggested, edging closer to the door. "We can order some food. Are you okay with Uber Eats or will that be a problem?"

"Your lips are purple," he said, touching them.

"Oh, the red wine—"

"It's in the lines above your lip," he said, sounding turned on. She was embarrassed and wiped her mouth.

"Don't be self-conscious," he whispered. "I told you, I like older women."

"Should we go into the living room?" she asked again.

"What for?" he said, kissing her. His tongue slipped inside her mouth like a hookworm. She was still holding her glass of wine. She was worried about her breath.

"Isn't this why I'm here?" he said, pulling away.

"It's just that I'm starving."

"I'll give you something to eat," he said, and grabbed his crotch.

She laughed nervously. "I thought we could continue getting to know each other over dinner—"

He snickered and took the wineglass from her hand. "There are plenty of ways we can get to know each other," he said, setting the glass down on her bedside table. "I want you, Virginia. Consider yourself lucky. How many women your age can say that?"

He kissed her again, hard. It was like being muzzled. His hand went to her right breast, at first over her pink sweater, squeezing it like an orange, and then he ripped open the cardigan and all the pretty pearl buttons went flying.

"Can we slow down?" She was starting to panic.

He ignored her and unfastened her bra. She just stood there, doing nothing. He was twice her size. "You should consider yourself lucky," he said, "that I can actually get it up with someone your age."

He was probably right.

"Impressive tits," he breathed, taking one of them in his mouth and sucking it until she cried out from the pain. "Did you have them done?"

"No."

"You're aging well, Virginia. A little too well, even."

"Can we stop for a minute?" she asked him, trying to make her voice sound calm. Inside, she felt anything but calm. Her heart was pounding, her pulse racing. She was suppressing a scream, and yet all she managed was "Can we stop for a minute?"

The incongruity of it was stunning, even as it was happening. Outwardly, she just stood there while he mauled and sucked her breasts, chewed on her nipples, pulled her head back by the hair. "This is a bit too rough for me," she told him when he started unzipping his jeans.

"Okay, sure," he said. "We'll slow it down."

She felt herself breathe again for a moment, but then he was pulling her toward the bed.

"Can we just go in the living room and order some food?"

"After."

He tugged her by the arm and they fell onto the mattress together, the full weight of him pressing down on her body. His fly was open and she could feel his hardness against her groin.

This is the part where, in the remembering, she wishes she had done something—*anything*. This is the moment for which she hates herself the most. *She let him.* When he slid her pants off her, she let him. When he shoved two fingers inside of her, she let him. When he said, "You old dry fucking cunt," she didn't respond. She just lay there and let him. She let him. She let him.

After a while, he stopped what he was doing and sat up abruptly and started fishing around his pockets for a condom. She rolled over to the other side of the bed, the side closest to the window, but he caught her arm and dragged her back.

"Lou, please—stop—"

Did she even say that out loud? She has no idea anymore. Maybe not. She said it to herself, that's for sure. She meant to say it out loud. Maybe she did. She realized then his name probably wasn't Lou, that she probably wasn't the first woman he'd done this to.

"You're the one who invited me up here," he said, releasing her arm to tear open the condom wrapper. "You've been flirting with me all day. Don't pretend you don't want this. I hate games."

While he was preoccupied with the wrapper, she crawled away from him again and got off the bed, ensnared in the duvet and top sheet, but now she was trapped between the bed and the window. She watched, transfixed, as he put on the condom. "Please don't," she said, in a voice so small and thin the words disappeared in the space between them.

Unperturbed, Lou Geffen stood up, wielding his hard-on like a sword. He was huge. Every part of him was huge and monstrous. His long teeth and chin, his towering frame, his weapon-like penis. He pushed Virginia against the wall without a word and the back of her head banged the window. She whimpered.

"Stop playing hard to get," he said, his words hot in her ear. "You can't do better than a guy like me, Virginia. Look at yourself." He pinched the loose, sagging skin beneath her arms, on her neck, across her lower abdomen—pointing out the spots she'd never been able to tone or firm up after sixty—and he said, "It's over for you, old woman. We both know you want this, so stop playing the victim."

Tears were burning her cheeks.

"Old bitch," he muttered.

She instinctively raised her knee to his balls with as much force as she could muster, which admittedly wasn't much. Still, he winced and bent over to catch his breath. When he stood back up and collected himself, she could see the rage in his eyes. Not just rage, but revulsion. *Old bitch.* She understood that he despised and desired her equally. She attempted to climb back onto the bed and scramble to the other side, but he caught her and lifted her off the ground, grabbing the sheet and duvet with her. Although he had probably meant to throw her onto the bed, he overshot it—or underestimated his own strength—and heaved her right over it. It happened so fast, perhaps it was only seconds before she crashed to the floor with the wineglass and the lamp from her bedside table, and yet when she replays it in her mind now, she imagines herself soaring through the air in slow motion, suspended above the bed like a bird.

Lou watched her land from the other side of the room, and for a moment she thought she might be able to escape. *Run, run!* But she couldn't move. The pain engulfed her, she thought she must be paralyzed. She wondered if she would ever walk again and then succumbed to blackness.

The next thing she remembers is he was fucking her on the floor, amid the shards of glass and spilled wine and her own blood. Her feet were tangled in the sheet. She was in and out of consciousness, one moment aware of her body on the ground, the brutality of what was happening, the incomprehensible pain shooting through her left side; the next moment, she was floating above the entire scene, staring down at Lou Geffen's back, at her own legs splayed out beneath him. In and out she went, in and out.

Is this dying? she wondered.

She never fought. She lay still as a corpse until he shuddered violently and cried out her name and collapsed on top of her, panting into the side of her face. Pinned beneath him, with his damp chest hair chafing her skin, she knew powerlessness in its most visceral, unvarnished form.

And still, it was her fault. *She* was the one who called herself Bangin'Boomer. *She* was the one who flirted with him over coffee (he was right about that). *She* invited him back to her place. *She* had considered it a triumph to have wrangled a man in his forties, some twenty years younger than her. *She* was the one who lay there and let him do whatever he wanted. *She* let him do it. *She* instigated the whole thing and then did nothing to stop it. *She. She, she.*

She closes her eyes, waiting for the self-hatred to ebb. Waiting for the flashbacks to diffuse into gentle waves of cannabis-steeped oblivion.

23

Arden and Joshua pull off 95 in Mamaroneck, not too far from Rye, to gas up and get water. Arden, who didn't eat breakfast again and is starving, grabs a couple of bags of chips, a handful of mini Cracker Barrel cheese squares, and two bottles of Perrier, and then waits outside in the sun, scrolling her Instagram feed. She's vaguely aware of how subpar the posts make her feel, but her finger just keeps swiping and swiping, past the stunning yogi in a spectacular Bound Side Crow pose, her golden abs glistening with sweat; past @*missredwinelover* posing on the beach at the Four Seasons Wailea, the wind whipping her hair and blowing her caftan up around her thighs; past the adorable puppy sleeping on a rumpled all-white bed, sunlight dappling the mise-en-scène. She's numb to the endless ticker tape of filtered perfection, and yet not numb enough that she can't feel the belly flop of self-esteem happening inside her. She wonders for the millionth time what this habit of scrolling Instagram has cost her daughter and an entire generation of young girls whose brains are like Silly Putty.

"Ready?"

She looks up from her phone to find Joshua standing by the driver's side of the car, waiting for her. He's wearing a banana-yellow Lacoste shirt with a popped collar, rolled-up navy Chinos, Topsiders, and no socks. This morning, when he emerged from his room dressed and ready to go, she laughed at him and said, "The *Preppy Handbook* called, they want their ensemble back."

"When in Rye," he responded, unfazed.

She's still wearing the same sundress from yesterday, but she feels pretty in it, and if Joshua doesn't mind it a second day in a row—he told her that when she said she had nothing to wear—neither does she.

Back in the car, Joshua rips open a bag of Doritos as he veers back onto the highway.

"Let me," she says, taking the chips away so he can concentrate on merging back into the traffic. She lowers the music—hip-hop, always hip-hop—and turns to face him.

"I feel like I cheated on Scott last night," she blurts.

"It's been almost two years."

"I enjoyed being with you. I'm not saying I didn't. It was great. I'm just feeling really guilty."

For a while Joshua is quiet, then he says, "I'm not sure what to say to that."

"Me neither," she says, and they leave it there.

Joshua takes a slight detour to downtown Rye, pointing out this and that—his former barber, the best ice cream in Westchester County, the Square House Museum, behind which he felt up a girl named Sarah Levy on a school trip. Arden realizes, as he's talking, that he wants to show her more of who he is. He wants her to know him better, and this realization makes her feel giddy and guilty and afraid all at the same time. This was supposed to be a one-night stand, nothing more. She wants it to be just that, and she doesn't.

"So, you basically grew up here," she says, looking out the window as they make their way along tree-dappled Purchase Street, past flapping American flags, a café boasting ORGANIC—LOCAL—ALL NATURAL, a handful of small boutiques, an oyster bar, a Starbucks on the corner with a soft-yellow facade.

"We moved here when I was fourteen," he says. "Larry and my mom bought a house and we moved in with him the year before they were married."

He points to a charming baby-blue Colonial that looks like a hotel and says, "This is Larry's office. I clerked here every summer during law school."

"It's strange," she says. "I know I've been here before—my mother used to take me with her when she had her meetings with him—but I don't remember any of this at all. At least not the outside."

"What do you remember?"

"The wood floor in his office. I would play jacks and they would get stuck in the cracks. I remember he had this gigantic wooden desk and a wall of books. It made me think he was important, like the president of the United States. I once told my mom that and she laughed. But I was bored a lot of the time." She turns to Joshua. "He used to give me these donuts as a treat, but then he'd get super annoyed at all the powdered sugar on the floor, and he'd make his secretary clean it up with a Dustbuster."

"Sounds like Larry."

"I remember he had a TV and a VCR in his office. There was no cable or anything, so one day I asked him if he had any videos I could watch. He put on *Jane Fonda's Workout.*"

"He always loved Jane Fonda."

"I didn't remember the town being this pretty."

Joshua's parents live in Rye Brook, which, Joshua explains to Arden, is a village in the township of Rye—not to be confused with the city of Rye—and very close to Port Chester, which has a fantastic food scene along the waterfront. Maybe, he suggests, they can go there after seeing his parents.

Arden looks at him and smiles, a tentative smile, which he immediately reads and says, "Or not. You'll probably want to get back to Brooklyn."

When they reach the end of Purchase Street, Joshua turns onto the Hutchinson River Parkway, a quiet stretch of road on which there are no other travelers, and then takes another turn onto a deep country road flanked by soaring trees.

"I didn't realize it was so rural," she says, lowering her window to let in the smell of summer air.

"It's more like rural suburbia."

Larry and Althea's house is on a woodsy cul-de-sac, with several acres of dazzling green lawn between it and the next property. The house itself is painted pale cream with a prominent circular porch and a turret, both made of stone. The turret is capped with an upside-down cone, a peculiar hybrid of medieval castle and traditional New England Colonial.

"Interesting architecture," Arden remarks as Joshua comes to a stop in the driveway.

"Mom loved the rocking-chair porch," he says, shrugging.

"I never would have pictured you living here as a kid."

"Why not?"

"You seem more urban to me."

"I was only here four years," he says. "Besides, I like to think I was already too old to be gentrified."

From inside the vestibule, Joshua calls out to his mother. When no one answers, he leads Arden through a very beige foyer, past the formal living/dining room with a lacquer table long enough to seat two dozen people, and into the kitchen, where a handful of caterers and waitstaff in crisp white shirts and black pants are bustling around in a well-choreographed dance of food preparation.

"Mary, I'm starving. What have you made me to eat?" Joshua says, wrapping his arms around a small Filipino woman pulling a tray of spring rolls out of the oven. Then, turning to Arden, he says, "Mary is the best chef in Westchester County."

Mary rolls her eyes and slaps Joshua's hand away from her spring rolls, but he manages to steal one anyway. "Your parents are outside," she tells him.

"Did you make me Malagkit for dessert?"

"Of course," she says. "I even made you extra to take home."

He kisses her cheek, and she says something in Tagalog, which makes him laugh, and then Joshua and Arden go outside through the sliding glass door. The backyard smells of barbecuing meat and fresh garlic, where another chef is grilling marinated shrimp and pork kebabs.

"How many people are coming?" Arden asks Joshua, looking around at at least a dozen rental tables set up on the expansive lawn.

"I don't know. Fifty?"

"Fifty?"

"In less than an hour, this yard will be a sea of white hair, Lilly Pulitzer dresses, and madras golf pants."

Larry and Althea are seated at a teak table underneath an enormous white umbrella by the pool, sipping lime-filled cocktails. Althea is wearing a very short tennis dress, showing off beautiful legs the color of a frappuccino. She has long, thick black hair, which is braided and hangs down to her lower back, and flawless sun-kissed skin. She could be Joshua's sister.

Spotting Joshua and Arden, she jumps to her feet and hugs them both, Joshua first and then Arden. "I'm so sorry for your loss, dear," she says, looking at her with big brown eyes. "Larry told me your husband passed."

"Thank you."

"And with three kids." She shakes her head, as people often do. "You're so young to be a widow."

"Mom—"

"It's fine," Arden says, touching Joshua's hand and then pulling hers away very quickly, too quickly for it to go unnoticed.

Larry gets to his feet, shakes Joshua's hand, lightly pecks Arden on the cheek. His few remaining strands of hair are shimmering blue-black in the sun, freshly dyed, like a spray-painted nest. The harsh August light is not kind on his face; nothing is camouflaged, despite his best attempts.

"I'm going to change," Althea says. "I just came from a tournament."

"Your mother is ranked twenty-eighth after today's win," Larry tells Joshua.

"That's just for women over sixty," Althea deflects. "I have too much time on my hands, obviously."

"That's really impressive," Arden says.

Larry throws an arm over Joshua's shoulder and says, "Let's go inside. I'll make you both a drink and then we can talk in my office."

Stopping in the kitchen, Larry lines up three tumblers on the counter and then ladles sangria from a glass punch bowl, making sure an orange slice lands in each glass. He hands one to Arden and she takes a sip, not really a fan of red wine, but it's delicious. Sweet and fruity, with almost no taste of alcohol.

Larry's office is masculine, opulent, slightly dated. The walls are burgundy, a little darker than the color of their sangria, with built-in bookcases and brass sconces on either side of them. A stately antique desk sits in front of wide bay windows that overlook a gully at the edge of their property, and two shiny, tufted brown leather club chairs face each other on a Persian rug of deep reds and greens. The desk, which is about the size of a standard dining table, is filled with framed photographs of him and Althea—on their wedding day, in their tennis whites, at Joshua's graduation, on various trips. There's also a banker's lamp perched over a leather-framed blotter, a fancy chess set, and a signed baseball sitting in what looks like a frosted glass soap dish.

"First, let me congratulate you on your win," Larry says, with a flash of his gleaming white crowns. He leans back against his desk and crosses one ankle over the other.

"Not a win yet," Joshua says.

"It's a major victory, son. Getting access to Bruce's DNA *postmortem*? It's a home run is what it is. It makes me wish I'd taken the case on contingency."

He winks at Joshua, and Arden is almost certain they have an arrangement in which Larry will be very well compensated for the referral.

"So, what's next?" he wants to know.

"Well, assuming Arden is a genetic match to Bruce, we have the kinship hearing to deal with."

Larry finishes his sangria in one gulp. "It's like drinking Kool-Aid," he says, picking up the orange slice with his fingers and sucking the alcohol out of it.

"Lar, why didn't you subpoena Jane Knoppers?" Joshua asks him, sitting down on one of the leather chairs and motioning for Arden to take the other one.

"Subpoena the maid? What for?"

"She was the nanny, and she was sleeping with Wallace at the same time as he was seeing Virginia. She *knew* about Virginia."

"I didn't think it added anything to our case."

"Seriously?"

"They would have skewered her, Josh. Painted her as a jealous, vindictive slut. She had no credibility in proving Virginia was Wallace's lover."

"She overheard Wallace's wife accusing him of sleeping with Virginia."

Larry looks surprised at this bit of information. "Son of a bitch," he mutters. "She never told me that. Still, there was nothing to gain. Ashforth's lawyer would have shredded her testimony. We didn't stand a chance in Westchester County, not in those days. It was a different world, totally stacked against a single mother of an illegitimate child. Virginia was the villain and nothing I did or said could change that. Jamie Ashforth and his lawyer knew it, and they capitalized on it."

"They're evil," Arden says.

"Nah. The Ashforths aren't evil." Larry waves a ringed hand in the air, holding court in that pompous, self-appreciative way of his. "I'm going to give you kids some free advice. The Ashforths are not the ones you need to worry about. They're just people. They're humans, like the rest of us. *Greed* is the true enemy."

He pauses a moment for effect, allowing his wisdom to hover importantly in the air. "Greed is what will destroy you in the end. Can't you already feel it taking hold of you?"

Arden shudders in spite of her irritation. Larry is watching her in a way that makes her feel as though she's been called into the principal's office.

"Arden is entitled to a share of her father's estate," Joshua says. "That doesn't make her greedy."

"Not yet."

Arden and Joshua look at each other; neither of them says anything.

"Listen, I did think of something," Larry says, brightening. "Ashforth had a personal assistant. I interviewed her years ago, but she'd signed an NDA and it was ironclad. She did his dirty work, but she was very loyal. I can email you her name. Maybe worth seeing if she's still alive? If she's willing to talk now?"

"Why would she?" Joshua says, reaching over to untwist the strap of Arden's dress. Arden looks up at Larry just as Joshua retracts his hand and clears his throat. Larry is watching them; there's something in his eyes—a knowing, some subtle perception. "Not to be crass," he says, ignoring whatever is going on between Arden and Joshua, "but you could bribe her."

"Bribe her? With what?"

"With your winnings."

"We're not doing that," Joshua says. "We won't need to bribe anyone when we have a positive DNA match."

"Better to be overprepared. Why not have more evidence than you think you need?"

Arden's phone buzzes from inside the pocket of her dress. She pulls it out and glances at the number. "I have to take this," she says. "It's my sister. She's watching my kids."

Arden gets up and steps out of the room. "Tate? Is everything okay?"

"Everything is fine now—"

"*Now?* What do you mean? What happened? Did Wyatt have an allergic reaction?"

"No, Wyatt's fine. It's—Ivey—"

"Ivey? What happened?"

"She's fine, Arden, really. Everything is all right; she just had a bit too much to drink last night."

"What do you mean?" Arden cries. "She doesn't drink. Where was she?"

"She was at her friend Nikki's house for a sleepover."

"You didn't tell me she was sleeping over at Nikki's!"

"I didn't think I needed to. I thought it was perfectly innocent."

"Where did they get the alcohol?"

"I guess they snuck it from the parents' liquor cabinet. The mom called me around eleven last night."

"And you're only telling me *now?*"

"Arden, calm down. I picked her up and brought her home and she puked and passed out. She's hungover but she's fine. I promised her I wouldn't tell you, and I didn't want to upset you after your win in court yesterday, but then I started feeling guilty."

Arden takes a breath. *So this is starting already.*

"She's a teenager, Arden. You had to know this was coming."

"Let me speak to her."

"She's asleep. Let her sleep it off."

"My flight is first thing in the morning. I should be home by eleven. Do not let her out of the house."

"This is perfectly normal, Arden. I was fourteen the first time I got pass-out drunk."

Arden can't remember her first time, but it feels to her like it was much, much later, maybe sixteen. *I'm not ready for this.*

"Is everything good over there?" Tate asks her. "Did you celebrate last night?"

"A little," Arden manages, racked afresh with guilt. She was fucking her lawyer while her baby girl was getting plastered. "I have to go," she says, feeling agitated. "I'll see you tomorrow."

She shoves her phone in her pocket and turns to go back inside Larry's office with a terrible feeling of dread pressing down on her. She stops

short when she hears Larry and Joshua arguing and instead hangs back
to eavesdrop.

"You have to stop," Larry is saying, not even bothering to whisper.
"I shouldn't have to spell this out, but you can't sleep with your clients,
Joshua."

Fuck.

"*You* did," Joshua says.

"It was a different world back then."

"You keep saying that, but it seems like a convenient excuse for a lot
of things."

"Times were different is what I'm saying."

"You slept with her goddamn *mother*!"

"And it was a fucking mess, Joshua."

She reaches for the wall to steady herself just as one of the caterers
passes by on her way to the powder room. "You all right, ma'am?"

Arden nods but doesn't manage to get any words out. Her face feels
like it's on fire.

"You know better," Larry is saying to Joshua, more softly now. "It's stupid
and shortsighted. I can't believe we're even having this conversation—"

Arden barges into the room then and Larry immediately shuts up
and smiles and Joshua says something inane about fishing. She looks
directly at Larry. "You and my mother were sleeping together?"

He doesn't respond.

"Of course you were," she says, furious.

"It was a long time ago, kiddo."

"You ruined her marriage."

"Arden, you can't be that naïve."

"Is that why you kept pushing her to keep going with the lawsuit?"

"*Pushing* her? You've got it all wrong. She was doing it for *you*. Your
rightful inheritance is what made her want to keep going. It's what made
us both keep going. The sex was—just—"

"Her way of paying you?"

"I'm sure the implication of that would hurt her deeply."

"That is the last thing I care about."

"We were together all the time, long hours, weekends. She was a
beautiful woman. It was inevitable." His eyes dart over to Joshua. "Surely

you can understand how an attraction can develop working so closely with someone?"

"My husband is dead!" she cries. "I'm not married to another man. Although, I will say"—and she turns to Joshua, who looks like a petrified animal in a trap—"this is quite a service the two of you are providing, preying on vulnerable women. Contingency, with sex on the side. Or maybe sex as payment."

"Virginia was not a vulnerable woman," Larry says, almost with a laugh. "And being married was not an issue for her. I'm sorry, it just wasn't. She felt their marriage was over."

"Did my father know?"

Larry is silent. She remembers how uncharacteristically hostile Hal was at the Chinese restaurant when they first met with Larry. It all makes sense now. *He's always known.*

"Arden, their marriage was already over."

"How can you possibly know that?"

"It was over for your mother."

No wonder Hal was so upset last night. He's probably reliving what Virginia did to him, and for that Arden feels truly horrible.

"Arden, I'm sorry you heard that," Joshua says, standing up and approaching her.

"So am I," she says, turning and fleeing the room.

She grabs her bag from the foyer console on her way out, aware of Joshua following her. "Leave me alone," she says, not even bothering to look at him.

Outside, on the front porch, he reaches for her arm and says, "Hang on a sec."

"*You knew,*" she cries. "You've known all along."

"It wasn't my place to tell you," he says. "It has nothing to do with me."

"I feel so stupid."

"Why?"

"Do you and Larry fuck all your clients? Is that how he mentored you?"

"Stop it."

She pulls her phone out of her pocket and slides over to the Uber app.

"What are you doing?"

She doesn't answer.

"Arden—"

"I'm leaving."

"You're taking an Uber back to Brooklyn?"

She has another plan.

"Arden, please. We won yesterday. We're celebrating. Things are good."

"Things are not good. I feel like an idiot."

"Why? Because we slept together? Or because your mother slept with Larry?"

"Yes."

"They have nothing to do with each other."

"It's humiliating. My mother and I are both such idiots. I never wanted to be like her." She's saying this more to herself. She's ashamed, embarrassed. Hal was right. Poor Hal. *Poor Hal!*

"So, now what?" he says, following her down the front steps.

"I'll call you when I get the DNA results."

Her phone vibrates. *Hector is on his way.*

"Arden, this is insane. You can't take an Uber to Brooklyn. It'll cost a fortune."

"I can afford it," she says. "I won, remember?"

"You're being ridiculous."

She doesn't respond.

"Please, let me take you home."

"Stay. Your mother wants you here. I'll be fine."

"Arden—"

"I'm taking an Uber. You can wait here with me if you want."

Joshua gives a dramatic sigh and shakes his head, but he eventually gives up and goes back inside the house, leaving her by herself to wait until her ride shows up.

Once in the car, Hector offers her a bottle of water, a mint. Asks her if she'd like to hear hip-hop, top forty, or classical music. "No, thank you," she says to all of it, and then turns away from the window.

It takes them about twenty minutes to get to Denby. To Arden's surprise, there are no gates to keep her out of the Ashforth property, just a winding, tree-lined road carved into the woods that eventually leads to a sprawling, cedar-shingle colonial at the top of the hill overlooking Long Island Sound.

"You live here?" Hector asks, gazing up at the absurdly grand estate.

"Oh no, no," she says. "I'm just visiting family."

He nods, impressed. She almost asks him if he'd be willing to wait for her and then drive her to Brooklyn, but on the outside chance Jamie Ashforth invites her in, she thanks him and gets out of the car with no plan as to how she's going to get back to the city.

Before going up to the front door, Arden slips off her mules and sneaks across the lawn, around to the side of the house. She continues past tennis courts and a fenced-in pool area with a cluster of canvas-curtained cabanas and a black marble waterfall flowing into a hot tub, and then she stops at an oversized glass window, through which she glimpses a palatial interior with soaring skylit ceilings and water views from every angle.

Peering inside the house, she has the strangest feeling of having been here before. Nothing specific, just an intuition that not only has she been here but that she's stared through this exact window.

This was my father's house.

She's suddenly certain that Virginia brought her here once, when she was very young, perhaps four or five, and they snuck around the grounds and looked inside, just like she's doing now; and although it's not a fully fleshed-out memory, she has a vague, dreamlike recollection of Virginia saying something like *Your father lived here before he died. One day, you'll live in a house just like this.*

There doesn't appear to be anyone home, which she should have figured would be the case on a Saturday in August. A family like the Ashforths would most likely be in the Hamptons or the Greek islands with all the other billionaires. Determined, Arden goes back around to the front of the house, puts her shoes on, and approaches the front door. On the assumption that no one will answer, she brazenly presses the bell and waits, feeling more confident than she probably should.

To her surprise, the door opens to a slight, bespectacled man with a shiny bald pate, gleaming in the sunlight like a polished marble floor.

Arden's mind races. *A half uncle she doesn't know about? A second cousin?*

"I'm Arden," she says, trying to sound composed. "Jamie's half sister. And you are—"

"I'm the house manager," he says with a whiff of attitude, scrutinizing her from behind his glasses. "The Ashforths are in Lyford Cay."

"I see," she says, disappointed. "Would you tell them—" She stops herself midsentence, reconsidering. "Never mind. Thank you."

"Mr. Ashforth is a good man," the house manager says sternly. "He's a philanthropist. He gives money to people who deserve it."

The door closes in her face, but not before she hears him mutter the word "parasite" under his breath. She stands there reeling. Her face is hot.

"Arden?"

She spins around to find Joshua leaning against his car, looking exactly as he had earlier today at the gas station. *Could that really have been only a few hours ago?* So much has happened since her victory in court yesterday, it feels like time has stretched into another dimension—she took the DNA test, slept with Joshua, found out her mother had had an affair with Larry Lasker, was berated by her half brother's *house manager*, and has to go home tomorrow to deal with her now officially teenage daughter, who got wasted for the first time last night.

"Need a ride?" Joshua says.

She didn't even hear him pull up, but she's relieved he's here and that she doesn't have to wait around for an Uber on the Ashforths' front lawn. She gets in his car without speaking. It's taking all her energy not to cry.

Joshua has the good sense not to speak. He starts the car and speeds off, and Arden has the feeling that the rude house manager is watching her from one of those massive picture windows. She doesn't turn around.

After a while, when they're back on the highway to Manhattan, Joshua says, "What, exactly, were you hoping to accomplish with that visit?"

"I have no idea."

"Who was that guy?"

"The house manager. He called me a parasite."

Joshua is quiet.

"I really just wanted to see where they live," Arden says. "But when I got there, I don't know, I just felt the compulsion to knock on the door."

"Did you think they'd invite you inside for lemonade?"

"I don't know what I thought. Obviously, I wasn't thinking." She opens her window to let in some air and says, "They're in Lyford Cay. Where is that?"

"The Bahamas. Probably a good thing he wasn't home."

"Did I fuck up?" she asks him.

"We may hear from Ashforth's lawyer. We'll get a warning."

"I'm sorry."

They drive in silence again. Arden is relieved not to have to talk about anything. It's been a wretched afternoon and she probably owes Joshua another apology for leaving his mother's house in a huff. It's not his fault Larry slept with her mother. She can hardly blame him for keeping that to himself either, but she doesn't want to reopen that conversation. Or any conversation.

Joshua turns on the radio and starts singing along softly with Kendrick Lamar. Arden rests her forehead against the glass window, which feels cool against her skin. She's starting to like his music.

24

Arden wakes up hours before her alarm goes off, after a restless sleep that was mostly disrupted by ruminations over Ivey and the results of the DNA test, which should be coming in today. It's Monday, five in the morning. She swings her legs out of bed and tiptoes to the bathroom, not wanting to wake Wyatt and Ali.

She turns on the shower and steps inside, relieved to have surrendered the battle of trying to sleep. The hot water rains down on her and feels resplendent. She shuts her eyes and succumbs to a sleepy trance, but it doesn't take long before the cycle of worrying starts up again, sabotaging her brief, meditative moment. *What if the DNA isn't a match? What if, after all the years of anguish, obsession, and heartbreak, Wallace Ashforth isn't even her father? Knowing Virginia, it could be any number of men from Toronto to New York.*

And then there's Ivey. They spoke yesterday when Arden got home. It was more of a one-sided conversation, Arden lecturing and raising her voice, welling up with tears. "What would your father think?" she said at one point, immediately regretting it. Ivey just stared back at her, stone-faced. She didn't say much at all.

"I just want you to make good choices," Arden said.

"I don't want to make good choices."

Well, then. Arden grounded her for two weeks and took away her phone. Ivey tried to stay stoic, but the loss of her phone triggered hysterical rage. *"I hate you! You're the worst mother! No one's parents take their kids' phones away! Daddy would never do this to me! You weren't even here! Everyone my age drinks!"*

Arden dumps a handful of shampoo into the palm of her hand, slathering it angrily into her scalp. She thinks about Scott, which makes her even angrier. *I wasn't supposed to be doing this on my own.* She's not sure if she's mad at him or at the universe or both. *Help me get through this.* Not even sure who she's praying to—Scott or the universe or both.

This, meaning everything. Ivey, her mother, the court case, the DNA results, Joshua. *Joshua.* She hasn't heard from him since he dropped her off at Hal's on Saturday. They had a terse parting, neither of them mentioning the night they spent together or Larry's bombshell about his affair with her mother. It was all just left hanging in the wind, unresolved, immutable. She hasn't spoken about it to Virginia either. After dealing with Ivey yesterday, Arden had nothing left in the tank for yet another unpleasant conversation.

She rinses her hair and some of the suds get in her eyes, stinging them to the point of tears. She swears under her breath, feeling defeated on all fronts, even by her shampoo.

Downstairs, she makes herself an espresso, gulps it in one shot, and then drops a slice of brioche bread into the toaster. When it pops, she butters it, sits down at the table, and stares at it, unable to eat. The caffeine has made her even more jittery, along with the dread that was already brewing.

She passes the next few hours on her phone, in the usual soul-sucking rabbit hole of Instagram, Twitter, and panic-inducing headlines. At eight, glazed from all her scrolling, she decides to bring breakfast upstairs to Ivey. She's troubled by the way they left things and now feels the urge to make it right. She can't stand the unbearable discomfort of her children's pain and suffering, which inevitably compels her to fix it swiftly and at all costs. Their unhappiness, big or small, is something she simply can't sit with for any amount of time. She can't remember if it's always been like this or if it's worse since Scott died.

She fills a tray with peanut butter on toast, a sliced orange, and a mug of hot chocolate and goes upstairs to make peace with her eldest daughter. She can hear the twins in her room, already up and on their tablets. She knocks softly on Ivey's door and then carefully opens it. Ivey is asleep on her stomach, diagonal across the bed, with Stinky, the stuffed bunny she's had since birth, nestled under her nose. With her adolescent body hidden under the duvet and her messy hair fanned out around her, she could be the same toddler of a decade ago. Even the way she still presses Stinky's long, dirty ear to her nostrils hasn't changed. If only she could stay sleeping, Arden thinks.

She sets the tray down on the nightstand and gently touches Ivey's shoulder. "Good morning, darling," she whispers.

Ivey doesn't stir. Arden sits down next to her on the edge of the bed and strokes her hair, the way she used to when Ivey was little. "Iveeeeeee," she coos. "Time to wake up. You start camp today."

Back in January, when Ivey was slightly more open-minded and less defiant, she agreed to let Arden sign her up for a weeklong creative arts camp in August. Now that it's here, she hasn't stopped complaining about it. She doesn't want to ride the bus with the little kids; she doesn't want her days to be so "structured"; she doesn't even like art; she doesn't know anyone who's going; none of her friends go to day camp—they all go to sleepaway camp for the entire summer.

"Ives?"

Ivey lets out a soft moan and rolls to the other side of the bed. Arden lies down and snuggles up to her under the duvet. Her body is warm. The back of her hair is a nest of snarls, which Arden gently untangles. "Time for camp," she whispers.

"No."

"It'll be fun," Arden lies. "Keep an open mind."

"You're ruining my summer."

"What if you love it? What if you make new friends?"

"I have enough friends."

"Well, you're registered, and it's paid for, and you agreed to go months ago."

"I've changed my mind."

"It doesn't work that way," Arden says, rubbing Ivey's back. "Come on, my love. I brought you breakfast in bed."

Ivey turns and looks at Arden over her shoulder. "Hot chocolate?"

"And brioche toast."

Ivey sits up and stretches. She inhales a deep whiff of Stinky's ear. "Thank you, Mama," she says, and Arden marvels at how she can weave back and forth between sweet little girl and raging hormonal witch in the span of a single breath.

Ivey holds out her arms to take the tray, and as Arden is laying it on her lap, she notices something on Ivey's left arm. "Ivey, what is that?" she says, pointing to a dark welt on her daughter's pale skin.

Ivey glances at the wound, which is blistering. "I burned it on the stove."

"Your *upper* arm? How the hell did you manage that?"

Ivey nibbles on her toast and doesn't answer.

"You had that other burn a couple of months ago," Arden says, her tone turning accusatory, panicked. "You said you burned it making cookies?"

"I'm a spaz."

"I don't understand how you could have burned yourself up here on your bicep!" she says, reaching for Ivey's arm to inspect it. Ivey jerks it away.

"Let me see it."

"Leave me alone."

Arden feels like she's being sucked into a black hole. Something doesn't add up. She gets out of the bed and rips off the duvet off, exposing Ivey's bare legs.

"Stop it!" Ivey shrieks.

Arden gasps.

"Get out of my room!"

"What are you doing to yourself, Ivey?"

There are at least half a dozen burn marks up and down her skinny legs, all in different stages of healing. Some are fresh and raw, others faded to varying degrees. The biggest one is the size of a quarter; the smallest no bigger than a cigarette tip. "How long have you been doing this?"

"Get out of my room!"

"Ivey, please. You're scaring me—"

Ivey rolls her eyes. "You're so dramatic."

Arden springs for the bedside table before Ivey can stop her and pulls open the drawer, where two Bic lighters are rolling around amid the packs of gum, stickers, hair elastics, barrettes, lip gloss.

"Those are for my candles!" Ivey screams.

"Bullshit!"

"Get out!"

"Ivey, how could you do this to your beautiful body? Is this why you're always in sweatpants? You've been hiding your legs? How long have you been doing this?"

Ivey's expression changes from defiance to rage, and before Arden can stop her, she throws the breakfast tray across her room. The ceramic mug shatters, spilling hot chocolate everywhere, spreading slowly into Ivey's clothes, which are in heaps all over the floor. Miraculously, the plate spins like a top but doesn't break. The toast flies off and lands under the bed. Arden watches, frozen, as though it's all happening in slow motion. She turns back to Ivey. The look on Ivey's face frightens her. It's not just the depth of anger in her eyes, but the audacity of her rebellion. Unlike Arden, there is no fear in Ivey's face, not in her cold stare, not in the impudent smirk on her face.

Arden grabs the two lighters—Ivey laughs at this pathetic gesture—and she rushes out of the room, too traumatized to tell Ivey to clean up the mess. She pokes her head into her room and is relieved to find the twins unfazed in her bed, headphones on, transfixed by their devices.

Downstairs, she throws the lighters in the trash and then takes the trash out to the garage. Her instinct is to get in her car and drive. Anywhere. Away from here, away from what Ivey has become, just to regroup. Instead, she starts walking, first around the block and then down to the park at Cheltenham and Mildenhall. *Breathe, breathe.* She knows she's got to get the twins ready for camp, but she doesn't feel stable enough to go back home. She circles the small park a couple of times, watching as a young mother reads to her pigtailed toddler on the grass. *Oh, those days!* What Arden wouldn't give to trade places with her.

When did the self-harm start? she wonders. How did she miss it? She's been too damn self-absorbed, just like her own mother was when Arden was a teenager. The lawsuit, the infatuation with Joshua, taking care of Virginia. Ivey's been hurting herself for months right under her nose and Arden didn't have a goddamn clue. Now she's drinking. What's next? *Meth?* This is where her mind takes her.

The morning sun is already hot on the back of her neck. She savors the warmth. They're calling for temperatures in the high nineties, a heat warning. She realizes she's still wearing what she slept in last night—Scott's old boxer shorts and a Raptors T-shirt—with Ivey's rubber slides. She wishes she'd thrown on a baseball cap to hide from the world, and just as she has that thought, one of the school moms out walking her dog calls to her from across the street. "Morning, Arden!"

"Morning, Sheila!"

"It's going to be a scorcher today!"

"I'm already feeling it!"

"Stay cool!"

"You too!"

Arden checks the time and reluctantly heads back in the direction of home to attend to the twins. Their bus will be here in twenty minutes. She keeps her head down as she climbs the gently sloped hill, her heels thwapping against the slides, a cyclone of emotions swirling inside her, mostly anger. And then she realizes, in an unwanted moment of clarity, that her anger, which has become more acute and consuming lately, *is* toward Scott. The universe is too intangible a concept to blame; it cannot be the container for her pain and rage. Had Scott taken better care of himself, *had he listened to her*, had he put his family before his status and fortune-seeking, he would be here with her now. Ivey wouldn't be acting out; they'd be the semihappy and mostly normal family they'd always been. *If, if, if.*

She doesn't even notice the sprinkler on her neighbor's lawn, which douses her in a gentle wave of water as she passes by, dampening her clothes and hair. She glances up, jarred back into the world. She wipes her face. The water feels good in the heat, a slight reprieve from the humidity, which is already heavier than it was when she left the house. She can feel her body working harder to breathe, harder to move.

Stay cool! It's going to be a scorcher!

The ridiculous things people say to one another. This is what she's thinking as she approaches her house, but then the moment she turns up her front walk, she remembers. *Ivey.* The blistering burns all over her body. *What the hell do you do about a teenage girl over whom you've lost total control?* She's never felt so powerless.

She lets herself inside the house and the first thing she hears is laughter from the kitchen. She finds all three kids at the table, dressed in their camp T-shirts, eating breakfast. Ivey is pouring milk into her cereal bowl. She's wearing mascara and lip gloss, her thick hair in a loose bun on top of her head. She doesn't make eye contact with Arden, but her missive is clear. She's not only going to camp, but she also got the twins ready in Arden's absence. Arden understands these to be conciliatory acts. *Ivey still cares.* She hasn't gone completely off the rails yet. She has enough respect for Arden to have made the decision to stay inside some invisible but clearly demarcated boundary. Arden doesn't say anything. For today, at least, she'll settle for a truce.

"Where were you, Mom?" Wyatt asks her.

"How come you're wet?" Ali wants to know.

"I was hot, so I went under the Footes' sprinkler."

"That's weird."

"Did you brush your teeth?" Arden asks them.

"No," they answer at the same time, and then there's a knock at the door and it's the camp counselor, letting them know the bus is waiting for them.

As soon as the kids are gone, she pops an English muffin in the toaster for Virginia and puts on a pot of coffee. Virginia won't drink espresso; it has to be regular coffee, with the filters and the percolating, which annoys Arden a little more than usual this morning. When everything is ready—light raspberry jam on the muffin, black coffee, meds—Arden carries it to her room on a tray.

"Morning, Mom."

"Morning, darling." Virginia sits up with a little less effort than usual. Maybe she's finally starting to improve. She made almost zero progress the first couple of months after the accident, mostly due to stubbornness, depression, and lack of effort, but since she started attending those seniors' meetings, her mobility seems to have turned a corner. She still insists that Arden bring her breakfast—she's especially stiff and sore in the mornings—and since Arden is already used to making breakfast for the kids, one more mouth is no real bother.

Arden sets the tray down, her second service of the morning. Virginia looks up at her and smiles. Her teeth are a little yellow from neglect and there's a plate-sized disc of gray hair on her head from where her roots have grown in. She looks older. She looks her age for the first time in her life. Virginia doesn't mention any disturbing noises, so she must have slept through Ivey's fit. *Thank you, edible marijuana gummies*, Arden thinks.

"Is this the Bonne Maman jam?" she asks Arden.

"It's Smucker's. We ran out of the fancy one."

Virginia looks disappointed. She bites into her English muffin and makes little smacking noises as she chews.

"You had an affair with Larry Lasker," Arden blurts, standing over Virginia with her arms folded across her chest. "*While* you were still with Hal."

Virginia stops chewing. There's a smudge of jam in the corner of her mouth. She doesn't look at Arden; she doesn't move at all.

"You cheated on him and that's why your marriage ended."

"It was already over," Virginia says softly.

"I doubt Hal would agree."

"You don't know anything about that time, Arden."

"You cheated on the only father I ever had, the only man in my life who was solid and safe and good to us."

"Arden, it's not that simple."

"It was the only stability we ever knew," Arden continues, not ready to stand down. "You never cared about stability, though. It bored you. Hal was kind to you, and he loved you so much, and we finally had some security for a change, but you couldn't stand being a housewife, could you?"

"You don't know what you're talking about," Virginia says. "It was the inheritance that destroyed our relationship, and I did that for *you*, Arden."

"Why did you sleep with Lasker?"

"I only ever wanted a stable family for you girls," Virginia says. "I wanted the little house and the backyard and the husband—"

"But you threw it away! *Why?*"

"Did you tell Hal that you know?" Virginia asks her.

"No. What would be the point?"

Virginia pushes the tray off her lap, sliding it down the length of the bed.

"You need to eat, Mom."

"Please leave me alone, Arden. I'm not up to this right now."

"Neither am I," she says, holding back what happened with Ivey. No grandmother should ever have to know something like that about her precious grandchild. She would never understand it. Arden doesn't even understand it.

"I'm sorry you found out," Virginia says. "Was it Joshua who told you?"

"I overheard them talking. We were at Larry's."

"You were at Larry's? In Rye?"

"It was his wedding anniversary. Joshua invited me."

Virginia looks up at her then, a flash of recognition in her eyes, a kind of maternal leeriness. She says nothing, but in her face Arden can see she knows, or at least suspects, something has transpired between Joshua and Arden. She has an intimacy radar, Virginia does. A deep intuition about all matters sexual. Or maybe Arden is just being paranoid. Regardless, she senses the subtlest whiff of a power shift.

"Eat your breakfast," Arden says, softening.

"I don't want it. Just take it."

"What about your exercises?"

"Later."

Arden lingers there a moment, feeling bad now for having bullied Virginia and taken all her rage and frustration over Ivey out on her. She really is still so frail. Arden could have waited to confront her.

"Just so you know," Virginia says, "Hal and I are good. Our marriage really was over and the decision was mutual. I'm not saying my affair with Larry didn't hurt him; it did. And I regretted it deeply. But I made my amends, and he forgave me, and we'll always love each other, just more like a brother and sister, which was really the problem all along."

Arden sighs, a full-body sigh from the depth of her diaphragm. "I didn't mean to attack you like that—just—"

"I know. It's okay."

"Should I leave the tray?"

Virginia reaches for the coffee and meds, which Arden has meticulously distributed into separate compartments of a plastic ice cube tray. "I'll just have the coffee," Virginia says, wrapping her bony fingers around the handle of the mug. Arden notices her mother's hand is trembling, which makes Arden feel even worse.

"Mom, did you ever take me to Denby when I was little?"

Virginia sits up a little. "I did," she says. "I wondered if you remembered. You were about five, I think."

"We crept around the grounds and looked inside, right?"

"We did. Jamie was already living there at that point."

"I went there when I was in Rye."

"And?"

"It's pretty spectacular," Arden says. "No one was home except their house manager. He called me a parasite."

"Parasite," Virginia snorts. "You're Wallace's fucking daughter."

"It kind of made me angry, seeing that mansion, the estate. Compared to how we grew up?"

"Now you understand what I was fighting for."

Arden carries the tray back to the kitchen and dumps it on the counter without bothering to clean up. She settles herself at the table, where her laptop is already set up, types "self-harm," and watches, stunned, as a seemingly endless stream of links pop up on the screen. She clicks one of the articles called "Understanding Why Girls Self-Harm" and immediately wishes she'd opted to bury her head and bank on Ivey outgrowing this, the way she outgrew thumb-sucking and nail-biting. As she reads, she starts to feel a pulsating pain behind her eyes and has to stop midway through the article to get up and swallow two aspirin. She washes them down with a glass of warm tap water, standing at the sink and staring out the window at the pale blue sky, which is full of tiny white clouds that look like suds. She wonders, not that it matters now, if she should have put Ivey in therapy right after Scott died. Virginia and Tate thought she was too young and that Arden should wait and see how things went, but maybe they've missed the window. Maybe the time for counseling was while her grief was still raw, while she was still more innocent, a preemptive strike against future behaviors like self-harm, rather than a reactionary measure.

Arden pulls herself away from the window and returns to the table. She resumes reading, descending quickly into self-blame. Words and phrases—*perfectionism, low self-esteem, lonely, impulsive, anxious, unhealthy risk-taker*—leap off the screen, piercing her maternal heart. Before she ever had children, she vowed she would raise daughters with high self-esteem. She once believed it was possible to have control over how your kids turned out. What a farce. What an egregious lack of humility. She types "treatment for self-harm" and this, at least, feels a little more proactive and solution-oriented, even though the very first sentence is literally a personal attack: *Never, ever say to your child, "How could you do that to yourself?"*

She spends far too long at the table, alternately reading depressing articles that make her want to curl into a ball for the next ten years, scrolling social media, and letting her mind drift off into distracting little fantasies in which, having finally won her inheritance, she's staying at the George V hotel in Paris with Joshua in a suite overlooking the Eiffel Tower. Her stomach is rumbling, reminding her she hasn't eaten anything today, but she still can't eat.

When an email notification pops up in the upper right corner of her screen, interrupting her reverie, her heart seizes. It's from the lab. Without opening it, she jumps up and starts pacing around the kitchen. *This is it. This is it. Please, let me be an Ashforth.*

"Arden?!"

Her mother yelling from the other room.

"*Arden?* Would you mind bringing me an iced tea with lemon? I'm so hot!"

Arden hesitates, staring at the unopened email. "Come and get it, Mom! You should be moving more! You need to be up and about!"

Silence.

Arden hunches over her laptop and opens the email attachment. She quickly scans the numbers in search of the one Joshua told her to look for, the one that makes or breaks her case. Her breath feels suspended in her body, trapped somewhere between her throat and her lungs. She's gripping the ledge of the table. She can feel her heart beating, uneven, fast, reverberating like a heavy bass inside her chest. And then she sees it in bold, the relevant number, the only thing that matters anymore.

"Some nurse," her mother mutters, shuffling up behind her.

Arden spins around. Virginia is leaning on her walker, looking sweaty and put out. Her gray-blond hair is damp against her forehead, which is heavily lined lately, probably due to the prolonged absence of the regular Botox injections she claims she's never had.

"I just got the DNA results," Arden murmurs, so feebly she's not even sure she said the words out loud. "Look."

"I don't need to see them," Virginia says, pushing her chin out. "I already know."

25

In some ways, the real miracle is not so much that she knows she's an Ashforth now, but the way the news has brought her family together over the last few days. There's been a levity around the house that hasn't been there in a very long time. Where before there was a general sense of dread and impending doom in the air, the past few days have been infused with hope and optimism, as though things may just work out for them after all. It's not just about the money; it's more a reminder that maybe life isn't supposed to suck all the time. Maybe they're supposed to have some happiness and good fortune in equal measure to the shit. Even the children understand that those DNA results could mean an easier life for them, a better, brighter future.

That night, they celebrated. Even Virginia was happy and relaxed. She drank champagne and giggled like her old self, as though she'd finally done something right. The assault, Ivey's burns, their collective grief, all of it felt somewhat diffused by their relief and excitement. What did it really mean? Were they millionaires now? the kids wanted to know. "I think we probably will be soon," Arden said, daring to say it out loud, to make the declaration. Why shouldn't she? She's a goddamn Ashforth.

"Can we go to Hawaii again?" Ivey wanted to know. "Can I get a real camera? And a new phone?"

"You can go to college, how about that?" Arden said, laughing. She'd also decided, though she didn't say it out loud, that she was going to find Ivey the very best therapist in Toronto and fix her. That's what money can do for people, not just pay for vacations and Apple products and houses.

Tate went out and bought champagne. Not prosecco, but Veuve Clicquot. They made tacos and blasted music. When the champagne was finished, Arden and Tate polished off two more bottles of wine, ending the night with a dance party in the den. The kids danced until they were sweaty and limp, and then eventually fell asleep on the couch with Virginia, who'd been snoring since her last glass of bubbly. Arden snuck away to call Joshua while Ivey and Tate were still lip-syncing to Dua Lipa.

She'd texted him earlier. **98.4% match.** That's all she wrote. He called her within seconds, but Tate and Virginia and the kids had joined her in the kitchen at that point and they were all screaming and clamoring around her. She told him she'd call him back. They still haven't really spoken since they slept together. Their final conversation was the one in which she accused him of lying to her about Larry and Virginia and sexually preying on her. They've got a long road ahead with the inheritance case, so it's in their best interest to pretend it never happened and move forward as professionally as possible, which is too bad. The sex was fun, the flirtation even more so. They have chemistry, which makes walking away from their fling a little heartbreaking.

Joshua picked up after the first ring. "Congratulations, Ms. Ashforth-Moore."

"That has a good ring to it," she said, slurring just a little.

"Bruce is your half brother."

"It's official."

"How does it feel to finally have irrefutable proof?"

"Validating."

"I'll bet."

"What's next?" she asked him, wishing he were here with her. Or she were there with him. "When can I see you again?" It was the alcohol speaking. After she said it, she was partly relieved, partly mortified.

"We present the results at the kinship hearing, among other things, which I'm working on. But we can talk about that when you're sober."

"I'm sober-*ish*," she said, giggling.

"I'm glad you're celebrating. You deserve it."

"Are we going to talk about what happened?"

"Which event are you referring to?"

"All of them," she said. "Sleeping together, my mother and Larry's affair, my ill-conceived visit to Denby."

"Arden, I owe you an apology. Multiple apologies. I want you to know I take full responsibility. We should never have slept together. It was poor judgment on my part."

"On *both* our parts," she said, annoyed. "I'm not the victim here. You didn't seduce me."

"No, I guess not."

Arden felt herself deflating like a punctured raft. Not that she didn't agree with him, but she wanted to keep doing the wrong thing for as long as it felt good. Turns out he's the one with more pragmatism and self-restraint.

"As long as we're on the same page," he said. He did not address what happened in Denby.

Arden could hear the music blaring from the other room and suddenly all she wanted was to be with her family, enjoying the first good news they've had in far too long. She agreed to a FaceTime meeting with Joshua next week and then she hung up and went back to the den, where Tate and Ivey were still partying. Tate was holding two El Paso taco shells in either hand, nibbling one and using the other one as a microphone.

"You're eating gluten!" Arden cried.

"Who fucking cares?" Tate shouted. "We're going to be rich!"

Ivey held out her hands for Arden to join them and Arden went to them and let them swallow her into their little circle, and they swayed and held on to each other and laughed, and Arden forgot about everything else, including Joshua, and she was happy.

She's rehashing that conversation with Joshua in her mind as she turns onto Pottery Road, half listening to Ivey sing along to AJR. She can't even remember the last time Ivey wanted to go for a drive with her. She was floored when Ivey suggested they head down to Leslieville for a coffee. "Just me and you?" Arden said, trying not to sound as astonished and desperately grateful as she felt.

"Yeah. We can walk around Queen Street."

Arden did not need convincing. She didn't want to whitewash the severity of Ivey's problems, but the offer to spend time together felt to her like a peace offering, possibly even a signal that the worst was behind them. Every day she scans Ivey's flesh for new burn marks. Apart from the old ones, which are healing to a soft, faded purple, there's nothing new. She's wearing shorts today. She's been going to camp. She wanted to go for a drive with Arden. Maybe it's over.

Arden finds a spot right in front of their favorite coffee shop. The tables outside are filled with young families, parked strollers, toddlers running around. She remembers when this part of town was seedy and impoverished, and it wasn't that long ago either. Now it's about as gentrified and exclusive as North Toronto. "Can we get croissants at Bonjour Brioche?" Ivey asks her, stepping onto the sidewalk one lanky heron's leg at a time.

"Of course. We'll bring a box of them home."

Inside, Arden orders two iced lattes, one decaf for Ivey. Ivey rolls her eyes and mutters something about needing the caffeine today. "It's not like it's a drug," she complains.

"It certainly is," Arden says, thinking about the stunning migraines she gets when she skips her daily dose. "You're not even fourteen yet."

"Arden?"

Arden turns around. "Adam, hey! How are you?"

Adam Power was one of Scott's colleagues. They were decent friends, not super close; they went to the pub next door to work every Tuesday night with a few of the other brokers, but that was the extent of it. She hasn't seen or heard from Adam since the funeral, but she doesn't take it personally. Scott wasn't a very committed friend. He always said that between his family and his job, he didn't have time for a social life.

Adam hasn't changed much in two years. He's got a flat-top army buzz cut, he's buff and fit, with an upside-down triangle for a torso, and he's impeccably dressed. Scott used to say Adam had the stockbroker gene in his DNA, right down to his last name.

"You must be Ivory," Adam says, flashing a nervous smile. His left front tooth is a shade grayer than the rest, probably an old crown.

"*Ivey*," she corrects.

"Sorry, Ivey. My bad."

Adam orders his coffee and then they all shuffle to the other end of the bar to wait.

"How are you guys doing?" he asks Arden.

"We're managing," she says, never quite sure how much to divulge about her life. Adam doesn't really want her to be honest and share how hard it's been, how lonely she gets, how in debt they are. He wants to know she's moving on, dating again, finding happiness in her second chapter. No one wants to be made aware of how fragile their happiness is.

"Did you guys ever meet with Molly about your inheritance?" he asks her.

"Sorry, who?"

"Molly Goldman? She's married to an old college buddy of mine. Scott mentioned your situation before he died, and then . . ."

"My situation?"

"With your father's inheritance. Molly's an estate lawyer in Buffalo."

"Scott talked to you about that?"

"I just assumed you knew. He said you guys had an opportunity to inherit but that it was super complicated. I gave him Molly's name—"

"When?"

"Oh, geez. It must have been a couple of months before he died. Late spring? We were at the pub. I remember I had just gotten back from Florida. We have a time-share on Sanibel Island; we go every Memorial Day."

"What did Scott tell you, exactly?"

"Uh, well, he'd had a lot to drink. He was his usual stressed self and I asked him what was up. I mean, I knew he was having some cash-flow problems—"

Cash-flow problems? Was that how Scott had euphemized the titanic debt he'd accrued? Arden feels a slash of rage lacerate her good mood, but she bites her tongue.

"Eventually, he started talking," Adam continues. "He told me your father was some New York millionaire and that your mother had been suing for your share of the inheritance since, like, the eighties. He said there was some new law or loophole—or maybe someone had recently died? Your uncle or something? Anyway, he thought there might be an opening to try again and that's when I suggested he reach out to Molly."

"And that was in the spring before he died?"

"Pretty sure. I'm sorry if I've upset you, Arden."

"Oh no, no." She looks at Ivey, who's watching her carefully, and she makes herself smile. "Not at all. I'm just curious because he never mentioned a Molly to me."

"I guess he never got around to calling her. I'm not in touch with them much, other than sporadically on Facebook. I didn't follow up or anything."

"Molly Goldman is her name?"

"Yeah, last I heard she was practicing in Buffalo, but they also have a place in Gravenhurst—"

"Gravenhurst?" Arden's mind is racing. Gravenhurst is in Muskoka, about a half-hour drive from Port Carling, where Scott had his last lunch at Turtle Jack's.

Adam grabs his coffee and says, "It was good to see you, Arden. And Ivory."

"Ivey."

"Ivey. Sorry. You look well, Arden. Take care."

They watch him bumble out of the coffee shop and fling himself into the crowd on Queen Street, quickly disappearing.

"What was that about?" Ivey says.

"I have no idea."

"Dad knew about the inheritance before you did?"

Arden shakes her head, agitated. "It's news to me."

Arden speeds home along the Bayview Extension, stewing. She just wants to get back to her laptop. If it hadn't been for Ivey, she would have Googled Molly Goldman on her phone at the coffee shop, but Ivey was watching her like a hawk. After their coffees, Ivey still wanted to pick up those croissants at Bonjour Brioche and then stroll along Queen Street, not the least bit perturbed about Adam Power's bombshell. Arden, grateful for any shreds of time Ivey was willing to spend in her company, gritted her teeth and went along.

Once home, Arden settles in her office and searches Molly Goldman Estate Law Buffalo. In a matter of seconds, there she is, smiling confidently in her LinkedIn profile, her long blond hair cascading over her shoulders. *The mystery blonde from Turtle Jack's.*

Arden stares at her screen, not sure how to feel about Molly Goldman. She's very pretty, midthirties, wearing sexy power glasses. *Scott, what the hell were you up to?*

And then she remembers something. She starts ransacking her desk until she finds the envelope from Laird Storage buried in the top-right drawer, long forgotten in the pile of mail she's been neglecting for months.

She rips it open, stunned to find an invoice dated March 1, 2018, for rent on a storage unit in Scott's name. It doesn't make any sense. *An invoice dated a year and a half after his death?*

Here's what Arden missed at the time the bill arrived: *they've never had a storage unit!* It never even occurred to her until now to probe any further. She just put the envelope aside with the rest of her neglected mail and didn't think twice about the address on the upper-left corner. She still has no idea how it all connects to Molly Goldman, other than the unifying theme of Scott's deception.

26

Arden gusts into Virginia's room with her usual purposeful demeanor. "I need you to come somewhere with me," she says, dragging the walker over to the bed with her.

"Good morning to you too."

"Something's going on and I have to get to the bottom of it and Tate's at work and I don't want to go alone."

"Arden, take a breath."

Arden does not take a breath. "We have to go now while the kids are at camp."

"Go where?"

"Laird Storage."

"Why?"

"I'll explain everything in the car. Can you just get dressed? How long do you need?"

"At least an hour."

"You don't need an hour to get dressed. Don't worry about your makeup and hair. Just put on this sweatsuit." Arden grabs a pale-pink sweatsuit draped over the upholstered rocking chair in the corner and tosses it at Virginia.

"Am I allowed to brush my teeth?" Virginia says, slowly swinging her legs over the bed. Mornings are the worst. Hayley says she may feel stiff for the rest of her life if she doesn't put more effort into her physio.

"Just hurry," Arden says impatiently. "I'll make you a coffee and some toast to take with you."

"I have to eat in the car?"

Arden doesn't answer. Virginia slides off the bed and starts pulling her sweatpants on one leg at a time. It feels like she's been here forever, living in her daughter's guest room like an invalid. No money for her own place, no desire to return to work and sell shoes again, no motivation one way or another. The elder abuse group helps. She likes the people; they're kind and supportive. When she's having coffee with Bonnie, Jean, and Lois after a meeting, she feels more like her old self, sparks of the old Virginia spunk and optimism reawakening. It never lasts, though. The moment she gets back to Arden's, all her energy and enthusiasm seep away, leaving just an apathetic husk in the bed. She can't stand this version of herself—the invalid, the victim, the burden. She worries that if she doesn't start to improve soon—physically and mentally—her family's going to put her through an intervention.

"*Mommmm?!*" Arden shouts from the kitchen. "Let's go!"

Virginia puts on the sweatshirt and doesn't bother to brush her teeth or comb her hair. Who cares? She won't get out of the car.

"What's going on?" she asks Arden as they're pulling out of the driveway. She's got a piece of dry toast wrapped in tinfoil in one hand, and a reusable cup of black coffee in the other. Arden didn't even bother to add milk.

"Scott had a storage unit."

"So?"

"I didn't know about it," Arden says. "He kept it from me."

"Are you sure he deliberately kept it from you, or maybe he just didn't think it was something he had to share with you? It's just a storage unit."

"That's not how our marriage worked," Arden says, gratingly self-righteous. "He would have mentioned it. Besides, why would he even need a storage unit? We have a basement *and* a garage. It's because he didn't want me to know what was in it."

"What could possibly be in it that he wanted to keep from you?"

"That's what we're about to find out."

"Maybe you're blowing this out of proportion."

"There's more," Arden says. "I'm pretty sure he met with an estate lawyer the day he died."

"Why?"

Arden rolls her eyes. "He obviously met with her about my inheritance."

"I don't understand."

"I ran into a colleague of Scott's yesterday," Arden explains. "Do you remember Adam Power from the funeral? Buzz cut? Buff? Anyway, apparently he gave Scott the name of an estate lawyer because Scott told him we were considering filing a new petition for my share of the estate."

"Were you?"

"*No, Mom!* That's my point. Scott was doing it behind my back."

Virginia has a sip of her coffee, which is disappointingly bitter and watery, and then sets it down in the cup holder. Not sure what to say, she touches Arden's hand for support. They drive the rest of the way in silence.

When they arrive at the storage facility, Arden gets out of the car and goes over to the passenger side to help Virginia out.

"I'll wait in the car," Virginia says.

"Please come in with me?"

Virginia can't refuse. She eases her legs out of the car and holds out her arms to let Arden pull her up.

"Thank you," Arden whispers, kissing Virginia's cheek. Virginia softens, forgiving her for the dry toast and shitty coffee and for sometimes being a bully.

The woman in the front office looks up when they enter. She's got bright green hair and a bull ring in her nose, and she's wearing a T-shirt that says I WISH I WAS A CAT BECAUSE THE FATTER YOU ARE, THE MORE PEOPLE LIKE YOU. Arden immediately proceeds to lay out the invoice that brought her here, Scott's death certificate, their marriage certificate, and her driver's license.

"I'm here to empty my husband's storage unit," Arden says. "He passed away in 2016, but I just got this invoice from you in March?"

Green Hair looks at the invoice and then types Scott's name into her computer. She reads what's popped up on her screen, clicks a few times, and then prints something out.

"This is his statement," she says, handing the printout to Arden between her chipped black fingernails. "He started renting one of our three-by-four units in August 2016 at fifty-five dollars a month. He prepaid in cash for eighteen months, which brought us to February twenty-eighth, two thousand eighteen."

Arden looks at Virginia, perplexed. Virginia shrugs, equally confused.

"It's a good thing you showed up when you did," Green Hair says, "or his stuff would have been sold at auction. We clear out the units after six months of deliquency."

Arden looks over the statement. "August 2016 was a few months after Bruce Ashforth died," she says. "Larry Lasker started following Jamie Ashforth's intestacy hearing as soon as Bruce died. Maybe Scott was doing the same thing, planning for at least a year and half of probate?"

"Behind your back?"

Arden glances over at Green Hair, who is looking quite engaged in their conversation, and says, "I'll pay this and clear out his space."

Green Hair nods and carefully reviews all of Arden's ID, first the marriage certificate and then, lingering a little longer than necessary, if you ask Virginia, the death certificate. She hands Arden a key and tells them where to go.

Virginia hobbles along behind Arden down aisle F toward the very end, unit F16.

"This is it," Arden says, inserting the key and flinging open the door to reveal a tiny space, not much bigger than a closet. The room is empty except for a half a dozen file boxes on the floor.

Arden immediately bends down to open the one marked, BUNT V. ASHFORTH APPEAL—'91.

"Can't you do that at home?" Virginia says, resenting that her day's been hijacked.

"He's obviously gone to great lengths to keep me from finding out about this," Arden mutters, haphazardly pulling out files. "Can you imagine how much time and effort he must have put into getting all these transcripts? It looks like he's got one for every single one of your petitions."

"I don't understand any of this," Virginia says, leaning against the wall. She didn't bring her walker today—Hayley told her to start leaving it at home—but this probably wasn't the best day to listen to Hayley.

"Because he knew I would never go after my inheritance," Arden says. "Not after what I went through when you tried. We fought about it once."

"Your childhood wasn't that tragic, was it?"

"You weren't there."

Virginia ignores the dig. "He wouldn't have been able file a petition without you," she says. "It doesn't make sense."

Arden looks up, her eyes rimmed red. "I assume from all this," she says, gesturing to the boxes, "he was doing his research and biding his time, waiting for Bruce's intestacy verdict, and then he was going to present me with his argument for filing again."

She continues to flip through the manila folders, scanning the papers too quickly to be able to read or retain anything. Virginia isn't sure what the point of any of this is. "My hip hurts," she says. "Can we please go home and do this? I need to rest."

Arden sighs and Virginia feels guilty for being a nuisance.

"I can help you sort through these at home," she offers.

Arden slaps the lid back on and rises to her feet. She picks up two of the boxes and motions for Virginia to follow her out to the car.

When Virginia is settled in the passenger seat, Arden makes two more trips, packing all the file boxes into the trunk.

"He must have been so desperate," Virginia says when they're back on the road. "Financially, I mean."

"Maybe he was always counting on my inheritance."

"Oh, Arden. You know that's not true."

"Do I?" she says, her voice sounding shaky. "Who knows how long he was waiting for an opportunity to get his hands on my inheritance? Maybe it was always his plan."

"Arden, if it was money he was after, he would have married a rich girl, not a girl with virtually no chance of inheriting from her biological father after a decade of failed attempts in court! You're not thinking straight. Bruce's intestacy came long after you met Scott."

"From the contents of that storage unit, I would say Scott was pretty damned invested in my inheritance."

"He loved you," Virginia says. "If he got fixated on the Ashforth money, it must have been because he was in serious debt and he didn't know what else to do."

Arden doesn't say anything. Her knuckles are white from gripping the steering wheel so hard.

Virginia watches as Arden pulls the lid off the box labeled ASHFORTH V. SLOMINSKI & THE PARKINSON'S FOUNDATION and throws it to the floor alongside all the boxes she hauled in from the car by herself. She attacks the contents with silent rage, examining page after page of the hearing transcript. Virginia can see that Scott has highlighted parts and scribbled notes in the margins.

"He was teaching himself estate law," Arden mutters, turning her frenetic attention to the next box, PRECEDENT & CASE STUDIES/NY TRUST & ESTATE LAW. "I mean, look at all these notes. He was even studying relevant estate cases. He was *becoming* a lawyer!"

"He was doing it for you," Virginia says gently, trying to be helpful. "You know he was only looking out for his family."

"But to lie to me all that time? What else was he hiding from me?"

"Arden, you stand to inherit *a lot* of money. Scott did what he did for the same reason I did it—for the same reason *you're* doing it now. Your share of your father's estate will change your lives forever. We all want the same thing. We always have."

"I just wish he would have told me."

"You said yourself you would have said no," Virginia reminds her. "Obviously, he was preparing to come to you with a solid case."

Arden looks down at all the papers in front of her and with one sweep of her arm pushes them off the table so they cascade to the floor in a waterfall of white. She starts to cry. Not silent, stoic tears, but loud sobs that turn into hiccups, like when she was a little girl. Virginia slides her chair over, wraps her arms around Arden, and murmurs, "Let it all out."

Virginia heard somewhere that it's the best thing you can say to a crying child: *Let it all out.* And while she's happy she can be here for Arden in this way, to hold her and be a safe space place for her to unleash her grief, Virginia feels a dreadful amount of shame. *I caused this,* she thinks. *My selfishness, my poor choices, and my grasping are the cause of my daughter's anguish.*

Arden pulls away abruptly and stands up. "Sorry," she says, wiping her nose with the back of her hand. "I'll be right back."

She leaves the room and Virginia can hear her closing the powder-room door down the hall. She gazes wearily at all the boxes, transcripts from the appeals, kinship hearings, probates, and precedents, all of it scrawled over with Scott's obsessive notes. *I created this monster.* Will the same thing happen to Arden too? Has it already?

With some difficulty, she reaches down for one of the transcripts strewn on the floor. PROBATE—WHITE PLAINS, 1988.

> Your Honor, the petitioner must inherit according to the law of descent and distribution and the recent amendment to Domestic Relations 117—
>
> That is debatable. What I can't wrap my head around, Mr. Lasker, is that in your interpretation of DR117—
>
> The legislature's, Your Honor.
>
> Mr. Lasker, the purpose of our being here is to interpret the legislature to the best of our ability. According to your interpretation, your client would be allowed to inherit from her natural parent as well as from her adoptive parent. I'm playing devil's advocate here, but was not the goal of 117 to treat everyone the same?
>
> There is, most definitely, this double-dip, which is unavoidable, Your Honor, but historically the rights of the illegitimate child have always been secondary—if not altogether ignored—in favor of the natural-born heirs. Are we really concerned about discrimination against the natural-born children here?

Virginia remembers how optimistic Lasker was after the domestic relations clause was amended, which would have given Arden the right to inherit from Wallace Ashforth despite having been adopted by Hal. But they lost that hearing anyway. They lost every single one after that too. Maybe Virginia should have stopped there and made the decision to accept their quiet life in Brooklyn. Maybe it all would have unfolded differently.

"You want tea?" Arden says, returning to the kitchen composed.

"Please."

Arden fills the kettle with water and plugs it in, then drops two tea bags into two mugs.

"Look at this," Virginia says, noticing a name scribbled on the back of the collated transcript. "Emma Merritt."

"Who?"

"She was Wallace's personal assistant. Scott wrote her name down here."

"Larry mentioned an assistant when I was in Rye," Arden says. "I thought you were his assistant. How many did he have?"

"I was a secretary in his private pool. Emma was the keeper of all his secrets. She breathed rarefied air."

"Meaning?"

"If I got flowers from Wallace on my birthday, it was Emma who would have arranged it. Emma booked the hotels, transferred the old secretaries into different pools when Wallace was done with them. It was Emma who handled the wife, Geraldine. Emma knew more about him than Geraldine did. She was professional and stealthy, always by his side."

"Were they having an affair, do you think?"

"Oh God, no." Virginia chuckles, remembering her. Emma Merritt was as asexual a creature as Virginia had ever known. She had a broad face and thin lips, like a Jim Henson Muppet, and a shapeless body she hid under boxy blazers and calf-length skirts. She used to wear her hair in a short, unflattering bob when all the other women in the office were sporting the Farrah Fawcett look.

"So, she was basically in charge of managing all of Wallace's affairs?" Arden says.

"You could say that. She did other things too."

Arden shakes her head. Virginia can't quite read her expression, but it feels disparaging. "What?" she says. "I know you want to say something."

"How were you okay with being one of his concubines?" Arden asks her. "Didn't it bother you?"

"I was in love with him," Virginia says, trying not to sound defensive. "He was a very powerful, very charismatic man. And he loved me, too, by the way."

"He had an assistant to *oversee his sex addiction!*"

Virginia sighs. Everything is an addiction with this generation. The kettle whistles and Arden unplugs it.

"Why do you think Scott wrote her name down?" she says, pouring boiling water into their mugs.

"He must have come across it somewhere in all these transcripts," Virginia guesses, still smarting from Arden's sex addiction comment. "Larry called her as a witness at one point, but she was a vault. That's what we used to call her at the office. The Vault."

"Larry mentioned that too," Arden says, setting their mugs on the table and sitting down.

Virginia dances her tea bag around in the liquid by its string, watching as the water turns golden brown.

"I feel like Scott was a stranger," Arden murmurs, staring at the name "Emma Merritt" in his now extinct handwriting.

"Don't rewrite history," Virginia says. "He was not a stranger."

Arden shrugs. "I'm going to Buffalo," she tells her mother. "I need to speak to that estate lawyer and find out what the hell was going on before he died."

27

Driving across the Peace Bridge from Fort Erie, Arden gazes out at the blue expanse of the Niagara River and thinks about the weekend shopping trips she used to take with Virginia when she was a teenager. They used to go at least twice a year for Christmas and back-to-school shopping. They always stayed at a subpar motel in Tonawanda and watched American TV reruns. (Virginia was obsessed with *The Mary Tyler Moore Show*, and Arden loved *Bewitched* and *The Brady Bunch*.) Dinner was the $5.99 prime rib special at Denny's, breakfast was always IHOP—neither chain had come to Canada yet, so it was a real treat—and then it was shopping at the Walden Galleria, where Arden would spend hours roaming the GAP, American Eagle, and JCPenney. On Arden's sixteenth birthday, Virginia drove to their favorite Denny's in Buffalo for the free birthday dinner and a shopping spree at the Outlets in Niagara Falls. It was one of the best birthdays of Arden's life, mostly because it was so unexpected; she savored every moment of having Virginia all to herself.

Molly Goldman's office is in a yellow brick low-rise on Delaware Avenue. Arden arrives a few minutes early for her appointment and takes the extra time to grab a much-needed iced coffee next door and rehearse what she's going to say. *You were the last one to see him alive* feels a bit dramatic, but it's the truth. She wonders if Molly Goldman even knows that Scott died right after they had lunch. Arden arranged the appointment through Molly's assistant, saying only that she was Scott's widow and that Molly had met with Scott a couple of years back, having been referred by his colleague and mutual acquaintance Adam Power. The meeting was booked presumably to discuss Arden's inheritance case, and as far as Arden knows, she's paying for this consultation.

She rides the elevator to the fourth floor, introduces herself to the receptionist, and is instructed to have a seat on one of the generic black Staples chairs in the front office. After a few minutes of scrolling on her phone, Molly Goldman appears with an outstretched arm and a smile that reads slightly commiserative, as though they've both lost Scott. Arden stands, very much on her guard, and they shake hands.

"I'm really sorry to hear about Scott," Molly says, sounding sincere.

She's even more attractive in person. Tall, slender, with high cheekbones and honey-blond hair. What the LinkedIn photo does not capture is her warmth. Scott must have been captivated, Arden thinks, with a clench of possessiveness.

Arden follows Molly into the inner sanctum, down a short corridor to her office. They sit opposite each other, Molly behind a glass-top desk with brass A-frame legs, and Arden in a soft pink suede armchair.

"Thank you for meeting with me," Arden says, nervously swirling the ice in her cup.

"Tell me how I can help?"

"Scott died two years ago."

Molly nods solemnly. She already knew. "When my assistant mentioned you were Scott's widow, I was absolutely shocked."

"You didn't know before that?"

"I had no idea."

"I figured Adam would have told you."

"My husband and Adam aren't really in touch, other than a like here and there on Facebook," she says. "It's not something he would have reached out about."

"You were the last person to see Scott alive."

Molly's eyes widen. Her mouth falls open as though to say something, but she doesn't. *She didn't know.*

"He had a heart attack on his boat," Arden says.

Molly covers her mouth with her hand, muffling a gasp. Arden lets her absorb the news for a few seconds. They sit in a not-uncomfortable silence until Molly finally says, "I'm *so* sorry." As though it's somehow her fault she was the last one to see Scott alive instead of Arden. "He was so excited to get out on that boat . . ."

At this, Arden bursts into tears. Now it's her turn to apologize. "I didn't mean to do that—"

Molly pushes a box of Kleenex across her desk. "Please. Don't apologize."

"I'm here to find out why he contacted you and what you discussed about my inheritance case," Arden says, pulling herself together. "Scott never told me he was meeting with you. He never told me he'd been following the Ashforths or that he wanted me to file a petition. He was doing it all on his own."

Molly tips her head to one side. If she's surprised, her expression does not reveal it. She may have thought Arden came here looking for a lawyer, not on an investigative mission; if so, she doesn't reveal her disappointment either. "Scott and I met under the premise that you needed an estate lawyer to file a petition naming you a distributee of your half brother's estate, which I came to find out was quite substantial."

"Did he say why he needed a new lawyer?" Arden asks her. "My mother already had an estate lawyer in Westchester County, someone who knew the case backward and forward."

"I think he felt that the original lawyer was part of the problem," Molly explains. "From what he told me, he didn't have much confidence in your mother's lawyer. He wanted someone younger, better versed in all the new DNA technology. It helped that I have a place in Ontario but practice law in the state of New York. The way he presented the opportunity made a lot of sense."

Molly leans forward in her ergonomic swivel chair and rests her elbows on the glass desk. "On the other hand, he may also have just been picking my brain."

"How do you mean?"

"Well, Adam Power gave Scott my name. I felt at times, over the course of our lunch meeting, that Scott was dangling the carrot of possibly hiring me, when he was really just trying to decide if the case was worth pursuing. When I never heard from him again, I concluded I must have been right."

"And did you think it was?"

"Worth pursuing?"

"Yes. I mean, is that what you told Scott?"

"I'll tell you exactly what I told Scott," she says. "I told him it could be a while before Bruce Ashforth's estate was settled. He had just started tracking that intestacy hearing, and I warned him that it could be years before there was a verdict."

"You were right about that."

"I also told him that if Bruce's death was ruled intestate, I thought you had an excellent chance of inheriting."

"Really?"

"Absolutely," Molly says, brightening. "I felt that if we could get a posthumous test of Bruce's DNA and prove you were a match, we could have convinced the surrogate to make you a distributee."

It's strange hearing Molly Goldman say "we," as in her and Scott; as though it was already *their* case and had little to do with Arden. She harbors no ill will toward Molly Goldman for this, but the confirmation of Scott's surreptitious pursuit of Arden's fortune feels somehow sinister, deepening her sense of betrayal. She can feel the burrowing of resentment inside her.

"From what I gather," Molly continues, "your lawyer has done exactly that."

"You've been following."

"Hard to avoid in the New York estate law circles," she says. "I also had a personal interest. I had hoped to throw my hat in the ring."

"I'm sorry."

"My God, don't be sorry. You lost your husband."

Arden blows her nose, hovering on an emotional precipice. "So, you think I can win?"

"I think you have an excellent shot. The posthumous testing was a big hurdle."

"I appreciate that," Arden says, allowing herself a swell of hope.

"Of course."

The pity she sees in Molly's blue eyes makes Arden want to flee. Pity is unbearable, especially from other women. She stands up and smooths out her wrinkled linen pants. "Thank you for making the time," she says. "And I expect you to bill me, please."

"Don't be absurd," Molly says, dismissing the offer.

Arden is about to leave but stops at the door. She turns back around and says, "How was he that day? How did he look? What was his mood like? Do you remember?"

"I do remember," Molly says. "He was animated and excited to get on his boat. He pointed it out to me, told me he was going out to Lake Joe. Considering I didn't know him, he struck me as someone who was in great spirits, happy to be at the cottage. He was suntanned and—" Molly stops herself and lowers her eyes.

"And?"

"I was going to say healthy."

Arden blinks, letting her eyes stay closed an extra second or two.

"When you said heart attack"—Molly shakes her head—"honestly, I was shocked."

"I've always imagined him being stressed and upset that day," Arden confesses. "Not himself."

"I didn't know him, but that wasn't my impression."

Arden thanks her again and Molly wishes her good luck with the hearing, and she leaves, gutted. She supposes she should be relieved he wasn't having an affair—and she *is*, of course—but this secret makes her wonder if there was anything else he was keeping from her.

28

Tate helps Virginia out of the car and hands her the cane. "I'll be at the coffee shop on the corner," she says. "Text me when you're done or come join me."

Virginia takes the cane and starts heading up the front walk to the church, moving at an impressive clip. Progress at last. She's not ready for yoga yet, but she's no longer ruling it out for the rest of her life either.

The usual crowd is already seated around the table when she arrives, along with a newcomer she's never seen before, a white-haired woman in Birkenstocks with a straw hat on her lap. Jean waves at Virginia and Virginia waves back. She likes being here. She's never shared with the group before, and although she doesn't necessarily feel like she belongs here, she does find it to be a place of great comfort. For the one hour she's here each week, the voices in her head fall silent and she's able to hear other people's voices for a change. Their stories, delivered with no ulterior motive other than to heal and disclosed with heartbreaking vulnerability, temporarily mollify Virginia's anxiety with the gift of their perspective. She admires their courage, though she herself has never dared to speak.

Today, with the sun streaming in through the horizontal slats of the venetian blinds, the group says a serenity prayer and then Leah reads a passage from *It's Not Your Fault: Forgiveness and Elder Abuse*, and then opens it up to the group.

"My name is Reva," the newcomer says. "I'm a seventy-eight-year-old widow."

"Hi, Reva. Welcome."

Reva is quiet for a moment as she acknowledges the group's welcome. "After my husband died," she begins, "my friends encouraged me to go online."

At this, Virginia perks up.

"I was looking for some companionship, so I joined an internet chatroom for widows and widowers. I met some lovely people, but I got very close to one gentleman in particular, Dan, from Seattle." She pauses briefly to dab her eyes with a tissue. "We never met, but I fell in love with him. He was charming and witty, and we shared all the same interests. Opera, baking, gardening. We started sharing photos, recipes, music recommendations. We talked about meeting in person, but he was going through some challenging personal stuff, so we shelved the idea for a while."

Reva gazes out the window, tears coming down her cheeks. "It's so embarrassing," she admits. "I was so naïve, so lonely. One day, after we'd been corresponding for a few weeks, he told me his daughter had multiple myeloma. That's how it started. He didn't ask for anything at first. He would just mention every so often that she didn't have insurance and they were trying to figure out how to cover the costs. He said they were going to need at least a hundred thousand dollars to keep her alive for the first year, and he didn't know when he'd ever be able to meet me. I actually believed him. You can figure out the rest," she says, lowering her gaze to avoid making eye contact with anyone, bracing herself against judgment or recrimination.

"Gene, my husband, he left me a substantial nest egg," she continues, fiddling nervously with her straw hat. "I would have been well taken care of for the rest of my life if I hadn't . . ."

Jean slides over the Kleenex box.

"Gene would be so angry with me," Reva says, her eyes filling with tears again. "I've lost everything. I'm totally broke."

Here, Reva breaks down, crying freely as if she's known these people her entire life. Virginia marvels at her fortitude, though perhaps it's this sort of blind trust and openness that landed her in the room in the first place.

"I've been too ashamed to tell anyone," she confesses. "None of my friends know. I haven't said a word to the police. Dan is still at large, preying on other idiots like me."

"It's not your fault," Leah says. (She's the only one allowed to speak after a share.) "And thank you for your honesty, Reva. I'd be happy to speak with you one-on-one after the meeting."

"Thank you for sharing," the group echoes.

Bonnie shares next, then Lois, Elaine, Alfred, Jean. At last, they come to Virginia.

"We still have some time left," Leah says. "Did you want to share, Virginia?"

Virginia glances over at Reva and inexplicably bursts into tears. Someone slides the Kleenex box toward her. "I'm sorry," she sobs. "This isn't like me."

"Take your time. We're *here*."

After several minutes of uncontrollable crying, Virginia glances up at Jean and Jean winks at her, and Virginia can feel the compassion emanating from each and every one of them, like a current of warm air. In that moment, she feels safe and grounded for the first time since the assault.

"My name is Virginia," she says, her voice little more than a quiver. "I haven't shared before, so I'm a little nervous. I've had a hard time identifying with all of you. I mean, I appreciate all your sharing and I know I'm a victim just like the rest of you, but it's the label I struggle with. I'm not saying I don't think I'm old—I know I am—but when I hear 'elder abuse,' it doesn't really resonate. It sounds too . . . polite. Like a euphemism or something."

She stops to collect her thoughts; she's off on a tangent, not sure at all where she's going with this. The words are simply falling from her lips without her usual filter, a barrage of everything she's kept in lockdown for so long.

"Jean was right," Virginia says, looking over at Jean. "At my first meeting, she said to me, '*You were raped, Virginia.*'"

She looks over at Leah, sheepish. "Sorry, Leah, I didn't mean to cross talk, but I *was* raped. And I get it: because I'm sixty-five, it falls under the umbrella of 'elder abuse'—and I suppose it's all just fucking semantics anyway—but I can't seem to connect what happened to me, which was brutal and violent and horrific, with these pamphlets and these books about old people with dementia."

She glances around the room, rallying for solidarity, hoping she isn't offending anyone. "I'm not trying to diminish anyone else's experience," she says. "Alfred, I know your wife was also raped, and any kind of abuse is horrific, of course. I'm not saying I'm worse off than anyone else, but what I am trying to say is . . . what I'm really needing to say is . . . I was raped."

She lets the statement hang there in the room, dense as fog, giving it space outside her body to exist. She's held it inside for so long, sealed off in airless jars and shoved into the dark corners of her psyche, desperate to forget, to move on, to go back to being Virginia.

"We met on a dating site for seniors," she explains. "My username was Bangin' Boomer."

Some of the others chuckle, which makes Virginia feel slightly less ashamed. "I guess you could say I got what I asked for," she says, believing it to the core. "I didn't even think to wonder why a man in his forties was on a dating app for old people. He was the youngest guy by three decades. I thought he was open-minded. I thought it was noble that he didn't care about age and, frankly, I was flattered that of all the women on the site he chose me. It didn't even occur to me that his interest in me was just some sick fetish."

Reva is nodding her agreement. Alfred and Bonnie's eyes are rimmed with tears. Sitting among these delicate, bruised souls, of which Virginia is certainly one, it's hard for her now to recall what it was like to feel desirable or confident or powerful. Aging will slowly strip a woman of those traits over time, but Lou Geffen incinerated them in one night. What he took from her feels less like theft and more like murder. To say he stole her trust in humanity and her self-worth minimizes the truth of it. It's more dire and encompassing than that; a part of her is dead. He effectively snuffed out the woman who was at least in possession of some dignity.

"That's what I've become," Virginia tells the group. "The object of a monster's predilection for old women."

She wants to tell them: *I used to be beautiful! Men used to worship me! I used to have value!*

Instead, she says, "He called me a decrepit old whore. He told me I should consider myself lucky that he was interested in me, and I believed him. I still believe him. I haven't said a word to anybody because who would believe that a man like him would ever rape an old woman like me?"

Lying on the floor after Lou Geffen had finished with her, Virginia thought about how her father had once called her a pretty moron and how she'd known, even back then, that men had all the power. As she'd made her way in the world, she had no delusions about that. Their admiration, attention, and approval would become her holy grail, her drug of choice. She was at least clever enough to figure out where *her* power lay, which was in her beauty and her body. She's been using them ever since, with some degree of success. She's never had a problem getting a man; it's always been sustaining their attention (or hers) that has proven to be her downfall. She's waited on the precipice of her own life for more than six decades, marking time, standing by, chasing, vision-boarding, all to wind up pulverized and alone on the floor of her tiny bedroom.

She's been hard on herself over the years—justifiably, the girls might argue—but as she lay there, post-assault, contemplating her sixty-five years on earth and the legacy she would be leaving behind, she was suddenly aware that her usual guilt was laced with something deeper and darker—*shame.* For as long as she could remember, she'd made men her primary purpose—attracting them, enthralling them, hanging on to them. For the first time in her life, she wondered what message that had conveyed to her daughters about *themselves.*

Her cell phone had begun to buzz from the kitchen table. There was no way she could get to it. She still had the landline, even though the girls had been telling her to get rid of it. She liked an old-fashioned phone. It was sitting on her bedside table, just a little more than arm's length away. She looked up at it, but it hurt just to lift her head, which she'd smashed on the hardwood. For all she knew, there was bleeding inside her brain.

She knew she had to get to a hospital. She couldn't let herself die there, not like that. She managed to prop herself up on her good elbow and reach for the hardcover book on the table—*Adult Children of Emotionally Immature Parents.* With as much strength as she could rally, she pulled the book down, which dragged the old phone with it, crashing to the floor beside her. She called 911.

She forced herself to stay conscious by singing to herself. If she was concussed or bleeding internally, passing out would mean certain death. She sang until the paramedics burst through her front door.

Many times I've gazed along the open road . . .

West used to play guitar and sing to her. He knew a few Zeppelin songs; they were the only songs he knew. "Over the Hills and Far Away," "Ramble On," "Going to California." Those were good days, those hippie days. The world was a bright, clear bubble of possibility; all that mattered to them was freedom. She hadn't fucked anything up yet. She wondered in that moment what West was doing with his life, abstractly, not really caring one way or another.

"If I were to ever see that animal again," she tells the group, "I think I would murder him. I don't mean to sound melodramatic, but I think I could bash in his skull without any hesitation or remorse."

Her eyes dart around the table as she takes the group's temperature. She's not trying to shock anyone, but her truth is finally coming out and she can't stop now, any more than she could stop *him*. "I wish you could have known me before this," she says. "I miss the old Virginia. I'm grieving her at the same time as I'm trying to move forward. I miss the sense of power I used to have, even though I see now it was only ever an illusion."

The days of misinterpreting her beauty and desirability as power are over. Lou Geffen woke her up; he smashed her to the floor and raped her and degraded her, and in so doing he taught her that she is and always has been powerless. Whatever self-worth she managed to accumulate over the course of her life and to preserve in a world that isn't very kind to women, *he* nearly destroyed.

"I don't know if I've made any sense," she apologizes. "I just want you all to know I appreciate you and you've all really helped me, even if I've never said anything before. I really hope I didn't offend anyone because I really do admire all of you. So, thank you for listening."

After the meeting, Leah pulls Virginia aside and says, "Have you considered a rape support group?"

Virginia shakes her head. "I think that would be worse. An old woman like me? It would be far too humiliating. Everyone would wonder what the hell I was doing there."

"You said yourself what happened to you has nothing to do with your age."

"It does and it doesn't. My age has everything to do with how I'm going to heal and get on with my life."

"Only if you let it, Virginia. Do you have a good therapist?"

"I have a physiotherapist," she quips, grateful for Hayley's peppermint-scented wisdom, which is what got her here.

"That's not what I mean." Leah reaches for a pen and scribbles a name on the back of her card. "Don't let him win," she says, looking deeply at Virginia. "For all of them, and for yourself, do not let him win."

It hadn't occurred to Virginia that not going after him was tantamount to letting him win. She's already lost. No matter what happens now, she never wins.

29

"They're here."

"Who's here?"

"Your brother and his wife."

Arden follows Joshua's gaze across the courtroom to where Jamie and Caroline Ashforth are seated at the end of the mahogany table, looking moneyed and aloof and smug. As soon as Arden lays eyes on them, it's like a vacuum sucks the air right out of her chest.

She recognizes Caroline Ashforth from her Instagram feed and various clippings of her and Jamie at social gatherings. Her face is a dewy pillow of Juvéderm, with small moguls of filler around her mouth and blue doll eyes, where the skin is tightly pulled back and stapled behind her pearl-studded ears. Her hair is bleached Barbie-white and piled high on her head in a strangely old-fashioned hairdo, a combination of beehive and ponytail, like a country singer from the seventies or a Texan pageant queen. She's wearing coral lipstick to match her coral caftan, a billowing sheet of silk that drowns her size 0 frame. *Who wears a caftan to court?* Arden thinks. Even from this close, she could be anywhere from thirty-five to sixty years old; her age is indiscernible, which one must assume is the point.

Jamie, whom she's never seen in person before, is wearing a white chambray buttondown shirt and jeans, more casual than she would have expected. His silver hair is thick and wavy, swept back from his face, which is suntanned and healthy. He's handsomer in person than in the photos she's seen. She knows he's about sixty, but he could easily be a decade younger. He looks fit and athletic—probably a lot of golf and tennis and time spent on yachts in the Mediterranean. She hates him.

Hates the smugness oozing from his entitled pores, hates his wing-tip
loafers worn without socks, hates the obnoxious, oversized gold DG logo
on his sunglasses, which are perched on his head as though he's going
sailing as soon as court lets out.

"Breathe," Joshua whispers.

"How do you know I'm not?"

"I just know."

She takes a breath. Joshua gives her a nudge and she realizes they're
both still standing in the doorway. She enters the courtroom, keeping
her head down, deliberately not making eye contact with the Ashforths.
Once seated, she stares straight ahead. She can feel her heart pumping a
little too fast through her cotton blazer. She was already nervous for day
one of the kinship hearing; having Jamie Ashforth in the room, quietly
hating her guts, has discombobulated her even more.

She wants to look over and stare. She wants to study him for similar-
ities and idiosyncrasies—he's her *blood brother* after all—but she's afraid
to make eye contact. She keeps her gaze fixed straight ahead.

"Is he looking over here?" she asks Joshua.

"No. He's talking to Fistler."

"What's *she* doing?"

"Texting, I think."

Judge Lull appears before them and Arden notices him spot the Ashforths at the other end of the table. A fleeting look of surprise passes
across his eyes, and then he turns his attention to lining up his bifocals
and lozenges and tissue pack.

"Good morning, everyone," he says. He's shaved his beard since the
last hearing, leaving only a small white triangle on his chin. "Just for the
record, my name is Dale Lull and I'm the surrogate presiding over this
matter. This is an official hearing of the court, so there is a court clerk,
Helen Chuong, recording these proceedings."

Joshua leans in and whispers, "Are you okay? I know the past twenty-
four hours have been a lot—"

Arden is still reeling from last night's bombshell. Joshua arranged
to pick her up at Newark Airport so he could prepare her for today's
hearing. They were on their way to Hal's place when he ambushed her.
He said she needed to know everything in advance of the hearing, that

he'd only just found out himself . . . "It's good for our case," he said. "Her testimony will clinch this for us. I'm sorry to be the one to have to break this to you . . ." Arden could barely process what he was telling her.

She decided against confronting her mother last night—she was too emotional and overwhelmed—and instead she let Joshua handle Virginia. He ended up staying at Hal's late into the night, grilling Virginia over the phone and coaching Arden on how to get through Fistler's cross-examination. She'll deal with the personal fallout of Joshua's revelation *after* the hearings. Until then, she's doing the most pragmatic thing available to her—shoving this new information into a tiny mental compartment at the back of her skull and ignoring it.

"Kinship hearings are often complicated and confusing," Judge Lull begins. "The purpose is to determine blood relatives and establish proof of heirship. Although it may seem as simple as testifying how the claimant is related to the decedent, we all know it's never that simple."

Arden's phone vibrates in the pocket of her blazer. She glances down at a text message from Tate. Good luck, sis. It's almost over. If only. She certainly won't miss this musty chamber with its shrouds of red velvet, sea of mahogany, and portraits of creepy former surrogates staring down at her like they think she's a gold digger.

"The framework for analyzing kinship issues lays out formal rules for the inheritance process," Lull continues. "The statute describes how to build a family tree in order to identify the distributees who qualify as heirs of the decedent. I'll read that for you now—"

He puts on his bifocals and clears his throat. "'Spouses and children have the highest priority. If no spouse or issue survive, the priority for inheritance consists of, in descending order, parents, siblings/nieces/nephews, grandparents, uncles/aunts/first cousins, and first cousins once removed. A decedent's relatives of the half-blood are treated as if they were relatives of the whole blood.'"

When he's finished reading, he glances up and makes eye contact with Arden. Stupidly, she smiles. A knee-jerk reaction, likes she's flirting with him.

"In the context of the Ashforth matter," Lull continues, "this hearing will specifically determine if Arden Moore is a distributee of the decedent, Bruce Alastair Ashforth, and whether she is entitled to share in his estate.

Proof must be submitted here to establish this relationship and her right to inherit. The burden is on the alleged heir to prove, by a preponderance of the evidence, that she is a distributee. The interesting thing about this hearing is the DNA evidence, a state-of-the-art medical technology that has forever changed our understanding of kinship."

Arden's knee is bouncing nervously. Joshua reaches out and places his hand on it to stop her. "Sorry," she whispers.

"We're good," he says, leaning close and speaking into her ear. "Try to relax."

"I've received your submissions," Judge Lull says. "I believe the parties have agreed to the admission into evidence of two exhibits. One has been labeled Petitioner's Exhibit 1 and it is records from a lab called CityLab, which consist of DNA records for Arden Moore. And then we have Petitioner's Exhibit 2, which is a family tree. Is that correct?"

"Yes, Your Honor," Joshua says. "The lab report is twenty-four pages, and the family tree is three."

"Perfect," Lull says. "That's exactly what I have here."

Arden is staring so intently at the tone-on-tone houndstooth pattern of Joshua's suit jacket that the small checks begin to blur. She knows how important the thoroughness and accuracy of that family tree is, even with a DNA match. Joshua says the family tree must provide a clear, unbroken connection from one generation to the next.

"I'm also told you have three witnesses today—Arden Moore, Emma Merritt, and Dr. Barry Fingerhut—and that there may be a fourth witness who would call in via Skype."

"Correct, Your Honor. Virginia Bunt was not able to travel for health reasons, but she is standing by remotely in case we need to call her as a witness."

Arden and Joshua exchange looks. The plan is to keep Virginia *off* the stand. Fistler would tear her apart—her infidelity, her relationship with Bryce Beekhoff, her colossal thirty-year-old lie, which they've only just found out about.

"Mr. Fistler, you've listed two witnesses here—"

Judge Lull rattles off the names of Fistler's experts, the scientists who will refute Arden's DNA results and try to prove they do not meet reasonable scientific standards. Joshua has emphatically instructed her that they're just a couple of hired guns whose purpose here today is to discredit Joshua's DNA expert, Dr. Fingerhut, and for her not to worry too much about what they say on the stand. He also told her if the DNA results are determined *not* to be conclusive, Fistler will subpoena Virginia to testify, at which point, he warned her, Fistler will attack Virginia's credibility on all fronts by publicly humiliating her and exposing both her sexual history and her failed legal crusade to "shake down" the Ashforths.

But Joshua is an optimist. He believes in the science. He believes in the absolute, unimpeachable conclusiveness of Arden's DNA results, and so he's confident Virginia will be spared having to testify. All Arden can do is trust him.

"All right," Judge Lull continues, "Emma Merritt and Dr. Fingerhut are listed as witnesses, so I'm going to ask that they actually leave the courtroom for now while the testimony of Arden Moore is taking place." He scans the gallery. "Please don't take any offense: these are the rules we follow here. Because you're going to be testifying later, you can't hear the testimony of the other witness, so could you please leave the courtroom?"

At the back of the gallery, Dr. Fingerhut and a small, elderly woman rise from their seats, and she shuffles slowly out of the courtroom with his help.

"I should tell you I've reserved this whole day for our hearing," he tells the court. "Are we ready to proceed?"

"We are, Your Honor."

Moments later, Arden finds herself sitting in the witness box, ready for direct examination. Joshua painstakingly prepped her for this, but he could not have prepared her for the dry mouth, perspiration, and palpitating heart that are making it almost impossible for her to concentrate.

"Mrs. Moore, do you have a profession?"

"I'm a mother of three."

"Can you please speak up, Mrs. Moore?"

"I'm a mother of three. An *at-home* mother. That's my profession."

"Did you know the decedent, Bruce Ashforth?"

"I did not."

"Yet you've filed a petition in this proceeding asserting that you are the half sister of Mr. Ashforth," Joshua says, speaking calmly and slowly, his eyes never leaving hers. "Can you please tell us what the basis of your assertion is?"

"Sure. Yes. It would be based on DNA markers."

"Your Honor, I refer you to Exhibit 1."

Arden has no idea how much times passes while she's answering Joshua's questions. She trusts him and they fall into a smooth rhythm; question, answer, question, answer. The family tree is presented, more questions. Lob, return. It's all friendly fire. She feels okay, as long as Joshua is holding her in his unwavering gaze. She never looks away from him.

And then Joshua's turn ends, and she watches him take a seat, and in his place Fistler stands and approaches the witness box. She's still staring at Joshua, he at her. *Stay with me, you've got this, I'm here.*

"Good morning, Mrs. Moore," Fistler says, super friendly, like they've just bumped into each other on the street.

"Good morning."

"What is your earliest recollection of Bruce Ashforth?"

Arden blinks. Panic engulfs her. Joshua bobs his head encouragingly, mouthing, *It's okay.*

"As I told the court," she says, "I never met Bruce Ashforth. The Ashforths shunned me from the day I was born."

"You never had contact with him? Not even once."

"No."

"No visits, no correspondence, no phone calls? Not even a birthday card?"

"No, nothing."

"So, you're saying absolutely no open and notorious relationship whatsoever?"

"Correct."

"You claim that Wallace Ashforth was your natural father?"

"Yes. He was."

"But you have no proof of that."

"Objection, Your Honor. We've presented our proof in the form of a DNA marker test, which shows that the witness and the decedent share the same biological father."

"I plan to challenge the quality of the DNA testing and its conformity to a reputable standard," Fistler argues. "But I'll get to that later. For now,

Mrs. Moore, I just want to reiterate that, other than this questionable DNA marker test, you have absolutely no basis for filing this claim. You never met the decedent, you had no relationship with him whatsoever— nor any of the Ashforths, for that matter—and your entire case hinges on the fact that your mother, Virginia Bunt—a woman who effectively has been trying, and failing, to get her hands on the Ashforth fortune for more than thirty years—supposedly slept with Wallace Ashforth in the seventies. Is that correct?"

"Objection," Joshua says.

"Sustained."

"In fact, Mrs. Moore, isn't it fair to say there is absolutely zero concrete evidence to show that your mother ever had sexual relations with Wallace Ashforth other than *her* word, which we all know is unreliable at best? Isn't this hearing just a cash grab based on some fantasy your mother concocted more than three decades ago?"

"Objection!" Joshua repeats, flying out of his seat. Judge Lull bangs his gavel.

"Sustained!" he barks. "Mr. Fistler, this is your last chance. If these antics of yours are an effort to impress your clients, I strongly recommend you change course. You are not doing them any favors."

"Apologies, Your Honor."

But it's too late for Arden. Fistler has already deeply embarrassed her in front of everyone in the courtroom.

Later, when Joshua calls Emma Merritt to the stand, Arden braces herself for more ignominy. About the same time she discovered Emma's name scribbled in Scott's secret stash of legal documents, Larry emailed Joshua the name of Wallace's personal secretary—*Emma Merritt*. It was serendipitous enough that Joshua immediately went looking for her and found her living at a seniors' residence in New Jersey.

"Mrs. Merritt, I'm going to ask you to raise your right hand," Judge Lull instructs. "Do you swear to affirm that the testimony you're about to give in this court today is the truth, the whole truth, and nothing but the truth?"

"Yes, Your Honor." Emma Merritt stands at about four foot eleven at best. Slight and frangible, with spotted, trembling hands, it's a miracle she's managed to get here, and yet when she speaks, her voice is strong and clear, unflinching.

"Mrs. Merritt, can you please state your relationship to the decedent, Bruce Ashforth?"

"Bruce was my former boss's son."

"And who was your former boss?"

"Wallace Ashforth."

"What did you do for Mr. Ashforth?"

"I was his personal assistant from 1961 until he died in 1980."

"Your Honor," Fistler interrupts. "I fail to see how this has anything to do with the claimant's relationship to the decedent, *Bruce* Ashforth."

"Mr. Fistler has thrown into question the verity of Virginia Bunt's claim that she had a sexual relationship with Wallace Ashforth and that she became pregnant with his child," Joshua explains. "Mrs. Merritt is here to refute that argument and establish chronology."

"Go ahead."

"Thank you, Your Honor. Mrs. Merritt, please describe what you did for Wallace Ashforth in your role as his personal assistant."

"I booked his appointments—doctors, dentists, tailors, and the like. I made all his travel arrangements, his dinner plans, did his shopping for him. I basically managed his entire life in and out of the office."

"In that capacity, I assume you had information about Mr. Ashforth's personal life that no one else would have been privy to?"

"Correct."

"Objection, Your Honor," Fistler says, looking bored.

"Move along, Mr. James. I'm looking for new evidence here."

"Mrs. Merritt, were you aware of a sexual affair between Wallace Ashforth and his secretary, Virginia Bunt, from about 1977 to his death in 1980?"

"I was, yes."

"You're sure about that? It was almost forty years ago, and I mean no disrespect here, but you are, I believe, eighty-eight years old?"

Emma Merritt chuckles. "I'm one hundred percent certain. I managed their affair for years. It's not something one forgets."

"What do you mean exactly when you say you 'managed' their affair?"

"I handled all the logistics," she says matter-of-factly. "I ordered the flowers—daisies were her favorite—I chose the jewelry, booked their hotel rooms, wrote the cards for him to sign. I was the one who handled Mrs. Ashforth when she called looking for him."

Arden steals a peek at Jamie from across the table. His face is impassive, which doesn't surprise her. She knows enough about him to know he would never give her the satisfaction of a reaction.

"And you're sure of the dates?" Joshua says.

"Yes, I'm sure of the dates. I was the gatekeeper between his wife and all his lovers. That was my job."

"All his lovers, of which Virginia Bunt was one?"

"She was. The longest, in fact. And for a time, the only."

"Do you know if Wallace Ashforth knew she was pregnant?"

"Objection!"

"I'll rephrase. Did *you* know that Virginia Bunt found out she was pregnant in June of 1980?"

"I did."

Fistler jumps up and barks something that Arden doesn't quite catch. Judge Lull orders him back to his seat. Even knowing this was coming, it still feels surreal hearing the circumstances of her birth discussed by strangers in a courtroom, as though it's got nothing to do with her. She feels oddly detached, like she's watching a Shonda Rhimes drama on TV, and yet at the same time she's aware that the numbness she's experiencing is a protective reaction that will inevitably dissolve—or combust—at some point.

"Mrs. Merritt, how did you find out Virginia was pregnant?" Joshua asks her.

"Wallace asked me to arrange the abortion."

There's a detonation of whispers in the gallery, where the press is frantically scribbling notes and typing into phones. As their soft gasps billow in the air, Arden is keenly aware that her personal humiliation is their big scoop. She closes her eyes, wishing for a lever that would drop her down through a trapdoor in the floor. What will this mean to her children? The twins may still be too young to understand, but Ivey—vulnerable, angry, insecure Ivey—might perceive this as an indirect rejection.

"Wallace Ashforth *asked you* to arrange an abortion for Virginia Bunt?"

"He did, yes."

He wanted to extinguish my existence before I even entered the world, Arden thinks. Talk about an ego neutralizer. Everything she thought she knew about her father—"Uncle Wally," Baldie—was a myth. Not only did he know Virginia was pregnant, but he wanted her to terminate it. He wanted her to terminate *Arden*. The naïve child in her has always believed that if he had lived long enough to know about her, he would have chosen to be in her life. The truth is so much more devastating. Virginia spun a tale that preserved Wallace's memory in a far better light than he ever deserved.

Virginia will argue she did it to protect Arden, and that may be so. The reality of her father's deplorable rejection and coldhearted indifference would be a difficult conversation for any mother to have with her child, but Virginia knows the stakes here.

"Did he come right out and say it?" Joshua probes. "Did he use the word 'abortion'?"

"No one ever used the word 'abortion' back then," Emma says. "But I knew what he meant."

"Objection."

"Mrs. Merritt, let's take a step back for a moment. I want to get this right for the court; it's very important. Did Wallace Ashforth actually tell you that Virginia Bunt was pregnant with his child?"

"Objection!" Fistler shouts. "There is no way Wallace Ashforth or Virginia Bunt could have known at that time that she was pregnant *with his child*! We *still* don't know that because she had multiple sexual partners at the time. That's why we're *here*."

"Mr. James, be very careful here."

"Apologies, Your Honor," Joshua says. "Mrs. Merritt, did Wallace Ashforth tell you that Virginia Bunt was pregnant?"

"Yes, he did."

"When was that?"

"In the summer of 1980. I'm very sure about that because he died that September. It was just after the July Fourth long weekend, when he was back in the city for work."

"Back from where?"

"They had a summer house in Maine. Cape Elizabeth. The family would stay there from June until Labor Day, but Mr. Wallace used to come into the city every couple of weeks for work."

"So he was in Manhattan in early July when he asked you to arrange the abortion for Ms. Bunt?"

"Correct. He'd spent the night with Virginia when he got back from Maine, which was typical, and that's when she told him."

"And you know this how?"

"I booked their room at the Bossert."

"The Bossert was a hotel?"

"Correct."

"Go on."

"The next morning, he came into my office, told me Virginia was pregnant, and asked me to take care of it."

"And by 'take care of it,' you understood that to mean you were to arrange an abortion?"

"Objection."

"You can answer the question, Mrs. Merritt."

"Correct," she says. "It was not the first one I'd arranged for him."

A soft chorus of gasps undulates throughout the courtroom.

"You're saying Wallace Ashforth had gotten *other women* pregnant before Virginia Bunt?"

"Objection!" Fistler is on his feet again, red-faced.

"I'll rephrase my question. Wallace Ashforth *asked* you to arrange other abortions for him prior to Virginia Bunt's?"

"Yes, twice."

"And you did?"

"Yes. I did whatever he told me to do. That was my job."

"And so that morning, when he came into your office . . ."

"Wallace told me he had a problem. Actually, he said, '*We* have a problem.' And I said, 'Shall I call Dr. Blau?' Blau was the doctor at the abortion clinic we used."

"So, Wallace Ashforth had an abortion clinic in his Rolodex?"

"He did."

"Objection!"

"We get it, Mr. James. Move on, please."

"What did Wallace tell you about his conversation with Virginia Bunt, the one in which she told him she was pregnant?"

"Your Honor!" Fistler cries. "This is all hearsay."

"Mr. James, find a different way to get where you're going."

"Mrs. Merritt, is there anything else you remember about your conversation with Wallace that morning that you can share with the court?"

"I asked Mr. Ashforth if he was sure the baby was his, and he said, 'Looks like it.'"

"That's hardly ironclad proof," Fistler interrupts.

"Our DNA results are the ironclad proof," Joshua says calmly. "I'm just establishing here that there was in fact a sexual relationship between Virginia Bunt and Wallace Ashforth, and that Ms. Bunt did become pregnant with the petitioner, Arden Moore, during the course of that affair, which goes to chronology."

"Please continue, Mr. James. I'm getting hungry."

"Mrs. Merritt, did you ever end up booking that abortion for Virginia Bunt?"

"I did not."

"Why not?"

"She refused."

"Did you ever speak to her directly about it?"

"I did not. I only communicated with Mr. Ashforth. He said he was trying to persuade her to do the right thing, but she wanted to keep her baby."

"By 'do the right thing,' you mean have an abortion?"

"Exactly."

"Did he say how he was trying to persuade her?"

"He offered her money, like he did the others."

"But she wouldn't accept his money, would she?"

"Objection!" Fistler roars. "This is all speculation!"

"Mr. Ashforth *told me* that Virginia Bunt would not accept any money from him and that she was going to keep her baby with or without his help."

"Virginia Bunt doesn't sound like a gold digger to me," Joshua says, smiling in Fistler's direction. "Why come forward now, Mrs. Merritt?"

"You asked me to, sir."

"But why not thirty years ago, when Virginia Bunt was the one filing the petition on behalf of her daughter?"

"I'd signed a nondisclosure agreement," Emma Merritt says, speaking right into the microphone. "Wallace's son, Jamie Ashforth, threatened to sue me if I said anything. He threatened my family, my employment at the time. Everything short of my life."

"And now?"

"I'm eighty-eight years old, as you just told the court. I'm alone now; I've got no money. There's nothing for the Ashforths to take. Maybe I'm trying to clear my conscience before I die, but if the DNA proves that Mrs. Moore is Wallace's daughter, then she should have what's rightfully hers."

"Nothing further, Your Honor."

Fistler is on his feet before Joshua even sits down, sidling up to the witness box like a wolf about to pounce on a little mouse. "I must say, Mrs. Merritt, you have an awfully impressive memory for a woman just two years shy of her *ninetieth* birthday."

"Is there a question?" Joshua wants to know.

"You can't really expect this court to believe that you remember a conversation *verbatim* from *thirty-eight* years ago, can you?" Fistler asks her. "Isn't it true that Mr. James over there spent a fair amount of time helping you *prepare* what you were going to say today?"

"He prepared me," she says, lifting her eyes to look directly into his, a noble frailty about her that holds the entire courtroom captive. "He told me what to expect from you, but he certainly didn't have to tell me what *I* remember from *my own life.*"

When Judge Lull breaks for lunch, the Ashforths are the first ones out of the courtroom without even a glance in Arden's direction. Fistler makes a beeline for Joshua, effectively blocking his path out of the courtroom. "A word?" he says, not even bothering to acknowledge Arden.

"Sure," Joshua responds, playing it cool. Arden knows him well enough to know he's probably erupting inside, knowing an offer to settle is probably forthcoming.

Joshua turns to Arden, keeping his expression solemn but unable to hide the glint of triumph in his eyes and says, "I'll meet you by the fountain. Will you get me a hot dog?"

She nods and watches him exit the courtroom with Fistler right behind him, both striding with bravado and masculine confidence that makes her feel small and extraneous.

30

"What did he say?" Arden wants to know, handing Joshua a cold hot dog. She's sitting on the ledge of the fountain in City Hall Park—*their* spot—nursing a ginger ale. "It's been over half an hour!"

Joshua is beaming. He takes half the hot dog in his mouth, chews in silence for an irritatingly long time, and then wipes the mustard out of the corner of his mouth. "Sorry," he says. "I'm starving. Did you eat something? We have a long afternoon ahead of us."

"What did Fistler want? Do they want to settle?"

"He made an offer."

"How much? A *good offer*? What does this mean?" She's practically screaming.

"No. It was a terrible, insulting offer, but I'm obligated to present it to you."

"How terrible?"

"A hundred grand."

Her mouth opens.

"Exactly."

"*A hundred grand?*"

"He offered to settle for 'nuisance value.' I told him a hundred grand wouldn't even put one of your kids through college."

"And what did he say?"

"He said, 'Isn't college cheap in Canada?'"

"Will they negotiate?"

"Not anywhere near what you're owed."

"So that's it?"

"He threatened to eviscerate your mother. He said if you don't settle, he'll go to the tabloids. I warned you this would be their strategy—"

"The tabloids?"

"The *Daily News*, the *Post*—"

"I know what they are."

"The more graphic the testimony, the better the coverage."

"Graphic?"

"I prepped both of you for this, remember?"

"You mean he's going to ask her if Wallace ever ejaculated inside her?"

"Among other things."

"Fuck."

"Arden, you're missing the point. *They're scared.* They're making an offer because our DNA results are solid. Fistler's not stupid. He's making threats because he's about to lose and he knows it. I don't even think your mother is going to have to testify. We used the most reputable lab in the city. Not even their hotshot experts can discredit our lab."

"So, we shouldn't counteroffer?"

"Hell, no! You're entitled to *millions*, and you want to settle for at best a couple of hundred thousand? They're banking on your desperation."

"I *am* desperate."

"Not as desperate as they are."

"Can you guarantee that?"

Joshua shrugs. "You know nothing is guaranteed in a probate case," he says. "But I'm confident we're going to win."

The buzz outside the Surrogate's Court is significantly amped up in the afternoon due to the splashy return of Jamie and Caroline Ashforth in a chauffeur-driven Jaguar. Caroline Ashforth has long been one of those famous-for-being-famous socialites, an Instagram fashion icon and fixture on the philanthropic circuit. As she releases one Jimmy Choo–clad foot at a time onto the sidewalk, the photographers swarm her. "*Caroline! Caroline!*" All Arden can see from across the road is the top of her Barbie-blond bun. Even Jamie is completely obscured by the frenzy to get at his wife.

Arden and Joshua hang back as the paparazzi follow the Ashforths inside the courthouse, casting themselves around Caroline like a fishing net.

"Ignore them," Joshua says as they climb the cement steps.

"Who? The Ashforths or the journalists?"

"Both."

"Do you think it will be over tomorrow?"

"I do."

"And then it's all up to Lull."

"He's on our side."

"How can you tell? I can't read him at all."

"He understands the significance of DNA. Everything else is just a dog-and-pony show."

"Is that what this morning was?"

After age-shaming poor Emma Merritt, Fistler doesn't just attempt to discredit Arden's DNA results; he vilifies Dr. Fingerhut, outright accusing him of mishandling the chain of custody and implying that Fingerhut was being paid to show a match between Arden and Bruce Ashforth. Fistler's own scientists argue that Bruce's postmortem DNA had disintegrated significantly enough as to render the DNA unreliable. Listening to their experts, even Arden starts to doubt the validity of her test results and has to fight back tears in front of Judge Lull and Jamie and Caroline Ashforth.

"Ignore them," Joshua whispers, noticing her panicked expression. "This is all very standard."

Still, it feels like her entire case is unraveling. Results she thought were foolproof now seem muddied, questionable. Although Fingerhut manages to keep his composure, Arden is convinced Fistler has succeeded in planting enough doubt to sway Lull over to his side.

Surprisingly, Fistler does not subpoena Virginia to testify this round. Instead, Judge Lull says, "I'll hear closing statements now. Mr. Fistler, you're up."

Arden looks over at Joshua, reaches for his pen and scribbles, *Why isn't he calling my mother?*

"He's probably concerned about how it will look to bully another ailing, elderly woman over Skype," Josh whispers. "I'm sure he's keeping her in his back pocket for the appeals, though."

Fistler stands up, walks over to the bench, and turns to face Arden. He's so close she can smell the leathery scent of his cologne.

"*Shakedown*," he proclaims, directing the word squarely at Arden. "That's what this is. We all know it. We've been here before. This is an elaborate, costly, and time-consuming shakedown."

He pauses for a beat, letting the word hang in the air.

"At no point in this hearing has the petitioner proved the existence of any relationship with Bruce Ashforth or any of the Ashforths, for that matter. And why is that? *Because there never was one.* They never even met!"

Fistler settles his gaze on Arden, his expression one of plain disgust. Arden shrinks in her chair, can feel her face heating up.

"All we've got is some very questionable DNA extracted *posthumously* from Bruce Ashforth's brain tissue. This is what we're supposed to base this decision on? My client is being asked to give away half of his brother's estate—*his* family's inheritance—to a perfect stranger, based on some decomposing DNA tissue from *a pickle jar*?"

Joshua snickers.

"DNA notwithstanding," Fistler continues, "the petitioner, Arden Moore, is a *stranger* to the Ashforth family. There's been no contact throughout her entire life, let alone an open and notorious relationship, which should be the very foundation of any determination of kinship. The petitioner is a gold digger, plain and simple. She was recruited by her mother, a con artist going back forty years, to make a cash grab for the Ashforth inheritance. Perhaps Virginia Bunt did sleep with her boss, Wallace Ashforth—*if* we can trust her word or the memory of their eighty-eight-year-old witness—but that does not entitle Mrs. Moore to a penny of the Ashforth estate. It's preposterous."

Arden glances sideways at Joshua to gauge his reaction, and he gives her that cocky half nod, half wink she was hoping for.

Unable to resist, she looks past Joshua and locks eyes with Jamie Ashforth. She freezes for a moment, caught in his death stare, eyes like two black holes from which no light radiates.

Jamie turns away and leans over to whisper something in Caroline's ear. Caroline, cool as can be in her *Golden Girls* caftan, doesn't react other than to raise an immaculately groomed eyebrow. She looks right at Arden and smirks. It's like high school and the Ashforths are the popular kids and Arden is the misfit no one wants at their table. *They're laughing at me.*

"Thank you, Mr. Fistler," the judge says, sounding disinterested. Arden relaxes. Fistler's character assassination is over.

"Mr. James? Your turn."

Joshua stands, smooths his pants, buttons his suit jacket. He smiles. It's a gorgeous smile. A winning smile.

"Times have changed," he says, strikingly attractive in his low-key, self-assured way. Where Fistler comes across brash and predatory, Joshua is unflappably poised. His voice is calm and warm, like a solid handshake from someone you can trust. Arden can't be the only one here who finds him reassuring, amiable. Her spirits rally as he takes center stage.

"We know that DNA profiling provides evidence of a highly reliable kind when determining biological relations," he says. "In this case, we tested the genetic tissue of the deceased, Bruce Ashforth, the petitioner, Arden Moore, and her mother, Virginia Bunt. We have the results of a DNA marker test that show a ninety-eight point four percent match between the petitioner and the decedent on the paternal side.

"Mr. Fistler just concluded his very thin argument by stating: 'DNA notwithstanding.' Unfortunately for Jamie Ashforth, there is no longer *any* world in which DNA evidence can be considered 'notwithstanding.' Perhaps that was so before the legislation was amended, back when Mr. Fistler was in his heyday, but as you are aware, it's no longer necessary to prove there was ever an open and acknowledged relationship between the alleged heir and the decedent. I say this for the benefit of the other parties who may not be familiar with the 2010 amendment. The advances in genetic testing necessitated a radical change to our legislation in this regard, which means that claimants who didn't stand a chance ten years ago are guaranteed at least a fair shot at taking advantage of genetic testing now."

Joshua holds up the document before the court. "Our statutes in New York create a rebuttable presumption that if the genetic marker test shows at least ninety-five percent probability of paternity, it creates a rebuttal presumption of paternity. Which means the court *must* conclude that kinship exists between Bruce Ashforth and Arden Moore. There's either a zero percent match or a ninety-five percent match. Nothing in between."

Joshua sets the document down and stares at the floor for a moment, presumably deep in thought. "Mr. Fistler attempted to discredit our DNA results," he continues. "But the truth is it's virtually impossible to challenge the results from any reputable lab in this day and age. Dr. Fingerhut and his lab technicians keep copious, meticulous notes and provide an affidavit confirming chain of custody. Mrs. Moore provided identification and was photographed by the lab, both of which are included with the printout of our results."

Joshua shrugs. "This is as straightforward a case as I've ever seen," he concludes. "Here are the facts. Arden Moore is Bruce Alastair Ashforth's sister. We've got a ninety-eight point four percent DNA match that is irrefutable. Bruce died intestate. Under New York's intestate succession laws, if the decedent has no spouse, children, or parents, the siblings inherit everything. We also know, according to the New York Estates, Powers and Trusts Law, that half relatives inherit as if they were whole. The sibling with whom she shares a father has the same right to the property as she would if she had both parents in common. Arden Moore has been denied her rightful share of her biological father's fortune for her entire life. Thanks to the many advances in DNA testing since her mother filed that first petition on her behalf in the eighties, we can now set this right."

With that, he takes his seat next to Arden. She reaches for his hand, squeezing it tightly, needing something to hold on to, something to keep her tethered to her seat.

"I agree with Mr. James," Judge Lull says. "Times have indeed changed, and we have science and technology to thank for that. We've heard a lot of evidence from the responder's expert scientist about the validity of embalmed DNA, but at the end of the day, a ninety-nine percent match from a reputable lab is extremely compelling. I'm certainly not here to make it more difficult for nonmarital relations to inherit. I'm going to render a ruling that is in line with both the 2010 amendments to the statute while still being consistent with the legislature's intention to prevent baseless claims of kinship. To that end, I will be ready to submit my verdict in writing within the next thirty days."

Gavel bang. Arden and Joshua look at each other. It's over, at least until the appeal.

31

The courtroom begins to empty. Joshua and Arden stay seated, waiting out the fray beyond those doors. They watch everyone slowly file out, the din of multiple hushed conversations tinkling like wind chimes. The only other people left in the courtroom are Jamie and Caroline Ashforth, no doubt also trying to avoid the voracious scrum that awaits them on Center Street.

"I think I need to say something to him," Arden says, speaking softly in Joshua's ear.

"Is that a good idea?"

"It can't make things worse, can it?"

"I'm not sure about that."

"He's my brother," she says. "And now he has proof of that. He's heard it; he's seen it with his own eyes. I mean, maybe this is the time to hold out an olive branch?"

Joshua gives her a look. He doesn't even have to say the words.

"I need some closure," she says.

"Why? What do you hope to get from him that will bring you closure?"

"Nothing. I just want to say my piece."

"Come on, Arden."

"What?"

"'Say your piece'? What does that even mean? *I* just said your piece for you in my closing statement. Don't you think you should give him some space now?"

"I need to say something. I'll regret it if I don't."

Joshua sighs.

"Don't sigh at me."

"He's not going to welcome you into the family fold, Arden."

"I have no expectation of that."

"You sure?"

"I just want him to know I'm not a bad person, that I've got three kids to support. And that I'm open to him meeting them one day. I'm open to us getting to know each other . . ."

Joshua rubs his temples. She can tell he's exasperated with her.

"Give me five minutes," she says. "I have to do this."

She gets up and marches across the room to the other end of the mahogany table—the last time she will be in its regal presence.

"Jamie?" Her voice a hamster squeak. "Can I speak with you for a moment?"

He looks up at her, momentarily startled, his disdain for her as flagrant as his money. He's not nearly as handsome up close as the sum of his parts from across the table. His nose is too narrow and pinched at the tip, his lips are sinking into his mouth. She sees nothing of herself in his features, no resemblance at all.

"Whatever you have to say to me you can say in front of my wife," he says.

"I just wanted to say . . . I mean, this isn't even about us, really. It's our parents who landed us here, and I'm willing—"

"First off, if you win this round, we're going to appeal. Your dirty play to posthumously test my brother's DNA is not going to fly in the court of appeals the way it did with this moron Lull. My plan is to keep you in court for another thirty years. I've got the means, and I've already made it my life's mission to make sure you and your mother wind up with nothing. I'm just getting started."

His hatred knocks the breath out of her. She doesn't even react, just stands there like a mannequin, blank.

"Will you excuse me?" Caroline says to Jamie. "I'll wait for you in the car, Jame. I don't have the stomach for this."

She gets up and turns to Arden, their faces so close Arden can practically taste Caroline's perfume. Her skin is as smooth as a bar of soap. "You don't know who you're dealing with," Caroline says softly, her tone as light and nonchalant as if she were sharing a recipe.

"Neither do you," Arden responds, desperately out of her depth.

Caroline lets out a disparaging laugh. "You're a pathetic woman," she says, dissecting Arden's soul with her Ginsu eyes. "*Truly pathetic.*"

Arden doesn't retaliate. It's like her tongue's been cut out of her mouth. Instead, she numbly watches Caroline cross the courtroom, her heels echoing off the high ceilings, and hates herself for not having had the quick-wittedness to fire back. Something. Anything. *What's with your stupid beehive hairdo? Can't you afford a stylist?* But all the words evaporate on her tongue.

"Anything else?" Jamie says.

"Wallace was my father too. You and I are *blood.*"

He laughs, revealing two cream-colored canine teeth. "That will soon be disproved," he says. "Wallace is not your father, not in any way that matters. You will never lay a hand on his money. Not a cent."

"Why do we have to be enemies?" she asks, with the first fissure of compassion she's felt toward him since this whole thing began. It must have been difficult for him as a kid to witness his mother's suffering at the hands of a philandering father. The shame and hurt of Wallace's infidelity is still reverberating in his life today, so she understands that his anger is not entirely unreasonable. It's just not *her* fault.

"Stay away from my wife, my home, and my children," Jamie tells her. "If you ever set foot on my property again, I'll get a restraining order, which I should have done the first time you trespassed. Your mother is a gold-digging whore, and she's led you down a very dark and dangerous path, as you will soon discover. Do you understand? *I'm just getting started.*"

"What did I ever do to you?"

"My father never wanted you to be born. Had *he* lived, you wouldn't have. He would have eventually convinced your mother to get rid of you. He would have bought her a fur coat or a pair of diamond earrings or written her a check, and she would have terminated the pregnancy and fucked off once and for all like the others. I'll admit, you got lucky when his plane went down. I can see how a hustler like your mother would see an opportunity there. But I'll tell you something: even if it's true and we are related—"

"We *are* related!"

"—blood does not make you part of this family. It does not change the fact that my father never wanted you nor does it change the fact that you are the unwanted bastard child of two people who used to occasionally fuck in a seedy hotel. *You are an accident.* So do me a favor and stop trying to claim my family name as your own. You are not an Ashforth. You don't get to be an Ashforth, ever. That is not your identity to claim."

Reeling, Arden stumbles away, humiliated.

"You okay?" Joshua says.

She's vaguely aware of Jamie Ashforth leaving the courtroom, dares not open her mouth until he's gone. Her whole body is shaking.

"What did he say?"

Without a word, she drops into a chair and takes few breaths. Joshua puts his arm around her, gently pulls her into an embrace, and she releases a deluge of tears onto his suit jacket. He doesn't say anything for a while, doesn't try to make her stop or pull herself together. At one point, he touches her hair and murmurs, "It's okay. You've been through a lot."

"You were right," she admits. "I shouldn't have tried to talk to him."

"He's an asshole, Arden. You don't need him."

"I get that he hates me," she admits. "I'd hate the kid of someone my father screwed forty years ago and is now coming after my money. It's just that he was supposed to finally let me in. I thought if I won . . ."

Even as the words are leaving her mouth, she realizes how pervasive and entrenched this longing has always been inside her. She's wanted the Ashforth stamp of approval to validate and affirm her worth since the day she found out she was Wallace Ashforth's daughter. Maybe she thought the money would accomplish that, or a victory in court, but she sees now that the Ashforths are a dry well. Their acceptance of her both into their family fold and as a human being are as preposterously unattainable as Wallace Ashforth coming back to life. They were never going to let her in. *They never will.* She's been giving them way too much power for far too long. And in that moment, as the door closes behind Jamie and Candice Ashforth, Arden feels liberated.

"You're right," she says, a curtain of optimism opening inside her. "I don't need him in my life. I don't need his approval. We have nothing to do with each other."

"Other than he's your half brother."

"He just told me I'm nothing, that I don't even exist to him. That I don't exist, *period*." She's smiling now, feeling strangely calm.

"And you're happy about that?"

"Jamie Ashforth just said out loud what I've been running from my entire life," she explains. "From the time Carrie Stein called me a bastard in elementary school, I've been running from that truth. At the same time, I've been trying to figure out an identity for myself to prove her wrong. To prove the *Ashforths* wrong. Do you see?"

"Not really, no."

"The thing I feared most just happened, and look! I'm still here. I survived."

"Meeting Jamie Ashforth?"

"No. Being *rejected* by Jamie Ashforth, right to my face. I always thought if I could just get access to him, have a conversation, look into his eyes, I could win him over. I hadn't realized until now how much I've wanted my brothers to acknowledge that I *belong*, that I'm their blood. The fact that they wouldn't has always meant that something must be wrong with *me*. That they've all been right all along—even Carrie Stein—and I really am a nobody."

"Who is this Carrie Stein?"

"Jamie Ashforth has no idea who I am," she says, ignoring him. "He has a story about me, just like he had a story about my mother. I'm a gold digger, a parasite; that's his perception. He's entitled to his version, that Wallace destroyed his family for my mother. But I don't need him to hand me some identity I thought I was entitled to or that was owed to me. I'm a mother of three beautiful kids, a wife, a sister, a daughter. The Ashforth name doesn't define me. *Fuck them.* Biology is bullshit."

"Well, except in the case of our hearing," Joshua reminds her. "In this case, biology is everything."

"You know what I mean."

"You don't *need* the Ashforths, but you still want their money."

"*My* money," she says. "And that's all I want from them."

"I'm really digging this new, empowered Arden."

"Me too," she says, feeling lighter.

"When do you go back to Toronto?"

"Sunday."

"Let's go out and celebrate," he says. "We did it. We won."

"Not according to Jamie. He's just getting started."

"We won another round. We're playing the long game here, Arden. Remember? You've got to stay focused on the endgame. Lull has just made it very clear that the Ashforth money and power cannot defeat our DNA evidence."

"That's not what Jamie thinks."

"It doesn't matter what he thinks. It's not the eighties anymore. We may have to wait awhile, let the appeals play out, but no judge will reverse today's decision."

"Celebrating still feels premature."

"You heard Lull. He said he would deliver a verdict that was relevant and in line with the statute. His exact words."

"While also protecting the Ashforths from scam artists like me."

"You were fantastic, Emma Merritt was a rock star, Fingerhut was impressive—"

"And you were brilliant."

"Wasn't I?"

"Superb."

"Dinner?" he presses. "We can celebrate the new, liberated you."

"When you put it that way . . ."

"Why don't we go back to my place and order in?"

She looks at him, not quite sure what the invitation implies, but his expression is perfectly, calculatingly opaque. He offers no context, leaving her to draw her own conclusion. Buddies? Lawyer-client? Occasional lovers?

A few spicy tuna rolls, a bottle of wine, and a sexy sideways glance later, Joshua is ripping open a condom wrapper and Arden is flopping backward onto his bed with her panties around her knees like a string cat's cradle. It turns out the answer to her question was "All of the above."

Afterward, she falls fast asleep in a sweaty spoon, happily forgetting the day's drama, and doesn't stir until Joshua gently nudges her awake in the morning. "Do you want breakfast?" he asks her, drawing circles on her shoulder.

"What time is it?"

"Ten thirty."

"Shit."

"Eggs?"

"Does that mean we have to leave the bed?"

"I can make them and bring them to you."

"I'd rather you stay."

He settles back in bed, and she rolls over, resting her head on the soft slope of his lower abdomen. "You smell like sex," she murmurs.

"That's your fault."

Outtakes from court yesterday drift back into her consciousness, mostly Jamie Ashforth's parting words, which resurface in a crest of despair. "You are the unwanted bastard child of two people who used to occasionally fuck in a seedy hotel. *You are an accident.*"

And then she remembers her post-castigation epiphany, and she relaxes, reminding herself that Jamie Ashforth is nothing to her, that he holds no power, that who she is is so much more than a name or a DNA test. "I'm starving," she says. "Are the eggs still on offer?"

They both get out of bed, and she sets two places at the island while he cracks a few eggs into a glass bowl, chops some ham and green onion, and throws in a lump of goat cheese. It's all very civilized, this urban tableau playing out in his modern, millennial condo with the Statue of Liberty gazing at them enviously from her perch in New York Harbor.

"Now what?" she asks him.

"You go home to Toronto and wait for my call. As soon as I get the verdict—"

"No, I mean . . . in the context of us. Of *this*." Gesturing to his bedroom, where moments ago they were lying in a tangled knot of naked limbs. "Now that the hearings are over . . ."

"You mean are *we* over too?"

"I guess so."

"I need some caffeine for this conversation," he says, popping two pods into his espresso machine. He presses a button and two lovely streams of black liquid fill two ceramic shot glasses.

"I think you're great," he says, handing her an espresso.

"Oh God." She laughs. "Please don't."

"Don't what? Obviously, there's chemistry here."

"But?"

"For one thing, you live in Toronto and I live in New York."

"And?"

"And you're a widow."

She cocks her head. "*And?*"

He downs his espresso in one gulp, like it's a shot of tequila. "I mean, you know I can't do three kids," he says, whisking the eggs with some milk. "You know that, right?"

She watches him pour the eggs into a warm pan and drop two pieces of bread into the toaster. She likes watching him cook for her, make her coffee. "I don't recall asking you to parent them," she says, sipping her espresso.

"You're a package deal, Arden. And let's be honest, I can't follow your husband. I can't be the guy to fill his shoes."

"Technically, you did follow him," she points out. "And here we are."

"I don't just mean sex. I mean I can't be your next serious relationship. I'm not built for that kind of responsibility."

"Who's talking about a serious relationship?"

"What are you talking about, then?"

"I'm not sure."

"Intermittent sexual rendezvous? Phone sex?"

"That sounds pretty good."

"Really?"

"Why not?"

"You'd be open to that?"

"I've been married for most of my adult life," she says. "I'm almost forty. I'm not looking for the same things I wanted in my twenties."

"What are you looking for?"

"Well, I *wasn't* looking for anything. But now . . . I enjoy hanging out with you. I'm attracted to you. I like having sex with you when we see each other."

"When would we see each other?"

"My father lives here," she reminds him. "I'm here often enough."

"I really like where this is going," he says, brightening. "No part of me wants this to end."

"Me too."

"Really? I just don't want you to—"

"Fall in love with you?"

"I was going to say be disappointed in me. Parenting isn't in my DNA."

"You've been very transparent about that."

"I'm not Scott," he says. "I don't want to let you down."

He removes the eggs from the stove, grinds some pepper over them, and tosses in a handful of kosher salt. He serves them each a plate, adds the toast, and joins her at the island.

"Scott occasionally let me down," she admits.

Joshua looks up at her but doesn't probe.

"Do you remember when I told you he was seen having lunch with some woman just before he went out on the boat?" she says, scooping a spoon of eggs onto her toast.

"Of course."

"Well, it turns out she was an estate lawyer."

"He met with an estate lawyer right before he died? Isn't that a strange coincidence?"

"The meeting was about *my* inheritance."

"What do you mean?"

"I found out he'd been tracking the Ashforths as far back as Bruce's death. He was following the same probate hearing Larry was following, waiting to see how the intestacy case would play out."

"And you didn't know?"

"I had no idea."

"Why didn't he tell you?"

"I guess he didn't think I'd agree to file a petition," she says, "so he started gathering information, speaking to a lawyer, researching precedent. He even rented a storage unit to stash all his research so I wouldn't find out. Clearly, he was planning to present me with an opportunity I couldn't turn down."

"You just found all this out?"

"Recently."

"How do you feel about it?"

"Obviously I'm relieved he wasn't having an affair," she says. "You know how much the mystery blond was bothering me. But there's something unsettling about how secretive he was at the end, you know? The storage space, the meetings behind my back. That's not the kind of marriage I thought we had."

"I guess he wanted to be sure there was a solid case before he brought it to you."

"It bothers me that he was so obsessed with my father's fortune."

"He was right, though, wasn't he? You *are* entitled to that money. And if you don't mind me saying so, *you've* been obsessed with it yourself, haven't you?"

Arden sets down her fork. "It's different."

"How?"

"It's my inheritance. Besides, he was keeping things from me."

"It sounds to me like he was looking out for you without burdening you before it was necessary."

Arden considers Joshua's point, acknowledges to herself there may be some validity in it. "He made some really bad decisions," she says. "He compromised our family's security. It was this constant cycle of spend, get into debt, make more. Spend, get into debt, make more . . ."

She trails off. Joshua is watching her.

"I'm angry," she says softly. "I'm really angry."

"No kidding."

"It's not just because he was plotting to ambush me into filing a petition," she admits, allowing herself, finally, to acknowledge the full weight of her hurt. "Sometimes I feel like he let us down."

Joshua slides his barstool closer to hers. "I'm not an expert or anything," he says, "but maybe you should see a shrink or a grief counselor or something?"

"I have."

"And you talked about your anger? How you feel like he let you down?"

"God, no."

"Maybe it's time to go back? I'm sure grief has a lot of layers."

"The last time I went to see someone, I was just looking for a way to get through the day," she says. "My anger at Scott wasn't even on my radar. I couldn't even *think* those thoughts, let alone say them out loud to someone."

"Well, you just did."

"I know, and now I feel super guilty. How can I be angry with him? He's *dead*."

Joshua touches her cheek, smudges her tears away with his thumb.

"You're a pretty good shrink," she tells him.

"It's part of the job."

"Is fucking me part of the job too?" she teases.

"Ideally."

Her phone rings, startling her. Normally she has it set to vibrate. She reaches for it with a clamp of panic in her chest. She doesn't recognize the number. "Hello?"

"Arden? It's Julie Robbins."

"Who?"

"Nate's mom?"

"Oh, Julie. Hi! Is everything okay?"

"Wyatt is on his way to the hospital with my husband—"

Her heart drops. "What happened?"

"They were playing in the basement and Nate called me down because Wyatt's face was swollen and he was breaking out in hives."

"You gave him nuts?"

"No, or course not. But I haven't had a chance to check the basement yet . . . I don't know . . . my two-year-old might have left something down there . . . I don't know . . . I'm sorry, Arden. He didn't have his Epi-Pen with him. He's at Sunnybrook."

Fucking Virginia. No Epi-Pen.

"Julie, I'm in New York. I'm getting on the next flight out. Please, *please* tell Mark to stay with Wyatt until I get there. My sister's in Denver and my mother can't drive—"

"Of course."

"And please, can you have Mark call me with an update? And text me his number? You said they went to Sunnybrook? I'm going to be freaking out until I hear from him."

"Yes. Of course. I'm so sorry."

Arden starts collecting her things, reining in her hysteria. *Here we go again. Here we go again.* Blazer on floor, skirt, purse, phone. She's been through this exact scenario before, first with Virginia, now Wyatt. The emergency phone call, the race to the airport, the tense journey straight from Newark to the hospital in Toronto. *I can't keep doing this.*

"What happened?"

She looks up at Joshua, remembering he's there. "Wyatt's in the hospital. His peanut allergy. I have to get on the next flight home."

"I'll book them right now."

"'Them?'"

"I'm coming with you."

"You don't have to do that."

"I'm not letting you go alone."

"I'll be fine. It's an hour-and-a-half flight. I know this isn't your thing."

"What airline do you fly? Parker?"

"Porter."

She calls Hal. "Wyatt's in the hospital," she tells him, slipping on her shoes. "He had a reaction. Can you pack my things and meet me at Newark in an hour? My passport's in my nightstand."

"Do you want me to come with you?"

"It's okay. Joshua offered."

Dead air.

"I'll see you soon," she says, in no mood for Hal's judgmental silence. She hangs up and checks her phone for a text from Mark Robbins or Virginia. Nothing.

32

She finds her boy alone in one of the emergency room beds, hooked up to a beeping machine, playing on his tablet. Instant relief. "My sweet magpie," she says, kissing his forehead and squeezing his hand.

"Hi, Mom." Not even looking up from his game.

"How do you feel?"

"Fine."

"Put your tablet down and talk to me. What happened?"

"I was just playing Lego with Nate and then I had that feeling like my throat was closing and it was hard to breathe."

"Why didn't you have your Epi-Pen? Grandma knows you have to take it with you everywhere."

"It's not her fault," Wyatt says. "She asked me if I had it and I said yes."

"Why did you lie?"

"I didn't. It was on the table at the door. When Mrs. Robbins came, I forgot to take it." Wyatt notices Joshua standing in the doorway and says, "Who's that?"

"That's Joshua, my lawyer."

Joshua waves and says, "Hey, buddy."

"You brought your lawyer?"

"He's also my friend. How do you feel now, darling?"

"Fine. Can I finish my game now?"

Arden and Joshua pull two chairs over to keep him company while they wait for the doctor. After about an hour, a young woman who barely looks older than Ivey pokes her head into the room and says, "I'm Dr. Edrisinghe. I'm one of the residents."

Arden almost tells her to go away and send in a grown-up doctor, but she restrains herself.

"He's doing much better," Dr. Edrisinghe says. "But we're going to admit him and keep him overnight so that we can monitor him. We want to make sure he remains stable over the next eight hours."

"But he's okay?"

"We gave him more epinephrine and a shot of steroids," she explains. "He's going to be fine. I'm going to arrange his room for the night. Just buzz one of the nurses if you need anything."

Arden reaches over to stroke Wyatt's damp hair. He's pale and heavy-lidded.

"You're sure you didn't put anything in your mouth?" she asks him.

"No."

"Do you remember touching anything sticky or—"

"I don't know," he says impatiently.

She wants to say, *Do you see how it can happen when you least expect it?*

"Am I going to have this forever?" he asks her, rolling his head to look at her.

"I don't know. I think there's a seventy-five percent chance you could outgrow it."

She touches his cheek, which is still warm, and takes the tablet from him. He doesn't argue. His eyes close; he yawns. She watches him sleep to make sure his chest rises and falls with every breath.

She gets home just after eight, anxious to see Ivey and Ali. Joshua stayed at the hospital with Wyatt, so she figures she has about an hour before his generosity starts to wane.

"Hello?!" she calls out.

Ali dashes out from the den and is jumping into her arms before the front door even closes. "Mama!" she cries, overjoyed. "You're home! Is Wyatt okay?"

"Wyatt's fine."

"Grandma says he tricked her and left his Epi-Pen here on purpose."

"He just forgot it, that's all."

"I believe Grandma."

"You do, do you?"

"She says she told him to take it."

"I did," Virginia says, hobbling toward them. "I reminded him multiple times. I'm sure he had it in his hands before he left."

"It's okay, Mom."

"How is he? I feel sick about it."

"He's fine."

"I told him at least twice to take it with him."

"I know," Arden says, and then turns to Ali and sends her upstairs to pack an overnight bag for Wyatt.

"You're never going to trust me again," Virginia says, tearing up. "But I'm telling you the truth."

Arden doesn't say anything for a moment, but the segue is too irresistible. "Speaking of the truth," she says. "Yesterday's hearing was full of surprises."

Virginia visibly flinches but tries to cover her discomfort with a stoic expression.

"You had to know it was all going to come out," Arden says.

Virginia sighs by way of an answer.

"Why didn't you tell me that Wallace Ashforth wanted you to have an abortion?"

"How does a mother tell such a thing to her child?"

"You lied."

"It was a lie conceived of good intention."

"So, you made up a whole story about him dying before he found out you were pregnant?"

"Yes," Virginia says defiantly. "And you would have done the same thing for your daughter."

"If he hadn't died, would you have gone through with it?"

"The abortion?"

"I know he was going to pay you lots of money."

"Arden! My God! Of course not." Tears spring to Virginia's eyes. "How could you even ask me that? I was having you no matter what. Ask Emma Merritt if you haven't already. No amount of money would have persuaded me not to have you! And I told her as much. I told him too. And his wife, Geraldine."

"So, it's true he got Emma Merritt to make the arrangements and then try to bribe you?"

"Yes, that's how it happened."

"You were one of many women he got pregnant," Arden says, softening her tone. "Did you know?"

"I knew, but I also knew he really loved me. We did have something special. He was a philanderer, and he was never going to leave Geraldine, I know that now. But he loved me, Arden, and I loved him. He promised to always take care of me. Whether you believe me or not, you were conceived in love."

"Sometimes I wish you'd never gone after my inheritance."

"Why? You're entitled to that money."

"It's not about the money," Arden says. "You taught me to believe that my worth had to come from *out there*." She points to the air, at nothing in particular. "You made me believe I needed their validation to be okay, that my identity and my existence were contingent on their acceptance."

"I never intended for that to happen."

"I know, Mom. I really do. I know you were trying to protect me, and provide for me, and that you believed in your heart that the money and the name were rightfully mine."

"They're not worth it, Arden. The Ashforths aren't worth it."

"I know that."

"Whether you forgive me or not, everything I ever did was to better your life."

"Of course I forgive you," Arden says. "I mean, I can even understand why you had to lie."

"Really?"

"I'm a mother, too, Mom."

Virginia flings out her arms and Arden lets herself be hugged, too tightly, while her mother sobs noisily onto the padded shoulder of her blazer.

"Where's Ivey?"

"Her room," Virginia sniffles, pulling herself together. "Where else? She spends an awful lot of time in there."

"She's a teenager."

"I remember you girls being out way more."

Arden bites her tongue. She's not sure how her mother remembers anything about their teen years, since she was almost never home, but all she says is "I'll go check on her."

Upstairs, she knocks lightly on Ivey's door and pushes it open without waiting for a response. Big mistake. Ivey—sitting on the edge of her bed in only a bra and underwear—lets out a bloodcurdling scream. "What are you doing? You can't just barge into my room like that!"

Arden notices the lighter in Ivey's hand at the same time she notices the fresh burn, blistering on the pale skin of her upper thigh. "Ivey—"

"Mom, go away!"

Arden doesn't move, but she doesn't panic either. *Don't react,* she tells herself. "Your brother is okay," she says, ignoring the burn.

Ivey looks up at her, suspicious.

"They're going to keep him in the hospital overnight to make sure everything is fine."

"That's good."

Arden sits down on the bed.

"Grandma told him to take his Epi-Pen," Ivey says, looking down at the floor.

"I know."

"Wyatt deliberately left it here."

"We don't know that."

Ivey looks at Arden out of the corner of her eye, obviously bracing for the lecture and the hysteria.

"Are you okay?" Arden asks her.

"Yeah. Why wouldn't I be?"

Because you just held a flame to your flesh until it swelled and blistered.

"I'm sorry I wasn't here."

Ivey shrugs.

"The hearings are over now," Arden tells her. "I don't have to go back to New York for a while."

Ivey doesn't say anything.

"Can we just run some cool water on that burn?" Arden says gently. "It'll help with the pain."

"I don't want the pain to go away!"

"What does that even mean?"

"You don't get it. Can you just go, please?"

"Can you help me to understand?" Arden asks her, using all her will-power to sound calm.

"No."

"Does it distract you from your real pain?" Arden asks her.

Ivey rolls her eyes but doesn't shoot down the hypothesis.

"I'm guessing the physical pain kind of drowns out the pain inside you."

Ivey shrugs, which Arden takes as progress. At least she's listening, hasn't turned back into the little girl from *The Exorcist* yet.

"It makes sense," Arden says. "When Daddy first died, I was taking these sleeping pills."

Ivey looks up at her, surprised.

"At first, I took them to help me sleep, but, really, they made my grief kind of blur and fade into the background. Is that kind of what it's like when you harm yourself?"

Tears are sliding down Ivey's cheeks. Arden's heart shatters, but she stays calm. The last thing Ivey needs is for her mother to lose her shit right now.

"I can imagine that when you're feeling the physical pain of the burn, your sadness is just a little more bearable."

At this, Ivey finally breaks. She starts to wail, the way she used to as a baby, and Arden pulls her into her arms.

"It's just too much," Ivey sobs. "If Wyatt dies, I don't think I can live through that."

Arden resists the urge to talk Ivey out of her fear and pain, to tell her everything's going to be all right. She has no idea if that's true, and Ivey wouldn't believe it anyway. She's fresh out of solutions. She's got no advice, no wisdom, no more Mom moves.

Ivey lets the lighter fall out of her hand. It drops to the floor and skitters under the bed. She cries and cries, and Arden doesn't interrupt her. She offers up not a single platitude or false promise. For now, all she can think to do is be quiet and give Ivey the safe space to purge some of her grief she's been attempting to burn into submission.

Arden returns to the hospital much later than she'd promised Joshua. Joshua assured her in a string of texts that he was fine—catching up on work, watching the Blue Jays—but she stills feels guilty as she rushes down the corridor to Wyatt's room.

She opens the door and hears voices deep in conversation. She hesitates before entering.

"And then it's like someone's pressing on my throat and I can't breathe." Wyatt's voice.

"Sounds awful, dude."

Arden peaks inside. Joshua is sitting on a chair next to Wyatt's bed. Wyatt is sitting up.

"Do you want me to turn off the TV so you can fall back to sleep?" Joshua says. "Or we can find a show to watch? I like to watch TV after I have a nightmare. It distracts me, makes me forget the bad stuff."

"You have nightmares too?"

"Sure. Everyone does."

"I had a lot of nightmares after my dad died," Wyatt says. "So did my sister. That's why we sleep with our mom."

"I know exactly how you feel."

"Did your dad die?"

"No, but he left when I was a kid."

Arden quietly moves inside the room but stays back to listen unobserved.

"How come he left?" Wyatt wants to know, sounding incredulous.

"I don't know. One night I woke up in the middle of the night and heard our front door close. I ran out to check and my dad was dragging a suitcase down the front steps. I called out to him, but he didn't hear me."

"What did you do?"

"I followed him outside, but I was too late. He got in a cab and drove away. I ran after the cab in my pajamas, all the way to the end of the block, but he never stopped."

"Why? Why didn't he even say goodbye?"

After a long silence, Joshua says softly, "I guess he must have been really unhappy with his life."

"My dad had a heart attack."

"Your mom told me."

"When I went into anaphylactic shock, I thought maybe I'd at least get to see my dad."

Gut stab. Arden winces.

"You're going to be just fine," Joshua says. "A lot of kids have peanut allergies."

"Mine is *life-threatening*," Wyatt says dramatically, quoting Arden. She's obviously succeeded in drilling that into his little head, which may or may not be a good thing.

"Will you lie down beside me till I fall asleep?" Wyatt asks Joshua.

"On this little bed?"

"Yeah."

"Uh, sure."

Arden can hear some shuffling. She waits a bit, not even sure why she's not stepping in to rescue Joshua. Maybe she wants him to see it's not so bad, parenting. Not for her sake, but for his future partner. She's moved by his vulnerability, by the way he so openly shared his wound with Wyatt. He doesn't know it yet, but he will make a good partner—and possibly parent—to someone down the road, when he's ready.

33

Virginia is having Sunday brunch with the girls. They're meeting at their usual spot in Yorkville, on the top floor of Holt's overlooking Bloor Street. It feels almost normal. Hell, it feels *good*.

Virginia is improving, which is to say she's finally starting to see a slim beam of light on the horizon. The elder abuse group has helped to lift her out of the black despair of a few months ago, to the point where she finally felt ready to book her first appointment with a therapist. It's out of her comfort zone—her father used to say therapy was for weak-minded imbeciles—but she's come to see that the only way to recover from her trauma is to work through it. She has no idea what that looks like or how long it will take, but so long as her health plan pays for it, she's willing to give it her all.

There's been some rebuilding to do with Arden. In the aftermath of Emma Merritt's testimony and the shock she inflicted on Arden, Virginia's had to do some hard soul-searching. While Virginia's primary motive for never telling Arden the truth was to protect her, she was also very much vested in her own version of history. Indeed, she rewrote their love story in her imagination and came to believe it with total conviction. With Wallace gone, there was no one to challenge her story. The more Virginia repeated it to her daughters, the more the story was solidified as fact. The story Arden has always believed—that Wallace died before he ever found out Virginia was pregnant—ultimately became Virginia's truth. Out of that lie, she launched her crusade to get Arden what she deserved. Had she known she was undermining Arden's self-esteem with every petition she filed, she would have stopped. Well, she likes to think she would have, anyway.

Still, they both know it wasn't just the legal campaigns that imprinted on the girls' psyches that their worth came from outside themselves. Is anyone really that enlightened as to believe otherwise, to know better? Virginia was trained to search for her worth in men. How could she pass on any other strategy to her daughters? It was always *When I find my soulmate. When this or that man loves me. When I'm married. When he leaves his wife. When we get the money . . .*

This is what she grapples with now. She's still not fully healed. She can't work, she's definitely finished with men. So where does that leave her? What's next?

Uncovering the answer to that question seems to be the direction in which she's going. It's bloody uncomfortable, and she's got these two circus mirrors in Tate and Arden constantly showing her where she's flawed and how her cockeyed beliefs have shaped all their lives, but the only other path available to her is backward, and she's damn well not going there.

"Have you spoken to Joshua?" Tate asks Arden. "When does he think you'll get the verdict?"

"Any day," Arden says, pressing her fork down onto the milky white skin of her poached egg until it squirts yolk all over the plate. "But he keeps preparing me for the fact that I won't see any money for a little while."

"What's 'a little while'?" Virginia asks, adding milk to her coffee.

"Joshua says the judge has to issue a report listing all of Bruce's heirs within thirty days of his verdict, and then we'll have a better idea."

"I thought you and Jamie were the only heirs?"

"So far, we are."

"This all sounds quite vague," Virginia says.

"Anyone have anything else they want to talk about?" Arden snaps.

"Actually, I do," Tate says, brightening. "We chose our egg donor."

Virginia clasps her hands over her heart. "You're going to have a baby?"

"We're going to try."

"Do you have a picture of the donor?" Virginia asks. "Does she look like you?"

"Does that matter?"

Obviously, Virginia is supposed to say no, but that would be a lie. "Is she pretty?"

"I told you, Mom, we don't get to see what she looks like, but she meets all our criteria. She's twenty-seven; she's fair, with blue eyes. She plays violin, she ran track, and she had a 3.8 GPA in college. I feel like all our bases are covered."

"What about alcoholism?"

"No history."

"Cancer?"

"Just one grandfather."

"That's better than most," Virginia says pragmatically. "Do you worry the baby won't have your DNA?"

"What did Arden's DNA ever do for her?" Tate says. "Look, we were prepared to adopt. At least this way our child will have Tanvir's genes. The doctor gave us super high odds with a donor, Tan's sperm is in mint condition, and I'm good to go other than my shitty eggs and caffeine addiction, which I'm planning to quit starting tomorrow. All signs point to this maybe working out for us."

"When do you start?"

"November. If all goes well, I'll only have to be in Denver for about ten days for the transfer."

Virginia realizes she's crying. She wipes her face with her napkin. "I'm so happy," she says, patting under her eyes. "I'm going to be a grandmother again."

"You're sure you're up for motherhood?" Arden asks Tate. "Do you maybe want to spend some more time with Ivey before you make your final decision?"

"I want to be a mother," Tate says, sounding slightly defensive. "I've given it a lot of thought, and I really do."

"It's a new beginning for all of us," Virginia says, feeling flushed with joy. "Let's order some mimosas and celebrate."

She leans over to flag their server, and that's when she spots him at the opposite end of the restaurant. There's a woman sitting beside him in the booth, and two boys across from them, about Ivey's age. *His wife and kids?* There's a wedding band on his finger that wasn't there on their date. Her heart starts to pound—hard, fast, loud, drowning out the din in the restaurant until the noise blends into one long wail in the background and everything outside her field of view blurs. She tries to slow down her breathing to steady her racing heart but finds she's not able to breathe at all. She can hear the girls' voices—distorted, faraway—trying to reach her. She's swirling, plunging down a vortex.

"Mom? Are you okay? Mom? What's wrong?"

"My heart is beating too fast."

"Are you having a panic attack?"

"It's him." She manages to point across the room to where he's sitting, enjoying a stack of pancakes with—presumably—his wife and kids. *Lou Geffen*. Her monster.

"Who?"

Virginia is hyperventilating, gasping for air. She can feel someone's hand on her back, stroking her. A voice whispering, "It's okay, Mom. Just breathe. Keep breathing."

"He's here," she says, gripping the table. "Lou Geffen is here."

"Who the fuck is *Lou Geffen?"* Tate's voice.

"Do the four-count breathing Hayley taught you," Arden says. "Breathe in, one-two-three-four. Hold, one-two-three-four. And release, one-two-three-four."

Virginia does her four-count breathing. Arden puts a glass of cold water to her lips, and she sips. She has no idea how much time passes, but eventually her heartbeat starts to settle into its usual rhythm and her breathing returns to normal. When she comes back to the present, Arden and Tate are both watching her, panic-stricken. Arden is sitting beside her, still rubbing her back.

"Better?" Arden says.

Virginia nods.

"Is it the guy who raped you?" Tate says. "Is that who you saw?"

Virginia nods again, slowly, and challenges herself to look over at him. He's talking, loudly. He talked a lot on their date, likes the sound of his own voice. He looks exactly the way she remembers him from her nightmares—extraordinarily tall, even seated in the booth; broad-chested and bald, with a long face and chin. *You know you want it, you decrepit old whore.*

Watching him interact with his family, Virginia starts to feel angry. At first, the anger is intellectual and shows up in her head framed as a question. *How dare he?* How dare he enjoy Sunday brunch with his wife and kids after what he did to her. How dare he even *have* a wife and kids. How dare he shovel pancakes into his mouth as though everything is normal and he's not a rapist? The more questions she asks herself, the more the anger begins to transmute inside her body into feelings, like scalding water coursing through her veins. She feels hot, inside and out. Rage roiling beneath the surface of her skin. "I have to say something."

"I'm coming with you," Tate says.

"No. Just let me do this my way."

"We should call the police," Arden says. "We can have him arrested."

"We can't have him arrested," Virginia says. "At least not yet. Not like this."

"You can't let him get away with what he did."

"I get that," Virginia says. It's taken her a while, but seeing him here, living a normal life of blissful impunity, is the thrust she needed.

She grabs her phone, squeezes Arden's hand, and slides out of the booth. She limps across the restaurant, her back slightly bent forward, and she can imagine how old she must look. *He did this to me.*

When she reaches his booth, coming up behind his sons to face him, she feels suddenly fearless. Emboldened by the presence of her daughters, whom she can sense behind her, supporting and cheering her on, she takes a breath and looks him right in the eye.

"Hi, Lou," she says. "Remember me? Virginia Bunt?" The words flow, divinely inspired. She feels solidly *in* her body, but someone—some*thing*—is speaking for and through her. "Or you may remember me better as *Bangin'Boomer*?"

Lou pretends to look blank. The wife is watching her. The two boys are playing on their phones, hunched over, oblivious. One of them is wearing a Lawrence Park soccer jersey with the name "Silber" above his number.

"We went to the Beanerie in Liberty Village?" Virginia says. "I'm the one who ordered the small black coffee in a large cup? It really bothered you."

"I think you've got the wrong guy," Lou says, smiling easily. "My name's not Lou."

She isn't at all surprised by how smooth he is. Calm and cool, ready to defuse her with his charisma. He's been here before.

"Let me jog your memory," she says. "You told me marriage was a death knell, so I assume this can't be your wife."

At this, the two sons look up. Lou quickly hands the boys some cash and tells them to go to the ice cream shop down the street and he'll meet them there. The boys look at Virginia, bemused, and shuffle out of the restaurant.

"Your husband is a rapist," Virginia tells the wife. "I need you to know that. He raped me and beat me and left me for dead."

"Get the fuck away from our table," the wife says. "Who is this old psycho, Randy?"

"I have no idea," he says, acting dumb and innocent, comically flummoxed.

Virginia starts searching her phone for the screenshot of his SilvrFoxes profile. She knows she saved it in a folder in her iCloud drive, in a file called Evidence, but she's so nervous, she keeps thumbing different icons and opening the wrong apps—Utilities, Skype, Weather.

"I said leave us the fuck alone!" the wife repeats.

Finally, Virginia manages to open the right folder, and there it is. She holds up her phone, flashing the screenshot in front of their faces. "OldDogNewTricks," she says, relieved. "His username."

She watches with satisfaction as the wife's expression changes in an instant from unequivocal conviction to doubt.

"He lies about his age," Virginia continues. "He pretends he's older than he is so he can prey on older women. I'm sure I'm not the first."

"What is she talking about, Randy?"

"This is absolutely outrageous," he says. "That is not me, I've never been on a dating site, let alone to 'prey' on old women. Whoever did this to you—and I'm sorry for what you've been through, ma'am—but whoever did this to you has stolen my photo. Do you think I'd be so stupid as to use my own photo if I was going to rape you?"

The wife looks relieved. She's nodding her head with renewed vigor.

"You raped me," Virginia says, holding steady. "You shattered my hip and it had to be replaced and I'm only now getting back on my feet after nearly seven months. You are the man in the photo, the same man who showed up at the Beanerie for coffee and then came back to my place and beat the shit out of me so badly I still walk with a limp. I don't know if you ever biked Hawaii or if you really are a doctor, but you are a rapist and I'm going to prove it."

To the wife, she says, "Search his computer. I'm sure you'll find all kinds of interesting things."

"Let's get out of here, Stace." Lou/Randy reaches for his wallet and tosses two twenties on the table.

The wife, poor Stace, doesn't move.

"Let's go. *Now.*" He stands up, towering above them. He *is* intimidating. Virginia never stood a chance.

"You're married to a rapist," Virginia tells the wife. "I know this must be hard to hear, and it's not your fault, but now you know, so you can't pretend."

"Get away from us!" the wife cries, and she looks past Virginia, wildly flailing her arms to get a server's attention. "Excuse me! Can someone please help? This woman is harassing us!"

Tate rushes over to Virginia's side and puts her arm around her mother's waist. "You okay, Mom?"

"I didn't go to the police because I'm old and I thought no one would believe that someone like you would rape someone like me," Virginia tells Lou. "I can see Stacey is confused. She knows you raped me, deep down, she really does, but she's confused because I'm old and she's much younger than me and she doesn't understand it." Looking at the wife, she says, "I know you believe me. Deep down, you *know* what he is."

"Get away from us before I call the police," the wife threatens, and Virginia laughs. She laughs so hard because she's ready for whatever they throw at her.

"Call them," she says, and she snaps a couple of photos of him and his wife for good measure. "I'll see you in court, Randy Silber. I'm going to press charges and expose you for the rapist that you are. And whether I win or lose in court, anyone who knows what a creep you are—and you *really* are a creep—will know that I'm telling the truth. And I will find all the other women you raped that have been too afraid to come forward, and together we will take down your life."

When she sits back down at her table, after Lou Geffen and his wife have fled the restaurant in a fluster of embarrassment and self-righteous indignation, Virginia melts down. With Arden and Tate on either side of her, sandwiching her protectively, she weeps.

"We're so proud of you, Mom."

"I don't even know what I just said."

"You said you were going to press charges and take down his life."

"I don't know what I was thinking," she says. "I can't do that. They'll put *me* on trial. With my sexual history? They'll humiliate me, make it all my fault. That's what they do. And who would believe that a young guy like him would rape an old woman like me? No one. That's who. I'm the one who will be publicly shamed, not him. Look what happened with that TV news anchor in Vancouver last year. He was acquitted of everything and there were *three women* involved."

"Mom. Take a breath."

"I have no proof. A screenshot of his profile—"

"We kept your sheets, Mom. Maybe his DNA is on them."

"You kept the sheets?"

Tate and Arden nod at the same time.

"He used a condom, but I remember feeling sticky. It could have been blood, but maybe the condom ripped?"

"And we'll find other women," Arden says. "We'll go to SilvrFoxes. We'll report him. Even if you don't win in court, you will ruin his life as he knows it."

"I have friends at all the magazines and papers," Tate says. "*Maclean's*, *Chatelaine*, the *Globe*. This is a story, Mom. A dating app rapist preying on elderly women? You can publicly crucify him."

"If there's enough evidence."

"You have to at least try," Arden says. "I feel like you'll be able to live with whatever outcome if you at least try, instead of staying silent and pretending it never happened. Then he gets away with it for sure."

Virginia considers what Jean from the group is always telling her: "Whatever you bury, you bury alive."

She doesn't want this thing living inside of her anymore.

34

ON MONDAY MORNING, AFTER SATURDAY'S DRAMATIC BRUNCH, ARDEN wakes up and checks her phone to see if Joshua has texted with news. Still nothing. Judge Lull seems to be taking his time with his decision, which, Arden has concluded, can't bode well.

Life must go on, she tells herself, as she has every morning since the last hearing. After Wyatt's stint at the hospital, she made a commitment to live as though she'd never filed the petition in the first place. No more putting life on hold, she promised the kids. The money, as wonderful and welcome as it would be, will neither make nor break their family. Those were her words to them: *The money, as wonderful and welcome as it would be, will neither make nor break our family.*

She felt they needed to hear this from her. She needed to hear herself say it and mean it.

To that end, she gets out of bed with a feeling of resolve that sends her straight to her computer. She made another commitment to herself when she got back from New York, which is to finally pursue an interest that has been percolating for quite some time and register for Christie's six-week online art law course. She hasn't told a soul what she's planning and has no intention of sharing it with anyone in her family until she's completed the course. Her track record on commitment is abysmal, and she doesn't want to have to convince Tate or Virginia of her enthusiasm or determination. Doesn't want to have to tell them, *This time I mean it.*

But this time she means it. She had coffee with Hana from the gallery the other day, after which she made two rather momentous decisions. First, Hana offered Arden the manager position, and she accepted. "I've got two babies running the gallery and they're going to bankrupt me," Hana complained. "I need someone mature and reliable who's not on TikTok all day. Someone the artists and clients can respect. I need *you*."

Before Arden could even debate the full-time hours, Hana offered to let her work four days a week. With Virginia still living at her house, Arden felt confident accepting the job. She figures Virginia can help out after school, get the kids to their activities, and make them dinner. For once, Arden didn't vacillate or waver or ask for more time; she simply said, "I'll do it."

As they continued to talk about Hana's legal nightmare with Della Feasby, the idea began to crystallize in Arden's mind.

"I mean, everyone in the city knows when you're dealing with designers you *have* to give them a ten or twenty percent discount," Hana said. "Ultimately it comes off the artist's commission. It's standard. Everyone in our industry offers a designer discount. And she *knew* that when we signed her on. She was so grateful to have representation."

"Isn't it in her contract?"

"I mean, sort of. Not really."

"'Sort of. Not really'?"

Hana sighed. "It's not exactly the most formal contract," she admitted. "I wrote it up myself. I put in something about her getting a commission based on what the piece goes for, but she's claiming that means the full price, even though we both know *she knew* it would be off the sale price."

"But that's not clear in the contract?"

"No, and that's why she's suing me. She knows I wrote it myself, and her new wife is some big lawyer in Calgary, so now she's asking to be compensated for, like, *eight years'* worth of designer discounts plus this, that, and the other. They're bullying me and making me out to be a scammer, and all of this is coming out of my pocket."

"Didn't your lawyer review the contract before you both signed it?"

"I didn't have a lawyer at the time," Hana said. "I've never had an issue before. I have a standard contract that I wrote myself and my artists have always had integrity."

Their conversation validated Arden's desire to combine her love of art and her newfound interest in law, and the decision to enroll in the course at Christie's came to life. Hal and Joshua called it early on, but Arden kept pushing it away. *Too old, too late, too many kids.* But she hasn't been able to get it out of her mind. The program at Christie's is not a degree by any stretch. It's only a six-week course and at best would give her a better understanding of how law affects the art industry and where she might be most needed. She would still have to finish her degree, and then law school. It could be a decade before she could work in law. She would be in her late forties.

And yet.

She has no clue where all this might lead, *if* it ever leads to anything. It's just a stepping-stone, a way for her to figure out what she wants to do with her life, to dip her toe back into school. She may even decide to open her own gallery one day. If the last couple of years have taught her anything it's that she's more interested in the journey this time. All she knows is that *not* pursuing this career path is not an option. The same way *not* filing the petition for her inheritance was not an option. She may come to these decisions ass-backward, resisting every step of the way, but at least she's finally making them.

Her idea of herself is slowly changing, as is her place in the world—or at least what she believed her place to be. Turns out her identity was never set in stone. It's a dynamic thing, expansive, capable of shape-shifting. Mother and wife were never enough to contain all of who she is and can become. As she contemplates this, she realizes she has amends to make.

She reaches for her phone.

"What's up?" Tate says. "I'm at work."

"We never really finished our conversation the other day," Arden says.

"Which one?"

"When you made your announcement about trying for a baby."

"Running into mom's rapist kind of hijacked my news."

"I owe you an apology."

"You do?"

"When you told us, my reaction was a little—"

"Snide?"

Arden was hoping Tate hadn't noticed. "I'm sorry," she says. "I didn't mean to make light of it. I know how huge this is for you."

Tate doesn't offer up any kind of absolution, so Arden plods on. "I shouldn't have asked you if you were ready for motherhood like that."

"It's a valid question."

"I made light of your desire to be a mother. *Me.* A mother of three. Like it's *my* thing and not yours. That wasn't fair."

Tate doesn't say anything. She sniffs, and Arden wonders if she might be crying, but this is Tate, so probably not.

"We've both had our lanes our whole lives," Arden explains. "I'm the mom and you're the career woman. I'm the caregiver and you're the type A. It's our dynamic. No one is one-upping the other, and I think we both like it that way."

"Are you saying you feel threatened by me having a baby?" Tate asks her.

"'Threatened' is a bit strong."

"You're not comfortable with it."

"Look, I know this is my shit to deal with," Arden says. "You're going to be a great mother. I'm genuinely happy for you. And I'm sorry I didn't say that the other day."

Tate doesn't say anything, but now Arden is certain she can hear muffled sniffling.

"Are you crying, Tate?"

No response.

"Tate? You don't cry. Talk to me."

"I'm scared," Tate admits, breaking down. "What if it doesn't work? What if I *can't* have a baby?"

"It'll work. You're using a fertile young egg, and you said this place in Colorado is one of the best in North America."

"*What if it works?*" Tate cries. "What if I have a kid and I'm terrible at it and it ruins my life and it turns out I never was meant for motherhood? What if I'm worse than *Mom*?"

Arden pauses for a moment and then thoughtfully says, "I'll raise your kid if it doesn't work out for you."

Tate laughs. "I don't know if I'm mother material," she says. "You're such a natural. You're so good at it."

"I'm not so sure anymore," she says, thinking of Ivey.

"Arden, you're a great mother. And I'm going to need your help."

"You really want this, don't you?"

"I mean, yeah. I really do. I want to experience being a mother. I want a baby. It's just not what I ever *thought* I wanted."

"I guess you didn't get the memo either," Arden says. "Apparently, we're allowed to change our minds whenever we want."

When her phone vibrates in her hand and she sees Joshua's number, it comes back to her full force. *The verdict.* She'd actually forgotten about it for a few minutes.

"Tate, it's Joshua. I have to take it."

"Shit. Oh my God."

"I'll call you right back." She disconnects Tate and answers Joshua.

"You got a minute?" He sounds serious.

"Of course I've got a minute," she says impatiently.

"Lull's decision is in."

Her blood pressure spikes. She feels light-headed, short of breath. All that BS about the money not making or breaking her family comes back to her and she is very much aware of just how badly she's been relying on this inheritance. *"And?"*

He pauses a beat, playing with her, and then says, "Congratulations." She can hear him smiling through the phone. "We won."

She puts her hand to her heart, worried it may pop out of her chest.

"You there, Arden?"

"Yes, just trying to stave off a heart attack."

He laughs.

"What's next? When do we get the money?"

"Like I told you, the judge will issue a report within thirty days, listing the identity and relationship of Bruce's heirs based on the evidence we submitted."

"So, thirty days?"

"Not quite. The family tree is still open."

"What does that mean?"

"There may still be alleged distributees out there," he says. "Technically, it hasn't been sufficiently proven that you and Jamie are the only heirs. Before any money is awarded, there has to be an appropriate search for other existing heirs."

"For how long?"

"Three years."

"*Three years?*" Arden cries.

"From the time of Bruce's death," he clarifies. "So that's already two years gone. After that, no one else can come forward and claim. That's when you'll get your share of the money."

"Why are you just telling me this now?" she asks him, doing the math, calculating everything and everyone she owes, including that line of credit that's been her albatross since Scott died. *One more year?*

"I've kept you on a need-to-know basis," he says.

Now seems like a really appropriate time for her mantra. *The money, as wonderful and welcome as it would be, will neither make nor break our family.*

"Okay," she says, mustering her resolve. "I can wait." She's got a real job now. It's going to be all right.

"Assuming Jamie's appeal is out of the way."

"Right. The appeal. So he could still win."

"You've been decreed a rightful heir, Arden. Ashforth can't exert any influence anymore, not over DNA. You just have to be patient now."

"I can do that."

"Go tell your people. This is a victory."

"Thank you," she says. "For taking this on, for doing it on contingency."

"Thank you for trusting me."

"To be fair, I didn't really have a choice."

They both laugh.

"I'll see you at Hal's vernissage in November," she says, her voice dropping, turning a little flirty. "We'll celebrate."

"I'm counting the days," he says, switching from his lawyerly voice to his sex voice.

She hangs up and sits by herself with the news for a little while. It occurs to her that it's the fourth of September, one day after Labor Day, two years since Scott died. She can't help but think he's had something to do with this, that he's orchestrated this win on his death anniversary, a wink from heaven or wherever he is.

The reality of being a multimillionaire feels surreal, but she can wrap her head around that later, when and if the money is finally in her hands. As for being legally decreed an Ashforth heir, well, that feels deliciously vindicating. While she'd like to believe she wouldn't have cared either way, the truth is she does care. Not because it validates her or provides some brand-new and improved identity, but because the court has finally acknowledged her bloodline and her birth father. It means something to her, if for no other reason than to exonerate her mother. Biology may still be bullshit, in the sense that no father could have loved her more than Hal did, but her mother poured her blood and guts into proving biology. Arden is glad to be able to give her this gift of redemption, belated as it may be.

She gets up from her desk and heads down the hall to Virginia's room. Her mother will be the first to know that at long last the Bunt women have triumphed.

Death is not the end. There remains the litigation over the estate.
—AMBROSE BIERCE

35

ON WHAT WOULD HAVE BEEN SCOTT'S THIRTY-EIGHTH BIRTHDAY, ARDEN, the kids, Virginia, and Hal trudge to Mount Pleasant Cemetery on foot. It's a cold, bright morning, and when they arrive at Scott's niche beside the pond, Arden crouches down on the concrete and places her bouquet of white roses in front of his name.

As she stares at it, engraved in small serif letters on the smooth granite façade, she feels a flood of emotion. It's been one hell of a year, and she thinks he would be proud of her. She's accomplished more on her own in the last year than she would ever have thought possible. He used to say she was capable of anything she set her mind to, but she never believed him. The saddest part is he had to die for him to be proven right.

She hopes he's watching over her the way people always say loved ones do after they die. She's starting to think it might be true, that perhaps he's the one who's infused her with strength and courage, managing the people, places, and things that would best facilitate her growth. Maybe dead people can arrange winning verdicts and new jobs and the right people showing up along the way.

Lately, she's been jotting down memories, the ones she's terrified to forget. She writes them on scraps of paper, Post-it Notes or receipts, toilet paper, and then she stuffs them between the pages of *Photography Across Time*. They're just random moments, small ones and big ones alike, moments she wants to share with the kids when they're older and have mostly forgotten their childhoods. They're going to forget a lot of things, if they haven't already. She wants to be able to sit around the Thanksgiving table one day and read them out loud, bringing Scott back to life for them. Like the time they were watching *The Wizard of Oz* with Ivey for the first time.

"Where's the color, Daddy?" They were still at the black-and-white part of the movie, which Ivey had never seen before.

"Movies were black-and-white in the old days," he said.

Ivey pondered that for a minute and then said, "Was *life* black-and-white in the old days?"

God, how they'd laughed.

The other day she remembered some of Scott's speech from their wedding, and she wrote that down, too, and tucked it inside the memory book.

"The woman I'm marrying has a special pair of glasses," he'd said, rousing everyone to tears. "Every time she puts on those glasses, she only sees the best in me. I hope I can live up to the man that only you can see, baby."

She remembers being loved by him with such conviction, that day and throughout their entire marriage. She doesn't remember ever *not* feeling that way with him.

As the hearings begin to recede, her feeling of betrayal over his covert investigation into her inheritance has shifted into something much closer to compassion. Scott didn't have a devious bone in his body. He didn't want the money for himself; he wanted it for their family and their future, just like she did. They've always been working for the same cause, which, ironically, Joshua is the one to have pointed out to her. With the clarity of time, she's come to understand that what she misconstrued as betrayal was simply desperation. Scott would have done anything to protect and provide for his family, and sometimes that desperation led him to make misguided choices. For that, she forgives him.

She reaches out and touches his niche. The kids are surprisingly quiet, almost reverential. This is what she holds on to: *their love for each other was real*. She's at peace knowing that theirs was a good and solid marriage. They were not just going through the motions like some couples she knows. They weren't miserable in each other's company or staying for the sake of the kids; they never experienced the demise of humor and mutual respect and good sex. They did not grow bored with each other or disenchanted or indifferent. He died right in the middle of their love story. It wasn't perfect, but it was nowhere near its denouement.

Another memory she wrote about: the hiking trip in Santa Barbara. They were on a trail nestled between the Santa Ynez Mountains and the Pacific Ocean. Scott had Ivey on his shoulders, which was no small feat. She was about five at the time, not exactly a baby. She'd tripped on a rock and scraped her knees, so Scott had agreed to carry her for a while so they wouldn't have to turn back.

At a certain point along the trail, the sea came into view and shimmered before them in the distance. The air was chilly, but the sun was keeping them warm. Their family was still in its larval stage. They only had Ivey, but they'd been trying for a long time to have another baby. They were both excited to expand the family.

Scott and Ivey were up ahead of her. Arden was happily trailing behind them, watching Ivey play bongo drums on Scott's head. She let out a laugh that filled the air for a split second before it was drowned out by a piercing squawk. Out of nowhere, three birds swooped out of the sky and landed on the rugged peak where Scott and Arden were standing. They were squeaking loudly to one another, a grating noise like the sound of bare feet in wet Crocs. Ivey blocked her ears.

"What the penguins saying, Daddy?"

"They're not penguins," Scott said as he lifted her off his shoulders. "They're magpies. They're saying *mag-mag-mag*!"

They were boisterous little creatures, black and white, with royal blue wings and bright yellow bills. They were hopping around, noisy and rambunctious.

"That's the baby," Ivey said, pointing to the smallest magpie. "That's the daddy and that's the mommy!"

"Aren't magpies bad luck?" Arden said. They had the five-hour flight home the next day.

"Haven't you ever heard that nursery rhyme?" Scott said. "One for sorrow, two for joy, three for a girl, four for a boy?"

"No."

"Ivey's going to have a little sister."

"I've never known you to be superstitious," Arden said, just as another magpie landed right in front of them, blabbing with the same zeal and enthusiasm as his friends. *Mag! Mag! Mag!*

"There four of them!" Ivey cried. "We're having a brother!"

Three months later, staring at the ultrasound, they were dumbfounded to see not one but two fetuses, a boy and a girl. She'd been pregnant in Santa Barbara and hadn't known it. From that moment on, they always called the twins their magpies.

She traces the words on his plaque, words she chose. How do you sum up a person's life in one sentence, let alone what that person meant to you? It took her over a year to finally get it engraved, and still it doesn't convey nearly enough.

SCOTT MOORE
A MAN OF INTEGRITY, ZEST & HUMOR,
WHO LOVED WITH HIS WHOLE HEART.
FOREVER MISSED BY HIS BELOVED FAMILY.

After spending some quiet moments at the niche, the twins start getting restless and run off to read the tombstones around the cemetery. Virginia and Ivey stroll over to the fountain so Virginia can sit down and rest.

Hal stays with Arden. He links his arm in hers and she rests her head on his shoulder.

"I've given a lot of thought to your offer," he says. "And I've decided I'd really prefer to stay in my house."

"I knew you'd say that."

"I love that shitty little house," he says. "All my memories of you and your mother are in it. And my studio . . . that studio is part of me. It's too late in my life for a big move."

"I figured."

"I'm a simple man," he says. After a beat, he asks her, "Are we good?"

"Of course we are. Why wouldn't we be?"

"I was hard on you."

Arden's heart surges. "I deserved it," she says. "I was going down the same path as Mom, and you knew it."

"At least you're getting a happy ending."

Arden turns to him. "I know it opened up a lot of old wounds for you," she says. "I know about Mom and Lasker."

Hal nods. "I thought that might come out."

"You lost so much," she says. "I'm sorry if I was insensitive about that."

"*You* lost more," he says, pulling her into his arms.

"You're my father," she reminds him, her words a little muffled in his scarf. "You always have been, and nothing has changed."

36

MAY 2019

VIRGINIA OPENS THE FRONT DOOR AND STEPS OUTSIDE, BREATHING IN THE spring air, which is humid and sweet. Hal's gardener is trimming the shrubs.

"Morning, Enzo," she calls out to him.

"Hey, Virginia." He raises a muscular arm to wave at her.

She's back living in Brooklyn with Hal these days, a poignant full circle. The difference this time is she and Hal are just roommates. Hal prefers to call them companions, but Virginia thinks that makes them sound like a couple of old people who have settled into a platonic relationship until they die. Hal says roommates makes them sound like they're still in college. Better that, she says. Anyway, it's a temporary arrangement, until Arden wins her last appeal and can finally buy Virginia a Park Slope brownstone, which is where she's chosen to live out her days.

It's been nearly eight months since she pressed charges against Lou Geffen (real name: Randy Silber). Thanks to his son's soccer jersey, she had a name when she went to the police. After that, it was a blur of interviews for the *Star*, the *Globe*, *Maclean's*. There was also a TV interview with W5—part of a story on elder abuse and cyberdating—that inadvertently made Virginia the face of elder abuse.

After all the media attention, two more women came forward, both in their late sixties, with stories identical to Virginia's. Early in the new year, after a six-month investigation, Randy Silber turned himself in. He was charged with three counts of sexual assault and then promptly released on bail, back into his life, where he's been ever since.

The pretrial is scheduled for October. She's had plenty of time to change her mind about testifying, but after everything she's already been through, there's not a chance of that happening.

Her lawyer has warned her—*everyone* has warned her—that her dignity is going to take a beating, but hasn't it already? If she doesn't go through with testifying, Randy Silber will be free to rape again. She's more than willing to put her reputation on trial to destroy his. Besides, she's done it so many times before, for a far less significant cause, and this time she has the support of her daughters, her friends from the group, Hayley, and Hal. She's never felt less alone. And when it's done, whether she triumphs in court or not, she will leave Toronto once and for all and settle permanently in Brooklyn, in her own brownstone, and enjoy the retirement Arden has graciously offered her and that, frankly, she's worked damn hard for and deserves.

"Summer's around the corner," Enzo says. "Can you smell it?"

"I sure can," she says, coming down the front steps and sitting on the last one. She likes watching Enzo work. He's very buff, probably in his late fifties. He's a little younger than her, but nothing outrageous.

"Did you change your hair?" he asks her, looking up from the shrubs.

She touches her head, remembering she went back to blond over the weekend. No more gray for the first time since the rape. "I did my highlights," she admits, blushing.

"I like it blond like that. It suits you."

"Thank you for noticing."

"That's my job."

"Paying attention to—" She almost says "old women" but stops herself. She's practicing being kinder to herself. "—to women's hair?"

"To beauty," he says, gazing at the garden where the flowers he planted are blooming.

He's flirting with her. *Duh*, Virginia.

She practices staying in her body. *Don't check out.* She closes her eyes and lets the sun wash over her, warming her skin. *Stay here.* She learned in the group to surf the uncomfortable feelings like a wave. The waves always crest and subside, and as she allows herself to take in Enzo's compliment without shutting down, her heart rate slows down and the feeling of impending danger begins to pass.

"It makes you look younger."

"Thank you, Enzo," she says, reacquainting herself with her flirty voice.

She's not dead inside. It felt like that for a while, but the very fact that she's noticing the beads of sweat trickling down the back of Enzo's neck signals that her body may be emerging from its trauma-induced retraction.

"What are those?" she asks Enzo, pointing to a cluster of light-pink blossoms.

"Those are azaleas," Enzo says. "Hal really likes them."

"They smell wonderful."

She leans over for a whiff of them, and as she does, her hand grazes Enzo's. She's very aware of him watching her. Maybe she's still capable of lust, possibly even love. Her heart opens and she feels like the old Virginia.

She's recently come to appreciate how good she'd once felt in her body, even as it was aging and morphing into an older, more imperfect version of itself. She used to get so caught up trying to find a partner, she often took for granted what a gift it was to feel so free and uninhibited, to enjoy sex and seek pleasure without apology. It was fun; it was *enough*. She sees that now. She always thought she needed a man—from a young age, the world told her she was supposed to have one—but, truly, she'd been content as a single, sexual, senior badass.

Perhaps she can get there again.

Arden steps outside at that precise moment, coffee in hand, and sits down on the top step of the porch. "Mom, are you flirting with Enzo?"

"I'm too old to flirt!" Virginia says, winking at Enzo.

She joins Arden on the stoop, aware that her old spark of mischievousness is back, her self-confidence mending.

"Are you ready to go look at that brownstone?" Arden asks her.

"Am I ever."

Arden squeezes Virginia's hand and they smile at each other, and it's like they're reading each other's minds. *Finally*. The inheritance is starting to feel a little more tangible, at least enough for Arden to have suggested a preliminary house-hunting expedition.

Arden pulls her phone out of her pocket to call the Uber and it chimes in her hand with an incoming text.

"One of the kids?" Virginia says.

Arden is silent, reading. When she looks up, her lightly tanned face is alarmingly drained of color.

"Arden, what is it?" *Panic.* "Is it one of the kids?"

Arden shakes her head, zombie-like, ashen.

"What then? You're scaring me."

"The Family Tree."

"What about it? Whose family tree?"

"That was Joshua," she says. "Someone has come forward."

"What do you mean? Who's come forward?"

"Another potential heir."

"What? *Who?*" Virginia's heart is slamming against her chest. "It's too late! You already won!"

"They had three years from the time of Bruce's death to come forward. Remember, I told you that?"

Virginia shrugs. "Vaguely."

"Well, someone claiming to be Wallace's son has come forward. It's not quite three years since Bruce died, so he's filed a petition."

"He can't be Wallace's son. Why didn't he come forward sooner? Where was he in the eighties when I was in probate and it was all over the news? He's a fraud, Arden. This won't change anything."

"Maybe he was waiting to see if my request to test Bruce's DNA would be granted."

"He can't be Wallace's son," Virginia repeats, more to herself. She needs Arden to be the only one.

"It's all on hold," Arden says, stunned.

"What does that mean?"

"Joshua is going to file the claim. He must believe him."

"What about *your* share of the inheritance?"

"It's on hold. That's all I know."

"You're still getting the money, though?"

"I think so, but less, obviously. And God only knows when. Maybe more people will come forward. Why should we be surprised?"

Virginia closes her eyes. "This can't be happening," she murmurs, and starts to cry.

Arden takes her hand and squeezes it, the color slowly returning to her cheeks. *She's so beautiful*, Virginia thinks. *How did I manage to create this magnificent, resilient creature?*

"We're going to be okay," Arden says, sounding sanguine. "Think about what we've been through in the past couple of years and look at us now. We're *here*, Mom. We're good. You're flirting with the gardener . . ."

Virginia giggles softly through her tears, gazing over at Enzo's lovely muscles and inhaling the sweet smell of azalea in the air, and she has to acknowledge that, yes, life can be delicate and cruel, but there remains through it all a deep inner well of tranquility that can always be accessed with a gently lowered bucket, a well that cannot be contaminated or drained, not by the Ashforths, not by the Lou Geffens, not even by their own unenlightened humanness.

She's still watching Enzo happily snipping his bushes, and he looks up and smiles at her, and she smiles back, and for a split second she knows Arden is right. They're going to be just fine.

ACKNOWLEDGMENTS

I'd like to thank the very generous Thomas Sciacca for his legal expertise. When I needed an estate lawyer from New York, I sent him a cold email asking for his help. I never imagined he would give so much of his time to help a writer from Toronto, but he did. He not only read the manuscript and spoke to me over the phone at great length, he also sent copious detailed notes, corrected everything that need correcting, and patiently answered all my questions throughout the writing of the novel. I am so very grateful to you, Thomas. (Your signed copies are on the way!)

Thank you to Sarah Ried and Sarah Stein, the two Sarahs who helped shape this novel into its current form. I am very appreciative of your support and guidance. (And, Sarah Stein, thank you for a lovely afternoon in NYC that inspired me to jump right into the next one!)

Thank to my longtime agent and friend, Bev Slopen. You've championed my career from the very beginning, and I will always treasure that. Thank you to Samantha Haywood and Carolyn Forde for welcoming me into the transatlantic family. I am so excited for the next phase of this journey. Marissa Stapley, I can't thank you enough for being a friend and an inspiration, for always saying yes and helping out a fellow writer. Your success and generosity continue to awe me. Here's to many more "moments."

Yet another huge debt of gratitude to Billy Mernit, my extraordinary "first reader," editor, and mentor. Not only do you make all my books better, but your insights have made my writing better over the years. Not a day goes by that I don't thank the writing gods for bringing us together at not one but two of your UCLA screenwriting courses.

I would also like to mention the Emerging Artist Gallery in the novel is inspired by Toronto's Art Interiors, owned by Lisa Diamond Katz and Shira Wood.

I'm so blessed to have a village of people in my life, all of whom make it possible for me to write. Marvyn, thank you for taking care of . . . well, everything. You are a true partner in every sense of the word. I love you. Thank you, RARA, for taking care of my home life and my family. Thank you to my entire staff at Au Lit, especially my brilliant managers, who allow me to go off and write books. I couldn't do it without you. Thank you to my spiritual team—Sandra, Sassy, Kam T, Bonnie, Hayley. (See dedication.) You are my people.

And thank you, Jessie and Luke, the loves of my life. You give all of it meaning.

ABOUT THE AUTHOR

JOANNA GOODMAN is the author of the novels *The Forgotten Daughter*, *The Home for Unwanted Girls*, and *The Finishing School*. Originally from Montreal, she now lives in Toronto with her husband and two children.

Read More by
JOANNA GOODMAN

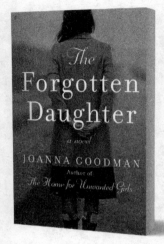

THE FORGOTTEN DAUGHTER
A Novel

"Resonant and relevant. . . . The characters, complex and flawed, love and fight so fiercely that it's hard not to be drawn into their passionate orbits and to feel, even slightly, a glimmer of hope as they refuse to give up on the ideal of happiness." —*Kirkus Reviews*

A tale of love and suspense following the lives of two women reckoning with their pasts and the choices that will define their futures.

THE HOME FOR UNWANTED GIRLS
A Novel

"A study of how love persists through the most trying of circumstances." —*Booklist*

The story of a young unwed mother who is forcibly separated from her daughter at birth and the lengths to which they go to find each other.

THE FINISHING SCHOOL
A Novel

"*The Finishing School* pulls back the curtain to expose a fascinating world of desire, betrayal, and dangerous secrets." —Lou Berney, Edgar Award–winning author of *November Road*

A successful writer returns to her elite Swiss boarding school to get to the bottom of a tragic accident that took place while she was a student twenty years earlier.